THE THRONE OF THE GODS

Raven Son: Book Five

NICHOLAS KOTAR

WAYSTONE
PRESS

Therefore, I will allot him a portion with the great,
And he will divide the booty with the strong;
Because he poured out himself to death,
And was numbered with the transgressors.

Isaiah 53:12

*For while gentle silence embraced everything and night at its own speed
was half over, Your all-powerful Word leaped from heaven, from the
royal throne, into the midst of a doomed land, a relentless warrior
carrying the sharp sword of Your irrevocable command.*

Wisdom of Solomon 18:14-15

For my mother

PART I

Ascent

PRELUDE

And behold, the Creator of the gods sat on his throne and spoke the Realms into existence. His word became matter, his heart became soul, and his spirit became spirit. And the songs of the gods below him were beautiful and good, filling the chaos into forms pleasing to eye and soul and spirit. Then the Creator of the Realms spoke. A word so still, so small, that the Powers strained to hear it.

"Behold, I leave the throne vacant and go to my house. Whoever wills to take my place on the throne, behold, it is vacant. But to the violent who would take it, know this. The crown is heavy, and the seat is onerous. Nevertheless, the Throne of the Gods suffers violence, and the violent take it by force."

Apocryphal Book of the Raven
Author: Unknown

FIFTEEN YEARS before the revelation of the Raven in the Heart of the World...

Rogned, prince of Karila, balanced on the tip of the highest point in his land. Before him plunged a sheer fall, thousands of feet down to jagged, teeth-shaped rocks. Behind him a narrow spur was all that kept him from another drop, down to a tarn said to be so deep that the bottom grazed the bones of the great serpent that formed the backbone of the world.

Something beyond the water pulled at him, calling with the intensity of a love song. He forced himself to look away.

Rogned had never quite appreciated the name of this crag —the Fang of the Giant—until this moment. It did not take a wild leap of the imagination to feel the stone heaving underneath him, as though an invisible upper jaw were coming down to meet the upward thrust of the Fang, to crush him before depositing him into a giant's gizzard.

The thought thrilled him: to be churned up and swallowed by the divine. It was what he had come here for, after all.

It had taken him most of the morning to climb the pockmarked Fang, through the bone-cutting winter wind and the ice-flecked mist. He thought he would never again hear anything other than the howl of the wind.

Better that than the screams of the dying in war, he thought.

From the top of the Fang he looked down at the green earth, and all sound ceased. The clouds tore apart slowly, silently. Three shafts of sunlight shot down into the land below him, and the tarn's frozen surface flashed.

Tears filled his eyes. He gritted his teeth until his jaw ached. Something like curdled milk filled him inside, something that would burst if he didn't let it out. He roared.

"How dare you reveal the land's beauty now?" he cried aloud to the Heights. "Now, when the grass and the rocks will be defiled with blood!"

No answer came from the Heights.

A flock of ravens flew underneath Rogned, bringing into sharp relief the army of five thousand Nebesti who were marching on Karila, his beloved home. Just three hundred fighting Karilans stood in the pass between the Fang and the Needle—an impossibly thin pillar of rock that reached half as high as the Fang. Kneeling, the Karilans faced the Needle—sacred to their old gods, who had been suppressed by the victorious Vasyllian invaders, hundreds of years ago. But then Vasyllia fell, ending the confederacy of the three city-states of Vasyllia, Nebesta, and Karila. What followed was internecine slaughter, a war that was about to end with the total destruction of Karila, the runt of the three. How fitting that Nebesta, jealous first daughter of Vasyllia, would do the deed.

"Rogned!"

The voice was hardly more than a whisper in the howl of the wind. Rogned turned around, careful not to slip. The man who had followed him was past the first flower of youth, and his eyes were as deep as the tarn. Those eyes were filled with more pain, sorrow, and anguish than anything Rogned had ever seen. They called him the Healer. He healed everyone but himself.

"I was hoping you'd follow, Voran," said Rogned. "I wasn't sure you'd believed me."

"Have you finally lost your mind? I know you artisans are impulsive, but this?"

"It's halfway to the Heights," said Rogned, not trying to hide the elation that rose inside him. *Not long now.* Images from last night's dream flowed through his mind—a wing the color of lapis lazuli, an eye that blazed golden fire, the simultaneous pain and elation of the thrust of a giant sword through his heart.

A muffled roar rose up on a draft of warm wind. Rogned thought he could smell the stench of the sweat and fear of his people.

The Nebesti were no longer advancing in their perfect ranks. They were throwing themselves chaotically at the three hundred defenders of the city of Karila. Even from here, Rogned could smell their war lust.

"Quickly, Voran. This may be our only chance."

Voran's face blanched at the sight of the knife, which

Rogned had pulled out of his boot in a smooth, practiced motion. He had rehearsed this moment many times during the last week.

"Rogned!" Voran's hands shook. The deep purple of the shadows under his eyes made the paleness of his face ghostlike. "You're mad! Just because of a few dreams? You can't force an encounter with the Heights. High Beings come to you in their own time. You're just going to kill yourself."

"That's the idea," said Rogned. He sliced the knife across his left wrist. It hardly hurt at all, to his astonishment. It was even pleasant to feel the hot blood on his frozen skin.

"I promised myself no one else in your family would die!" Voran screamed as he ran to stop Rogned, nearly falling off the edge in his haste.

Too late.

A wave of exhaustion swept Rogned into unconsciousness. He fell, and there was no bottom. He kept falling and falling and . . . Rogned awoke in mid-fall.

What in all the . . .

He was no longer falling.

White sand as far as the eye could see. It crackled under him as he rose up from a crouching position. Now it felt more like glass than sand. Rogned's hands were covered in the stuff. Before he realized what he was doing, he licked his right thumb.

His eyes grew large in surprise.

Salt.

Then the immensity of the landscape pressed in on him from all sides, along with a smell like rotten eggs. There was nothing but salt—ranging from white to grey to slightly pink— in all directions. The sky above him looked like a mirror image of the salt. Perhaps the sky in this place was not blue.

Where am I?

A scented breeze played with his hair. His mind processed the smells—impossible in their profusion and intensity. There was orange there, and lilac, and morning grass after a spring downpour, and logs burning on the coldest evening of the year, and—

Rogned was running before his mind registered it. No, he wasn't running. There was no word for this. Each step was a leap miles long, as though his essence strove to tear itself out of his body and to dissipate in the perfection of that smell ahead of him.

His mind hiccupped—there was no other way to describe the way it was functioning as it tried to sift through the everything he saw, smelled, felt. But below thought, deeper, in the throbbing warmth of his chest, longing burned him.

I am going home. The thought rang out like a choir singing from a mountain peak.

Before his limping thoughts could retort—*what is home?*—something formed out of the shimmering mirages rising from the salt. A riot of color, spinning wildly, yet anchored more firmly than a mountain. A tower of white, whiter than any white he had ever seen. Walls encircling it. Seven of them, each made of stone that shimmered; and Rogned somehow knew it was harder than any stone he had ever seen in Karila. Set in the center of each encircling wall was a gate. They were too far away for him to make out the details, but they reminded him of what he thought diamonds must look like. He had only heard of diamonds in stories.

Trees, laden with red fruits with a golden innerglow, seemed to embrace him as he sped into their groves. They grew directly from the salt. Their smell—pomegranate mixed with cinnamon and honey—finally slowed him down. That and the winged giant with a sword made of lightning.

The giant's skin looked like marble—marble that was living tissue, not stone. His eyes shone bronze, and six wings of gold, lapis, emerald, ruby, silver, and topaz flickered in constant movement about his body. The lightning sword looked like a part of his arm, something as much belonging to him as the presence that emanated from him. The presence felt like a mountain about to fall on an ant.

Rogned fell on his knees, though the shaking of his hands was more joy than fear.

"You," Rogned whispered. His voice sounded foreign to this place. He didn't belong here, and he was beginning to realize how mad he had been. And yet . . . how had he gotten here?

The giant spoke. "You came too early, child. My call was only a whisper. A preparation for a later time. No mortal can gain access to the Gardens of Aer before death."

"There will not be a later time," said Rogned, gathering courage from the shards of what was left of him after the voice of the giant had shattered him. "Karila is about to be wiped off the map. And I know my lessons: 'Those who take the Heights by force—they are the only ones worthy of it.'"

The giant laughed. Rogned had to look down at himself to make sure he had not burst into flame from its power.

"You quote scripture at me? I am of the Palymi, the highest order of the Powers that encircle the throne of the Unknown Father. We *inspired* that scripture."

"Then you know why I am here."

Something shifted in the Power's living-marble face, as though he were listening to a wind miles away.

"So you took the scriptures literally. You poor fool. You're not ready."

"I demand that the Heights answer the groan of Karila. We have been pushed back, inch by inch, forced to give up our lands, our very way of life to those who would exterminate us. I demand audience before the throne of the Unknown Father."

"You're lying."

If wind were a living thing with an emotion like anger, then it might have come close to what pressed Rogned to the salt-earth in that moment.

"You do not come here with a desire for justice. Do you not realize that I can see through you?"

Images and emotions bubbled up, pressing on his brain. His elder brother Karakul's dead body on top of a pyre. The fury Rogned had felt at seeing it. The urge for vengeance that boiled inside. The desire to tear down Vasyllia for what it had done to his brother. The burning madness of artistic creation. The sense of being possessed by an outside force when he sculpted. The feeling of power over the whole earth, as though he could turn it inside out at his own whim. The thought that he so often pushed down, though he gave himself over to it in his dreams—*I am touched by the divine. Only I can stop the war.*

Rogned grabbed his head, trying to ward off the onslaught of his own thoughts. His heart beat savagely, as if it were going to burst.

"Pride, anger, vengeance. Smallness of mind. Of such are the Gardens of Aer?" The giant seemed to grow even higher. "Raw metal in my hands. That's what you are. Don't you understand? Until you've been tempered, the fire of my power will melt you, not make you stronger."

"And what of courage?" Rogned pushed himself up to his feet, grinding his teeth against the power pushing him down. "What man has courage like mine? I'm not doing it for myself! I do it for little Nadina, the five-year-old who lost both her parents in a raid by the Nebesti last week. For my brother, who was murdered by a man he loved like a father. For all those innocents who are being destroyed, wiped off this good earth, punished for crimes and sins they didn't commit."

The sword flashed upward. Rogned's anger blazed out of him so hot, he thought he would be immolated in it.

"No! I know you, Palymi," Rogned said. "You guide my hand when I sculpt. That work of putting chaos into a form more perfect than creation itself—you and I have done that together. Don't deny it! I *know* you. You will give this to me, because it is the only way left. The war will tear the land apart. There will be no one left to worship at any altar."

The sword plunged into his heart. Rogned screamed.

Through the firelight of that agony, he saw the giant step aside. The first gate to the Gardens of Aer stood open before him. Flowers and trees of color and variety that he could never have imagined—they beckoned to him. No human love impelled like this. Rogned rose up, through the agony, and ran to the door . . .

The world yanked up from underneath him, and wet mist covered his face.

"THERE!" Voran gasped, hovering over Rogned. The shadows under his eyes were even darker than before. "I made a promise to you, Rogned, when you were a boy. Did you forget? I will not let you die in vain. Not after your brother died. I loved him, you know. He was the brother I never had . . ."

Rogned couldn't understand what Voran was saying. All he heard in his head was the song of the paradise birds nesting in the Gardens of Aer; all he could smell was the tuberose and lavender and . . .

A foul wind inundated him with the coppery smell of blood. Rogned gagged, his hands flailing. He grabbed Voran's head and squeezed it. Every muscle in his body strained. He screamed.

"Rogned, I brought you back. You won't die now." Voran wheezed, trying to pull apart Rogned's hands. He was too weak.

"What have you done?" screamed Rogned. It echoed, the sound bouncing around them as though they were in a cavern. "I was so . . . so close!"

He threw Voran aside, not even caring anymore if he fell off the edge of the Fang. The clouds above him churned with wind, pregnant with sleet. He reached for them. He could feel them between his hands like clay, like stone melting in his hands, forming into a shape. He gasped. Pleasure filled him, a rip current to the wave of disgust that now fell off him like rainwater. He . . . *sculpted the clouds.*

After the waves of pleasure had risen so high that his breath caught in his throat, he finally exhaled. The sun broke through the sculpture of fog and mist and ice and snow that he had made and that covered the expanse of the entire sky. It was the most beautiful thing he had ever done. The most beautiful thing any human being had ever done. He felt the Palymi's sword in his chest again.

"Yes," he said aloud, as his mind unmoored from his body. The word sounded distant, as though someone else were saying it. "I know now. Beauty *will* save this world."

THREE DAYS LATER, Rogned woke up. He lay inside a battle tent on the most comfortable pallet he had ever felt. He was so confused, he hadn't even remembered his own name at first. Voran had explained everything to him—how the sculpture he had created had stopped all the warriors in their tracks. How all of them had put their arms down, some of them openly weeping at the sight, some in such fear that they ran away screaming. The leaders of both sides had immediately come together to discuss terms of peace.

"Everyone agreed," said Voran. "You, Rogned, could be the only one to lead a new, unified army of the Three Cities. You've ended the internecine war. They're calling you the prophet-prince already."

FOOD no longer tasted like food. Even the salt in the barren wasteland bordering the Gardens of Aer had teased his sense of taste with hints of pomegranate and mint. Food was like sand now. Drink couldn't fill Rogned—it only left a gaping abyss inside that seemed to grow with every goblet. People's conversation grated like cracked cymbals. Voran's company, which he had treasured only weeks before, preferring it to the company of anyone else, cut at him like knife thrusts. The only comfort he had was in walking, alone, among the sharp rocks.

There was whispering life in those rocks, a sliver of that same power that pulsed through the lands bordering the Gardens of Aer. He would stand before the Fang, his hands pressed to the cold stone, and the twisting agony in his chest, like thorns slowly burrowing into flesh, would fade to a dull ache.

One evening, he was walking back to the now unified camp of the two armies. They would soon begin the long journey to a place Voran called Ghavan Isle, to be presented as the new army of the Three Cities to Dar-in-Exile Mirnían of Vasyllia. It had been Voran's idea, of course. But Rogned supported it. As much as he could muster support for anything these days.

The hundreds of campfires looked like clouds of fireflies. And they felt just as ephemeral. The two armies couldn't possibly remain this friendly for long. Rogned wanted nothing to do with the coming war for Vasyllia's reclamation. Not yet, at least. He wanted his final, fading memories of the Palymi's presence.

He drifted through the knots of waiting warriors—eating, drinking, laughing, telling stories, simply staring into the night. He avoided them, as though he were an incarnate wind. As he passed by them, he heard snatches of conversation.

". . . like a tower . . . just like old Nebesta, but greater by far . . ."

". . . a watchtower on top, the fires reaching up higher than anything . . . a beacon to the Heights . . ."

They were talking about his sculpture, he realized. But something was wrong. These men were Nebesti, but in the adjoining Karila camp, two old men were mumbling to each other in archaic Karilan:

". . . the rusted blade reforged, held in the hand of a Karakul reborn . . ."

"Yes, I recognized his face. Of course Rogned would put his own brother on the greatest work of art any man had ever made . . ."

They were talking about the same sculpture. But . . .

With a sinking feeling, Rogned realized he had no memory of the sculpting. Not the process, not the form, not even what it looked like.

He rushed back to his tent. The firelight threw back two shadows inside. Rogned heard Voran talking to the chief of Nebesta's armies, a hard man named Yarpolk Dolgoruk.

"Are you mad? We all saw it! It was Vasyllia restored, every stone of it more glorious than it had ever been in years past!"

Yarpolk sniggered. "You *would* see that, you fanatic. Can't you get it through your thick skull? Vasyllia is fallen. And if we ever come near it again, I would prefer to take each stone apart and pulverize it, not to put it all back together again!"

"What did you see, then?" challenged Voran, but Rogned heard a note of doubt in his voice.

"The River Nebestaala, a perfect sun rising over it. Two spears of fire and light crossed above it."

"That's . . . wait . . . that's . . ."

Rogned fled. He thought he knew what had happened. His heart plunged to his feet.

Every person saw what he needed most in the sculpture.

There would be no peace. There would be no end to war. As soon as everyone realized what had happened, the old tribalism would cause fissures in the new unity. There could be no unity behind a prophet-prince who gave a different prophecy for each of his followers.

What madness! He could never lead. What was he thinking?

It struck him like a punch in the face—intense, shrieking longing. The Garden. It called to him.

What are you doing, playing power games? You can only help them in one way. Voran stopped you the first time. Now is the time to finish the journey.

Was it his own thought? Rogned didn't care anymore.

ROGNED STOOD on the Fang in the light of the full moon. The tarn below him sparkled in the moonlight. There was music in the air, faint, barely audible, like a lone violin droning a single, plangent note. He recognized it. It was coming from the other side of the water. All he needed to do was jump.

He jumped.

Voran clung to the edge of the world with the tips of his fingers. It bucked under him like an angry colt. He closed his eyes, but that only made the cosmos itself spin sideways, at the same moment as the hard muscle of his palms cramped.

He opened his eyes, focusing on the grain of the brownish-grey rock in front of his face. There were flecks of pink there. Pink, like the upturned palm of Sabíana as he reached down to kiss it.

Focus!

Digging his fingers into the rock as though he could will it to become clay, he strained his shoulders, lifting himself inch by inch over the final hurdle, onto a flat ledge. Leading with his right shoulder, scraping his body over the wet moss on the tip of the ledge, he pushed with his feet, scrabbling up the rock face until he flipped over his shoulder, landing with a squelching thud onto his back. A wet cold creeped up from his back to his shoulders and down his legs. His eyes still closed, he reached out with his fingers. Cold water stung them.

A voice called out from behind him.

"How dare you reveal the land's beauty now? Now, when the grass and the rocks will be defiled with blood!"

Voran's head spun with a fierce sense of having been in this place once before. He turned over onto his knees, careful not to fall. He now realized where he was.

How did I get here?

The Fang of the Giant, this place was called. It was the tallest tor in Karila, a land of tors. Voran had been here once before, a long time ago, when he still had hope for the reclamation of his land from the demonic power that had presided over its fall. That was a time when he had still carried Tarin's blade, which he had hoped to pledge to the service of Rogned, prince of Karila. But Rogned, like nearly everyone Voran knew, had fallen to treachery. How long had it been? Fifteen years?

Except . . . there stood Rogned. His shoulder-length black hair whipped across his face by the wind, Rogned peered over the edge of the Fang, his shoulders tense. It was exactly the same pose, the same wind, the same . . . everything.

Pummeled forward by an internal compulsion stronger than his own will, Voran found himself reenacting the scene, just as it had occurred so many years ago.

"Rogned!" he heard himself call out, barely audible in the ripping sound of the wind.

Rogned turned. The sharp lines of his cheekbones, the deep set of his dark eyes, with their slightly oversized whites— he looked exactly the same.

"I was hoping you'd follow, Voran," said Rogned. "I wasn't sure you'd believed me."

The memory washed over Voran, pulling from his mouth the same words he spoke to Rogned fifteen years ago:

"Have you finally lost your mind? I know you craftsmen are impulsive, but this?"

"It's halfway to the Heights," said Rogned. Inspiration rose from him like the steam from his mouth in the frigid air.

Voran scrunched his eyes shut, balling his hands into fists and knuckling his eyelids. It wasn't real. This had all happened already, and he had no desire to relive this part of his life. Rogned was the younger brother of Karakul, one of several to die in the ill-fated embassy to Karila led by Otchigen. Voran had made a promise to himself that nothing would ever happen to Rogned. It had proved to be a false promise, in a life full of them.

"Quickly, Voran," said Rogned. "This may be our only chance."

Voran felt his face go hot at the sight—so familiar, and still so shocking—of Rogned's knife, which he had pulled out of his boot in a smooth motion, clearly much rehearsed. The fool had thought that committing suicide would force an encounter with a Palymi he had seen in his dreams.

"Rogned!" Voran's hands shook, in spite of himself. "You're mad. Just because of a few dreams? You can't force an encounter with the Heights. High Beings come to you in their own time."

Voran knew what would come next—the eldritch light in Rogned's eyes, the swift passage of the knife over his exposed wrist, the angry spurt of blood.

Except . . .

Rogned stood in place, then smiled. His face . . . twisted.

Voran's stomach churned with mixed fear and disgust.

An all-too-familiar voice issued from the still-liquid features of the changing face before him.

"You were wrong, of course, my rat. You *can* force an encounter with the Heights. Rogned only proved it."

The Raven, having completed his transformation, stood before Voran with an expression of smug self-satisfaction, his hands held loosely at his sides, palms-out, his head cocked to the side slightly, like a trained bird gauging the reaction of its master to a newly learned trick.

Voran sagged into the ground and leaned back, no longer

caring about the plunge, thousands of feet deep. He closed his eyes and let himself fall.

As he expected, he snapped awake, just as his back thumped against the now familiar wall of rock looming over him, slightly curved, like the cupped hand of a motherly giant. Once again, Voran was swathed in furs against the mountain winter. Once again, his eyes alighted on the young, handsome features of the Raven—not the demonic overlord of Vasyllia, but the strange trickster who had abducted him from the Heart of the World and dropped him in the middle of a foreign mountain range. The Raven beamed cherubically from within a king's assortment of woolen clothes and furs.

They had trudged through knee-high snows and skirted around crevasses, each a mile deep, for about a week now. Voran was finding it difficult to distinguish the days, not only because of the never-ending panorama of grey peaks and white snows that blinded him with the sun during all hours of the day, but because his nights were filled with variations on the kind of vivid dream that he had just escaped from. Sometimes he woke up to the thought that he wasn't sure which was real —this world or the dreams.

But this was the first time that the Raven had appeared in one of them.

Voran considered that realization. It should probably have worried him more than it did. But he was finding it difficult to muster the strength for anything other than the simmering fury at his heart—a rage that came up roaring at the slightest remembrance of what happened in the Heart of the World.

"Are you ever going to tell me where we're going?" asked Voran, mainly to provide some contrast with the constant shriek of wind in his ears.

"I've told you," said the Raven, as he made a tent shape from the improbably dry logs that always seemed to appear out of nowhere. "We're going to storm the Heights of Aer."

He said it with the same inflection as one might say, "We're going to have dinner."

Voran shook his head and leaned his head back against the rock face.

Images that usually had the good grace to wait behind his eyelids now crowded into his waking mind—the dead body of his nephew, Antomír, the face of Sabíana as she realized that she had been healed by Voran, the three Powers opening veiled curtains of water that were doors to other places and times, the Harbinger revealing the true name of the god Voran had worshiped as the Creator, who had turned out to be nothing more than an aspect of Vasyllia's eternal enemy, the Raven. The same Raven who now conjured fire from his fingertips to light a campfire thousands of feet above ground, in an unknown wasteland of rock and ice.

Voran realized, a bit distantly, that his fingers were digging into his knees painfully, that his entire body was like a tightly strung bow, that his teeth were carving out holes in one another from the grinding.

"I must say I'm impressed with your calmness, Voran," teased the Raven. "Naturally, I've never been human, but I imagine I'd be a little bit more tense if I were in your place."

"Don't mistake calmness for serenity, Raven."

"Ah. Good. Saving your energy for the times ahead, yes?"

"Something like that."

In fact, it took a nearly constant force of will to prevent his chest from exploding from anger, to stop the feral curse that lay curled up, waiting, at the back of his throat. There were no words in Vasylli, or probably in the tongue of any race, to express the depth of his anger at the Powers who had toyed with him for two decades, who had stood by and watched as his entire world, everything he held dear, collapsed in a heap of lies and futility.

He remembered the face of the boy, also named Voran, whom he had seen in his travels with Tarin. He was a pockmarked child, damaged by war, and he had broken Voran's heart, so many long years ago. The boy—not a boy anymore, he reminded himself— was probably dead of disease or the sword by now. And all for what?

To distract himself, he spoke aloud again.

"Are you real, Raven? Or are you some sort of sickness in my mind?"

The Raven chuckled.

"You should try to expand your mind a bit. Why does it have to be one or the other?"

Voran felt himself, almost without control, burst into sudden motion. With both hands he grabbed one of the burning logs by its unlit end and attacked the Raven, showering him with blows that raised a cloud of sparks dancing around the spinning ice crystals that glittered in the pale sunlight.

The Raven cringed under the blows as though he were nothing but flesh and bone. Voran felt the dull thudding of the wood against something like flesh. It enraged him, even as it poured a rich elation into his chest—warm like fresh mead. There was great pleasure in beating the Raven.

Something chuckled inside Voran's mind, something that was not his own thought. He recoiled, dropping the log. It fell into snow and hissed. Through the cloud thrown up by the log, Voran saw that the Raven's face was bloody, the bruises already forming. The chuckling in Voran's head echoed, then attached itself to the lips of the Raven. The wounds closed up, right before Voran's eyes, in a parody of quick healing.

"Good, good," hissed the Raven in the ancient voice of his hungry, formless self. It was obscene and unsettling, coming out of the mouth of a seemingly young man. "You see? I only want what you want. Pleasure at power. Imagine what I can give you when we take the Heights together."

Voran heaved, as if to vomit, but nothing came out. In that moment, he remembered that he had not eaten in days.

"Raven!" His voice was jagged, dried out by lack of food and the frigid air. "I don't pretend to know what your goal is. But don't you think it's time we stopped playing and spoke honestly to each other? If the Harbinger killed you, how are you here?"

The young man's voice returned. "You don't even know what you're asking, do you, my rat? But very well. Some straight talk."

He settled into his furs, like a bird ruffling its feathers. The likeness only made Voran's stomach churn with more disgust.

"You have to understand. The Harbinger, as you know him" —he mouthed the name with distaste, as though he had belched up some old undigested bits of beef—"he likes a bit of pageantry. Smoke and mirrors, you know? The shining white sword cleaving through my neck, separating my head from my body, and so on and so forth."

The image of the young-faced, golden-robed Harbinger holding up the shriveled head of the Raven flashed before Voran. He nodded.

"It didn't occur to you to wonder how that was even possible? After all, you've probably been told that I'm formless. The Great Changer, and all that. Hungering for physical form and possessing the bodies of lesser beings. Yes?"

Voran felt another brick in the edifice of his worldview crack.

"So why the decapitation, you ask? *How* the decapitation? I have no head, no body. Not even any hands with which to take the fruit."

Another image—the Raven scrambling up a cone-shaped rock, his taloned hands reaching for the last fruit on the burning trees, the one hope for the Living Water to continue to flow.

"Think about it! I had no physical form. You had expelled me from your body, thank you very much." The Raven's expression barely differed from that of a pouting child. "I could have taken the fruit while I possessed Antomír, it is true. But that's my great weakness, isn't it? An overweening sense of poetic justice. I really, really wanted *you* to pick the fruit."

Voran's head felt thick, his thoughts congealing like bad molasses. The Raven had nearly succeeded. If not for Khaidu, that wondrous Gumira child, he probably would have.

"So what are you saying, Raven?"

"The Harbinger didn't actually kill me. He couldn't. I had no body to kill."

"You're lying. I just beat the marrow out of your bones."

"Oh." A smile stretched the young man's face past human capacity, until it seemed the edges of his mouth would tear from the strain. "You wouldn't believe how flexible the human mind is! Just push a few levers and you can convince someone that they are drinking the best wine. Even if you reveal the truth to them: it's actually the piss of a cow. But they won't believe you. They're *sure* of what they tasted."

"An illusion, then. Fine. But what about the Harbinger? I find it hard to believe that you fooled the Powers."

"Do you? And what other great wisdom do you have concerning the essence of the gods?"

Voran had a strange sensation, as though he saw himself from the vantage point of heaven, a tiny speck on a mountain range that reached as far as the eye could see. He felt utterly, cosmically insignificant.

"Yes, exactly," said the Raven. "You are in no position to judge. Only to listen."

Voran took a deep breath. He nodded once, curt.

The Raven smiled, clearly enjoying himself.

"I mean, naturally I don't always tell the truth. Spinning half-truths is so much more fun. And sometimes I can't even untangle them, they get so complicated! Haha! But since we are to be partners in rebellion, I will give you some of the truth. Enough to prevent your tiny little skull from exploding."

He waved, and a rabbit hopped out of nowhere into their field of vision. The Raven put out his hand, inviting. The rabbit, its nose sniffing frantically, extended its long-eared head close, curious. The Raven's hand contorted in a way no human could, twisting the head of the rabbit right off its body in a split second. Voran yelped in surprise.

"So . . . did my hand twist the head of the rabbit off?"

Making a claw out of his other hand, the Raven plunged his fingernails into the fur of the mangled corpse. He pulled. The skin peeled off like an orange rind.

"Did my nails pull off this hide?"

He threw the skinned carcass down at Voran's feet, gesturing impatiently at him. In his shock, Voran didn't understand what was expected of him. Then he understood, to the curdling of his own blood. The Raven expected him to dress the rabbit for cooking.

"I don't actually have any fingers or nails, though. I'm a spirit in a world of forms. Formless, but definitely alive. It would of course be very disturbing to your puny mind if I showed what I actually look like. You have no frame of reference for it, for the power that throbs in me more intensely than the heart that beats in your chest. So I clothe it in an image that you can not only see, but also feel with your hands. Is that real? Is that not real?"

The Raven shrugged comically, like a storyteller does during a market-day spectacle.

"All you need to understand is that my will to live, to inhabit a form, is just as real as your desire for revenge. And so, we join forces toward our common goal."

Having dressed it, Voran held the skewered rabbit over the fire. It looked real enough. The juices hissed as they dripped into the flames.

"You still haven't explained how you fooled the Harbinger," said Voran. "I've felt the power of the Palymi's blade. It can sever spirit as well as flesh—I'm sure of it."

The Raven's eyes flashed black fire for a moment, and the entire sky seemed to go dark. Then he smiled again, though the threat still lurked behind his eyes.

"There's a hidden art that I mastered, many eons ago. In cases of extreme need, I can divide my self—my essence, if you will—into several places at once."

"The flask, you mean?" Voran remembered the strange, alluring nature of the thing that had looked like his old flask of Living Water, but had been another illusion—a kind of trap-door leading out to this land of endless mountains. "Why do I sense that you're only telling me part of the truth?"

The Raven adopted an expression of aggrieved shock.

"Spare me," Voran said. "I'll fill your story out, shall I? You *were*, in fact, dying. Your spirit essence oozing out of the wound inflicted by the Harbinger's sword. But since you had been inside me, possessing me, a part of you remained there. It's probably still there, now. And that means . . ."

Voran looked sharply at the Raven, who watched him, unblinking.

"I'm all that's keeping you alive."

The Raven slitted his eyes closed and growled.

"And I think there's more to it. Shall I?" Voran twisted the rabbit over the fire, enjoying the smell of roasted flesh. His mouth watered. "You have very little actual power left. Enough to conjure up vivid dreams and to appear before me in this"—Voran waved vaguely at the Raven, dismissive—"pathetic guise. But certainly not enough to do what's necessary."

The Raven's eyes closed a fraction, his expression growing more pleased.

"Whatever do you mean, my rat?"

"You can't just transport us directly to the Heights, can you?"

The Raven's silence, which stretched out a long time, was eloquence itself.

"So how are you going to . . . what expression do you keep

using? Storm the Heights?"

The Raven leaned toward Voran, cupping his hand over his mouth conspiratorially. Voran almost laughed aloud. It was as though the Raven only had an outside idea of what human expression was like, and his attempts were theatrical and exaggerated.

"Rogned," whispered the Raven.

Voran tensed.

"He's dead, Raven. Hanged by his own men."

"His body is, sure. But don't you realize that the Heights are beyond the material world? Closer to spirit than matter, in fact."

"Wait. Are you saying what I think you're saying?"

The Raven stood up and raised his hands in triumph. "And the penny drops! Yes. Rogned's body might have been hanged on the gallows by Yarpolk of Nebesta. But his spirit waits for you, even now, in the Heights of Aer. He traveled the forbidden road to the Heights, unlike all others who are fated to languish in the Realm of the Dead. And I will teach you to do the same, but in your body."

Voran stood up, barely able to suppress the excitement coursing through him.

"How? And be specific, you pathetic excuse for a god."

The Raven, it seemed, chose to ignore the slight.

"You know the story of the Children of the Priest-King?"

Voran shook his head.

"Oh, it's a good one! But very long. I'll give you the short version.

There once was a family. A very, very messed-up family. Cross-cultural marriages, magic fountains of water, prophecies, that sort of thing. The important thing is this: Four children of that family, called, for our purposes, the Children of the Priest-King, did what no other human beings ever did. They crossed through the Realm of the Dead and came as far as any human being in his body can: the gate of the Garden of Aer. At that first gate (there are, of course, seven), the Heights deigned to listen to their request, since they had braved dangers no human being ever has. And so on, and so forth."

"The point, Raven?"

"Ah! It was because of them that a Palymi was placed at the gate to the Garden. A Palymi with a flaming sword."

Voran gasped. "You can't be serious."

The Raven laughed and slapped his knee. "Yes! Rogned told you, didn't he? The Palymi who spoke through his sculpting. And you know what that Palymi did? He opened the gate for Rogned. That gate remains open to this day."

"How do you know?"

The young face assumed an expression so ancient, so knowing, that Voran stiffened. He really should try to remember who he was dealing with. Not a flippant young man, but the oldest, most ancient malice the Realms had ever known. A demonic force that had toppled an entire civilization. And now all that was left of it was lodged somewhere inside Voran's mind, manifesting as this . . . illusion.

Or at least that's what Voran *hoped* it was.

The Raven's voice assumed a chant-like quality, and Voran realized that the demon was quoting from some ancient lore, far beyond the knowledge of man and beast.

"And just beyond the gate is the center of all the Realms. A sea the size of an ocean, with an island anchored at its center. Upon that island stands the world-oak, its boughs entwined with Gamayun's tower, that reaches up into the Sea of Time. At the base of that oak stands a throne. Whoever sits in that throne calls upon himself the might of the Powers, to do his bidding for one day and one hour and one minute. Behold, it is called the Throne of the Gods."

The Raven turned back to Voran, and his eyes glowed. "And you will sit on that throne, Voran, son of Otchigen, and the Most High himself will bow to the footstool of your feet."

Voran couldn't help it. His heart leapt at the prospect.

ꕷ   2   ꕷ

Sabíana sat by a river of fire, transfixed by something no
other human being had ever seen. From the blazing
ripples rose a cone of rock crowned with three cherry trees, all
of them aflame without being consumed. Behind them, a
distant mountain range provided a hazy frame that made the
entire spectacle more like dream than reality. She felt the
shadow of the towering red-barks in the forest behind her,
though she couldn't see them.

The light of the trees in the Heart of the World flickered.
Two of the trees had shed their petals completely now, and
they stood bare and insignificant by the flaming river. The
central tree clung to its petals, which still burned brightly,
though not nearly as bright as the throbbing single fruit
hanging from the lowest branch. It looked full to bursting.

Sabíana stared intently at the fruit. She tried to understand
how the seeds of this fruit, when harvesting the flaming
waters, could transform that river into the lifeblood of the
Realms, the source of all life itself. She failed miserably.

By her side, a greatly diminished Lyna sat, her wings folded
over her eagle chest in a way that was decidedly human, not
birdlike. To Sabíana's left, the Harbinger stood, leaning on a

staff, looking for all the worlds like an old man bent by age, not one of the greatest Powers of all the Realms, capable of cutting down the power even of the Raven himself.

"I should feel wonder at this," Sabíana said, more to herself than to anyone else. "No one has ever seen this before, not in all man's history."

Instead, the deadness in her slithered out from her heart, crawling with icy fingers over the rest of her body. What did it matter that she was about to see a miracle? What was the point of miracles when the world itself had no meaning?

The fruit throbbed like a heart, then flashed in bright vermilion.

No one answered Sabíana, not even the Harbinger. At that moment, Sabíana missed Khaidu so much it ached inside her. The Gumira's sharp humor would have been a healing balm in this moment, more desired even than the physical healing Voran had given her body. But Khaidu had gone with Aglaia through one of the Palymi's doors, to the parting of the ways. They were intent on braving the Realm of the Dead, mad as that idea was.

But who is more mad? They who brave the dead lands, or we who wait for the lands of the living to wither and die?

It seemed an uncounted age that they sat there, the fruit slowly growing brighter and brighter. Then, in a flash that was as much music as it was light, the fruit burst open. Seeds like living sparks flew out over the waters. Every time they hit the water, a chord of light-music played in the still air. The animals of this place—squirrels, foxes, badgers—came to sit at the edge of the waters and stare in mute wonder, completely unafraid of their human companions. Their eyes reflected the sparks. Sabíana thought they looked wiser and more content than any human being could be.

"What now?" asked Lyna.

The Harbinger sighed and shook his head. "I do not know."

Sabíana turned her head sharply at the figure robed in grey, with grey beard and grey eyes—a figure so solid he seemed carved from marble.

"If *you* do not know, who does?"

"The normal life cycle of the trees presupposes many fruits, not one. The lifeblood of the Realms must be seeded regularly. Now, all the Realms hold their breath to see if another fruit will even grow."

He stopped. Sabíana jumped up, the anger needle-sharp inside her.

"What? Will the Realms start dying? What does that mean for all living things? What does it mean for Vasyllia? You suggested to Voran that we should hope! What hope do we have, if the Realms themselves begin to collapse?"

"The only hope anyone can have," said Lyna in a half-chant, looking blankly out over the waters. "The hope that the Heights intervene in time."

"That is no hope at all!" Sabíana paced along the bank, her hands twitching at her sides. "To sit and wait, and hope for deliverance? That is not the way!"

"No," said the Harbinger. "It is not. And I have not lied to you, Sabíana. You can choose where to go. Wherever you go, your healing will inspire others. Even before, when you were a child, you commanded the loyalty of men. Now, having come through a living death and back again, you can do wonders."

"You're suggesting I take the road to Raven's Bane, aren't you?" Sabíana faced the Harbinger, feeling an irrational desire to kick aside his staff.

"Yes."

"And what if I choose Vasyllia instead? What if I refuse to accept her demise?"

"That would be . . . far more dangerous."

"Ha! Who was it that urged me to take the difficult way, Harbinger? Who?"

The Harbinger bowed, and he had the decency, Sabíana thought, to look abashed.

"You must understand, my swan. Everything that occurred up to the moment when you came to the Heart of the World was foreseen, to some degree. The Powers have been straining to move events, in their limited ability to intervene, toward this moment. But there is no certainty from this moment on. I can prophesy no longer. No one can."

"And so, we are left to our own devices," Sabíana mumbled. Her mouth was sour with disgust.

"No," said Lyna. "You will have the Sirin." Her eyes were alight with some nonhuman emotion. "I will take the road to Raven's Bane, Sabíana. But I will not stop there. I will go to the habitations of my sisters. I will raise them for the cause of Sabíana, Darina of Vasyllia. For the Heart of the World, that it may rise again as a beacon for those who choose to live not for themselves, but for the impossible love of human souls. Wait for me in Vasyllia, my queen. I will come to you. And I will bring the final fruit from the Heart of the World, to be replanted in its proper place."

Sabíana's breath faltered as the light of Lyna's feathers caught the dancing spark-light of the seeds. Lyna sang, and the sparks danced in harmony. The animals cavorted in pure joy. To Sabíana's shock, she saw a mountain leopard dancing with a horned sheep as though they were family, not predator and prey. Lyna flew into the spinning veil of water leading to Raven's Bane. The door flashed as she passed and winked out.

Sabíana felt her cheeks with her fingers. They were wet. The deadness inside her cowered and began a slow retreat.

"I go to Vasyllia," she said to the Harbinger. "I go to save my city before it destroys itself."

He bowed before her, becoming even older and more frail than before. His staff outstretched, he pointed the way to the final door.

※ 3 ※

The combined armies of Ghavan and the lost clan of the Gumiren had marched for forty days. Adelaida, who had never walked more than half a circuit of Ghavan Isle at a time, was almost constantly overwhelmed. The ever-shifting land-scape, the impossible profusion of animal life, the sheer expanse of land with no sea anywhere near it—she couldn't have imagined it in her most frightening dreams. But that was nothing compared to the stench of corpses and burnt wood and sweaty leather that accompanied them nearly at every step as soon as they entered Nebesta. From battleground to battle-ground they trudged, from one hell to another. She wasn't sure if she had gone mad, or if the world itself had.

But all that was nothing compared to the palpable sense of wrongness that pressed upon her like a greasy, oversized hand on the nape of her neck. They had arrived at the border of Vasyllia.

A wall stood between Vasyllia and the rotting forests of Nebesta. On their side, the Nebesta side, every tree seemed diseased or dead of some slime-rot. It smelled like overripe fruit, but with an underlying taste of death, like a charnel house. But just beyond the wall, Vasyllia glistened green and brilliant. The warmth of the air on that side wafted over the wall occasionally, banishing the slime smell with faint traces of rosemary and pine.

How were two such opposites possible? How could Vasyllia look like a paradise of legend, even more perfect than her own Ghavan Isle, while its neighbor was a graveyard of humans, beasts, and growing things alike?

A hole gaped in the wall like a mouth of some dead monster. Even as they approached—Adelaida walking with her brother and sisters just a little behind the main host, near the supply carts—the warriors froze. Some of them took their helmets off. Others fell on their knees in what was clearly a gesture of reverence.

"What's going on?" asked Zabían, speaking for the first time in several days. For a moment, Adelaida's relief was so intense, she forgot that he had even asked a question. It was enough to hear his bright, ten-year-old voice. The color had come back somewhat to his cheeks, and his green eyes weren't quite so sunken. She tweaked his nose—so straight, just like mother's—and ruffled the slightly curling dark gold of his hair. It had been getting lighter by the day in the mountain sun.

Zabían had not taken well to the world outside Ghavan—even worse than the rest of his siblings. The horrors they had witnessed had weighed more heavily on him than on the others.

"I don't know. I'll go and see, little mushroom."

He smiled at the old joke, a fraying connection to the false world of their youth. Zabían had always loved to collect mushrooms.

Or had he?

After all, were they even born properly, like real human beings? Or had they been created whole cloth by the artifice of a mad demon? Was her entire remembered life nothing but a figment of *his* imagination? And what about now? Was their existence in the real world a curse, or an unexpected gift of some unknown Power on high?

Her breath came so shallow, it felt like she was drowning in the open air. She forced herself to take a breath so deep, her ribs ached from the stretch.

Such thoughts were still dangerous ground for her. She wasn't ready to think about all that yet.

Instead, she pushed gently against the shoulder of the nearest foot soldier. The metal, cold and thrilling to the touch, seemed to jump from her as the young soldier made way, pushing his fellows ahead of him with a soft word she didn't hear. Many bowed their heads with respect; some had a smile for what she imagined might be her youth and beauty.

She recognized Batuk, one of the leaders of the Gumiren, just ahead, stroking his horse. She approached him.

He was a stocky man, almost all muscle, from the bulge in either cheek all the way to the mutton-chop calves that seemed almost superhumanly large. The tension of that muscle-bound frame was reflected in the tightness around his eyes, which were dark and surprisingly sad, if you looked beyond the odd angle of his cheeks and the strangely overlong whiskers.

"Vohin Batuk, what is happening?" she asked, all formality.

He looked at her with cold eyes for a long moment. She almost expected him to turn away from her. And she wouldn't blame him. He was a hard man, and most of the warriors were afraid of him, some even spurning him openly. But from the first, she had sensed some deep wound inside him—probably somewhere deep in his eyes—and it drew her to him now.

When she didn't turn away from his unblinking gaze, Batuk softened—she saw it in the set of his shoulders and the sudden looseness of his hips.

"Vohin . . . that is a Vasylli term, yes? I am only Batuk. Please call me Batuk."

"Batuk," she smiled. "Why have we stopped?"

"Listen," he said, pointing with his head toward the front of the lines. "Can you hear?"

She could, to her surprise. Though Derzhava, the seer, was at least fifty yards ahead of them, Adelaida heard her voice clearly.

"Here Alienne, the Golden Lady of the Lows of Aer, gave her life for the love of her husband. Here, the foundation of all Realms cracked and moved, and time itself was rewritten. Here began the fall of the Raven, the rise of us who are his bane."

Adelaida shuddered. The memory of the Golden Lady left her with mixed feelings. The light that had accompanied her, the flame-like wings and godlike presence that shuddered in the air like a piper's low note—it had left Adelaida breathless, filled with emotions for which she hadn't yet found the words. But the coming of that Lady had changed something about Ghavan Isle, something Adelaida had never noticed, until she lost it.

Ghavan had been a place of patterns, of ritual and repetition. Adelaida had never considered it anything but normal. But then, the outside world broke in on Ghavan, and it was as though she and the rest of them had awoken from a dream that had lasted decades. And though the world outside was beautiful in places, Alienne had cracked open the egg of Adelaida's life. And the yolk was running out.

"Would you like to see?" asked Batuk. Adelaida didn't understand at first, but then he patted his horse's back invitingly. She nodded.

He picked her up as though she weighed nothing. The sensation was briefly exciting, like falling, but upward. The horse nickered, but held still. It was a chestnut-brown color with a light blond mane. A beautiful horse, easily led, even by Adelaida's slight legs.

"Thank you," she said to Batuk, a bit sheepish.

But then she saw Derzhava in Lebía's arms as she sat on a

warhorse, and all her attention was taken by the spectacle. For a moment, it was as if time stopped, as though everything she saw were a painting, more realistic than life itself. Derzhava, the woman who looked more like a sickly child with papery pale skin than a woman of twenty-something, was held in the arms of her mother Lebía, who in her queenly dress of sky blue, edged with gold, looked only a few years older than Adelaida herself. Mirnían, his curls resting on gold-plated scale armor, his grey eyes intent on Lebía, also looked too young to be her father. In his left arm, he held a helm that caught the sickly light of the greyish sun. The warriors of Vasyllia and the Steppe were frozen, intent on the vision of the seer speaking of events that made the Old Tales seem like quotidian affairs.

But where do I fit in all this? They have eyes for no one but each other.

She had started to feel it as soon as they left Ghavan. Lebía and Mirnían had grown closer to each other as they traveled, bound by common experiences conjured by the journey home. But those experiences were from a world where Adelaida should never have existed. And yet, here she was. Here they all were.

"If you frown like that, your eyes might pop out of their sockets," said Batuk.

Coming from the hard warrior, it was such a strange phrase that it snapped her back to herself. Surprised, she laughed. In that place, amid that ruin of the wall, it was the wrong thing to do. Immediately, she noticed that some of the warriors looked up at her with resentment, as though she had stolen something precious from them.

"Help me down, please," she said.

Batuk did.

THE NEXT FEW days were a blur of nearly constant pain. Adelaida had always prided herself on being a good climber. The spruce-covered white-stone hilltops of Ghavan Isle had been a favorite haunt. She could ascend the highest hill, to the point where the Great Sea sparkled like diamond-studded snakeskin between the boughs of the fir trees, just far enough to be dreamlike. But Vasyllia was not a hill country; it was a land of mountains.

These mountains towered like they had evil intent against all travelers. Every time her leg muscles twinged with new, never-before-experienced pain, she was sure she could make out looming and sneering faces in the towers of stone above her. But then, the defiles and drops and green-flecked land-scapes of river and valley *underneath* her took her breath away, and she thought she might drown in the simultaneous thrill of being so high and the tumbling fear of falling and dying.

It was all exhausting. But she had not only herself to think of. Zabían adjusted quickly, capering back and forth along the narrow path leading up to the Pass of Ardovían like one of the several mountain goats they saw scampering out of the way of the army. But the twins did not take it so well. When they had finally started to climb the mountains, Kachinka sat on the side of the road and refused to move forward. When pressed, she admitted that she had thought the mountains were strangely shaped clouds. When she realized what they actually were, the fear left her babbling and unable to move.

It was a pitiful spectacle—a slightly plump thirteen-year-old princess in a deep purple underdress with an ermine-fringed sleeveless kaftan over her shoulders sat on the icy mud, her snot mixing with the sleet that fell fitfully from the rising thunderheads above them.

Only Adelaida's years of practiced calmness had brought Kachinka back to some form of normality. That, and Marinka's presence, her half-intelligible twin-talk calming Kachinka, even as she herself couldn't stop from shuddering in her boots.

All of it left Adelaida twenty times as exhausted. It was hard enough dealing with the bubbling cauldron of her own thoughts and emotions and fears. Not to mention the sleeping anger deep inside her, threatening to explode. But she pushed herself onward, maintaining that calm demeanor and catching brief snatches of sleep while the troops rested.

It wasn't enough.

An evening three days after they had started the ascent into Vasyllia shone brilliant with a red sunset striped with purple clouds, as though the entire expanse of heaven were the piebald pelt of some mythical creature. A few stars twinkled uneasily near the horizon, which was visible only as a knife-shaped slit between razor peaks. Mist snaked through the valleys underneath the high road Adelaida traveled with the riders of the Gumiren.

The Steppe fighters found no advantage to being mounted in this terrain, and so walked next to their horses to lessen the strain on their animals' backs and legs. Adelaida appreciated the thought—she had always felt sorry that the horses needed to bear their burdens for so many long hours.

Adelaida sat on the edge of the road, her legs hanging perilously off the side of a cliff that would have dwarfed three Ghavan hills stacked on top of each other. She looked over the edge, then gasped as the air refused to enter her lungs. She could not see the bottom, so dark it was. She closed her eyes. The terror of the wide world, roiling inside her, subsided, but slowly. In its wake, like a drone held by a bagpiper between the choruses of a song, wonder grew, sparkling like the pinpoints of light in the rising darkness above her head. It was a terrible world, certainly. But it was beautiful beyond words.

Batuk, who was never very far, though he did not seek her company, had volunteered to bear the shriveled and broken form of Derzhava the Seer. Perhaps sensing Adelaida's emotion, he carried Derzhava and placed her on a specially prepared bed of furs next to Adelaida. Smiling at her quizzically, he walked back to his brothers, who were setting up camp under the shelter of an overhanging half-cave of rock.

Adelaida felt an onrush of gratitude so strong, it stung her eyes as a few tears came out. She hadn't realized how much she needed the calm, quiet company of Derzhava.

"How are you bearing the ascent, Derzhava? It must be hard on you, no?"

Derzhava's face was beautiful—pink-cheeked and smooth as a twelve-year-old girl's, though with a thinness that bespoke long illness. But that beauty was almost a mockery. Her arms were misshapen as old tree roots, with no hands but stumps. Her legs, shriveled and twisted into obscene shapes visible only as suggestions under the blankets covering her, were too short for her body.

"Adelaida," Derzhava said, smiling at her crookedly. "Let me tell you something your mother probably never told you. Pain of the heart, especially pain for others, is often heavier than pain of the body. The pain of my body is always there, and so my mind sometimes forgets about it, just as we often cease to notice what is in front of us always."

Adelaida smiled back, though she suspected that Derzhava was lying to make her feel better.

"How is Batuk caring for you?" she asked.

Derzhava's eyes grew distant for a moment, then focused again. "Yes, exactly. His pain, poor man, is far worse than mine."

Adelaida was confused by the apparent change of topic, but it was often thus with Derzhava, who seemed to see a world with deeper shadows and brighter colors than other people. Then a thought struck her.

"Are you saying he is . . . atoning for something by his good care of you?"

"That feeling had come into my heart, yes. You may not know this, dear one, but the Gumiren have very strict taboos about physical deformity. They leave deformed children to the tender mercies of the wild animals of the Steppe."

"How barbaric!" She couldn't help but recoil, even as she turned toward Batuk with a reproaching glance, as though he were personally responsible for his people's strange customs.

"They lead a hard life, little one. It is perhaps a mercy to such people to end their earthly sufferings early, hastening the dawn of the second life."

Adelaida did not agree. But she never liked to contradict anyone, so she didn't now.

Derzhava looked at her with a lopsided grin and laughed. Adelaida felt naked under her gaze.

"What?" she asked, confused.

"Do you allow me to speak my heart to you, Adelaida?"

Adelaida just looked at her, unsure of what to do. She still had a hard time getting used to Derzhava's mannered, formal speech.

"It might be painful," Derzhava said. "I think your inclination is to retreat. But let me speak, I beg you."

There was a stab of pain in that last phrase. Adelaida, overcome with pity for Derzhava, nodded.

"Everyone looks at you and sees a woman grown," Derzhava continued, "and a beauty, at that."

Adelaida felt the blush creep up her cheek, along with the discomfort that always accompanied any such compliments. She was grateful that it was getting dark.

"But you are a newly created baby. You, and your brother and sisters. The life you had in the egg-world of false Ghavan was not quite substantial. Your creator, the Artisan, never intended you to have any life other than a phantom half-life. But your second creator, whoever he might be, in giving you full life, did not shield you from the thorn that comes with it."

"Thorn?" Adelaida said, barely audible. "More like sword."

"Ah, I was right." There were tears on Derzhava's face, scarcely visible in the bluish twilight. "Is it enough for me to say to you that I understand what you are going through? The isolation of being something that only you know to be true. The weight of expectations from others that you can't even understand, much less fulfill."

It was as though a block of frozen snow fell off Adelaida's back. For a moment, her reticence to speak about the things of her deep heart fell away.

"Yes, Derzhava! It's more than that, though. I should be grateful, I know, that my siblings and I were given this gift. But I can't help but feel . . ."

She stopped, afraid once more. Would she ever stop being afraid?

"Go on, dear one."

"Well, it's . . . were we created by our parents? By a creator god? This Unknown Father that everyone seems to be pitting their hopes on now? Or are we the product of the Artisan's malice?"

"And if the last, then what?"

Adelaida's head spun. Suddenly, she was aware, with every part of her body and mind, that she was perched on the edge of the world, and a simple push from behind would be the end of her.

She breathed deeply.

"If we were created by an evil power, can we be anything but evil?" She didn't mean to include her siblings in that *we*. But to say *I* only—it was too much.

"Only in a world ruled by fate."

Derzhava left the rest—a myriad of possible explanations —silent. It seemed Adelaida would have to work it out for herself.

And for a sliver of a moment, Adelaida resented Derzhava.

But that emotion was shoved aside by shame. What had she been thinking? Derzhava, of all people, understood what it meant to be isolated, with no clear place in a world made for the strong and the healthy. Inside that shriveled tree stump of a body was a beautiful woman that no one ever looked at, much less saw and loved.

"I'm sorry, Derzhava. I've been selfish again. Let me make it up to you."

Derzhava's eyes were brimming with unshed tears as Adelaida got up and carried her back toward camp.

❧ 4 ☙

Khaidu breathed deeply and closed her eyes, savoring. *Yes.*

She hadn't realized how much she missed it—the smell of fresh grass in a soil-scented wind, reaching for miles in every direction. The Steppe.

Well, almost. Khaidu knew it wasn't exactly the Steppe. Instead of the roll and swell of the dappled long-grass of her home, here the shallow hills were covered with shorter blue-grass. At a distance, glimpsed through the shimmering door of the Palymi in the Garden, the grass had looked almost furry. But now, when she touched it with the tips her fingers, her eyes still closed, it felt rough, bristly. It reminded her of the downs of upper Karila. This place was probably not far from the place where she had first encountered the Majestva trapped in the bodies of eagles.

The memory of it—of those eternal Powers breaking free of their bonds like banners unfurling at a storm wind, then wreaking bloody havoc on their enslavers—seemed almost impossibly faint. As though it were some other Khaidu who had lived those distant days.

"AHEM!"

Khaidu, sitting on the earth with her useless legs awkwardly crossed in front of her, had almost forgotten the massive black wolf propping up her back. Actually, the wolf was a princess of Vasyllia, but in her *other* form. Whatever form she chose, Lady Aglaia of the Excessively Strong Character never did have any patience for simply *being*. Come to think of it, she never had any patience at all. Ever. Not even a little bit.

"What?" Khaidu complained. "Can't I enjoy myself for just one moment, wolf?"

It wasn't Khaidu's fault, after all. She had followed Aglaia to this place, yes. (What had she called it? The parting of the ways? Nothing here but bristly hills for miles.) But she had not followed the wolf from any burning desire to see the Realm of the Dead. Who in their right mind would want to go there?

For perhaps the hundredth time, she heard the question in her own head: *So why did you follow Aglaia, and not Sabíana?* Surely their bond—first the bond between hunter and eagle, and later the fierce love between women who would have been sisters in a more just world—was the more worthy of being honored. But Sabíana had been healed. And . . .

Aglaia made an animal-grunt that could have been anger or just more irritation. Khaidu wasn't in the mood to try to distinguish.

Sabíana . . .

Khaidu's heart twinged at the memory of seeing her standing straight, proud, and healed. No longer the broken thing, but truly a queen that would command armies. It wasn't that Khaidu was jealous, not exactly. But the foundation of their sisterhood—their common brokenness—it was gone. And Sabíana had found her Voran again.

Only to have him taken from her a second time, the voice retorted. *She could have leaned on you for support.*

Khaidu recoiled from that thought, unexpectedly. To be a burden to others—that was once her greatest fear. To be needed by someone like Sabíana had been liberating, invigorating. But now—it wasn't enough. She needed to find her own place, her own reason.

"YOU AGAIN!"

Khaidu almost fell to the ground at that booming voice behind her. It was definitely not Aglaia, not even at her angriest.

And it definitely wasn't female.

"If I keep my eyes closed, will it go away?" Khaidu whispered to Aglaia.

"And how has that strategy worked for you so far, wolfling?" Now there was definitely amusement behind the growl. It made Khaidu's shoulders relax a little.

Aglaia started to rise up to her forelegs, and Khaidu grabbed the thick fur on her shoulders, pulling herself back astride the wolf. As she did, she opened one eye, keeping the other closed just in case. But it shot open as soon as she saw . . .

A giant head, covered by a peaked helmet the size of a small mountain. It seemed to sprout from a set of shoulders so massive that Khaidu's ten brothers, their wives and children, their entire *tabun* of horses, and their yurts could have fit in their shadow. There were ancient engravings on the faded bronze armor—curlicues, swastikas, and other complex shapes for which she had no name. A matted black beard reached all the way to the shrubs at the point where the shoulders disappeared in rocky earth. The beard's ends were ensnared in the bushes, which twitched comically every time the head breathed.

Khaidu's own breath caught in her chest. It was hard to find the strength to exhale. The smell of burning wood flooded her memory. Giant faces painted onto wooden towers burning, the white paint chipping and turning lurid in the flames. She remembered the smoke engulfing a giant city beneath a mountain range. And she felt the same despair that she had when she had seen her entire tribe flee from a band of giant warriors and fire-breathing serpents. They had all fled. Leaving Khaidu and her cursed, dead legs behind.

This giant would probably be even more gargantuan, if the rest of his body weren't entombed in the bones of the world.

Khaidu felt a fellow tremor of fear go through Aglaia's body.

"Buyan, you're . . . not a head anymore. Or not *just* a head."

The giant opened his mouth, revealing teeth like cracked boulders. "Your son's japes were better. You're losing your touch, Aglaia."

"Does this mean . . . ?" Aglaia began, but she stopped.

"My sons are coming into their power, yes. No thanks to Voran. But perhaps that's for the best. It won't be long now."

Khaidu shuddered. If that head were any indication, this giant must be twice the size of those who destroyed the last refuge of her Gumiren clan.

"Will you let us pass, Buyan?" asked Aglaia, tense as a twig about to snap.

The eyes in that mountainous head seemed to catch fire, deep within.

"I haven't decided yet."

Khaidu's stomach churned and her head began to spin in that now familiar sensation of sympathy with another mind, another being. She reached out with her thoughts toward the giant head . . .

She saw a white-hot sun rising over a tundra. Sparkling in its light—brighter than any sun she had ever seen—was a land she could not even imagine. Green-brown grasses were dotted with cloverlike flowers of every conceivable color. Bumblebees lazily floated from one blossom to another, drunk on nectar. White-maned elk with antlers five times larger than their own bodies strode like helmed lords over the expanse. Birds of every size and plumage sang and danced in murmurations so vast that three quarters of the sky seethed with their music shapes. At the center of it all towered a mountain. No. It was a giant man—the center point of this profusion of natural light and color. The sun seemed to shine solely on him, and only then to be reflected on all other created things.

With a gasp, Khaidu recognized Buyan to be that mountainous man.

As she had done in the Heart of the World, Khaidu spoke more from a need to utter something already spoken than from her own desire. "You were there. At the beginning. The creation by the Unknown Father. You were there."

Utter stillness seemed to descend on the giant head. Its skin—so leathery and brown as to be little different from tree bark—faded to a sickly pink.

"What happened?" Khaidu continued, unable to stop. "You were a thing of beauty. A child of the Creator. How did you fall?"

Now the pink had coalesced into angry red in the giant's cheeks, which began to puff as though he were a bellows preparing to blast a furnace.

"No, I don't think I will let you pass, Aglaia."

His shoulder muscles tensed. The teeth in his rippling jaw ground like millstones. Any minute now, Khaidu knew, the vast power of that creature entombed in the earth would simply snuff them out of existence.

And yet, Khaidu could not contain the words tumbling out of her mouth.

"The way of earth-power. The way of your people. We Gumiren know it well. We were taught it by the Dark Father. It ends in madness, always. You will never recapture the purity of that first world, Buyan. Not if you follow the path you are on now."

The giant head was struck dumb. So was Aglaia, who had ceased all movement under Khaidu.

"No," said Khaidu, chuckling. "I'm not a seer. I just pay attention. Precious few people do that nowadays. And I've seen enough to know that you cannot make the pristine beauty of the first creation in the wake of destruction."

"You just watch me, little person," growled Buyan. "My sons and I will scrape every atom of humanity from this earth. Then we will level the mountains and burn the forests. From the canvas of that fresh soil, fertilized by the bodies of all you fallen creatures, will come a new life, clean and pure. The beasts will worship us once again. And the Powers above will finally leave us alone to our earthbound life."

"Yes," Khaidu said, sniggering in spite of herself. "And then horses will sprout antlers to go with their scaly wings."

"Wolfling," whispered Aglaia. "Perhaps it would be a good idea *not* to antagonize the one person who can lead us to the right path?"

And there it was. Which path was the right path? The path to the Realm of the Dead? But this Buyan was a creature of earth. Khaidu suspected he had no idea how to find that road, no matter that he presided over the waystone that was said to lead to all roads.

And to her eyes, the faded waystone looked like nothing more than a mossy stone with scratches on it made by ice and wind.

"Buyan," said Khaidu. "I want you to know what I will make happen. I, Khaidu, of the last true Gumiren to walk this earth, I will raid the Realm of the Dead. I will restore Gamayun to her tower. I will set all times to their right course."

Buyan laughed, but there was nothing but malice in that storm-like sound.

"I made you what you are, Aglaia. Have you forgotten? And now I unmake you. Be the beast you were when I found you."

He snapped his teeth together so hard, Khaidu was sure they would crack into pieces.

Aglaia yelped, as though someone had kicked her.

"Aglaia?"

She didn't answer.

"Aglaia!"

Buyan blew out a blast of hot, putrid air. Khaidu fell off Aglaia, who cowered in place like a dog brought to heel. To her horror, Khaidu noticed that Aglaia was panting. She never panted, or did anything so obviously beast-like.

"I summon the powers of the Realm of Earth," groaned Buyan, "the dark monsters that inhabit the shadows of the sleeping groves, and I command them, by the power of Earth that flows through my veins. You will seek Khaidu of the Gumiren. Her blood is yours."

At that, the ground shook with a roar so intense, it seemed to come from within the earth itself.

The hills around them seethed. Just a moment before, there was nothing but grass. Now, approaching from a distance, wild dogs and rabid foxes and lynxes and weasels the size of bobcats paced and lurched and tensed their haunches, their fangs bared, growling and yowling noises rising like a storm wind.

Khaidu dragged herself toward Aglaia. But the wolf bared her teeth at Khaidu.

"Aglaia, what's the matter?"

There was nothing of the human in the eyes of the wolf.

The ground trembled under their feet, then seethed, as though a massive snake shape passed a few feet beneath them. Groaning and other sounds Khaidu had no name for rose from inside the earth.

Khaidu grabbed the wolf's ears in a sudden movement. The wolf tried to snap at Khaidu, but she held on tight.

"It's me!" she said, and closed her eyes. With her thoughts, she reached into Aglaia's mind. It felt wrong, like unclothing someone without their permission. But she gritted her teeth and went further.

The yowls and yelps of the beasts around them were

getting closer. The ground surged under Khaidu like a rising wave.

There!

A tiny, quivering flame, deep inside the wolf. The only thing left of the human being known as Aglaia. With a last heave of energy—her head was splitting in pain, like a wedge of iron between her eyes—she blew on that flame. It grew, then sputtered to a simmer.

The strength was leaking out of Khaidu. She gripped Aglaia's mane with her fingers and tensed the rest of her body in readiness.

"Aglaia. I know you can hear me. Take us to safety. You hear? Take us to the Hag."

With a suddenness that cramped Khaidu's fingers and tensed them close to the breaking point, Aglaia leapt into the air, soaring more like a mountain goat than a wolf. The beasts were all launched in her wake, like arrows sprung from a bow.

Khaidu laughed for sheer pleasure.

Her joy was short-lived.

She had lost Aglaia.

$\maltese$ 5 $\maltese$

Adelaida was as good as her word. She took Derzhava into their own pavilion, which was not a soldier's tent. It was a fairy-tale fancy of star-studded, navy-colored drapery hung over ornate stakes with fine carvings of leaves and flowers. Even the lanterns were made of iron wrought into wild shapes. In such a place, the smell of bedsores stuck out like a gash on a child's skin.

At first, the mere sight of Derzhava's bedsores was enough to make both Kachinka and Marinka blanch. The smell actually made Marinka leave the tent once or twice, her hand covering her face, which had gone white as one of their bleached linen sheets. But the two ruddy-faced princesses— one thin as a reed, the other pleasantly tending toward plump —took to their work quickly. Soon they had taken charge of Derzhava's laundry, which had piled up in Batuk's too-manly care. By the end of the first day, Adelaida found herself physically tired, but with a kernel of joy in her heart that she had thought herself no longer capable of feeling.

The next morning dawned bright, almost stark, as though the sun were angry with them for something they had done— or were about to do. Adelaida had just finished boiling a pot of water for their morning tea when a loud commotion sounded outside—oxhorns, booted feet, and that worst of all sounds: swords unsheathed in large numbers.

In spite of the fear rising once again inside her, she made for the outside. Derzhava, who was asleep, surrounded by still-warm stones that had been baked all last evening to keep her cozy at night, cried out as if in pain. Adelaida jumped back inside. In spite of her condition, Derzhava never cried out from pain, ever. This must be serious.

Derzhava looked around with eyes glazed over in confusion for a full minute. Her hair was plastered to her scalp from sweat.

"You're alright, Derzhava. It's nothing, you're alright." Adelaida cooed in a tone of voice as familiar to her as breathing.

Derzhava's eyes affixed themselves to Adelaida's face, as though she were seeing her for the first time in her life. For an eternal moment, they stared at each other, Adelaida's panic rising, even as she did everything she knew to keep herself still. Then, Derzhava came back to herself.

"Adelaida," she said, her voice raspy as though she had been screaming for hours. "You need to take me outside. Now."

"Let me," said Batuk.

Adelaida hadn't heard him come in. But the sound of his voice was a cooling draught to her rising panic.

He stood at the entrance to the pavilion, holding up the flap with one hand. Seeing him framed by the sun, a dark shadow with a glowing nimbus, Adelaida was surprised by an immediate thought. She didn't think it coincidental that he should appear just at that moment. No, she knew—she didn't feel, she *knew*—that she was once again within the weave of a pattern woven outside her. It was *right* that Batuk was there at that moment. It was the only possibility.

The last time she had felt that way . . .

Something like icy water spread out from her heart to the tips of her fingers.

"Are you alright?" he asked, coming inside suddenly, letting the flap drop behind him.

"Please, Batuk," said Adelaida, willing herself to sound calm, hiding the rising panic in her chest. "Derzhava. *She* is distressed."

Adelaida followed Batuk outside, trying to ignore the beating of her heart, which she was sure everyone could hear.

She had no doubts anymore. The Artisan was here.

But what she saw on the road ahead of her banished even that thought, if only for a moment.

An army approached them down from the Pass of Ardovían. There was something . . . wrong about them.

"They've been defeated," said Batuk to her silent query, which he seemed to read in her eyes. "See the way their shoulders slump? They don't even hold their banners up."

The banners were striking—newly sewn, with a heraldic device of a river crowned by a sun rising, two gold spears crossed above the sun. But Batuk was right. They drooped almost as much as the men did.

By now, Batuk had approached the front of their lines, in time for Adelaida to hear Mirnían speak in an undertone to Lebía: "Nebesti. Perhaps Parfyon's men."

Parfyon. The name was not familiar to Adelaida, but it rang in the air. Something dangerous about it.

"Let them pass!" commanded her father, in a voice he never used in Ghavan.

A litter seemed to float in the midst of the trudging Nebesti. A dead man lay on top of it, dressed in the finest armor Adelaida had yet seen. He was withered, white-haired. As the corpse approached, Adelaida recoiled. He looked as though someone had literally sucked the life from him. And he smelled like old cabbage left out in the sun too long. Even the warriors couldn't help screwing their faces up from that stench.

Adelaida saw her mother make an expansive warding gesture. *That* frightened her. Lebía was rarely showy in her rituals.

"That is the husband of Alienne the Golden Lady," said Derzhava the Seer, in a voice very different from Derzhava, her friend. This was a deep declamation, a voice from another Realm. It made Adelaida want to fall on her knees. Several soldiers around her did just that.

Adelaida stood rooted in place, watching the funeral procession pass back down the mountain toward the blighted lands of Nebesta behind them. So many of the Nebesti were young, hardly even her own age. What would they do in a land that seemed incapable of growing a single blade of grass, much less a harvest?

And with the certitude of a much older woman, Adelaida felt sure that they would see these young warriors again. Though would it be as friends or foes?

"Sire!"

A young scout ran toward them from over the pass, his face red with exertion and excitement.

"What is it, my boy?" asked Mirnían.

"There's an army encamped below, in the valley."

"Another one?"

THE BANNERS of the army standing between them and Vasyllia were unfamiliar to Adelaida. It turned out they were unfamiliar to her mother as well, which surprised her. Her father, though, visibly changed when he saw them. It was as though he were a string on an instrument suddenly tuned up to the point of snapping.

"What is it, my love?" asked Lebía.

"I have read about that banner," he said. "It is the banner of the Children of the Priest-King."

Something jingled in Adelaida's memory. It was connected to that sense inside her, still present, that the Artisan was near.

"Highness," said one of the Ghavanites. "Look!"

Across the Vasyllia River, on the other side of the army of the Children, as her father had called them, was yet another army. Their banners bore a golden sun on a black field.

"Traitors!" Mirnían practically hissed. "They've taken the Dar's banner for their own, the bastards."

"Call them what they are," said Batuk next to Adelaida in a voice she hardly recognized for its suppressed fury. "They are the Fallen. Destined for the lowest pits of the Realm of the Dead."

"Then let us send them the quicker to it, eh?" said Etchigu, Batuk's elder brother. He was as wiry as Batuk was brawny, but energetic and constantly in movement. His long hair had feathers and bells woven into it, and they jingled every time he laughed, which was often. Even now, as he cursed those he called the Fallen, he laughed.

In a single moment, Adelaida saw all the glory and horror of war pass through Etchigu and Batuk's faces. She looked down at her hands. They were shaking.

The sun came out from behind a cloud. Adelaida instinctively looked up to it, grateful for the suddenness of the warmth that a mere appearance of sun gave in this winter country. Her breath stopped cold in her chest.

"What in all the—?" She exclaimed, in spite of herself. Everyone craned their necks to see. A mountainous figure in the shape of a warrior clad in crimson rode across the sky on a horse of dark cloud. The warrior held a spear whose tip was the sun itself. In the middle of the sky, just above them, it stopped. Then it turned and faced them for a long moment, before bowing directly at Mirnían. Then the clouds once again covered the sun, and the vision faded.

"The Powers are with us this day, my friends," said Mirnían, unsheathing his sword. "Time to write new songs for new days. Forward!"

The mass of armed men charged down the pass like water flowing down a hill—all that metal, still unscathed, shone, even though the sun was hidden, and the speed of the warriors made their helms seem to froth like waves. Batuk stood at the shore of that rising tide, his eyes reflecting its increasing fury. He turned back for a moment and smiled at Adelaida.

Glory and horror, she thought again.

"Your family's moment of triumph, eh?" said a voice from behind her, one she'd hoped she would never hear again in her life. Her skin crawled as she fought the simultaneous urges to turn toward the voice and run the other way.

She forced herself to turn. He looked as he always had in his shop in Ghavan Town—a nondescript man of about fifty with hands covered in dry clay, his beard more bush than human hair. Even the smell of old ale still hung around him like a cloud of mosquitoes. But his eyes had a pit of black fire in their fathomless depths. Her creator, the demon she had known as the Artisan.

"Surprised to see me, dear one?" He smiled.

The earth on which she stood seemed to crack with that gaping smile.

"What are you doing here?" she whispered, barely able to mouth the words.

"Vasyllia, my dear," he said. "Vasyllia is the key. Vasyllia has always been the key. And now's my time to take it."

❧ 6 ❧

ntomír gasped.

But he did not breathe.

That was strange.

Something bright flashed above him, like the first rays of the morning sun on Ghavan Isle's snows. For a long time, he didn't understand what he was seeing. The flashes continued, like a distant rain of fire. Though his thoughts were swimming in thick syrup, he nevertheless made out clear images in the murky expanse above him. He could not call it a sky.

Something flowed as water, but viewed as from beneath: the view of a fish looking up at the world outside its domain. As soon as that thought occurred to him, he made sense of the other images. Tree roots—immense and endlessly complex in their loops and intertwinings, but not connected to any soil he could see. Hanging in the expanse above. Beyond the roots, hazy, as though the roots themselves were translucent—which, he realized with a sinking feeling, they were—pillars of greyish-brown reached up into a latticework of rib vaulting.

No. That wasn't right. Those were trees. And he was . . . *below* them?

Light flashed vermilion-gold from one of the branches of a

distant tree—impossibly large and impossibly far away. The light grew suddenly, like the sun rising impossibly fast, then it split into hundreds of smaller flashes, also golden-red. They fell into that half-invisible river that made up most of the expanse above and winked out.

In that moment, Antomír gasped again from the utter foreignness of the spectacle. But again, he did not breathe.

Then, he remembered. That was the Garden in the Heart of the World . . . above him.

"I died," he said aloud. The noise was strange—dry and muted, like dry leaves being trodden underfoot.

Surprised by the fact that he actually heard his own voice —he hadn't thought the dead could speak—his eyes darted down and around him. He lay alone on the crest of hill covered in short grass. It was strangely colorless: a drab grey that was less color, more an absence of it. Rubbing the blades between his fingers, he tried to make sense of the feeling. It was . . . it was as though the grass were trying to be real grass, but not quite managing it. His whole life he had lived in a world of defined shape and color, but this place was a flattened etching of the real world in charcoal, drawn by a not-very-talented child.

His own hands didn't exactly look right, either, as though they were not quite substantial.

He hadn't known what to expect of the Realm of the Dead. But he hadn't expected it to be this . . . underwhelming.

Something groaned in the distance—a strange sound, like boulders rubbing against each other. He tried to screw up his eyes to focus on a blemish in the sky-that-was-not-a-sky. Not a blemish, a gash. A gash of green and red and blue seeping into this world of grey and black and bone-ashen.

For a brief second, he remembered red, the color of blood. He felt the piercing of a sharp point of stone in his chest. He heard the shattering madness of Gamayun's cry.

Yes. Gamayun is dead as well.

Wait, was she dead? She had been alive when he last saw her. What had put that thought into his mind?

Then he felt it. A shuddering inside his chest, like a heart trying its best to beat.

And he knew, he simply *knew*.

Gamayun is near.

He suspected he would find her near that gash of color. No, he knew she would be there, because he was drawn to it like a starving child to its mother's breast.

With a dull thud of dread—it was the most he could manage in this place—he thought, *What other horrors will be drawn to that place?*

Getting up from his lying position was the work of a thought. He walked down the hill toward the glittering gash of light. It throbbed in the distance like a parody of a heart.

THE SENSATION of walking through the Realm of the Dead was strange. Antomír remembered, but only dimly, that feet were supposed to connect to hard ground. Sometimes that ground, in life, was pebbly or sandy, and his feet would shift sideways as he tried to thrust them forward. He remembered how that used to annoy him, especially as a child, when playing games with his fellow children on the banks of Ghavan Isle. Now, his feet only seemed to make contact with the bristly-grassed earth—except it wasn't grass or earth at all, but only a shadow of both. If he were not using all his powers of concentration (and they were no more well-honed than that of a drunken man), he might as well have been floating.

The landscape was equally pervious to the senses. There were suggestions of vast mountains, but they could have been clouds, because they seemed to shift whenever he looked away from them. There were pockmarks in the ground everywhere, and his attention passed over them as unimportant. Except there seemed to be something writhing inside those holes. He tried concentrating on them, but terror stopped his eyes and forced them back to the indistinctness of the landscape.

The intensity, however brief, of the sensation of terror was like a slap of cold water to Antomír. He wanted to feel, even if it meant to be in terror. And so he forced himself to look at the pockmarks.

Immediately, he wished he hadn't. The writhing shapes were human, or vaguely resembling human, but with faces so contorted with pain that his arms actually tingled, his back actually sweated, and his face actually flushed.

So there was a hell, after all.

Except, not all the forms were suffering. Some were peacefully lying in place, their faces white and serene. Only the absolute stillness of their chests—no rising or falling—betrayed that they were dead.

He also saw, or thought he saw, some of the forms standing up and moving. But they were far away, indistinct, and if he looked at them, it was as though they weren't there, only visible in the narrow band of corner vision where monsters and ghosts reside in the Realm of the Living.

Antomír wondered if he were similarly invisible to other denizens of this not-land.

With that thought came memories of his life, but not things he would have expected. He smelled the inside of a freshly baked loaf of sourdough the moment after his own hands tore it apart, mixed with the honest smell of the baker's sweat and toil. He heard the distant, haunting chord of farmers singing as they threshed—a song that reveled in the sadness of the mundane as much as the joy of the coming festal season. He felt the smoothness of a baby's cheek under his index finger—almost the same feeling as butter, but without the oily residue.

All of those experiences—they had all occurred with other people, in communion. Other souls had been present, with whom he had pungent, star-bright moments of common experience that lingered in memory far longer than in the moment. And all of that was gone. Even the memories were like sand falling through his splayed fingers.

He rushed toward the throbbing vein of color, hoping against hope that there would be something of the real there. Something more substantial than this torturous half-existence. Even to be annihilated, to cease existing—even that was preferable to this.

Instead, what he saw filled him with the strongest semblance of emotion he had yet felt in the Realm of the Dead.

He froze in terror, unable for a long moment—if time even existed here—to move. Around him, dark forms of the dead writhed out of the pockmarked ground, looking more like monstrous earthworms than people. Half clawing the earth, half dragging themselves, they seemed to be pulled toward the gash of colored light by invisible cords. He felt it then: the same pulling, reaching deep into his chest, into the place where Gamayun's shadow heart had beaten in cacophony with his own, like a barbed hook. He felt no pain, but whatever control he had over his shadow limbs evaporated.

Rushing through the foggy air, which left no trace of wetness on his cheeks, he looked up again at the expanse above. The tree roots, so vivid before, had faded into a half-murk of slate grey, and the impression of water, which before had been vivid, was smudged into shifting shades of greyish color. If before he had glimpsed the cosmos itself, now he saw nothing but a child's painting destroyed by a careless brush of a dirty thumb. He looked ahead instead, back toward that gash of light, afraid suddenly that it too had disappeared.

No. If anything, all the light had been concentrated in that single gash of indeterminate shape and endless, kaleidoscopic color. It spun and twisted and turned in on itself, then out again, like a flower eating itself and blooming all at the same time. Sickeningly alluring before, it now grabbed him with all the intensity that he didn't feel inside. But what shape was it?

So intent was he on trying to figure out what it was that he missed the entirety of the picture rising before him.

If most of the dead land was something like a shadowy moorland, what Antomír now saw ahead of him was anything but. Rocks jutted out of the hills like broken jawbones. Behind them, fragments of mountains that looked like petrified shapes of animals tortured to the breaking point loomed over the rocks. There were holes in those petrified shapes, and they glowed with a sickly orange light, throbbing like hearts winding down to a slow death. Creeping things with many legs scurried along their edges.

Beyond even those mountains towered a lone, malformed peak of jagged stone. In the half-light of the Realm of the Dead, it was unclear what the tor was, whether it was rock-hard or a long accretion of packed dirt. In the shifting, throbbing light winking in and out of the holes, the peak seemed to be made of different shades of red and purple and even dull-dark green. Above that peak, the gash of light now looked like a gibbous moon—if the moon were a constantly shifting kaleidoscope of colors lit from within. Antomír felt simultaneous elation and terror as he beheld it.

He thought he knew what it was. His memories were congealing like gelatin in his mind. That shower of sparks he had seen in the sky. It must have been the last of the fruits on the trees in the Garden in the Heart of the World, the last seeding of the lifeblood of the Realms.

And it seemed that much of that lifeblood had flowed into the Realm of the Dead.

Now he understood the shape of the gash. It was like a goblet filled with wine that was liquid and fire at the same time. And it shook back and forth, splashing colored sparks onto the single peak.

For a moment, the peak looked like the statue of a woman

robed in a dress of many layers and folds. That toothlike summit could, in fact, be a crumbling semblance of a crown.

And just under that crown, the smoothness of the rock face could, in a certain light, be mistaken for an almost human face.

The goblet of fiery light faded.

Two slits of light opened in the peak, and they glowed yellow with pits of black fire.

Those were . . . those were *eyes.*

It was not a mountain.

It was . . .

It was a queen of stone and flesh and fire.

Bow before me.

Worship me.

I am queen.

I am mistress.

I am death.

And I will bring you new life.

She hadn't spoken. Not in any manner of speech Antomír knew. But the words resounded inside him. If Gamayun's voice in his head had been loud, this was deafening. When she spoke, it was as though nothing existed. Nothing but her voice.

All around him, Antomír saw the shuddering forms of the dead fall on their knees before the Queen of the Realm of the Dead. Antomír remained standing.

At that moment, the compulsion that had brought him to that place snapped, and he was left in the same half-freedom he had felt before.

She wants me to worship her freely, he thought.

And he had thought there would be blessed release in death.

Apparently not.

He chuckled.

At that sound, which echoed as though he had screamed in

a many-columned hall, all the crouching dead turned their heads toward him. They had faces, he saw, but the features were indistinct, claylike, as though waiting to be molded anew by a potter's hand. He wondered if his own face looked like that.

At that moment, Antomír saw that one other figure had not fallen on his knees—for it was a man, he could tell. And next to him was a strangely shaped dark creature, no taller than his hip. Something like long, trailing moss dangled from its head, though at this distance Antomír could make little out.

His pulse flared with the discordance of two hearts beating.

That was Gamayun. But who was that with her?

Bring them.

The horde of the dead seized Antomír with hands like icicles. He felt himself flow toward the Queen of the dead, as though a flood had overtaken him. He flew ever closer to those inexorable eyes of fire and unfathomable blackness. They never blinked once.

7

Battered, bruised, her shirtsleeves reduced to ragged strips of soil-stained linen, Khaidu was still better off than Aglaia. The she-wolf had gaping wounds in her haunch that had begun to stink in that half-honey, half-rotten fruit smell of sickening flesh. Her left foreleg was almost useless. It seemed to Khaidu that even dragging it was painful for the she-wolf.

And yet, things could have been much worse.

They had made it to the Hag's, after all. The beasts of Buyan had done everything they could to hinder their progress. But Aglaia was fearless, and after two days, even the stragglers had left them alone. Khaidu knew this was a temporary reprieve. All the more important to find the Hag and continue their journey to the Realm of the Dead.

Khaidu's memories of their first visit were indistinct. Other than a vague memory of mossy-trunked conifers that seemed half-alive, she remembered nothing of the clearing they now entered. It was ringed with tall, waxy-leaved holly trees that seemed to be a kind of barrier to all other trees. Oddly, the clearing wasn't covered in grass or shrubs, as it probably should have been. It was covered in a bed of old brown maple leaves.

Strange. There wasn't a maple in sight.

Add to that the ten . . . no . . . *fifteen* snowy owls sitting too still and too silent at various heights in the hollies all around the hut, and a hissing kind of non-sound that Khaidu had only really experienced once, during a rare snowfall in the Steppe, and Khaidu had the distinct sense that they had entered a different Realm than the real.

The hut itself only intensified that feeling.

She remembered that before it had teetered on two wooden platforms like thick chicken legs, but she hadn't remembered why. The hut sat in the middle of a tiny swamp, and there was no dry access to the single-gabled, one-room log hut except by a long ramp—little more than a bunch of sticks tied together haphazardly—leading to the shallow porch where the rocking chair lay upside down, its runners shattered, as by a lightning blast.

"Something's wrong," Khaidu said to Aglaia. She spoke to her with her hope still kindled, though her expectation that Aglaia would answer faded by the hour. The wolf didn't even acknowledge her words. Instead, she thumped down at the edge of the swamp, a few infuriating feet away from the ramp.

"Really?" Khaidu looked down at the panting muzzle. "You couldn't get just one foot closer?"

Aglaia turned her snout away and nestled her head down on the soft bed of leaves, which rustled pleasantly underneath her. That sound seemed to summon the smells appropriate to autumn—cinnamon loaves baking in the oven and hot, clove-tinged wine.

Wait. It was spring, wasn't it?

With that thought, storm clouds gathered overhead, thunder exploded, lightning flashed. It was very ostentatious. And very obvious.

"Come out, come out, wherever you are!" called Khaidu. "You can't fool me, old woman! I know you're softer than buttered toast on the inside."

A whistle, more like a shriek, pierced the air around them. The holly trees rocked back and forth as though their trunks were putty, not wood. A massive mortar flew into the clearing from inside the forest where they had just been. The pestle in the hands of the Hag was so large, it was a miracle she could even lift it. The whole picture was ridiculous, bordering on the comical. But you wouldn't know it judging by the seriousness of the old woman with three hairs on her head, two teeth in each jaw, and an expression that reminded Khaidu of a cat just after it had eaten a mouse.

"Ah! It's the boy again!" she cackled as the mortar crashed into the ground in the middle of the clearing, throwing up a shower of dry leaves, through which the Hag marched like a parody of a bride processing to church through falling rose petals.

Khaidu ground her teeth so hard that her temples ached. She didn't answer.

The Hag clapped her hands together and laughed in undisguised delight.

"Ah! You're different, little wolf-child! More self-control. Good thing, too. Or I might just regret having given you your tongue in the first place."

That did it.

"Control?" Khaidu seethed through clenched teeth. "I'll show you control. Just come right close enough for me to touch you. You'll see what sort of control these hands have over quarrelsome hags."

The Hag stopped, her eyes so wide they almost reached her forehead.

"Oof! Those arm muscles! Wow! You're really, really sure you're not a boy?"

"Let me guess," Khaidu mocked. "You're hungry again?"

The Hag rocked her head back and forth with a mocking expression. She even tutted aloud. Khaidu felt the scream starting to gather in her chest.

"No time for jests, eh, little wolf-child? Ah, it's just as well. Aglaia, dear, how goes it with you?"

The Hag came up to pat Aglaia on the head. She nearly lost her arm to the elbow at the sudden snap of Aglaia's jaws.

"Woah there, nelly!" The Hag flew back five paces and now stood on one leg like a bedraggled stork. "Wait a minute. Wolfie's not talking."

"Powers of observation," said Khaidu, dripping sarcasm. "Very, very keen. Like a hawk."

"Hmph! I'd be careful of wearing out your welcome, eh dearie? Remember the st-t-t-tutter?" the Hag mocked, and Khaidu had the good grace to feel a little abashed. Just a very, very little.

"Buyan?" asked the Hag, screwing up her eyes and tugging at the single curling hair on her warty chin.

Khaidu nodded. "It may be my fault. I reminded him of who he once had been."

The Hag's eyes, this time, not only tried to climbed up her forehead, but bulged out dangerously.

"You did *what*?"

"I couldn't help it. I saw it. The creation of the world, with Buyan the first child of the Unknown Father, the steward of the early worlds . . ."

The Hag ran up to Khaidu and shut her mouth with her bony fingers. They smelled of wet moss and upturned dirt. Not a bad smell, considering.

"Are you trying to bring a Bukavach down on me, you stupid child?"

"Are you telling me you're no match for a Bukavach?"

"You don't seem to get it. Things are much, much worse than they were last time."

She sighed deeply. The sigh went on so long, it seemed that her lungs had the capacity of a man three times her size. The trees rustled to her sigh, the owls hooted to it, and mice scampered from the leaf mold up and down the Hag's legs while she stood in place, still sighing.

"Oh, you'd better come in," she finally said. "And bring your dog."

Aglaia growled.

"Ah! There's something of the old woman left inside, is there? Good! Come on in, doggie!"

Aglaia leapt up and nipped at the Hag's heels. The Hag jumped and ran up the makeshift ramp, Aglaia hot on her heels.

Khaidu laughed.

It refreshed her like water, cooling the anger in her chest.

THE HAG'S rough wood table stood on four legs carved like undersea monsters—oversized, sleek fish with cat-teeth and frond-like protuberances flowing out of their gills. Similar curly fern fronds decorated the bare part of the table—of which there was very, very little. Nearly every inch of that table—and it took up three quarters of the hut's single room— was bedecked with pies baked into the shapes of swans, twelve-layered savory cakes with butter oozing out of fillings that looked full to bursting with sausage meat, brussels sprouts, fried leeks, and black mushrooms. And the smells! Truffle oil mixed with baked dough, undercut with the sharp, garlicky smell of seared meat seasoned with fresh thyme.

The tankards frothed with mead. The sliced vegetables glistened, bursting with juices.

Khaidu found herself seated at the table, not entirely sure how she had gotten there, her back propped against a tall chair lined with velvet. The warm, moist air inside the hut, plus the smells and the overwhelming sight of so much food—she couldn't help it. She almost fell asleep on the spot.

"Well, feel free to doze, wolf-child," chittered the Hag, a

pie the size of her head in hand already and halfway to her mouth. "But there won't be anything left when you wake up."

Khaidu shook herself and downed half a tankard. It was sweet and cinnamony, and the bubbles played in her stomach, tickling her from inside. She giggled.

They ate for a long time in silence. Although the Hag's manners left much to be desired, Khaidu felt herself enter into a kind of ritual space the more she sat and ate at the table. The candles, smelling faintly of beeswax and cloves, gave the room a golden light, reminiscent of her family's storytelling in the evenings under the setting sun. The food tasted exactly as it should—nothing too salty or too sweet. And it seemed as though her body absorbed the food as soon as she ate, leaving her neither overfilled nor with that nagging hunger that accompanies oversalted dainties. It was exactly what it was, what it should be.

In that place, at that moment, it was as though she were being healed.

She spared a few moments to check on Aglaia. Was it the play of the candlelight, mixed with the hypnotic rise and fall of the orange flames in the small firepit in the kitchen area, where the proverbial cauldron bubbled? Whatever it was, Khaidu could swear that the sores on the she-wolf's body were fading before her eyes.

The Hag, finally full, pulled out a long, bone-like pipe from her skirts. Khaidu squinted. It *was* bone, now that she looked at it. Some dusky, ivory-colored thigh bone carved into a leering face. It was frightfully ugly.

"A gift," said the Hag, patting the bowl affectionately. But she would say no more about that.

"So why the extra measures?" asked Khaidu.

The Hag raised an interrogative eyebrow.

"The broken rocking chair, the peeling paint on the door lintel, the state of the carving on the gable. You think I didn't notice that the rooster's head had cracked off?"

"Harumph." The Hag puffed and puffed, and the cloud of tobacco—it had an earthy tang to it—surrounded her head. In the glittering of utensils amid candlelight, her eyes glinted reddish. "I keep trying to remind you that you should be careful with the Powers. I'm not just some old woman, you know."

Khaidu smiled. "I've seen flaming trees in the Garden of the World. I've looked the Raven in the eyes. I've braved the bluster of Buyan. And I'm still here."

"Barely," the Hag said, her seriousness like a layer of ice suddenly forming on a lake.

Khaidu shrugged. "So what is it that I'm missing?"

"I shouldn't be telling you any of this," said the Hag, more to herself. "But I can't help myself. You remind me too much of someone I knew a long, long time ago."

"Who?" asked Khaidu, though she was pretty sure she knew the answer.

"Myself. I was young too, once. A long, long, long time ago."

Something of a sacred silence descended on the room, flavored with the chirping of crickets outside the window and the occasional hoot of one of the snowy owls.

"I wasn't always the doormat of the gods. There was a time when I consorted with the great ones. But I chose the wrong ones, again and again. And really, who could stand being good all the time? So boring.

"Anyway," she waved her claws in front of her face, as though there were a cloud of mayflies wafting there on a warm upswell. "That's neither here nor there. Except, I was there at the first big . . . well, *disagreement* of the Powers. You Gumiren worship what you do not know, yes? The Unknown Father?"

Khaidu nodded once, her body taut with attention.

"*I* know him well enough, you know. Haven't seen kith or kin of him in thousands of eons, but there you go. Different circles. Different Realms. But back then, he was closer to the

Powers, or maybe they were closer to him, I don't know. In any case, it was a glorious time. This feast here?"

She pointed at the table, still covered with food, with a single arthritic forefinger.

"Nothing compared. Can't even conjure up an illusion of those feasts. Incredible. But it wasn't enough for some of us. The Power you know as the Dark Father. He . . . she . . . they . . . how do I even talk about it?"

She shook her head, her eyes glowing in the light of the pipe's burning bowl.

"There was a big argument. And the Dark Father—the Raven, and some others—were exiled and stripped of both form and power. One of them, a particularly nasty bitch of a Power . . . Oooh. I hate her . . . it . . . whatever. She was consigned to the frozen depths of the Realm of the Dead. She called herself queen of that land, deciding that it was better to rule over hell than be a slave in heaven. But she's no queen of anything."

She sucked on her pipe, and blew out a blue-tinged cloud that seemed to twirl in the candlelight into forms like dancing maidens.

"Or . . . she wasn't. Not until recently."

"Why are you telling me this?" asked Khaidu, though not with her usual irritation. She was riveted, but she wasn't sure she was understanding everything.

"I've been watching you, little wolfie, from afar. I have eyes in dark places, you know. You are not as independent, as self-sufficient, as you would like all of us to think. You have lost some of your heart to someone."

Khaidu blushed. She felt it as a creeping heat on her cheeks. She slapped herself and growled at the Hag.

"Heh." The Hag was enjoying herself a little *too* much. "You don't even realize how much you've lost to him. So you'll be interested to know that his princeliness, the royal runt

Antomír, is at this very moment under the power of said Queen of the damned. And she's waking up."

A chill blew through the room. A shutter snapped in place, making Khaidu jump.

"That wouldn't be so bad in itself. She can be as awake as she likes, but the Realm of the Dead is the Realm of the Dead. No one comes out. Or . . . not until now."

"What?!"

"It's this infernal breaking of the borders between Realms. Everyone's been doing everything they can to make it worse. Even the Vasylli. This last one? The forging of a new covenant on Ghavan Isle? The pushing of Ghavan Isle out of the Lows of Aer into the real? The change of the flow of time? The death of Gamayun, the Day-Seer? The world is not an egg anymore. It's an omelette. And not a very tasty one at that."

She sighed.

"There's a particularly nasty crack in the wall between the Realm of the Dead and the rest of the Realms. And the Queen of the damned is planning to wedge it open just a little bit more."

"Why?"

"Weren't you listening? She's not a nice lady. *Unleash the minions of hell*—I think that's the phrase. Yes. Has a certain ring to it. Let the dead back out into the Realm of the Living! And you know what? The dead, they're not very nice. They've been cooped up in the dead lands—not a very nice *place*, for that matter—for times out of time. And they've stored up their malice long and hard."

"Hag, I need to go there."

The Hag shook her head and chuckled. "How did I know you would say something like that? Foolish, self-sacrificing, *noble*." That last word she said like a girl-child might say *snot*.

"Why can't you just dig yourself a nice little hole and wait out the inevitable firefight of the Powers? Maybe they won't notice you?"

"Or," said Khaidu, "we'll all burn under their tender disregard."

The Hag slitted her eyes at Khaidu and sucked her pipe.

"I hate it when you get poetic," she grumbled.

"You're the guardian of the ways, aren't you?" asked Khaidu. "You have access to doors to Realms that no one else has."

"And so what if I do? Maybe I've thrown away the keys?"

"Uh-uh. You wouldn't. You've been waiting."

"For the Gumira cripple and her talkative doggie? Not a chance."

Aglaia growled in the corner.

"We all have our roles in this play, Hag. Our roles are sometimes bigger than we are. And maybe that's a good thing. Your role, or one of them, is to open the doors to those who are worthy."

"And are you? Worthy?"

The Hag smiled, and it was not a very nice smile.

How to answer such a question?

"I owe all my worth to Aglaia. And Aglaia has lost everything because of me. The best I can do is find her grandson. Perhaps we will all find rest then."

Or be shut up in the Realm of the Dead forever.

Khaidu's breath caught at the enormity of that thought. To willingly go to hell, to brave the possibility of being shut in there for all time . . .

"If that's what it takes," she said. But even to herself, her words sounded hollow.

❧   8   ❦

oran stood in the middle of a marketplace. Everything around him was obscured by a veil of dust kicked up by hundreds of sandaled feet. The smell of it was like chalk mixed with sweat, but it tasted spicy, one of those exotic spices like tarragon or cumin. What he could see reminded him of no place he had ever seen before.

How did I get here?

The merchants' stalls were cobbled-together concoctions, hardly more than flat boards on wooden stilts, without even a single awning as protection from the sun. Instead, the mostly dark-skinned merchants wrapped white towels around their heads. Every once in a while, they would douse themselves with water from small buckets. To Voran's surprise, they also drank tea like it was water, and the steam coming from it made it clear that it was hot.

What sort of mad people drink hot tea in the middle of a desert?

He followed the line of buyers, which was surprisingly orderly for an otherwise chaotic scene. It seemed there were rules about which stall you visited in which order, and at least some of those rules were governed, Voran guessed, by status. Or at least that was the only thing he could think of to explain why the tall men with gold-fringed towels on their heads were given preference wherever they walked, and why they followed no discernible patterns when choosing vendors. He thought they must be warriors of some kind, but no swords hung at their hips, nor daggers. So . . . they were important for other reasons.

And was it fear or deference that he sensed as the shorter, less ornately dressed buyers moved out of their way?

What am I doing here?

Voran had no memory of coming here at all. In fact, the dimness about the edges of this place, the lack of details in the periphery of his vision, suggested that he was dreaming, not awake. But can one dream places that one has never visited?

Then he was sitting on a tiled bench that hugged a pool, from which a fountain of water burbled lazily. In such a desert place, it seemed strange to Voran that so much water was wasted on something that had no utility other than beauty.

Then it struck him that no, that was exactly the point. He was in a place that valued beauty over utility.

And it was beautiful, in its way—the tiles lining the floor of the pool were multicolored, arranged in an abstract design that at first seemed random, but the more you looked at it, the more it seemed to make some sort of pattern, just barely discernible on the level of intuition. There were sparkling stones set at odd intervals in the tilework. They looked like real gemstones.

The strangeness of the scene made him perk up, but it also caused an odd sensation of doubling inside him, as though it weren't his eyes doing the seeing. Out of the corner of his eyes, he noticed his own hands. They were black. Not with dirt. His skin was black.

So this was not his dream, then.

The fountain stood in the middle of a town square, lined on three sides with squat mud-brick buildings of a surprisingly rich red color. The tiles on the rooves were black. On the fourth side of the square stood a structure that must have been a kind of temple, though like nothing he had ever seen. Even the beehive shapes of the Karila houses of worship looked staid compared to these turrets, packed together like knives stuck into the ground with the blades up. The sight impressed Voran with the same kind of presence, an energy humming just below the surface of the tangible, that he had often felt in the Temple at Vasyllia.

There was only one difference. Hardly any people walked in this square. The ones who did moved furtively along the square's edges. They looked at Voran not at all, which made it all the more obvious that their attention was fixed on him. Well, he *was* dressed very differently from all of them. Their clothing was billowy, made of some semitransparent fabric in shades of off-white. He was in black leather calf-boots and a tunic of blue-dyed wool with geometric designs embroidered in wire thread around his neck and down the front, all the way to his belt.

It was all very strange, seeing from the eyes of someone who was definitely *not* Voran.

He should be sweltering from the heat. He wasn't.

"A pilgrim, eh?" said a voice from behind him.

Voran turned around to see an old man, fat as a watermelon, with the soil-dark skin and curling hair typical of all the people here. Except his hair was very rare, and very white. His garment—edged in the same golden trailing that marked out the tall, important men in the market—was soaked to the skin with sweat.

"You could say that," said the man from whose eyes Voran looked out. "Is it that obvious?"

The old man laughed—more the movement of a twitching, bouncing belly than a sound—and took off his straw hat, which had a wide brim edged in blue ribbon. He fanned himself lazily as he sat down next to Voran.

"Your timing could not be better," the old man said.

Voran took a breath to ask the man to explain, but a shriek cut him short.

A woman ran into the square from the temple complex. She was young, judging by the muscular, lithe form of her body that came into definition as she ran through the warm breeze, which was scented with cinnamon. Her face was veiled in a red-dyed version of the same billowy fabric everyone wore. It stood out like blood on a body.

Behind her, four of the important-looking men from the market walked into the square. Each of them led a child ahead of them. The children were hollow-eyed, as though drugged. They had scars on their exposed arms and legs—old wounds for such young skin. With a rush of shock, Voran recognized one of them, the only one that seemed unable to walk and was carried. But no, he had never seen her—he would have remembered. That amount of scarring, that twisted torso, and yet, that pure and innocent face. He would have remembered seeing it. So why did he feel he *knew* her?

Behind the children and the important men came a subdued, murmuring crowd of people of all shapes, sizes, and ages. The one common trait was their dark skin.

The woman had the look of a hunted animal as she stopped, not twenty feet from Voran. There was an edge of something sharper than defiance in her eyes. Something unpleasant. She looked directly at Voran, and her eyes creased in what he assumed was a smile, though there was so much malice intermixed with hatred and . . . was that lust? Voran's stomach dropped in disgust as he felt the man who was *not him* feel a corresponding rush of lust for the woman. There was something wrong with her. And, apparently, with him.

She pulled out a knife from her long skirts and raised it ostentatiously over her head. Everyone—the men, the children, the crowd—froze in place. Gasps led to a watchful silence in which Voran heard the faint tinkling of wind chimes somewhere in the distance.

"Not yet," said the old man next to Voran. His word seemed to have power. The woman stiffened in her unnatural pose, her knife suspended over her head like a pendulum in mid-swing.

Voran's fingers ached, and he realized his fists were balled, his knuckles white with tension. Something horrible was about to happen.

"Pilgrim? Will you do the honors?"

"Who is she?" the man asked. Voran thought he detected an edge of panic in his words. It was all profoundly unsettling, being behind the man's eyes, but not being able to feel his emotions or hear his thoughts.

"She is of the rising darkness. She practices an artifice that requires the blood of children."

"A sorceress?"

"Ah! A foreign word, yes? We call them communicants. They who commune bodily with the formless ones. She allows the formless ones into her body for their pleasure. In return, they give her gifts such as no human being feels. Pleasures that are not describable by human words. Or so she says."

The formless ones. Voran remembered the catechism of his master Tarin, the mad storytelling warrior-monk. The formless ones were the Powers who had followed the Raven in his rebellion against the Heights and who lost their natural forms as a punishment. They hungered for incarnation, even a temporary one. But whomever they possessed, they devoured. Voran had enough personal experience of them to last a lifetime.

"A small price to pay!" she shrieked, though her body was still rigid, the fingers grasping the knife turning white from the unnatural angle of her wrist. "This life is nothing but dirt, pain, and falsity. Everyone wears masks. Love is nothing but violence against another. And then, the abyss. The dimness of the Realm of the Dead. Where is the justice in that? At least I had a taste of the Heights in this life. And I was promised more. Much more."

"The Heights?" said the old man, chuckling. "Hardly. Those pleasures are not from on high, believe me."

He said it like he knew it from firsthand experience.

"What do you care?" The woman spat into the dusty ground. "You claim virtue in saving these children from me. But once I am gone, what will they have? The life of the streets, begging for money until they are old enough to obtain their living off their bodies? I took care of them. I fed them. When I needed them for my crafts, I put them to blessed sleep. You will see. When they come back to themselves, they will not rest until they find me. I am their mother."

Voran felt sick to his stomach. Not only because of what the woman said, but because he recognized that she was probably right about the children. He had seen enough during his travels to know that children paid the heaviest price for poverty and war.

"Well, you are *her* mother, that is true."

The old man pointed at the shriveled form of the child in the arms of one of the important men, whom Voran now recognized to be a member of a warrior caste.

A look in the woman's eyes confirmed for Voran the truth of that statement, as well as something she was not willing to say aloud. She hated that child. Why? Who was the child?

"Enough babble, woman," said the old man. "It is time."

"Please!" She shrieked. "Pilgrim! Pilgrim justice. I beg you."

"Will you grant her request?" asked the old man.

The pilgrim didn't answer, and Voran wondered what he was thinking. His body gave no indication what his thoughts were, or whether he had any thoughts at all.

"You *are* a pilgrim, yes?" The old man looked at him with sudden suspicion.

"Well . . . in a manner of speaking," the man's voice rumbled. "What is the pilgrim's justice in this land?"

"Ah!"

The old man's eyes, which had been half-closed from the bright sun, opened wide. They were too big for his face, and gave him a turtle-like appearance.

"This woman was found in the performance of the final rite. You know of it?"

The man shook his head. Voran now felt it as though his own head shook. That was unsettling.

"For her, it was the time for reckoning. She was to sacrifice the children, before taking her own life. The formless ones demand such worship. We took the children, cleansed them in the temple, and offered the woman the same cleansing."

"She didn't accept." Voran finished his thought. The pilgrim echoed it.

The old man shook his head.

"It is my word alone that prevents them from forcing her to take her own life."

"You have such power?"

The old man shook his head at Voran. "You are a fool, I think, to ask such questions."

Voran felt dizzy suddenly. From the heat? No, it was as though there was yet a third presence there, behind the pilgrim's eyes. A familiar presence now.

"Pilgrim's justice is simple," said the old man, now speaking as to an inferior creature. "Give her a clean death."

"Why do your own warriors not execute her?" the pilgrim asked, the panic bubbling inside Voran as the familiar presence grew closer.

The old man sighed. "We are the people of the fountain." He said it like it was the most obvious thing in the world. At the pilgrim's silent incomprehension, he sighed again. "We have no weapons. No swords. Nothing with which to take life."

"Why do you not exile her?"

The old man laughed, but it was bitter. "When one's house

is infested with poisonous snakes, does one simply let the snake out a mile outside the house?"

The children began to stir, while the important-looking men held them still by the shoulders. The crippled girl-child opened her eyes and moaned.

"Shouldn't the children be taken away?"

"Why? They must see the reckoning that comes of communing with the dark. It is of the cleansing. Else, the taint will haunt them for all days."

Voran didn't understand; he didn't think it was either sane or fair. It wasn't *their* fault that all this had happened to them.

Whose fault was it?

This is a dream. This has *to be a dream.*

"It is," said the Raven in Voran's head, compounding the feeling of vertigo he was already feeling. "It's my dream. Get out!"

As Voran silently screamed in the pilgrim's head, the man unsheathed his sword even as he walked. The woman's eyes filled with hatred.

"Abomination!" she spat as she shrieked it. "No! Anyone but him. He is cursed! *They* are cursed! I will not be killed by a cursed . . ."

Voran brought the sword down on her. The blood splattered warm over his face. Her scream grew and grew and grew until it filled his head and his chest and his heart and he fell down and down and down and . . .

He snapped awake. They were still in the mountains, under another overhanging cliff, in the never-ending gale of snow and ice and wind.

The Raven sniffed and rubbed a gloved hand against his mouth. There was a line of red still on the edge of his lips. Voran, confused, looked around but saw no rabbits, cooked or uncooked, anywhere in the vicinity.

"How did you . . ." the Raven said, but didn't finish his sentence.

Vaguely, Voran recalled flashes of the dream—a horror of macabre imagery of slaughter and death.

Voran's panic blossomed with the bile rising up his throat. Was the Raven feasting on his dreams?

Or . . .

Had he just *invaded* the dreams of the Raven?

The Raven leaned back against a stone and, for the first time since they had begun traveling, looked wary and defensive.

Voran couldn't help feeling a bit of triumph at that look. But how had he done it, if he *had* invaded the thoughts of the Raven? And how could he use it to his advantage?

THEY HAD BEEN TRAVELING the rugged wastes for days. Nothing about the never-ending expanse of rock, ice, and snows—occasionally broken up with a conifer stand here and there—reminded Voran of any place he knew. He had traveled mountains before with Tarin, but always there had been a way between the summits—roads leading through passes from valley to valley, so that the going, though long, had been beautiful, not punishing. Now, every step was on jagged rock, and Voran's attention was completely absorbed with finding a foothold. Every time exhaustion took its toll and he lost his footing, or whenever he looked away for a fraction of a second, an irregular spur of rock would rise up before him like a sudden mushroom, and the pain of that step would shoot up toward his hip like fire.

At the end of each day, Voran collapsed, unable to move his legs anymore. Added to the physical exhaustion was the mind-numbing sameness of every day. The Raven didn't speak while they walked, and Voran didn't seek out his conversation anyway. Soon Voran's thoughts turned to sludge, or his mind just repeated phrases that seemed to come out of nowhere. Things like "white is the snow and the snows are white" on a loop, again and again, until merely existing was a torture.

He tried to remember the word Tarin had given him, during their travels in the mountains. The word that conjured the presence of the divine. Said . . . sad . . . something. It was always dancing on the edge of his conscious thought, taunting. He forgot it entirely by the third day.

"Are you even sure of the way, Raven?" Voran asked, trying not to look at the blood still on the Raven's face.

"You didn't expect it to be easy, did you?" said the Raven, answering the question Voran had actually asked, as he did so often these days. That ease of communication, when they seemed to speak in answer to thoughts and words both, made Voran wonder, again, if the Raven was even real, or if Voran had finally gone mad.

Or if there was beginning to be little difference between him and the Raven at all.

"But there won't be much of me left if we continue like this," Voran complained. Vaguely, he imagined how much weight he must have lost, feeding only on scraps and the occasional rabbit.

"I will help you. Only together can we finish the journey. You might even say, only in union can we succeed."

Voran didn't like the threat behind those words. But he had chosen. He would see the journey to its end.

They continued onward.

ON A DAY when breathing itself became painful from the dryness and cold of the air, Voran finally saw a change in the landscape.

The mountains were gathering into pillars of stone, shrinking lower and lower as the land sloped downward into a distant promontory that shone dully green in the distance. Finally, Voran recognized where they were.

Just ahead of them, about a day's journey away, stood a needle-sharp crag surrounded by flatland. The Fang. They were approaching Karila from the west, from the long spur of the mountains that began in Vasyllia and formed the border north-to-south between lands belonging to the Three Cities and the lands known only as the Great Wild further west.

Seeing the Fang, Voran stopped, frozen by cold and indecision.

"What's the matter?" the Raven asked, stopping as well. He was untouched by the snow, his furs just as clean and shiny as the day he put them on.

"I can't . . . you can't make me go back. They will kill me. Karila has no love for me."

"And yet, that is our way."

"Why?"

The Raven cocked his head. "We are following in Rogned's footsteps, Voran. I thought you understood."

"I didn't realize we were literally going to follow . . ."

He realized the implications. Rogned had repeatedly tried to commit suicide during his ascendance, believing that by doing so, he would force an encounter with the Palymi that haunted his dreams. Was *that* what the Raven meant? Would he expect Voran to try to force an encounter with the Heights the way Rogned had?

"How badly do you want this?" asked the Raven, all seriousness.

Voran's head spun, and his vision went foggy for a moment. A fuzzy sensation filled his ears, as though someone were doing his best to shove cotton wool into his ear canal. A buzzing sound seemed to come out of him, filling the empty space around them.

"Why are you forcing me to relive this . . . this . . . it was the worst time of my life!"

"Boo-hoo!" Grabbing him by the shoulders, the Raven shoved his face right into Voran's. His breath was sweet, like strawberry mint. It made Voran feel even sicker. "I always suspected you were soft! Have you not been paying attention? Rogned opened the door to the Heights. If we are to follow him, we must follow his footsteps. There is no other way to storm the Heights. Not that I know of."

"You mean . . . ?"

The Raven smiled an adder's smile, and for a moment, his face looked like Aspidían's, the Vasyllian torturer who had taken everything away from Voran. "Oh yes." He pointed toward the tarn at the foot of the Fang. The site of Rogned's second suicide attempt. "Ready?"

Ready? Of course not. Voran could no longer tell the difference between the waking and the dreaming worlds. The Raven had total control over where they went and what they did. Even their dreams were becoming confused. And even when he thought he was doing as he chose, Voran's will still served the desires and plans of the Raven.

And now the demon wanted him to . . . what? Commit suicide by drowning?

How could he be ready? And why was he doing all this, anyway? Why was he so far from those he loved, so far from the one purpose that had guided and defined him for decades? For a mad chance at sitting in the throne of the Most High and commanding his Powers?

He would end up the same as Rogned, hanged from the neck by his own men.

That's exactly what the Raven is planning for you. The thought was spoken in a gentle whisper. Whether it was in Lyna's or Sabíana's voice, he couldn't tell anymore.

Voran took a deep breath and forced himself to think of the Garden in the Heart of the World. He recalled the Harbinger's hooded expression, how that supposedly all-powerful creature had proven himself to be no more potent than a phantom. The rage boiled inside Voran again. Years! He had given years to Adonais! And then, Adonais had turned out to be a great joke, and no one—no one!—had so much as bothered to warn him about it in advance.

They could not be good, these Powers that called themselves good. They were frauds, and so must be the one whom they serve. Unknown Father, indeed!

I will come to know you. I will take your throne, and I will make *you listen. I will* force *you to hear my plea.*

And then what?

The question, this time definitely in Sabíana's voice, lingered with no answer.

Voran turned to the Raven.

"I'm ready," he said.

End of Part I

PART II

Descent

INTERLUDE

The prince sat at the foot of the sage and said, "Give me a word, Master."

The sage stood still as a tree for three days and three nights. The fourth morning, he spoke.

"A time will come," he said, "when the bearer of the secret will empty himself to utter humiliation. The one who rose to the heights will descend into the waters.

"And there he will trample upon the heads of the dragons."

"The Tale of the Serpent and Gamayun"
Old Tales, Book II

~

Fifteen years ago . . .

Rogned, prince of Karila, struck the surface of the tarn, and it was like hammering a sheet of metal with his body. The initial shock dulled his mind, but with the enveloping cold of the tarn's icy water, the rush of the impact flashed like light-ning. He screamed. The water flowed into his mouth, and he choked. A vast darkness came up from the depth of the tarn and swallowed him like a jaw rimmed with layers upon layers of teeth.

Closing his eyes, he tried to release his body to his death.

Instead, light flashed somewhere below, leaving a reddish blur on the inside of his eyelids, along with a pressure against both sides of his head.

Was this the passage into the second life? Was that light his Palymi opening the door to the second terrace of the Gardens of Aer?

He opened his eyes, then realized, with a shock, that he was breathing. Underwater.

Impossible.

Palatial towers of coral rose from the floor of the tarn, embedded with rubies and emeralds that glistened between trailing arms of speckled anemones. Striped fish with wide eyes that looked perpetually surprised darted back and forth from holes in the coral towers, which looked like turret windows. The bottom, an incalculable distance away, seemed to be made not of sand, but of gold. Shimmering through the water was a dappled silvery-red light that was not coming from the sun.

Rogned looked up. He could see nothing above him, save for a pinprick of cold, white light. The moon? So far away?

A rumbling that was more felt than heard forced his eyes back down to the tarn floor. The towers were moving.

They weren't towers.

They were coral-encrusted appendages. No, they were *necks.* He was staring right at seven heads—half reptile, half fish, with cat-teeth and frond-like cilia lazily trailing behind what looked like gills, or tufted ears, he wasn't sure. The eyes were the size of a king's washbasin, black with pits of flickering red. And they were angry.

Rogned was suddenly bathed in red. The dragon—for it was a seven-headed undersea dragon—breathed fire underwater. It did not scorch Rogned, but the water around him boiled, and he found himself in the middle of a half-water, half-steam bubble of rainbow colors and a noise like waves crashing against a cliff. As he stared through the colored haze at the sinuous undulations of the dragon underneath him, it reached for him, snapping its jaws, but he was too far. The dragon seemed to be anchored to the tarn floor.

Then he saw a raven.

The sight was so strange that he rubbed his eyes, thinking that perhaps he was dreaming the whole thing. But no, it was a raven, and somehow it was flying, not swimming, darting in and out between the ponderous necks as they tried to catch it. It looked like an elephant trying to catch a gnat with its snout.

A sense of significance accompanied the appearance of the raven, a calm that preceded either storm or triumph. Rogned followed the raven as it flew in and out of view, finally disappearing below the dragon. All seven heads curled inward like a flower closing its petals for the night, and the jaws snapped shut on what looked like its own bloated body, which was anchored with kelp to a squat building made of copper. There was a single window or door in the house, and from it the raven emerged, still flying. It held an elaborate golden key in its beak.

The raven, still holding the key, flew up. Rogned reached out, his arms sluggish and slow in the turbid water. He reached for the key and grabbed it. It was cold as ice.

He heard a voice in his head.

"He shall trample on the heads of the dragons."

Feeling himself ridiculous, Rogned reached out with his feet to step on the heads of the dragon, who once again was reaching toward him with gaping jaws. But he couldn't reach them.

Instead, he felt the substance of the water between his fingers. And he remembered that water . . . water could become ice. He had always wanted to make a sculpture in ice.

The mad excitement boiled inside him again. The need to

create. He closed his eyes and caressed the water with his fingers, trying to sense it with every tiny atom of every finger.

In his mind's eye, he imagined that water was nothing but hot ice. And he was *so* cold. With a flash of pain in his chest where the Palymi had stabbed him, he felt the cold go out through his fingers in trailers, like ivy growing on a stone wall. The ice danced into a latticework that grew larger and more elaborate the closer it came to reaching the dragon, whose jaws snapped at the cage being woven around it. But the shattered cage only reformed around itself, until the ice hardened and thickened into columns like the pillars of a great temple. The dragon thrashed against it, but the prison held fast.

Underneath the vast, heaving bulk of the dragon, in the house of copper, Rogned saw something shining dully in the strange under-light of the waters. He swam lower as the dragon tried in vain to break through the cage, which shuddered but held firm.

As he swam up to the single window of the copper structure, he saw all the red-gold shimmer of that strange realm concentrated at a single point inside the house. Its light burning like a morning sun, a suit of gleaming armor lay on the floor. It was made entirely of copper plates connected by wire, with a peaked helmet sporting a large noseguard shaped like a sea serpent. The ear guards were the serpent's wings. A spear shuddered in the ground, as though it were a living thing trying to pull itself out and fly upward toward the enemy. Then there was the sword—ridiculously long, its edge glinting against the light of the armor. As elaborate as the rest of the armor was, the sword was simple—a straight two-edged blade in the Vasylli style with a leather-wrapped handle and an unadorned crossbar. But it was the sword, not the rest of the armor, that called to Rogned. His hands itched to hold it.

The window proved too small for him to push his body through. But there was a door with a keyhole. And he remembered the key in his hand. He reached out to unlock the door.

Then Rogned's chest constricted, and pain like a thousand knives stabbed him in both sides.

Spewing out water, he came up through the surface of the tarn, his neck held fast in something that felt like . . . teeth.

He felt himself dropped like a sack of potatoes on a hard surface. Pebbles. Lots of sharp pebbles were embedded in his elbows and back.

Through a fog, he saw the haggard face of Voran looking down at him with worry. Next to Voran's face hovered the black maw of a beast. Rogned scurried back like a crab in terror.

"It's only me, Rogned," said Aglaia. Her voice was tired and more than a little annoyed.

"Why can't you let me die?" asked Rogned.

Voran looked at him for a long time before answering.

"Rogned, you were almost frozen stiff when Aglaia pulled you out. I was sure we had lost you. It wasn't I who brought you back. Not this time."

Then, a flash of memory. *How had he forgotten?* He *had* opened the door. Only it led not to the chamber with the armor, but to a wooded plain before a white wall higher than the tallest trees. His Palymi stood there, opening a second gate, which had revealed a garden of peach trees whose sweetness he could smell even from that distance. The Palymi had stepped back to allow him to see. But rather than let him in, the great hand of living marble had pushed him back. It was at that moment that Aglaia had pulled him out.

"It seems I'm not done yet," said Rogned. "The Palymi brought me back. I suppose you'll have your prophet-prince after all."

Voran's expression was anything but joyful. Why? Wasn't that exactly what he wanted?

9

The accursed tarn glistened with the faint sunlight of early morning, as if the entire surface were steel, tempered to a wartime edge. The Fang towering over it was bathed in a fiery, orange light on the sun side, but was hooded in deep purple on the shadow side. Wafting on the gusting wind was a hint of lavender. Voran remembered that there had been fields of it growing wild nearby. The memory was tinted with loss, because the smell had once been like a punch in the face. Now, it was like the glancing touch of a feather on the nostril.

On the other side of the tarn, the rocky plain extended half a mile toward the next rise of tundra rock, which had always made Rogned think, Voran remembered, of a frozen wave of ocean water. Not that either Rogned or Voran had ever seen the ocean—only heard of it as an almost mythical place, beyond all human knowledge.

Voran couldn't see what hid under the half-wave of rock, because it was still shrouded in night. But he remembered well enough.

It had been the base camp of Rogned's ill-fated rise to prominence. He remembered what it had looked like: something like a forest clearing after rain, speckled with innumerable mushrooms sprung up overnight. But instead of mushrooms, here had stood different tents sporting a wild variety of colors, from plain canvas-grey to striped gold and red, the sizes and shapes just as varied as the colors, from the rounded and yurt-like tents fitting two or three native Karilans to the multitiered monstrosity of the Dolgoruki that actually had room for three flagpoles and a weathervane. The image of mushrooms was so strong in his recollection that Voran could taste fried chanterelles.

"You're *actually* smiling," said the Raven, his incredulity as exaggerated as all his emotions, so false in that preternaturally young and beautiful face.

"There are few happy memories in my past twenty years," growled Voran. "But I remember a morning like this, standing near here with my mother, holding a steaming clay pot of Karila butter tea, watching the sun paint the tops of the tents. It was a rare, quiet morning, full of hope, potential."

The Raven laughed scornfully at Voran. Voran felt a wave of disgust with himself at that sanguine memory. He didn't even bother rebuking the demon's laughter.

The sun had risen high enough to light the area where the base camp had stood. Voran, who had begun to walk forward, froze in place.

The tents—some of them, anyway—were still there. The color had leeched out of the fabrics, and most were tattered, making a strange symphony of swaying canvas and half-ripped flags on leaning poles. But what was surprising wasn't the tents —it was the presence of soldiers.

Even from this distance, they looked familiar. Most of them were dressed in the same kind of clothing they had worn those years ago—the billowy, roomy pantaloons and wide-sleeved tunics of the Karila. But Karilans loved extravagant colors, with no care for Vasyllian conventions concerning harmony or matching. The ancient clothing that these bedraggled creatures wore might've been brightly colored in some distant past. But not anymore.

The stooped shoulders, the quick, darting glances back and forth, the lack of laughter or loud noises of any kind—these men were not the hunters, but the hunted.

Voran felt their abandonment like a stone in his stomach. However indirectly, he was the cause of their misery.

And then, he knew.

"You want me to surrender to them. Is that it?"

The Raven clicked his tongue and rocked his head playfully.

"I always knew you'd catch up. Good to know that famous mind is working again."

"What about you, then?"

"Oh, this is the last you'll see me for some time, I'm afraid. Can't let them know we're in cahoots. Not yet. They might not understand. It's not every day you meet such a tolerant soul as yourself."

Voran snickered and shook his head. To his own surprise, he thought he might miss the company of the Raven. It was like dancing on the edge of a knife in shoes with thin leather soles, but the danger of it was strangely appealing.

"I suppose I'm just expected to let events unfold on their own, am I?"

"Oh no," said the Raven, and his eyes smoldered. "What am I? A Sirin? Or one of those mealy-mouthed Powers who serve, serve, serve? No—seize events with both hands. But to do that, you'll have to take the plunge first."

"Like Rogned," said Voran.

"Like Rogned," agreed the Raven. "See you soon, my rat."

VORAN APPROACHED the camp with both hands upraised. The first man to see him—a filthy-looking soldier with matted hair and livid sores at the corners of his mouth—exclaimed to the others in Karilan. Immediately, a party of five ruffians, blades unsheathed, approached from three different sides. At least two of them, Voran noted with interest, were blond, with light-colored eyes, wearing scale mail in the Nebesti manner.

Were these Dolgoruk's men? No, they were too young, and all the Nebesti had gone with Yarpolk back to Nebesta after Rogned had been hanged. So these must be something new. Perhaps some stragglers from Parfyon's ill-fated campaign.

Voran was surprised that Karilans and Nebesti were on speaking terms again. Then again, prey do not make for very discerning company.

"I am unarmed," called Voran as they moved in on him.

"That accent!" said a familiar voice in a strong Karilan accent. "I would know it anywhere. But it can't be."

An ancient Karilan, bowed almost double with age, hobbled into view from behind the company of soldiers who now surrounded Voran, blades extended. He was dressed in a dirty brown kaftan cinched with faded leather. He walked barefoot, his toes looking more like the roots of an old tree than anything human. A white beard shone starkly against his brown skin. The eyes, dull brown like mud puddles after a spring storm, still had the old sparkle to them, though it was very faded. It was the eyes that gave him away.

"It can't be," whispered Voran. "You should be long dead, old man."

"My hearing is just as good as before, little Otchigen-son."

That gave him away. It was Sagynduk, former special envoy of the Karila to the court of Vasyllia. He had had a complicated history with Otchigen, Voran's father. Voran himself had only seen him once, when the man was already in his ninetieth year, and he had looked about ready to fall over at a breath of wind even then. But special envoys, even former ones, had strange longevity. It was believed to originate from their being the guardians of the Blade of Covenant—an ancient relic of

Lassar's time that was a symbol of the union between the Three Cities, Karila and Vasyllia in particular.

But the Blade of Covenant had become an object of derision, the "rusted blade" that was so intimately connected with Voran's own family history. For it was the coming of this same Sagynduk, and the rusting of the Blade of Covenant, that had preceded his mother's disappearance and the long beginning of the fall of Vasyllia itself.

"What are you doing so far away from Vasyllia, Voran?" asked Sagynduk. He had not come any closer, nor did he say or do anything to make the soldiers feel any less tense.

Voran didn't blame him. Sagynduk was a fervent believer in the calling of Rogned. He had blamed Voran personally for Rogned's death.

"It's a long story, old man. And I haven't had anything to eat in days."

"You look it. And even from here, you smell it."

There was a hint of fond remembrance in the tone. The soldiers responded—instinctively, it seemed to Voran—by the barely perceptible loosening of their shoulder muscles. Old Sagynduk still had his charisma—that was certain.

"So will you extend the hospitality of the Karila to a wanderer?"

"I will extend the hospitality you deserve, traitor."

Sagynduk hadn't raised his voice or even changed his soft pattern of speech. But the soldiers acted as though he had. They shoved Voran to the ground and tied his arms behind him. A filthy bag was thrown over his head, the smell of onions and rotten bread predominant among other, unfamiliar stinks. Voran breathed through his nose, but crumbs of moldy meal blocked his breathing passages, and his breath caught until he began coughing fiercely.

But by that time, he had been lifted off his feet and was being carried somewhere, until he was dropped onto rocky ground, hard. The impact jarred his bones and made his gorge rise. He threw up into the bag. The smell, already horrible, was too much, and he passed out.

His last thought was the leering face of the Raven, laughing at him.

THE NEXT FEW days were like a drawn-out nightmare. Voran was kept covered under the same foul hood for what seemed like days. He wasn't allowed to remove it even when taken outside the camp to relieve himself. During the day, he simply sat in place, trying not to notice the stench of the bag on his head. All his other senses were accordingly sharpened, and nothing they perceived was promising. He heard nothing but Karilan, which he barely understood at all. He felt nothing but the bonds about his wrists, which cut into his skin and quickly started to itch and burn. He saw only dim shapes through the burlap, but he could tell that all of them were wearing swords.

They gave him no food, only foul-smelling water. Still, every time he drank, he felt a little bit of hope come back to him. Something about the whole situation—whether it was the Raven's influence or his own long-held hope, he wasn't sure anymore—suggested that things were not as hopeless as they seemed.

Sagynduk came every evening, but he wouldn't answer any of Voran's questions. He just sat in front of him, on the ground itself, apparently in silent judgment of Voran. Sagynduk's breathing, which always started out ragged after he walked in, soon regularized into a steady, repeating rhythm that had a soporific effect on Voran. He almost fell asleep a few times, but managed to catch himself from drifting off.

Right before the moments when he almost dropped off, Voran saw Tarin's old face screwed up in concentration, muttering the word that gave him peace. And Voran began to form the sound of it himself. *Saddai . . . Saddai . . .*

But he never could focus entirely on the word as he used to. It always escaped him, leaving him feeling empty.

Finally, in what was probably the fifth evening, Sagynduk took off the bag. He held a moldy piece of bread out to Voran.

"Thank you," said Voran. He meant it, too. And lest anyone think otherwise, he devoured it. It tasted as bad as it looked, but he forced his face to remain impassive.

Sagynduk nodded approvingly.

"You have been changed by your time in the wild," he said.

"*You* have not," answered Voran.

Sagynduk laughed—a short, rich sound, quickly cut off.

"I have been trying to find it in my heart to forgive you for Rogned's death."

"And?" Voran's jaw muscles were cramping from the toughness of the bread and the unfamiliar movement of chewing anything at all.

"No hope of that, I'm afraid. I think it is because I see your father's eyes behind your face."

"Is that a Karilan expression?"

"It is. It means nothing good for you."

Sagynduk resumed his stoic silence, punctuated by the regular rhythm of breathing through his nose, which whistled slightly.

"I will answer the question you refuse to ask, old man."

Sagynduk's mouth quirked in a not-quite-smile. "As arrogant as Otchigen ever was. Very well. Tell me what I should be asking."

"Why I came back to you, unarmed, and gave myself up for no good reason."

"Yes, I had been wondering. But I wouldn't have asked you. You are not trustworthy."

"Perhaps not," said Voran, smiling to himself. He had allied himself with the great enemy of mankind. Trustworthy he certainly was not. "Still, I will tell you. It is to raise up the cause of Rogned again."

"Rogned is dead."

"But what he stood for—a new way of living in this blighted world—is very much alive."

"Voran, you're not going to insult these white hairs on my chin by suggesting you are the savior of Karila, are you?"

"I was a fool to expect anyone else to do what I should have done from the beginning."

"And what is that, my arrogant once-friend?"

"I should never have placed my hope for salvation in a Karilan."

Sagynduk's face turned dark purple. Voran, who had hoped to bait the old man, felt a rush of gratification.

"Thank you for confirming that I have always been right about you people," said Sagynduk. "May the rusted blade crumble to dust at your feet."

It sounded like a ritual incantation, which it probably was, but it also suggested something interesting and unexpected to Voran.

"Wait, is that also just an expression? Or did I understand you correctly? The rusted blade is still whole?"

Sagynduk spit at Voran's feet. The spittle didn't quite reach them. Sagynduk rose up in a single, fluid motion and walked out of the yurt. He hadn't remembered to cover Voran's head with the bag.

"You're starting to understand, aren't you?" said the Raven, who had appeared by Voran's side, sitting cross-legged.

"Yes," said Voran, not without regret at having lost any remaining hope of ever winning Sagynduk's good favor. He hoped it was worth it.

"Don't you want to ask me? To see if you've guessed correctly?" probed the Raven.

"I wouldn't trust your words for a moment," said Voran. "The time for words is done. I will act. And either I will have chosen the right path, or my miserable life will be ended."

Something about what Sagynduk had said gave him an idea.

The rusted blade was at once a symbol for a lost peace and a sign of all that was wrong with the world. But a rusted blade that became whole again through a miracle of the Powers—that would be something spectacular. And if Voran were to be the one wielding a new Blade of Covenant, then there would be nothing he could not do. Would the Raven perform the miracle of restoring the blade? Was he even capable of it?

Voran guessed that the Raven was capable at least of creating the illusion of a restored blade. That should be enough. And if it wasn't, Voran was sure to face very swift justice at the hands of the Karila that he had effectively abandoned when Rogned died.

He sighed and put his head in his hands. The wholesome smell of his own dirty hands was infinitely better than the bag. "Raven, I am not sure which path—life or death—I am hoping for."

The Raven chuckled. "Oh, you're too valuable to me, my rat. You will die—all humans do, after all. But not for a while yet."

THE MORNING WAS STILL DARK when Voran's sleeping form was jostled awake by unsheathed swords. The soldiers holding them didn't bother to be careful, and he was cut in several places. Without a word or a sound of complaint, Voran got up. They did not put the bag on his head.

Outside the yurt, all the soldiers were mounted. Voran couldn't figure out where they had hidden the horses, until he saw an unfamiliar figure—someone dressed in the Karilan style, but with actual colors. That was unexpected and interesting.

"Hey," Voran pushed one of his guards with an elbow, which earned him a gaze that would have shriveled most men. "You're using me to buy your way back into Karila, aren't you?"

"Shut up, *meryn*."

Voran laughed. *Meryn* was an old Vasylli swear word, meaning "castrated horse."

"You do realize that's a Vasyllian insult, yes?"

"Do you?" said another guard.

"Fair point," said Voran.

The guards chuckled.

It was clear to Voran now. This band of ruffians, the remnants of Rogned's army, would naturally be out of favor in Karila itself. They had probably been living as outlaws, surviving by stealing and selling slaves to passing merchants. Voran's appearance had given them an unexpected chance to come back to Karila as heroes. Voran had no doubt that no matter who held power in Karila now, he would be thrilled to receive Voran as prisoner—the gift of a man who had raised Karila's hopes, only to see them dashed under the boots of the cursed Dolgoruki.

Voran wondered if the Raven had planned it this way, or if he was just a very experienced gambler. Or perhaps it was a bit of both. He seemed to know exactly what Sagynduk and the Karilans would do and how.

A chill passed over his heart for a moment. But no, he had made his decision. He would follow the Raven's way, even if it took him to the Realm of the Dead while he still breathed.

"Is that him?" asked the mounted Karilan, a young man dressed in light blue pantaloons and a bright red shirt tied at the throat with tasseled string. He was too young, surely, to know about Rogned, except as a legend.

Sagynduk, who sat mounted, uncomfortable, on a stocky mountain pony, didn't look at Voran. "This is the traitor. Do we have a bargain with your mistress?"

"She is your mistress as well, honored envoy," said the young man, with a strange flourish of his right hand.

Sagynduk breathed out in relief. It was what he had hoped to hear, evidently.

"Will you comfort an old man's pain?" asked Sagynduk. "Is the mistress disposed to this traitor's immediate or prolonged death?"

"Oh, very much the latter," said the young man, leering at Voran with eyebrows raised. There was something definitely wrong with him. The idea of pain pleased him, and probably excited him as well.

"Don't count on it, Sagynduk," said Voran. "We Vasylli have a way of staying alive longer than anyone expects."

"Yes." He countered. "Like cockroaches."

Laughter accompanied the movement of the entire party away from the Fang, alongside the hills.

And so it goes, thought Voran. Already he felt in his hand the imagined weight of Rogned's sword. And he knew exactly what he had to do.

❧ 10 ❧

Sabíana stood in her city and wept.

She didn't even bother to stop herself. This was not her city anymore.

Passing through the Harbinger's portal was strange, like awakening from a dream that seems more vivid than the waking world. Her disorientation wasn't helped by the sight before her.

It was all wrong. The seven towers that used to sparkle like different-toned gems every morning had been torn down. Instead of them, seven identically spaced protuberances that looked like chimneys leered over a blackened roof. The veined marble and malachite of the walls had been covered by some sort of off-white spackle that was cracking in some places and painted over in others. From a distance, as it was meant to be viewed, the former palace of the Dars of Vasyllia now looked like a squat, utilitarian building that could have easily passed for a public lavatory.

How had they managed to change so much in so little time?

Stranger still was the silence. The square before the palace, as indeed the courtyard inside the palace gates, was usually buzzing with human speech and movement. Now a few leaves rustled in a wind that seemed too lazy to play with them properly. The smells in this part of the third reach were always complex—the Dar's stables were nearby, and their heady mix of straw and manure, leather and human sweat, had always played mischievously with the perfumes of the courtiers and the occasional almondy whiff of the Dar's bakery. Now there was nothing but a stale suggestion of old dust. And this was outside!

"What are you doing out during quarantine?" barked a monotone voice. Its singular combination of emotionlessness and crudity marked the speaker even before she saw him: a dog-man, larger than most, his hand already pulling out a cat-o'-nine-tails.

The whip's appearance, calculated to intimidate, did nothing but disgust her. She certainly did not fear the flunkeys of Aspidían—though Aspidían himself was another matter.

She raised her hand, palm-out, at the hulking warrior. He stopped short, confused, like a dog whose leash has been yanked back. Sabíana had counted on it. It was one of Aspidían's signature conditioning gestures: hence the confusion in the dog-man's face. He responded to the gesture on the level of instinct, but whatever was left of his conscious mind was having trouble understanding how the gesture fit so badly with the face and body of a woman.

Then, something happened in the back of his eyes. For a flash, he was human again.

"Highness?" he whispered as he exhaled, barely audibly.

She felt the tears come again. "Yes," she said. "I have been healed. And I am back to make things right again."

He sighed, his face making a grimace as though he were trying to remember what smiling was like. It came out as pain. She lifted her hand up to her lips, trying to stifle the rising sobs. Would she ever be able to reclaim her city? And what had been left of her city, truly?

"Will you take me to your master?"

The moment of clarity in his eyes dimmed back to crudity. But rather than take her roughly as he was conditioned to, his touch was like a young lover's. She was grateful to him for that.

SABÍANA HAD OFTEN HAD STRANGE, unsettling dreams in the long years of her sickness. Even before she had been given, and had taken, the chance to escape her broken body in the form of the eagle (only to be captured by a certain recalcitrant Gumira by the name of Khaidu), her dream reality was more vivid than the dreary, everyday pain of the invalid. She had had dreams of herself as a fish swimming through an underwater ruin that looked vaguely like Vasyllia a thousand years into the future. However, the wondrous more often gave way to the horrible—pestilence and war and famine and many other variations on the theme of the death of her people and her city.

But never had her reality matched her dreams so well.

The palace had once been a true jewel. Carved out of the bones of the mountain, and only built on top of those bones in later generations, there was something organic about the way the rooms flowed into one another like caves. The decorations of the rooms and the halls had always been tasteful. Opulent, yes, but the colors were reminiscent of natural life. There were rooms painted and carved in orange and red tones, like the red-stone monoliths of distant Karila. There were rooms draped in blues and greens that shimmered like a pool of water on a spring day. There were dark red halls that seemed to glow from inner fire, like a lake of molten rock in a volcano.

But all of that had been . . . not removed, exactly. Vestiges remained. But all the colors were reduced to neutral off-white. All icons had been removed. Slogans of a rather crude simplicity were painted onto panels with no decoration other than the insipidity of the text itself. Things like "freedom ennobles, tyranny enslaves," which looked no more dignified than the words she and Mirnían had sometimes scribbled on the hallway walls during their childhood, to the horror of their chaperones.

There was nothing here but insipidity.

Not even the formerly present hum of malice, the always-thumping reality of the Raven's presence, remained in the palace. It was altogether a shell. A dead body already reeking, so that the hastily applied red paint on the lips only made it more horrible.

Most of these thoughts only flitted through Sabíana's mind as she was led by the dog-man, leaving not enough of an imprint in her heart to resonate. But her mind told her, through a rising haze of dread that throbbed in the increased beating of her heart, that she would have to process all of this later, and until she did, she would not be a proper challenger to Aspidían's verbal fencing. He would have the upper hand, even more than usual.

But she had no choice. It was the life of her city that hung in the balance—she was sure of it.

That thought left a wave of nausea in its wake, but what followed was familiar—a firmness, a steel-hard certitude, that it didn't matter who won this particular verbal duel. She would be the last woman standing, not because she was better or stronger or more adept than Aspidían, but because this was her city. These were her people. They were her blood and her bones. He was nothing but a passing fad.

Even if all the armies of the world swept over Vasyllia, she would remain to pick up the bones of her nation and pray for them to be knit together again.

But to whom? To whom would she pray now?

But before she could answer that impossible question, the dog-man stopped. They faced a pair of ceiling-high doors. The carved Sirin that used to be there had been . . . adapted . . . to a new figure. A woman wearing a skirt of leaves, smiling gap-toothed at the viewer. She was hideous—not by design, though, Sabíana felt, but because of a lack of talent. That made it somehow even more sickening—that someone actually thought there was enough beauty (surely not beauty?) in that figure to allow it to adorn the chamber where so many momentous and great decisions had been made in Vasyllia's long, storied history.

The doors opened inward, and Sabíana steeled herself for battle. Inside, she heard snatches of conversation:

"Locking them down is proving surprisingly easy."

"The same can't be said of the rats in the first reach, though."

"Why are you still worried about them? Just forget about the first reach. There are only two reaches now."

Sabíana looked up, expecting to see the fresco of the Covenant Tree, hoping to let its ancient presence fill her with the needed strength that she already felt leeching out of her. But the tree was not there. Instead, someone with even less artistic ability had scribbled what almost looked like a caricature—a muscle-bound, half-naked man reaching out toward the sun and grabbing it with a comically large fist. The sight was at the same time so pathetic and hilarious that she stopped in her tracks. Before she realized what she was doing, a short, barking laugh escaped her mouth.

Conversation ceased. Four haggard faces with hard eyes turned at her, annoyed. In the middle of them, on the far side of a table overloaded with maps and scraps of paper and parchment, Aspidían's cunning expression was transforming right before her eyes into open horror.

She smiled at that, but it was the wrong thing to do. It acted like a blow to Aspidían's face. His usual half-mocking calm was already reasserting itself.

"My lady!" he said, sketching a clearly mocking half-bow. "It seems we live in an age of miracles. May the heavens be blessed for your return."

If he had said, "The toilets need cleaning, wench," it would have better suited the hatred in his tone.

"What have you done to my city?" asked Sabíana. Secretly, her heart leaped to hear herself speak with such self-control, in spite of the bumblebees in her stomach.

"Ah. No preamble, then? Good." He smiled, and she was surprised to see actual warmth there. He must have been left with no one of even somewhat comparable wit. She felt sorry for him then.

"Aspidían, I thank you for keeping the peace in my convalescence. But don't you think it's time Vasyllia's Darina took her place?"

"Your place?" He stretched out his arms as though to embrace everyone in the room. "Does this look anything like the Vasyllia of the Dars?"

"No," she conceded. "It looks like a camp for refugees from a nomadic invasion."

He didn't like that. Not one bit.

"You have been absent for a long time, Darina," he said, putting a mocking emphasis on the title. "*Your* people are afflicted from without and within. From without, by an invading army, even worse than the Gumiren. From within, by a pestilence that not even our best leeches can name. They have never seen it before."

So that's why there were no people outside. Everyone had been shut in. Forcibly, it seemed. For a moment—a long moment—Aspidían's words had the desired effect. She was knocked off balance. It was nearly a fatal mistake.

"We have lived without you, Darina, for a long time," said one of the other men, whom she didn't recognize. "We now prefer the safety of self-governance."

She scoffed audibly at that. Aspidían looked like he wanted to choke the speaker for his badly chosen words.

"Yes, I see how safe you all are now. Free of the Gumiren, but, as Aspidían only just said, besieged on all sides. And no wonder. None of you have any training, any upbringing, in how to rule men. None of you have gone through the grueling hours, day after day, of studying the counsels of the Dars, of training for every eventuality, the *least* of which is war and pestilence!"

She stopped, and was pleased to hear her voice echo in the chamber, which normally was supposed to be filled with people, and still resonate like a cathedral.

The men's eyes were wide with shock at the sound of that echo, or at her words, though she doubted she had won anything yet.

"Will you be the fools remembered by history books as the ones who prevented the return of the Darina to her place, to the detriment of all Vasylli? Or would it comfort you, perhaps, if there would be no subsequent history of Vasyllia at all? At least, then, no one will remember you . . . or your *treachery!*"

It had the desired effect. Two of the four men fell on their knees before her.

Aspidían chuckled. It cracked the solemnity of the previous moment.

"Good, good," he said, and began to clap. "It's been a long time since anyone of Cassían's line had Cassían's fabled way with words."

He pounded his fist on the table. But the sound's suddenness was nothing compared to the sloughing off of the pleasantness from his face. He was no longer playing. Sabíana had to steel herself at what she knew was coming.

"You are brave, Sabíana, I grant you that. But either you are truly foolish, or your long disease has affected your wisdom. Look around you! There is nothing here that is left of your family's rule. If we have taken down even the visible icons of your presence, how do you think that reflects the hearts of the people of Vasyllia?"

She took a breath to answer, but he didn't give her the opening.

"I say this for your own safety. If you come out of this palace and show yourself to *your* people, they will give you the gift of Yadovír's death."

For a brief moment, a wave of sadness passed over his features, but they hardened anew, twice as fierce this time.

"In fact, I should do that. I should announce to the assembled reaches that the Darina who abandoned her city in its hour of need is here to cast judgment on the sons of Vasyllia who remained and who prevailed against the Gumiren. And not only against the Gumiren, but against the Raven *you* worshiped as a god!"

Her eyes shot wide open. How did he know about the true nature of Adonais?

"Yes!" he continued, his tone rising to a near-scream, like a volcano only seconds from erupting. "Everyone knows of the collusion of the Dars of Vasyllia with the Raven, and all to keep them in power!"

That didn't even make sense, she thought. But given the conviction of his tone, most people would believe Aspidían just long enough for her to be lynched publicly, even if afterward they would realize the folly of his words.

"Look at your city!" he said, walking to one of the many windows overlooking the second reach. "See what your kind has left as our inheritance! Only two reaches left free. An entire first reach of working people, without whom we will hardly be able to survive, walled off from the rest of the city, lest the plague spread and there be no one left. It is killing one person out of every four, Sabíana!"

And there it was. The misstep. Sabíana pounced.

"Have you told your followers here that you're using the entire first reach as a human buffer against the invasion?"

The blood drained from his face as he realized his mistake. All four of the other men turned on him with rising anger.

"Is that true?" asked one of them.

"What else have you not told them, Aspidían?" she said,

now sure of her footing again. "Have you perhaps failed to consider that the reason the Raven is gone has nothing to do with his defeat, but with something far, far worse?"

She took the table's edge and flipped it over. Aspidían had to jump back to avoid it falling on his feet.

"You know so much, do you? Why do you think, after bending all his age-old strength to taking Vasyllia, the Raven would abandon it?"

"He . . . he didn't. The will of the Vasyllian people . . ."

"Shut your lying mouth!" It was so uncharacteristic, coming from her, that Aspidían did as he was told. "There is a secret at the heart of Vasyllia, deep in the midst of Vasyllia Mountain. The source of all Living Water is here, under our very feet."

Aspidían chuckled. "That's . . . that's superstitious nonsense that we've outgrown, thanks to . . ."

"You would say that? You who have seen the power of the Raven made manifest in terrifying ways? You know that the world of the Powers is no prank."

"No," he said, and stepped on the overturned table as he moved toward her. "It is no prank. It is the great evil that we must fight. No more petty godlings for Vasyllia. We will stand against them. Vasyllia for Vasyllia!"

Nods of agreement came from the four followers.

"You think you can stand against the Powers?" Sabíana asked, shocked. "You need the help of the Powers if you're going to survive what's coming."

"No more gods!" roared Aspidían. "They need our worship for their power. Without it, they fade into insignificance. Well, no more!"

Sabíana couldn't believe her ears. He was spouting utter nonsense, but his followers were eating out of his hand like tame deer.

"What will you say to the Powers when they descend from the Heights to burn you? You are nothing."

"*They* are nothing! We have proven it. As soon as Vasyllia

ceased to worship him, the Raven lost his power. The gods are dependent on us! We need not give them our worship. We are self-sufficient!"

"You are mad. And you will burn," she said, but she hardly recognized her own voice.

"At least we will have the luxury of dying in fire. Like the heroes of old. You, on the other hand." He flicked a wrist, and two dog-men appeared out of the shadows of the colonnades lining both sides of the hall. "You will be among those to greet the invading force. May your fiery words convince them to turn back."

Sabíana's arms were seized by hands that felt like iron rings. They lifted her and carried her out of the hall to the soft applause of the four followers.

"Take her to the quarantine. Leave her to her beloved first reach."

Sabíana screamed her frustration. The dog-men reacted not at all.

❧ 11 ❧

delaida stood on a shelf of rock overlooking the downslope of the road down from the Pass of Ardovían to the valley that eventually led to Vasyllia. Most of the valley was shrouded in wispy clouds and dust kicked up by booted feet, but every once in a while, green swards dotted with bushy trees appeared, framed by cotton-wisps of cloud, and when the sun shone out from behind cloud cover, here and there diamonds sparkled: small lakes and a snake-river of deep blue.

Adelaida felt like she was overlooking a waterfall, with warriors instead of water flowing down the hillside. Next to her, half-seated, half-reclining in something that looked like a movable hammock, was Derzhava. They were the only still objects in a swarm of movement and noise and dust that choked her every time she tried to take a breath. The air tasted chalky and tinged with salt. Derzhava stared with eyes half-open down toward the valley, where Adelaida knew, more than saw, that two armies stood on the verge of exploding into a whorl of carnage and savagery.

Derzhava had been explaining the complicated politics of those she had called the Children of the Priest-King, and how they were actually followers of Antomír, a brother Adelaida

113

had never known she had. Only it seemed that Antomír was either dead or in some sort of mortal peril. Derzhava had refused to elaborate, though her body was rigid with fear, or some premonition

"Did I hear you right?" asked Adelaida. "The Children of the Priest-King ride . . . ride bears into battle?"

Derzhava chuckled. "Seems a strange steed, doesn't it? Apparently, they're not quite normal bears. Some sort of bond between them and their riders."

With a lurch of her stomach, Adelaida wondered if that bond was anything like the bond she seemed to share, whether she liked it or not, with the Artisan.

He had made himself invisible after letting her know of his presence, but a nagging nausea deep in the pit of her stomach never left her. She was sure he was there, though what he wanted with her, or with her father's armies, Adelaida preferred not to think about.

"And among them are some that are not bear riders? What did you call them? Monks?"

"From a place called Raven's Bane, yes. They're trained fighters. Both in body and in mind."

That was promising. Maybe one of them might be able to teach her how to keep the Artisan at bay.

"But why are the Vasylli fighting them, then? Shouldn't they be on the same side? If the Children of the Priest-King support Antomír, surely they'll support my father as Dar. And he's the true Dar of Vasyllia. Why is Vasyllia not welcoming us with open arms?"

"That is a question with no easy answer."

Derzhava's eyes shot open for a moment, though she still seemed to be gazing at something that was invisible to Adelaida.

Derzhava continued, though her voice was strained now. "Vasyllia is a fallen place. It's difficult for me to pierce through with my sight. I see . . . foggy darkness, something like an obelisk with wings, broken into pieces. A throne that is more an anti-throne. It stinks of blood. Old blood. And I sense a wild kind of elation. But there's nothing good about it."

"Have they overthrown the rule of the Raven?"

"No. I think the Raven has left them to their own devices. And they've chosen to rule themselves. No more Dar for Vasyllia—something like that."

"Who will rule, then?"

"The unscrupulous. The cunning. Those who can perform the magic trick of allowing the people the illusion that they rule themselves, while pulling their strings like puppeteers from behind the scenes."

Adelaida shuddered.

A bright light flashed from above. Adelaida strained her eyes to see, because it was as bright as the sun flying toward the earth, like an apple falling from the tree of heaven. No, not one apple. Many.

"What is . . . there are forms inside those suns!"

"They are not suns," wheezed Derzhava, her voice heavy. "They are . . . ancient evil."

Fifteen of these orbs alighted on the battlefield far below, between the bristling lines of bear riders and the shield walls of the rogue Vasylli behind several concentric half-circles of barriers, which looked, from this distance, like briars or twisted vines with thorns. The orbs faded to reveal slithering shapes, like dragons with spindly horse-legs, that shifted awkwardly into indeterminate forms, which somehow became giant warriors, their silver mail blazing in the light of the sun. The glare was now so bright that the tattered mist seemed to shrink, even flee from it.

Adelaida realized that her mouth was slightly open. Shaking herself from her shock, she was surprised to note that it wasn't the sudden appearance of serpent-giants that shocked her. It was their beauty. Surely nothing that beautiful could be evil.

"Someone *do* something!" shrieked Derzhava, her face sprouting droplets of sweat. "They are an ancient enemy of mankind."

Adelaida tried to comfort her, but felt hardly able to. In her desire to find some physical means of giving Derzhava comfort, she looked away from the battle. But there was nothing she could do. She caressed Derzhava, trying to comfort her, but Derzhava recoiled as though her whole body were ablaze with pain. Absurdly hurt by this gesture, Adelaida looked back at the battle. She didn't understand what she was seeing.

"Enemies? Are you sure?" she asked Derzhava. With a rush of excitement in her chest, Adelaida saw the giant warriors charge, not the forces of the Children, but the lines of the traitor-Vasylli defenders. A rescue! A divine rescue!

"I don't . . . I don't understand," Derzhava whispered. Now there were angry splotches of red on her cheeks and chin. "They cannot be trusted. I must . . . take me down there, Adelaida. I must speak to Mirnían."

"But . . . Derzhava, they're in the thick of it."

As though Adelaida had willed it into existence, the rush of the Ghavanite armies became a torrent, and a cry of unfettered joy rose up in song, loud and resonant, as if it were the banners of the Gumiren and Mirnían's house that were doing the singing, passing on the song in canon from one to another. It thrilled her, until her fingertips tingled.

Then, the carnage began.

In her head, Adelaida heard, "Let the feast begin." It was low, growling, like a lion who had only barely learned how to talk. Adelaida turned aside and was sick.

IT TOOK ADELAIDA, with Derzhava in her arms, what seemed like hours to navigate the onrush of warriors. Sometimes she was buoyed onward by the stream of soldiers, sometimes she and Derzhava seemed snagged, like a tree branch stuck on a boulder. If, from above, the flow of warriors toward their bloody destination had thrilled her, now, in the midst of them, she was terrified of being trampled underfoot. Every passing look, whether from warrior or engineer or physician, was tainted with annoyance at her intrusion into a world where she didn't belong.

What was she doing, really? Derzhava was hardly in a fit state. Her terror at the coming of the giants had seemed to addle her mind, but her body was not much better. The sweating was now profuse, her hair sticking to her scalp. Worse than that was a sickly stench, as though her body were rebelling against the battle by breaking down from the inside. But she had insisted.

"Take me to Mirnían, now!" she had said, in a tone of voice that brooked no opposition. The voice of the seer.

Adelaida was tall for a woman. She had never before thought it much of an advantage, but now it might have been the only thing that prevented the two of them from being overwhelmed by the bristling mass of steel-pointed humanity. The closer they came to the battle, the stranger the faces and the movements of the men around her were. At the top of the mountain, they had all been driven, like a thrown spear, toward a single point, their bodies and faces intent on the coming carnage. But now, some stood in place, their faces bloodied and pale with fear. Others ran the other way, some of them with limbs hacked off and blood flowing freely over their mail. The stench of sweat and blood rose in waves, along with warm upswells of air that smelled of sulfur.

Adelaida was sure she was going to be sick. But she couldn't. Derzhava took up all the available space in which she could throw up. And she had to take care of her.

It was enough. She found that space deep inside, that inner strength that was at its limit, and held fast. Vaguely she recognized that she would have to pay for this later through exhaustion and sleep. If they survived, that is. If any of them survived.

Soon her mind itself became numb with the intensity of the spectacle of blood and carnage. The closer they came to the battle lines, the more warriors lay on the ground, covered in blood and mud, clutching at limbs mutilated beyond recognition. Some were comforted by their fellows, but most were simply dazed, lying in place as their lifeblood fled from their bodies.

Why is no one helping them? This thought, like a trumpet blast, woke her up, and she felt her self-control flow back into her. She should be helping them. She should be taking control of the nurses.

But Derzhava's need came first.

"Adelaida! What are you doing here?"

It was Batuk.

Adelaida laughed at the perfect absurdity of running into him in the middle of battle. Maybe having a spirit bond, even with a mad demon, had its advantages.

"I need to find my father," she said, her voice barely audible above the pervasive roar of men screaming, bears roaring, and steel striking steel. There was also something deeper and more terrifying. Some sort of growl that seemed to come up from the earth itself, shaking it slightly.

"Come, I'll take you," said Batuk in his normal voice. She had no trouble hearing him, in spite of the battle noise. The swell of gratitude for his voice, his presence, even his round face, like a shallow bowl, made her smile like an idiot.

What she saw of his features behind his iron nose guard was grimy and splotched with dried blood. But he still cracked a smile at her. It filled her like warm mead on a winter's eve.

He was as good as his word. Taking Derzhava from her in one arm, in spite of the seer's groaning protests, he seized Adelaida's left hand in his right and plunged into the maelstrom that swirled around them. Adelaida lost all sense of direction. With the suddenly looming shapes of trees and the walls of mountain stone shading them, even up and down grew confused. Her nausea intensified. But she only stared at the men as she passed. The ones who caught her eyes, some of whom she recognized as having been annoyed at her passage before, now held on desperately to that shared glance of common humanity. Several times, she saw their eyes shed the horror that had filmed them. Some even got up and saluted her, before plunging back into the whorl of violence.

One of them—a young Gumir with a strange helmet that had a lining of fur both inside and out—smiled as she passed and burst into a song in their guttural language. Batuk twitched—she felt it in her hand—and without stopping, he rocked his head back on his neck and howled. But the howl descended into his chest and then forked in two, a deep overtone appearing that pierced through her. Her entire body sprouted gooseflesh from the sound.

All around her, the Gumiren started barking and whooping that war song. It was wild and brazen, and Adelaida thought she could float on the thickness of its sound. She whooped without words, her elation pouring out of her.

How could war be at once so horrifying and so thrilling?

The energy of all the warriors surrounding her shifted, their speed becoming manic, their impetus now more like an avalanche than a waterfall. It was terrifying, but she felt safe in Batuk's hands. And, she realized with a shock, she felt safe in her own skin. War was a natural habitat for her.

Was that because she was the creation of a demon?

Her stomach dropped, but the song brought it back up. No, she wouldn't think about that now. Now, there was Derzhava, and later would be the war, and the uncounted hours in the nursing tents. All other thoughts must be banished.

A tent of deep red velvet, edged in gold, stood on an

outcropping, sheltered partly by a rock wall with just enough of a vantage to see the carnage below. As they climbed up, Adelaida breathed in sharply at the sight. She saw the giants cleaving furrows in the lines of Vasylli, the bear riders picking off the stragglers like spearing frogs in a barrel. Her own Ghavanites and their Gumiren allies were pouring into the bottleneck in the very center of the fortified Vasylli lines, and they were widening it slowly.

The Vasylli were being overwhelmed.

But the losses on both sides were staggering.

"Come, Adelaida," said Batuk. She bowed her head to enter the comforting darkness of the tent.

It took her eyes a moment to adjust. Her ears adjusted first, to the chaotic wheezing of voices strained to their limit:

"Should we throw them at the buttresses there?"

"The bottleneck has to be a trap!"

"Everything hinges on the giants! We must follow their wake!"

"Whose side are they on, though? What if they turn on us?"

"I've had enough divine intervention to last me a lifetime."

In the light of three lanterns smoking dangerously, she saw a makeshift table. It was little more than a board laid on top of boxes. On top was a hastily sketched map with the pieces of a Gumir board game on it. The figures, which were obscure to Adelaida, seemed to represent cohorts of warriors. Mirnían leaned with both hands on the table. His expression was drawn, but the flush on his cheeks and his quick breathing revealed his excitement, not his confusion. Across from him, Lebía's eyes ran back and forth from his face to the board. Whenever she looked at him, her eyes shone. Adelaida's insides twisted and curdled at that look. She had never seen such a look shared between her father and mother.

"Adelaida? What are you doing here?"

Lebía had seen her, and the expression on her face—

annoyed concern and exasperation—was so familiar that Adelaida couldn't help but smile. She felt rooted on firm earth again.

"Do not trust the giants!" exclaimed Derzhava.

All the conversation, all the movement in the tent stopped as everyone recognized Derzhava's voice. Two of the young warriors on the other side of Mirnían fell on their knees, muttering something.

"Derzhava, your counsel is much appreciated," said Mirnían, all solicitude and concern. Adelaida saw that he was shocked at her physical state. "We are not sure exactly what to make of all this. It's a totally different kind of war than what I'm used to. Like a meat grinder."

"They prefer it that way. They don't take sides. All they care for is their objective."

"Which is?" asked Lebía, urgently.

"The Heart of the World."

Adelaida's heart raced, and it wasn't her body that was doing it. She felt the savage excitement of someone else pushing at her from outside.

"It's time you all heard the truth of what's going on here. I had my suspicions before. But now I am sure."

"But the battle, Derzhava?" pressed Mirnían, though not without gentle respect. "What do you see? I will follow your word in this as in all other things."

She took a deep breath, the whites in her eyes growing larger than humanly normal. Then she closed her eyes and hummed gently, in the depth of her stomach.

Everyone in the tent fell silent and stopped moving, as though a stray twitch might distract the vision of the seer.

Adelaida realized how, of all the armies present on this wild field of battle, they had the clearest advantage. A seer provided something no one else had, not even the giants—a vision, however dim, of the possible futures.

"If you would heed my words," said the seer in her strained, wheezy voice, "I would fall back and regroup, letting the giants and bear riders bear the brunt of the assault. Form shield lines and prevent any stragglers from escaping. Move forward, one foot at a time, only as far as the bear riders and giants advance further into Vasyllia lines. The giants' destination is forward; they shouldn't turn back on us. Not yet."

Mirnían nodded at Batuk, who saluted with a fist on his chest and ran outside. Adelaida felt part of her heart leave with him. She wondered at that. But that thought would have to wait. Along with so many others . . .

Derzhava groaned with pain, a whiteness passing over her face as vividly as though someone had painted it onto her face with a brush.

"Make way!" said Mirnían, and the tent exploded into motion as everyone tried to make the seer comfortable.

After everyone managed to get in everyone's way fifteen different times, and one of the lanterns fell halfway down to earth before it was caught at the last moment, the space inside rearranged itself so that the table was moved, the seer was central, and everyone sat around her, every ear and muscle intent on hearing what she had to say.

❦

The Tale of the Seer

I am continually astounded at the trust you all put in me. If you only knew the truth of who I am . . . or what I am . . . you would perhaps cease to listen. But it is now time for all bandages to be torn off for the sake of the body's health.

My name, Derzhava, means "power" in an ancient tongue. It is not my name. My true name would mean little to any of you, but it was once a rallying cry, of sorts. You see, I come from a time so ancient to all of you that it is no longer even remembered, either in tales or in histories.

How can that be, you ask?

You already know that the boundaries between Realms have been shattering because of the Raven. My own Realm is one not only distant in the count of days traveled, but in the count of millennia gone by. I am of the first People of the Fountain, who still live beyond the great Dune Sea, which itself lies beyond the Steppe. A land that your forefather Askoldír visited, but millennia after my own generation lived and died.

These bear riders that fight with Antomír . . . they are the distant *descendants* of my own people.

And yet, I am here. For I was bound, for good or ill, to a person . . . no longer a person, I suppose. Let us call her, for simplicity's sake, the Queen.

The Queen sought the ultimate transformation—from human to divine—but not through any means allowed by the Unknown Father. She tried to seize it with dark sorcery, to force it by her own will. Sorcery that involved . . . well, perhaps I shouldn't speak of it. Some things are better left to the darkness of the distant past.

She found a chink in the walls dividing the world of men from the world of the Powers. But what sort of Power seeks to go down, to descend to the world of the lower creatures? Certainly not the Powers that aspire to know the Unknown Father, that seek the gift of transfiguration. Only those with insatiable hunger, like the formless ones of the Raven, the changers of Nebesti lore, seek to break into the Realm of mankind, to feast on the innocents there.

These Powers gave the Queen a taste of pleasures not of this world, pleasures they claimed were the exclusive purview of the Powers. They lied. For all they are capable of giving is a phantom pleasure—heady and intense, but evanescent. And the Queen herself suspected that they lied. But she took the bait, for the promise of ascendance by her own will—this was too much to pass up.

I am the unfortunate child of the Queen. A child born not

of love, but of violence. A child born without form or comeli-ness. A child she hated, a child she hoped to use to gain the ultimate prize. Not immortality itself, but a source of endless power, an immortality of transformation in the Raven's image. You may have heard of it: amalgamation—the mixing of essences and forms into a single, unconquerable god.

My life was to be the payment, for I was a seer even from my childhood, given a mysterious power by some divine gift I never asked for nor understood. The Powers that my mother served hungered for what they believed my gift would give them: certain knowledge of the future and a clear path to seize the Throne of the Gods—a fabled place supposed to grant absolute power for a day. Only at the very last minute were her plans foiled, and yet, not completely.

One of those who wanted to use my mother for his own purposes, the demon some of you know as the Artisan, stole me at the last moment. He hid me in a place of his own making, a false paradise with no entry or exit. This place you all know as the place where the egg-reality of Ghavan existed —a place between the Realms. If not for Alienne and Lebía, I would have been sacrificed by a well-meaning but credulous Dar Cassían, and the original design of those Powers who sought to use my mother would have been fulfilled.

I should say, the design of those Powers and my mother herself. For though her body was executed for black magic, her soul was seized by those Powers that she served. And yet, she was not subsumed by them. She became a terrifying Power in her own right. One who even stood as high as the Raven.

In fact, the account you all know—the account of the Raven being punished for rebellion against the Heights—is not the complete story.

The Raven is but one part of the Great Changer who stood up in rebellion against the Creator, the Unknown Father, all those eons ago. There were three creatures that combined their forms to make up the Great Changer. The Raven was one, and perhaps the greatest. The Artisan was the second. And the third was the Queen. When their rebellion failed, they were each punished in a different way. The Artisan was banished to the false paradise of his own making. The Raven was stripped of any form, banished to outer darkness, and left to gnaw on the hunger that is never satiated. But the Queen, my mother. She was chained in the Realm of the Dead by unbreakable chains, to await the final Judgment of the Unknown Father.

She styled herself the Queen of the Realm of the Dead, but she was no more queen than the least serf who inhabited that land. And yet . . .

As the walls of the Realms began to crumble, the ancient plan of all three evil Powers became manifest. The Raven sought the Heart of the World, to drink the lifeblood of the world in human form. He believed it would make him immortal, and the first step of their plan would be complete. The second was to be my own sacrifice of blood to the Artisan, the creation of a false covenant that would undo the strength of Vasyllia.

Antomír foiled the plot of the Raven, and Lebía uncovered the wiles of the Artisan.

Yet Vasyllia still fell, and no one was able to stop the death of the trees in the Heart of the World. Now, all the Realms are dying. And still, we do not know the plan of my mother, the Queen, to escape her bondage. But believe me, she has bent all her intelligence, stretched out over eons, to the problem. Even now, she may have found a solution.

THE TENT WAS SO SILENT, there was a hiss, only irregularly interrupted by cries from outside. But even these seemed to be muted, as though the entire place had been wrapped in wool blankets. Terror reigned on all faces, on all high-strung shoulders, on all white knuckles being gripped so hard, Adelaida imagined she heard joints creaking in the quiet.

"This is . . . horrible." It was Mirnían, who looked like his entire life had suddenly been revealed as a vain parody of a life.

"Not one . . . but three," murmured Lebía to herself, as though unaware that she was speaking aloud.

"What hope have we of defeating . . . *three* ancient gods?" Etchigu wheezed in his raspy tenor. "And what about the giants?"

"Their appearance now," continued Derzhava, her face still flushed, her eyes still mostly whites, her voice still resounding unnaturally, "can only mean one thing—they know that the Great Changer will try to join its disparate parts again, to once again challenge the might of the Heights. Like all creatures of this Realm of Earth, they have no desire to see that happen . . ."

". . . For it is the lower Realms that burn when wars are waged in the Heights," finished Mirnían. To Adelaida, it sounded as though he were quoting an old tale or scripture.

"So they are . . . our allies?" Lebía ventured, disgusted at the very idea.

"They have no love for mankind," said Derzhava, and her voice was nearly ragged from some internal battle, "for they were the first creation of the Unknown Father, and though they fell from his grace, they begrudge the coming of the second sons."

"I never . . . second sons?" Mirnían seemed struck dumb by all these revelations.

"They will come to you with sweet words and manifestations of great power. But should they find what they seek, they will turn on you and scrape the earth dry of human existence. That is the secret desire of Buyan, their father."

"And yet," Adelaida was surprised to hear herself speak, almost as though her voice had decided before her head, "it was you, Father, who were given the omen of the great warrior in the sky. The Heights will fight for *you*."

Mirnían looked at her with wide eyes. For a moment, it seemed he didn't recognize her, or that she had perhaps grown a second head. Her hand reached up to her neck to check, just in case.

"Adelaida," he whispered. "You . . . yes. If anyone is proof that we are walking the straight path, you and your siblings are. You are our miracle."

She flushed so hot she was afraid her skin would burn off. Her eyes felt like lead weights, and the only place they could possibly look at was the ground at her feet.

"So," Mirnían's voice was strong again. Adelaida's heart flooded with pride at the sound of his voice. "We go onward. Keeping our heads on our shoulders, and our minds fixed to the Heights. Surely we haven't come through so much only to see our efforts crash against the walls of Vasyllia like waves."

"He's getting poetic again," said Lebía, to no one in particular. But her smile spoke volumes. "Watch out, Vasyllia."

Batuk chose that moment to enter. His face was flushed, and he wore a cocky smile that warmed Adelaida in places she hadn't felt warmth before. She flushed and looked away again.

"The giants have broken through the enemy lines. They and the bear riders are making short work of the remaining Vasylli."

"Remaining?" asked Mirnían.

"Word from the bear-rider scouts is that most of the Vasyllian army that held the pass fled a while back, with enough time to reach the city unmolested."

"They left their fellows to die, did they?" Etchigu asked, his voice dripping with scorn.

"Cowards," hissed Lebía. Her face was hard, more stony than Adelaida had ever seen it. Once again that elation at the madness of war took Adelaida. She shuddered involuntarily.

"Well, time to see what to make of our new allies," said

Mirnían, almost flippantly. He extended an arm to Lebía. They went out of the tent first, like the male and female personification of war itself, and the rest followed in awed silence.

~

ADELAIDA WAS LEFT ALONE with Derzhava. Batuk had just left them, though she felt that he remained just outside. She laid the shivering, shuddering form of the seer on a bed of kaftans and old banners that smelled faintly of camphor. Looking around, she found nothing that she could use as a towel, only a filthy rag on the rim of a rusted metal bowl with dirty water in it.

Wartime hygiene, she mused to herself.

Pouring the water on the packed earth, she threw aside the rag and took off her own head-covering. The temple rings got tangled in her curls, which she noticed were shamefully oily and unwashed, and she tugged at both with irritation. She realized that her hands were shaking visibly.

She took a breath.

Making a decision suddenly, she pulled on the edge of her head-covering, tearing a strip of linen from the upper layer. It was fairly clean. She had noticed that one of the warriors had been drinking out of a skin. It lay on the ground now, an arm's length from Derzhava's makeshift bed. Hoping that it wasn't wine, she reached for it and drank. It was water, and it was almost fresh, except for a tang of leather taste. It had probably been in that skin for a few days, at least.

It would have to do.

Derzhava stared off into space, wheezing like a sick animal, whimpering occasionally as spasms shook various parts of her twisted body.

Adelaida caressed her head. A bunch of hair came away with her hand.

Pushing down her disgust, Adelaida poured the lukewarm

water from the waterskin onto her head-covering and dabbed Derzhava's forehead. Derzhava's eyes shot toward her face, affixing themselves to her.

"It's me, Derzhava. You'll be alright. Batuk is just outside if you need anything."

"Bless . . ." Derzhava coughed pitifully. "Bless you, child."

It was strange to be called "child" by someone who looked so much like a child herself. But Adelaida had to remind herself that Derzhava was almost ten thousand years older than she was.

"Do you . . ." Adelaida hesitated, feeling, as she often did, the intensity of Derzhava's own confusion and disturbance. But something niggling deep in her chest told her to continue. "Do you remember your mother? Her face, I mean?"

"Yes. She was beautiful. Once."

The silence that followed was less heavy than before. Adelaida breathed into it, and decided to push some more.

"Did it hurt?"

"No. Yes." Derzhava's eyes clouded over. "I mean . . . I know it hurt, just as I know that water is wet. But I don't remember it. Only . . . there's a knot inside my chest that begins to unravel every time I think of it . . . and it's like there are killer bees inside, buzzing, waiting for me to open my heart completely so they can eat me."

Adelaida suppressed the shudder that threatened to make her hands shake violently.

"How did you forgive her?" she asked. As soon as she did, she knew it was the right thing to say.

"You are a miracle, truly," she said. "I have not felt the love of another human being since I was a child. Serafina—or I should say Alienne, I suppose—was kind to me, but she was a woman of iron. She had to be, after what happened to her."

Yes, thought Adelaida, *being immolated by your own husband might do that to you.*

"I must sleep, now," said Derzhava, and already her eyelids drooped.

~

BATUK STOOD AT ATTENTION, his sword hand gripping his pommel as though at any moment he expected an attack. But to Adelaida's eyes, the only creature he'd have to fight was one of the hundreds of buzzards that had already begun their feasting.

"She . . . ?" he asked Adelaida with the quiet intimacy of friends who don't need complete sentences to understand each other. Adelaida felt that freedom like a drink of water in the desert.

"Asleep," she answered, and breathed deeply. Immediately, she wished she hadn't. There were foul, squirming stenches on the wind that she had never before smelled. She had no desire to know what they were.

Something shuffled in the tent behind them.

"Poor thing," Batuk said. "Never a chance to rest."

"She is damaged in more than body," said Adelaida, and felt foolish for saying it.

Batuk took her right hand with his left.

"I meant you."

She sighed as she saw the light in his eyes. It was intense and sad and angry all at the same time. Here was another damaged creature, another who craved the healing power of touch. How would she ever manage to hold them all in her heart?

She must.

The shuffling behind them grew more jerky. Something about it . . . *smelled* wrong.

Her heart fell to her ankles.

She threw herself against the flap and almost fell into the tent.

Curled over the recumbent form of Derzhava, like an overgrown squirrel chewing its hoard of nuts, was the Artisan. His eyes were blazing red, and his teeth were bared over Derzhava's chest.

Adelaida knew she wouldn't be able to budge him. So she threw herself onto Derzhava's body.

"You'll have to kill me first," she said.

The Artisan wiped his mouth with grimy, long-nailed hands. He chuckled.

"I was too late. She was already dead."

Adelaida recoiled from Derzhava.

"You won't stop me, dear one. I am very, very hungry. And we are getting close to the place where I will be satiated forever."

She stood up at full height in front of him. He was so small, so pitiful before her. But his eyes blazed, and they were of ancient cunning.

"My life is now given to them. I defy you."

"Good luck with that," he said, and disappeared.

Adelaida fell on her knees in front of Derzhava. The emaciated form looked sucked dry, as though she had only been holding onto life by a thin thread, and a slight breath of wind snapped it. All that was left was a husk.

As she held her, she tried to find the tears. None came.

"Heights!"

It was one of the Ghavanite warriors, a young man. She didn't know his name.

"Get away from her, witch!"

Her thoughts thick and sluggish, Adelaida tried to make sense of what he meant.

"She . . . she's dead . . ." she began.

"You killed her!" he cried, his finger accusing louder than his voice. "You sucked the life out of her. I *saw* it!" At that moment, his eyes shifted, and Adelaida recognized the Artisan. He had possessed the body of the young warrior.

Behind him, Batuk's face was ashen, but without expression. The Artisan disappeared back into the young man, who grabbed Adelaida's hair.

"You'll pay for this! I know your wiles. We all do! You'll pay!"

Batuk grabbed the warrior's hand and yanked it behind his back. Picking him up like a sack of wheat, he threw him out.

Adelaida fought to control her breathing. She understood what the Artisan was doing. He was feasting on the forms of warriors from her father's army, using them up then discarding them when there was nothing left. And he would try to make it look like Adelaida was the murderer.

❧ 12 ❧

The absurd, luxurious dinner at the Hag's left Khaidu completely groggy. She didn't even remember making it to her bed—or what passed for a bed in the Hag's hut: a straw pallet on the floor. In the fog of her seemingly endless dreams, she remembered waking up to thoughts that the Hag was known to bake her visitors during their sleep. But no, she only did that to the boys—the Ivans, as she called them in her less guarded moments. In any case, Khaidu woke up in one piece. Aglaia lay next to her, panting cheerfully. Her wounds were almost completely healed.

"How long have I been sleeping?" Khaidu asked, more to the air than to Aglaia. But Aglaia's pant turned to something like laughter. It gave Khaidu quiet joy to know that the crotchety old Vasyllian noblewoman was still inside there, somewhere.

The Hag was nowhere to be seen. The sun caressed the slatted floor of the hut in rays that hung like drapery, thick and unmoving. Dust floated in midair like flecks of gold. Khaidu waved her hand gently through the light-drapery, and the dust motes danced around her fingers. She laughed. She hadn't felt this light and content in . . . well, she couldn't remember ever being this calm and happy.

Add to that the chirping and chittering and whooping of songbirds outside the hut and the whiff of fresh straw tickling her nostrils—Khaidu could stay here forever.

Antomír's dead face flashed in her memory, framed by falling rose petals in a garden full of trees as tall as towers. It was pale, but in her remembrance, a smile lingered, made horrible by the bit of blood seeping from the corner of his mouth.

She shuddered.

Could he truly be still alive in some way? What sort of life was it to abide for all ages in the land of shades and demons?

She would find out soon enough, she decided. No, she couldn't stay here, no matter how much the Hag was trying to make her. For she understood now that the perfect morning was yet another of the Hag's ruses. A gentle, kind ruse, to be sure, but a ruse nonetheless.

As though the Hag could smell the change inside Khaidu, she sniffed loudly as the rocking chair creaked on the porch. It was an invitation, Khaidu understood. She dragged herself with her arms, slowly, outside into a morning so perfect, it might as well have been a painting. The hollies were bursting with red berries, and songbirds with shiny blue heads chirped and sang and whooped in murmurations that seemed to paint an ever-shifting series of black-and-brown-and-white pictures against the cloud-covered sky. First a bird in flight, then a mountain, then a dragon with teeth bared—all these images flashed before Khaidu's mind as the birds painted the sky.

"I can't stay. I'm sorry," said Khaidu.

"It would be for your own protection," said the Hag, rocking steadily in the chair.

"And the people I love?"

Khaidu craned her neck to keep looking at the Hag's face floating above her.

The Hag sighed deeply. "What makes you think you can do anything at all? You're going up against some very, very nasty gods!"

"What else can I do, Hag? If I love anyone, I must act."

"You don't even know if you love him," whined the Hag, a wistful note in her voice.

At that moment, Khaidu knew. A fierce emotion welled up inside her. It was like fire, but without the pain. She knew.

"I do love him. And I am no . . ."

She paused, and the Hag gave another of her long, plangent sighs.

"Go ahead and say it," the Hag whispered.

"I am no coward."

The Hag growled into her bone-pipe as she huffed five times, ending in a sputtering mess of coughing.

"Neither am I. I will help you, foolish Gumir-child."

BEHIND THE HAG'S house stood a perfectly symmetrical wood hut, almost half the size of the Hag's house. It was already steaming heavily from every possible opening—a single window, fogged up completely, a chimney too long for such a small house, and even a crack or two in the wall. It smelled of roasted oak leaves—a musty, inviting smell that caused the rocks in Khaidu's shoulder muscles to soften into butter.

"Are you sure?" she asked the Hag. "I mean, why must I wash if I'm going to the Realm of the Dead. Seems a little . . . I don't know . . . excessive?"

The Hag harrumphed. "And you'd be the expert, I suppose."

Khaidu submitted, patting Aglaia gently on the head. The wolf lumbered toward the door.

"Leave all your clothes at the door," commanded the Hag.

"Why? What are you going to . . . ?"

"Listen, wolf-child. You've made your bed. Time to trust the only one who can actually get you where you want. Ever heard of that lovely word . . . *trust*?"

"Trust *you*?" Khaidu chuckled ruefully. "By the Unknown Father . . . I hope this is worth it, Aglaia."

The wolf under her whined and panted. She still seemed to be holding onto some vestige of her humanity.

Getting out of her clothes was harder than Khaidu expected. She had long ago learned how to manipulate the dead parts of her body into position so that her strong arms could do the necessary work. But either she was especially tired or her clothes were especially ruined, because it took her a very long time to get her clothes off completely. She undressed outside—a thing unheard of among the Gumiren—which didn't help in the least. Finally, after what seemed like hours, she was naked, shivering in the early spring cold, and very, very hot-faced. She could only imagine how ridiculously red her cheeks and neck were right now.

The Hag, uncharacteristically, made no comment at all on Khaidu's appearance. Instead, she just picked her up, opened the door to the little house, and walked in.

Inside was a sauna much larger than the small dimensions of the house suggested. More of the Hag's magic, Khaidu guessed. It had several shelves, all made of some fragrant wood that she didn't know the name of. Already it was blisteringly hot. Every inch of Khaidu's body itched wildly as her skin seemed to try to shrink in on herself.

"Hag, are you trying to roast me alive?"

"In a manner of speaking, little wolf. Don't worry. It won't take too long." She smiled her carnivorous smile, and Khaidu swallowed hard as her heart began to race. Whether it was the heat or the Hag's look, Khaidu tried not to think about it.

Instead, she just lay there, on a rough linen blanket on the top shelf of the sauna. The Hag proceeded to douse a bouquet of oak leaves in water that smelled faintly of lavender. With the wet leaves, she spritzed a pile of rocks in the corner, immediately raising a cloud of steam. She seemed pleased by that and plunged the bouquet into the water again, before spinning it around her head wildly, leering all the time. The hot air spun around with the oak leaves, and Khaidu's breath caught at the searing heat of the air, no longer caressing her—more like flogging her. She closed her eyes and tried to focus on deep breaths.

Then, something interesting happened. With her eyes closed, she became more aware of every inch of her skin with more intensity than when her eyes were open. And so, when the moment came when every single pore on her body gave up the struggle and opened up, she felt relief no less intensely than if the Hag had doused her with cold water.

Then the Hag did douse her with cold water.

Khaidu was sure that the Hag had killed her for real this time.

Then she felt the iron grip of the old woman lift her, and she opened her eyes.

"You're ready, little wolfing. That wasn't so bad now, was it?"

Khaidu had a very choice phrase ready for the old witch. But she decided she would be magnanimous, so she said nothing.

The Hag chuckled.

THE HAG DRESSED Khaidu in wide linen pantaloons of a deep green color and a colorless overshirt that she kept in place with a worn leather vest. Strangely enough, it all fit perfectly. But the look of it was strange to Khaidu, for she had always dressed in the flowing dresses and long wool overdresses of the Gumiren.

And yet the strangest moment—and for Khaidu the most

awkward—was yet to come. The Hag, having told her to sit still on a stool in the main hut, began to plait Khaidu's hair. No one had ever plaited her hair before, not even Mamai, not even in childhood. Khaidu imagined it used to be done among her people when they were at peace, but after the coming of the Dark Father, such things were left aside as useless at best, and dangerous at worst.

After all, to be pampered, even for a moment, invited weakness that could prove fatal.

But then the Hag began to sing. And her rough talking voice, like sandpaper, proved surprisingly moving as a song voice. There were centuries hidden in that song, centuries mostly of sadness and loss. But even in the tear-edged pain of that song, here was a quiet resilience, a beauty that could only be visible to someone who had lived for many eons, seeing the best and the worst the world has to offer.

And Khaidu released her tension into the Hag's bony hands. In that moment, the Hag was more like a mother to her than Mamai jani-Beg had ever been.

Then the Hag made a joke about stubborn wolf-children.

No, she was not a mother. She was a pest.

After the ritual of dressing—for everything about these last two days felt like a ritual to Khaidu—the Hag led them deeper into the forest, past the line of berry-laden hollies. Immediately, the light changed. It had already been a cloudy day, but inside the forest, the light almost completely disappeared. What remained of it had a glowing, greenish quality to it. Together with the smell of moss and dirt and the almost complete absence of recognizable sound, punctuated by an occasional groan of an old tree bending in a whispering wind, Khaidu was sure they were in a different Realm entirely. Had they already passed one of the doors?

The Hag was uncharacteristically silent and thoughtful. She kept puffing at her bone-pipe and stealing occasional looks either at Khaidu or at Aglaia. Each of these looks was quickly withdrawn and was always accompanied by a growl or a shake of the head. But she seemed to have decided not to try to convince "the stubborn wolf-child," as she was calling Khaidu more and more.

Finally, the light disappeared almost entirely. The trees pressed in on one another so tightly, it seemed to Khaidu that they were actually huddling closer to each other. And no wonder—an icy wind passed through the boughs, cutting through Khaidu's black woolen cape and hood, which had been the final gift of the Hag. No furs, no fire, nothing could withstand the deadening cold of that wind.

Khaidu knew without being told—it was the breath of the Realm of the Dead.

"We are close now," said the Hag.

Just ahead of them stood a monstrously fat oak tree. Two horses standing tail-to-toe would not have covered the breadth of that tree. And it *looked* fat—bulbous growths that seeped yellow-brown liquid dotted the trunk at odd intervals. If she looked at it peripherally, Khaidu thought that the growths looked like massive warts on a giant face, complete with protuberant lips and a knotted nose. But when she looked at it head-on, it was just a tree.

A small archway of complete darkness stood in the middle of the oak's trunk. In the shifting darkness, Khaidu at first thought it was some kind of parasitic vine with especially large leaves. But it didn't stir in the breathing of the icy wind. Then she realized that it was the source of the wind, tousling the few free strands of her hair almost as regularly as breathing.

"Wake up!" barked the Hag, and slapped the trunk hard. The tree shuddered, and a noise like a snore cut short rose from under the leaf mold at Aglaia's feet.

It *was* a face—now there was no mistaking it. And the darkness was a mouth, which now was closing very, very slowly.

"What has come over the world? Haven't I told you not to

sleep with your mouth open? Anyone could pass by and fall in!"

"I'm . . ." the voice was huffy and deep, barely audible except as a groan. "Sorry. Sooooo. Tiiiiired."

"Oh I can fix that," growled the Hag gleefully. "I'll just uproot you, shall I? Then you won't be tired anymore. You'll be dead."

"Noooooooo." It was more like a yawn than a yell. Khaidu stifled the urge to laugh. No matter how many times she encountered the absurdity of the magical, it never failed to amuse her.

"Lucky for you, I actually need that door today. Open wide, silly tree."

And it did. Slowly, almost like a nightmare, the archway creaked larger and larger, until it could easily have fit a mounted warrior with a peaked helmet. The edges of the arch were studded with roots and dripping dirt. They looked like cracked teeth.

I'm going to be swallowed. The thought loomed no less terrifyingly than the talking tree.

"Last chance, wolfling," said the Hag. Her eyes were definitely glowing now, reddish-brown in the green-tinged gloom. And yet, Khaidu wasn't afraid of her. She actually felt sorry for her. She didn't quite know why.

"I'm going, Hag."

The Hag nodded three times and sighed.

"Then you'll need this."

She pulled out three objects from her skirts, long and lumpy and bone-colored.

"Bone of eagle, bone of wolf, and bone of bear," she said. "But only use them in greatest need. The consequences of using them . . . Well, I won't tell you, but you have a good imagination."

She did. It would probably be something like what happened to Aglaia. Escape one danger, only to lose your tongue or your eyesight or your loved one. This old magic was always like that, Khaidu realized.

She decided she wouldn't use them. Not unless the fate of the whole world depended on it.

Then she chuckled at her own absurdity. She was already thinking like a heroine in an old wives' tale. Ridiculous.

"Thank you," she said, taking the bones and putting them into a pouch in her vest.

The Hag crossed her arms and took a long look at Khaidu. The lines between her eyebrows—or rather the place where her eyebrows should have been—were leaving shadows on her face, they were so deep.

"We won't see each other again, little wolf."

Khaidu nodded.

"Does that make you sad?" asked the Hag.

Khaidu said nothing, remaining unmoving on Aglaia's back.

"Well, get along with you. I don't expect you'll ever make it out. But perhaps you can make the one-way trip worth it."

As Khaidu felt her eyes widen with growing panic, the Hag slapped Aglaia on the flank. The wolf yelped and flew into the black hole. Khaidu had the distinct thought that she was being eaten alive and swallowed whole. She screamed. No noise came out.

❧ 13 ❧

Adelaida lay in Mirnían's battle tent, on Mirnían's bed, wide awake. It was the middle of the night after Derzhava's death, but she couldn't sleep. The face of the warrior who accused her of killing Derzhava seemed to hang in front of her, accusing. Even when she closed her eyes, she still saw it, as well as Derzhava's emaciated form and bulging eyes, which Adelaida herself had closed. They had refused to close all the way, leaving Derzhava with a confused expression that horrified Adelaida. Batuk had finally covered her with a blanket.

Batuk had immediately acted. He had taken the soldier who accused her into custody of the Gumiren, separating him from his fellow Ghavanites. Mirnían had cautiously approved of it, but Adelaida suspected that Batuk had a short leash only.

There would have to be a reckoning of some sort, she knew. She didn't know what to think. She almost believed the young warrior. Perhaps she *had* killed Derzhava without even knowing it. Was anything else possible for her, if she were the creation of the Artisan?

The tent flap blew aside as Zabían ran into the tent. Marinka and Kachinka followed, their arms around each other's waists as though they were not two sisters but a single creature. Their eyes were still hollow with terror and exhaustion.

Adelaida got up, immediately setting aside her own tiredness. She was grateful to them for forcing her out of her endlessly looping thoughts. Anything, even the twins' sour expressions, was better than being inside her own head.

Zabían jumped on the bed next to her, smiling.

"It's done. We won!"

Both twins rolled their eyes at Zabían. Kachinka said, "Well, it's over, at least."

Adelaida extended her arms out to the girls, who dissolved into tears and fell on her, nearly crushing her. They weren't little girls anymore.

"It's so horrible," said Kachinka.

"So many . . . they're so young . . . Why did they have to die?" sobbed Marinka.

"I can't . . . I want to go home," said Kachinka.

"And now they're saying that we have to deal with giants and serpents and . . ." wheezed Marinka.

"I want to go home!" shrieked Kachinka.

Then both of them wailed, one on each of Adelaida's shoulders.

She patted their heads and winked at Zabían. He shrugged his shoulders in that false modesty that he always put on when he felt mischievous, and giggled.

Adelaida smiled, but it felt hollow. Zabían didn't seem to notice.

"It is horrible, my dears. I know. I know." They probably hadn't heard about Derzhava yet. Would that make it even worse for them? They didn't really get to know her, not like Adelaida did. "But this is our life now. All we can hope is that it won't be for very long. Soon Father will retake Vasyllia. Then we will finally be home."

"Not my home," said Kachinka, pouting. Marinka nodded at Kachinka in solidarity.

"I think it's going to be great!" said Zabían.

Adelaida wondered if Zabían's cheerfulness weren't simply the inverse reaction to the girls'. She felt sorry for him and tried to include him in his sisters' hug. But she couldn't reach him past the twins.

He seemed to understand, and leaned into the common embrace with his head and sighed.

"My dears," said Adelaida. "No one asked us whether or not we wanted to come. It's true. But we have no other place to go. Ghavan is forever closed to us—"

"But *why?*" whined Kachinka.

Adelaida decided ignoring her would be best for all of them. "Think of Papa. Think of how hard it is for him to lead armies to kill his own people. Don't you realize that's what's going to happen? He's been raised his whole life to protect and nurture the Vasylli. And now they've turned on him, and he must kill a great many of them. Then, he must convince them that he did it for their own good. Imagine how hard that will be."

"He has Mama," said Marinka. "But who do we have?"

"You have me," said Adelaida. Inside, she felt a scream rising. Who would take care of *her?* But she forced herself to be calm.

"Here, lie down, my dears. There's enough room for you all."

Zabían cuddled between the twins. They fell asleep—all of them—even before Adelaida had finished covering them with the blanket.

She turned around to get some fresh air, then nearly jumped when she saw Lebía standing in the entrance, silently weeping. Adelaida's heart dropped.

"What now? Has something happened?" She ran up to Lebía, not knowing what to do with her hands.

Lebía pulled her into an embrace. "My girl. My dear girl. You carry so much on your shoulders. It's not fair."

Finally, Adelaida felt something break inside. Derzhava's face, Batuk's kindness, the children's inadvertent selfishness—it was too much. She sobbed, and it was loud. Too loud.

Lebía caressed her hair. "I won't be much of a mother for a long time, my girl. I am so pleased to see that you're taking my place with the children."

Adelaida's last bit of calm seemed to fade at those words. She swallowed hard, waited for the sob to fade. Then she pulled away from Lebía.

"I understand," Adelaida said, not recognizing her own voice. "Papa needs you."

"Not just Papa, my love," said Lebía, linking Adelaida's arm through her own. "All of Papa's close advisers, the Gumiren leaders, and eventually, all the people of Vasyllia. They will need a woman's calm touch to wipe away the pain of war. I have to provide that."

"I will be like a mother to them," said Adelaida, meaning the children. "Don't worry."

"Thank you, Adelaida. I don't deserve you."

Lebía's mind was already on other matters. Adelaida wanted to scream, to abandon herself to the weeping welling up inside her. But she couldn't.

"Mother," she said, gathering her courage. "Did we win the battle?"

Lebía sighed and sat on a stool, pulling Adelaida down on a neighboring one.

"I can't really say. The way to Vasyllia is open, yes. But will we now have to fight these bear-riding men and their giant allies? I don't know."

Suddenly, Adelaida realized that she hadn't heard anything about the fate of Antomír, Lebía's first son and her own brother.

"Mama," she ventured, carefully. She didn't know how to

relate to such a strange idea as a brother she had never met or even heard of, especially if he was now dead or wounded. "Mama, is my brother well?"

Lebía turned around to look at Zabían, her eyes slightly confused.

"No," said Adelaida. "Antomír."

Lebía seemed to gather herself into a single point. Her back straightened, and lines appeared on her face that Adelaida had not noticed before.

"Derzhava said to me that there was a chance he could be alive. But Derzhava is dead. And I fear, so is my son."

She would not say his name, it seemed.

"But you have not heard anything?"

"I have." Her voice was cold. "I spoke with Veles. He was his bodyguard from childhood. Veles is raving with grief, believes himself responsible for . . . Antomír's death. But even he has not seen him. Antomír seems to have disappeared."

"Then there is still hope."

Lebía chuckled—a cold, dead sound.

"I don't know. My heart tells me he is in the Realm of the Dead."

"Mama." Adelaida hugged her tightly. "Today we saw a Power of the Heights bow before the sword of my father. Maybe more miracles are in store."

"Maybe." She sighed, and tried to smile. It didn't work. "Come. There's to be a council of war. I think you should be there."

Adelaida would have loved nothing so much as a warm bed and maybe a cup of tea, but she nodded. They walked outside.

JUST OUTSIDE THE TENT, the world seemed to be on fire. A red moon hugged the tips of the mountains, almost too large to believe. At first Adelaida thought that they had perhaps come to a new world where the moon was always red, not off-white. But then she saw the corpses being burned in massive piles, the flames rising up higher than many trees. The smoke itself was red-tinged, and it was through that screen that the moon took on its sickly visage.

Adelaida was mesmerized by it. The features of the man in the moon, which always seemed to her to be a man singing, now seemed to be a man screaming from pain. She looked down, trying to focus on a mundane detail, any mundane detail at all. She found, instead, the eyes of her father.

Mirnían stared directly at her with a look she hardly recognized. There was sadness there, mixed with relief. But there was also something else she had never before noticed—age. Though he looked no older than his forty-something years, she remembered that he and Mama both had lived at least twenty years without aging in enchanted Ghavan.

If that meant that his return to Vasyllia had at first energized Mirnían with a sense of renewed youth, then the horrors of the battle had been enough to push down on him the full weight of the years he and Lebía had lost in an endless loop.

Adelaida smiled at Mirnían, and he smiled back, wanly. Something seemed to become ordered in his expression, and he nodded and looked away, visibly encouraged. That gave Adelaida enough self-confidence to look around. They stood on the highest point of the raised shelf of rock where they had pitched the royal tent. Below Mirnían, around him, behind him, was the morbid after-scene of war, made more horrible by the billowing smoke and smell of charred human flesh. Behind him stood an honor guard of two Vasylli Ghavanites, and Batuk and Etchigu to represent their people. Facing Mirnían directly, and so almost with his back to Adelaida and Lebía, was someone who looked like a mountain that had decided to sprout legs and walk. Two robed and hooded figures stood by him. They didn't move, but it was a stillness that suggested they could explode into movement at the slightest provocation.

Lebía twitched with surprise next to Adelaida. "Veles, is that you?" She unhooked her arm from Adelaida's waist and ran to the mountain man. He turned, revealing a pair of deeply sad amber eyes in a face like a crag, almost absurdly decorated with the most feminine, bouncy curls she had ever seen on a man.

But he smiled when he saw Lebía, and as they embraced the joy in his face was so bright, it seemed to Adelaida that his eyes actually lit up. For a brief moment, she saw the same outline of wings that Alienne of the Nebesti had revealed while still in Ghavan Isle. So he was also not quite human anymore, either. She wondered about his story. Was it as horrible and as wonderful as Alienne's?

As she had these thoughts, he turned to look at Adelaida, and wonder filled his eyes.

"Lebía," he said, though he seemed immediately abashed at using Mama's first name. "I don't understand. She looks like you."

Mirnían laughed. "It's a long story, old friend. I will tell it to you, sometime. But first, you must tell me your story. Where is my son?" And his face was no longer joyful, but stern and severe.

The man called Veles fell on both his knees. As he prostrated, he pulled out a sword from the scabbard of one of the robed figures who stood by him. It was a movement so graceful and quick, especially for a man so bulky, that Adelaida blinked, not quite believing her eyes.

He raised the sword, pommel first, to Mirnían.

"Highness, I have failed in my one and only duty. Through my own stupidity was Antomír taken away. I have lost him. I fear that he is already dead. I offer my life as recompense."

"Rise up, Veles," said Mirnían. "I do not accept it. If they wanted Antomír dead, then why did they not kill him here, on the field of battle? That would have been a much stronger gesture. Why take him away? That seems more an indication that they seek to use him as a hostage."

Veles remained on his knees. "So it would be, Highness. So it would be. If we were dealing simply with men. But I do not think that Antomír was taken by men. I believe he was taken by forces of the Raven."

Lebía interrupted. "Derzhava suggested the same."

"But why would the Raven want him?" asked Mirnían. Adelaida saw how hard it was for him to remain calm. Her heart longed to jump out of her chest and to fill his own pain with her comfort. She forced herself to stay in place. To her, who had always found it difficult to endure the pain of others when she could offer comfort, it was excruciating.

"He needs a vessel."

The man who spoke, one of the monks standing by Veles, was young, but very serious. He was dressed in dark, flowing robes that in the murk of the fire-flecked night seemed to melt into his long beard and hair, so that Adelaida couldn't quite make out where the man began, and where his clothing ended.

"We have long feared that he would try to find his permanent form in a human body, then give it immortality through the apples of the trees in the Heart of the World. That he chose your son's body for his purposes is . . ."

"It's understandable," said Lebía, bitterly. "The ultimate slap in the face to the ruling family of the city that worshiped him as though he were the creator god." She looked like she wanted to spit something foul-tasting from her mouth.

"But wouldn't we know?" Adelaida heard herself speaking. She would have to stop that, speaking without realizing she was doing it. It was very disturbing to that internal kernel of calm that needed constant care. "Wouldn't there be some sort of visible sign if the Raven achieved his purpose?"

Veles nodded approvingly. "I believe so. Though it could be only a matter of time. The Heart of the World is in the center of Vasyllia Mountain. It is no short or easy journey, even for those with supernatural help."

"And there is reason to hope that the Raven is not unopposed," said Veles's companion.

"Voran," agreed Mirnían.

Adelaida felt suddenly heavy, as though the weight of someone else's sadness fell on her like a waterfall. She felt the presence of the Artisan somewhere nearby. She was sure he was laughing at them all. Did she know why? Or was it just her morbid imagination?

"I don't think Antomír is alive," said Lebía. "But we can't sit here waiting one way or another. We have a different goal."

"Yes. And it would seem we share it. For now." This new voice was booming, low, coming from what Adelaida thought was the clouds. But when she looked up, she realized that there was a giant warrior standing in their midst, his outline flickering with flames that made his entire figure look slightly indistinct. Only his eyes, which were red-rimmed and hard, and his beard, which was like flowing gold, looked fully present.

At his appearance, Adelaida felt the presence of the Artisan fade away slightly. Was he avoiding the giants? She wondered if she could do something useful with that information.

"Do we?" asked Mirnían, his legs planted wide in the ground, his hand firm on his sheathed sword, ready for anything. He looked like an icon of a warrior-saint. A bloom of warmth grew in Adelaida's chest as she looked at him. "The last time I saw you, Zmei, you swore to destroy me."

"You are wrong, Mirnían," said the warrior. "My quarrel is not with you. It is with Voran. But I am willing to set aside even that long hatred if it means stopping what is about to happen."

"You still haven't said what your own endgame is, Zmei,"

pursued Lebía. She was standing by Adelaida again, and her arm shook on Adelaida's elbow, almost imperceptibly.

Zmei looked long and hard at Lebía, but she met his smoldering gaze head-on. After a long minute, he chuckled and inclined his head with respect.

"And you still haven't explained why we should trust you," said Veles. "You betrayed the Nebesti, your own allies."

"It is true," said Zmei. "But Parfyon's hatred had blinded him to the true objective. And that has always been Vasyllia."

"What do you want with our city?" asked Mirnían, the edge in his voice now more pronounced.

"We do not want your city," answered Zmei. But he seemed unwilling to say anything more.

The silence hung there, dangerous. No one moved. Even the creaking of a leather boot sounded threatening in the stillness.

"It is enough to say that our objective does not interfere with yours," said Zmei. "Do you dare ask more of me? You do not want me for an enemy."

"I had you for a friend once," said Mirnían. "Much good it did me."

Zmei leered at him.

"We do not fear you, serpent," said the monk. "We have long prepared to battle your kind."

"You cannot survive a battle with us," hissed Zmei, the fire in his eyes flaring.

"Survive?" The monk chuckled. "We do not intend to survive. Only to drag you, bodily if need be, into the lowest pits of the Realm of the Dead."

There was no bravado in his boasting, Adelaida sensed. He was young, but he spoke simply. He would do what he said, or die in the attempt.

Zmei seemed to sense it as well. His lip twisted, and Adelaida thought she saw a bit of smoke escape his lips.

"Very well," he said. "It is our belief that the Raven has

failed in his initial foray." He wouldn't say how he knew this to be true. "But the trees of the Heart did not survive his incursion. If you do not believe us, then you are foolish. Though many of you have forgotten who Buyan is, I remind you, he was the first-created one. The first warden of the Realm of Earth. We of his seed know when our home is dying."

Adelaida knew, down to the marrow in her bones, that he spoke truth.

"If that is so," said Mirnían, skeptical, "what do you hope to accomplish by going to Vasyllia?"

Zmei breathed deeply, clearly reluctant to answer.

"We know how to bring life back to the trees."

Everyone fell silent. Veles gasped audibly. Adelaida felt a terror like a strangling sensation around her chest. He wasn't telling the whole truth. And what he left out was very, very bad. She was sure of it.

"How?" Adelaida said, aloud. "How?!"

Zmei looked at her. To her surprise, he seemed abashed. But that faded, and all that was left was his pure contempt for the little people around him. He didn't answer her.

"You have a choice to make, Mirnían," said Zmei, turning away from Adelaida. "We go to Vasyllia. If we go alone, we will simply mow down everyone in our path. We can't tell you puny creatures one from another. You're all mice to be trampled. But if you ally with us, at least until we reach the wall of Vasyllia, then we giants agree to be placed in your hand, a weapon to be used against the followers of the Raven."

This whole time neither Batuk nor Etchigu had said anything, though Adelaida sensed that Batuk especially was furious. So furious, in fact, that his face was beet-red. Finally, he could contain himself no longer.

"Not one word, giant? Do you not know who we are?"

Zmei frowned in genuine incomprehension.

"We are the horse clan of Mamai jani-Beg of the Gumiren," said Etchigu, puffing his chest out in pride.

Zmei laughed. "That's supposed to mean something to me?"

"We are the ones," said Batuk, "that killed three of your brothers in the great city under the Steppe mountains."

Zmei's eyes grew huge; his nostrils now were definitely leaking grey smoke. "You?! Pestilence! I should burn you to ash right here!"

"It would cost you dearly, I think you know," said Etchigu. It wasn't bluster, Adelaida was surprised to see, judging by Zmei's impotent anger. There must be good reason why he didn't attack them, since it looked like the one thing he wanted to do more than anything else.

"Mirnían," Batuk turned to him, putting his back entirely to the giant. Adelaida even gasped at his courage. Her heart flipped in fear, too. She realized she didn't want anything bad to happen to him.

"These beasts are a foul race, worthy of no trust. But we Gumiren are practical. We understand that while we have a common enemy, we may march in ranks together, even with these filth. We will not stand in the way of alliance. Right now, it seems that getting to Vasyllia is the most important thing of all."

"Yes," whispered a voice behind Adelaida. She felt the presence of the Artisan. Quietly, she turned around, trying not to arouse any attention. In the shadow of the tent stood the young warrior who had attacked her. His eyes were no longer human, and his smile was very familiar.

"To Vasyllia. Yes." The excitement in the Artisan's voice was palpable.

Adelaida was torn in two. She recognized that there was wisdom in this alliance of convenience. But if everything they did only moved the Artisan's project forward, then what could they do? Retreat? Her heart felt like it was going to rip apart from the impossible strain of seeing two obvious, and opposite, realities be true at the same time.

"We are agreed, then," said Mirnían. "Batuk, your people have my respect and honor. Veles, can I count on the Children and the monks?"

He nodded. "We will share the spoils of the front lines, together with the giants. And if the serpents betray us, we will take it on ourselves to wipe their like from the face of this earth."

Zmei laughed, daring them to do so.

"Tomorrow we march," concluded Mirnían. "If the road is as open as I think it is, we will be at the wall in three days, four at the most. In those three days, we must devise a plan to overwhelm the strongest fortress in the Three Lands, and try to do it with minimal loss of life. Our task is not easy. But I believe we are meant to accomplish it. Rest now, my friends."

IT WAS QUIET AGAIN. Everyone had returned to their respective tents. Only a few of the soldiers still gathered bodies for burning. Adelaida was so tired that the inside of her head seemed to itch, and her fingers twitched without her being able to control them. And yet, she didn't sleep. She stood, arms crossed, watching the soldiers at their grim work. But her mind was elsewhere.

She listened with all her power, trying to hear something that would give her an indication of what she feared.

As the new allies had left for their beds, Adelaida had felt the air become charged with presence, with something like a hum, but just beyond hearing. No one else seemed to hear it. She had concentrated on it, and she had heard in it a growling, like a lion searching for prey in the desert.

The Artisan was growing hungry again. She wondered if his present vessel had already lost his usefulness.

Somehow, the connection she shared with him as his creation gave her some insight into his desires and thoughts, even when he wasn't speaking to her directly. And so she knew, on the level of a woman's intuition, that only she could stop him. All that remained was to figure out how.

She had no idea where he would strike next.

As she stood in place, trying with all her power to remain awake and aware of the world around her, she heard the plodding gait of Batuk behind her. For the first time, she was annoyed at him for coming at such an inopportune moment.

"You should rest, Adelaida," he said simply.

She couldn't argue with something so obvious. It made her more irritated. So she withdrew even further inside herself and didn't answer.

He stood by her, his elbow barely brushing against hers. Though he was a large man, she was almost as tall as he. Absurdly, that thought made her feel superior to him at that moment.

"You're not my protector, you know," she finally said. It sounded flippant, unworthy of her. She felt ashamed.

"I would like to be," he said, just as simply as before. He seemed not in the least perturbed by her irritation.

"Why?" she asked, and was ashamed to realize she was on the verge of tears.

She looked at him. She had never really paid much attention to the jagged scar that cut across his entire left eye, leaving it permanently closed and the skin around it puffy and inflamed. But now it intruded on her thoughts.

"This?" He pointed at the scar. "Yes, that is partly why."

She said nothing, sensing that he needed the space to finish his thought.

"I am a cruel, twisted creature, Adelaida. I was made for war. I am good at killing. So, I used to believe there was virtue in that, since it seemed I was created for such a purpose. But I was wrong to think that."

His breathing grew ragged. She wanted to touch him, but knew it would be the wrong thing to do.

"We Gumiren do not honor women above men. In our difficult lives, all are equally at the mercy of the Steppe. So power is what determines virtue. Or so I thought. But then, my actions led to the loss of my only sister. I have never forgiven myself for her loss."

In spite of herself, Adelaida felt another stab of annoyance. So was she then nothing but a reclamation project for Batuk? Did he not care for her as Adelaida? Only as a replacement for a lost sister? Her heart beat at her chest insistently, pushing out.

"But . . ." He shifted uneasily on his feet. "I am clumsy— forgive . . . not to say that I see you . . . Oh, how hard words are."

She felt ashamed at her coldness again. He meant well, she knew.

"When I lost Khaidu, my sister, I knew that even I was created to love, not to kill. My skill with violence . . . it is not meant to be a destructive force. I am meant to protect . . . those that I . . . that I love."

Adelaida found that she couldn't breathe.

At that moment, a scream cut across the silence like a jagged knife.

Adelaida was running even before Batuk could ask her what she was doing.

Fool, she said to herself. *Fool!*

She had allowed herself to lose concentration. And the Artisan had killed again, she knew.

The screaming, a half-gurgle now, continued, then cut off. Adelaida thought she knew which tent it was. She burst into it, heedless of who might be inside.

The Artisan, in the form of the old potter that she had known in Ghavan, crouched over the desiccated body of the young warrior who had called her a witch. He breathed in deeply, contentedly. He had feasted well. There was hardly anything left of the young man except skin, bones, and an expression of terror in his bulging, dead eyes.

"They don't last as long as they used to," the Artisan said to her. There was a plangent note in his tone, as though he were a father confiding in his daughter. It repulsed her.

Adelaida pushed him aside and leaned over the young man. She didn't know what to do, nudging him, pushing him, willing him to breathe. He was quite dead.

"Adelaida, what is this?" It was Mirnían's voice. He stood in the entryway of the tent, while Batuk held the flap open.

"Papa, I . . ." She found that she couldn't say anything.

Mirnían turned to Batuk, who had walked in behind him. "Don't let anyone near this place. On pain of your life!"

Batuk nodded once, deadly serious. Mirnían, his eyes filled with pain, crouched down to her.

"Adelaida, please, please tell me what is happening. I think it must be something terrible, something you can't control. Let me help you."

Adelaida looked over at the corner of the tent. The Artisan sat there, his eyes glowing. He shook his head and made a slicing gesture across his neck, then pointed at Mirnían. She understood. To save her father, she'd have to remain silent.

She said nothing, only closed the eyes of the dead boy. To her relief, they closed completely this time.

"Adelaida, you must tell me," said Mirnían, with a touch of desperation in his voice. "How can I protect you otherwise?"

She looked at her father, cut to her heart by the expression of fear and distrust on his face. She wanted to cry, to weep, to tell him what was happening. But she could not. She was not her own person anymore. From this moment, she would make it every day's unfailing work to stop the Artisan from taking another body. No matter what it took.

❧ 14 ❧

Antomír sat, or stood—he didn't know which one it was —in a room, or a hall, or a hole, one of such darkness that he could hear or see or feel nothing. Add to that the general indistinctness of the Realm of the Dead, and Antomír might as well have been chained in a dungeon. The effect was exactly the same.

He had lost consciousness, or whatever passed for consciousness here, as soon as the dead who served the Queen had seized him. She had told them to bring him to her. But whether they had failed or whether he was in some sort of holding cell, waiting to be released at her good pleasure, he had no idea.

All he could see and feel and taste and smell was absence. He couldn't even see his own hands in front of his face.

He should be terrified, he knew. But it was difficult to care here, where he had no body. This spirit-form that he found himself in, without a physical body to animate, tended to stasis. The best Antomír could muster in terms of emotion was a faint kind of frustration. But soon that frustration gave way to numbness that he knew was close to apathy. With his disembodied thoughts, he imagined that such apathy would lead to a kind of permanent oblivion. Even in his disembodied state, he recoiled from it. Or he did at first. If he didn't focus all of his attention on it, he seemed to slide back into it naturally.

To stop that from happening, even though he couldn't see his feet and hardly felt them, he walked. Forward or sideways or backward—it hardly mattered in this total absence of color, sound, or texture. In the darkness, he expected any second to crash into an equally invisible wall. Instead, he kept walking. He would almost have preferred crashing into something to continuing in this indeterminate half-state of nothingness.

He wondered what it meant that he still saw himself as a body, even if it was not as distinct as his physical self had been in life. Was there such a thing as a spirit-body? Or was this simply a projection of his consciousness, some sort of manifestation of what he believed himself to be?

And why were there so few other distinct spirit-forms in the Realm of the Dead? Most seemed no more distinct than mounds of flesh without expression or feature. Was that what he would become, the longer he persisted in this place of shadows?

Gradually, a hazy glow rose around Antomír, like a light-bearing mist rising from cold ground.

In a very distant place, there was something like a door or a window in the wall of blackness. At first, it registered only as a pinprick of color. He walked to it, even started to run, but he didn't seem to be getting much closer at all. Then, smells tickled his remembrance. Smoky tea and cherry blossoms. Sounds followed the smells, like auditory afterthoughts. They were good sounds—hearty, filling. That was the best he could do to describe them to himself.

Finally, the strange sounds joined into something he never expected to hear down here—laughter. And it was familiar laughter, to boot.

"Otar Svetlomír?" he said aloud.

Antomír thought he saw—still an impossible distance away, as though in a painting that hung suspended in a soaring wall of darkness—a pastoral scene by a river. The trees there were in early spring bloom, but the leaves weren't distinct. They looked like a caricature of the early greenery on alders glimpsed from a distance, when the translucent mass of new green looked like globs of paint on the grey canvas of alder bark. Here, the masses of leaves were even more paint-like, but like the work of a second-rate artist who preferred thick, crude brushstrokes to the mastery of the iconographer.

Sitting on a sawed-off stump, his chin leaning on a crooked staff, Otar Svetlomír smiled down at Antomír. He looked like he had been painted by an artist who was more interested in impressions than in verisimilitude. To his surprise, Antomír liked the way Otar Svetlomír looked in this form. After all, the old priest from Ghavan had always left a good impression, and the impression is exactly what this artist, if it was an artist, had captured in that living painting.

Once he reached a point where Otar Svetlomír was visible enough to speak to, Antomír couldn't get any closer, no matter how much he walked toward the living painting. So he stopped, more out of inertia than tiredness.

"My boy," said Otar Svetlomír. His joyful eyes now seemed brimming with tears. He held a cup of tea in one hand, and a round saucer in another. At that moment, Antomír remembered one of his favorite sayings: *If you wish to taste the far limits of what man is capable of, then stand on the edge of the abyss until you can stand it no longer. Then, go and have a cup of tea.*

That was exactly what he was doing.

Antomír wished he had a cup of tea of his own. But nothing materialized in his hands with the wishing.

"Why can't I join you, Otar?" asked Antomír.

"You will, eventually. I think. But it isn't your time yet."

"Time. Does time even exist here?"

Otar Svetlomír chuckled and pointed at Antomír with his cup. "Good point!"

Antomír brushed that off. It didn't make sense to his half-distinct thoughts.

"Otar, when we last spoke in Ghavan, when you appeared to me through the spring of water, what did you mean about the walls between Realms cracking? Are you saying there's a way out of here?"

"Not yet."

He said no more.

"Do you know when it will be?"

Otar Svetlomír put a finger across his lips and shushed him, as though Antomír were a small child.

"Even the walls have ears," he said, conspiratorially. It was such a strange thing to say in this place that Antomír wasn't sure that this was Otar Svetlomír at all, but perhaps some sort of illusion meant to confuse him. But why? What was the point of it?

"Otar, things were very bad in the Realm of the Living when I left it. And it seems things are just as bad here."

"Well, it is the Realm of the Dead. What did you expect? Some sort of paradise?"

Antomír had never really thought about life after death, except that he had some vague expectation that good people would get something nice and bad people would get something horrible and unpleasant. It was only fair. He would never have imagined the confusing and dark reality of the Realm of the Dead as it truly was.

"Is there nothing I can do?" asked Antomír, lamely.

"Ah!" Otar Svetlomír stood up and raised his hand in an exaggerated gesture. "In the midst of this doomed land, there is an all-powerful One that leaps from the Heights, a relentless warrior carrying the sword of irrevocable command."

"I have no sword," said Antomír. "Tell me where I can find this sword of irrevocable command."

Otar Svetlomír looked at him with sadness.

"Oh, not you, dear boy. No no no no. I was just quoting old prophecies. It is my opinion, and believe me, I have no pleasure in voicing it, but I don't think there's anything you can do at all."

"Please, Otar! There must be something. Give me a quest of some kind or I will fade into nothingness."

Otar Svetlomír sighed.

"My dear boy, there is nothing I can say. We are at the brink of some terrible catastrophe, even worse than everything that's already happened. Even here, even in the Realm of the Dead, I have continued my fervent prayers for the salvation of our people and of the Three Lands. But I no longer know whom to pray to. I have always been a man of Adonais. What does that make me, then? A worshiper of a demon?"

Antomír, for a moment, felt his entire self go stiff with terror. Something that had been nagging at him, some knowledge that was not his own, flooded his consciousness. He turned away from it, afraid that he would die a second time.

"Otar, I don't understand. What do you mean, the worshiper of a demon?"

Otar Svetlomír retreated even further into himself.

"So you're even less dead than I thought. The clarity of oblivion hasn't yet entered you."

The words were like ice, and for a moment, Antomír felt as though he had a body, and it was trembling.

"Tell me!" he shouted. No echo sounded in that dead space.

"Adonais is the Raven, my boy. I thought you knew."

He did know. He had just been turning away from that knowledge, the same way he had been turning away from all the rest of his new clarity.

He let go of the last vestiges of life.

It was like a candle going out.

Then, he awoke, fully embracing his death. And he knew.

He knew that the dead lands were indeed in an uproar,

with many of the unquiet souls gathering at the feet of the Queen. He also knew that she was not a great Power. Or at least, she had not been at first. In that dreadful nakedness that he guessed all the dead felt before each other, he saw that the Queen had once been human, a sorceress who dabbled in dark magic and who had eventually unleashed terrible forces that had subsumed her completely. And he knew then, as did all the denizens of that land, that the Queen was slowly widening a crack that would lead all the forces of the dead into the Realm of the Living.

Then he knew that the Queen and the Raven were part of the same force, the same driving need to possess living forms at any cost.

But if there were no Adonais, what could he do? What could the living Vasylli do? Otar Svetlomír was right. There was nothing to do but wait and be taken up by the wave of terror. There was indeed a way out of this place. All he needed to do was become a silent, hungry, insatiable pawn in the growing army of the Queen of the dead.

Even the thought itself was pushing him toward it. He felt hunger for his body; he remembered the taste of cherries; he smelled the salty air on Ghavan on a spring morning. He could have all of that. All he had to do was wait.

And then what? If he abandoned himself to become a thoughtless spirit in service to the Queen of the dead, he would be no better than one of the formless ones. The ones who possessed his grandfather Otchigen and left him as nothing more than an empty husk.

But what alternative was there?

There is no alternative.

The voice was inside him. The Queen had remembered his existence.

You are a king's son, a noble warrior. You need not become one of the formless ones with no self of their own. You can be my lieutenant, my chosen warrior.

You can be at the front lines of the war against the living.

"Why would I do that?" asked Antomír aloud.

The alternative is horrible.

He knew it would be. He could fight it for a time, the descent into formlessness. But there was nothing to hold onto here. However time was counted here, it would not be long before his sense of self would fade, and he would be nothing but that hunger that already gnawed at him, demanding to be filled.

"I don't care," he whispered. "I will not willingly join you."

There was no bravado or even bravery in his voice. He knew that he spoke simply from his heart. He, Antomír, who had for a time been a bear rider and an anointed one of a god he didn't even know, would never willingly become an enemy of everything he held dear. Better to simply fade.

He could not be held responsible if his selfless, formless spirit became a terror unleashed upon the world.

Except . . . his conscience seemed not to have died with his body. He knew it was not true. He knew that he would have to do everything in his power to remain himself, even without his body, even in this place of nothingness.

At that moment, as though his last thought had been a sword slash, his connection to the Queen was severed. He no longer felt her inside him, no longer heard the rumble of her inhuman voice. Everything faded again.

Antomír felt a strange sensation in his chest, something like the flutter of a second heart. Gamayun was near again. Though she had been the cause of his death, he suspected that here, she might help him hold onto himself, his inner self.

He turned toward the fluttering sensation and walked to it, like a blind man trying to find a loaf of bread by smelling for the bakery. It grew stronger and stronger. As it did, so did the light around him. It was coming directly from Gamayun. She was bathed in soft, red light, sitting on a stone in a field of other stones, facing away from Antomír. Next to her stood a man he had seen before.

"Who are you?" called Antomír. The man turned around. He was older than Antomír, but not by much. A tall, strong man of warrior caste. His eyes, however, were ancient and cold.

"I am Parfyon of the Nebesti," he said. "Welcome, Antomír. Your friend Gamayun has told me much about you."

ANTOMÍR DIDN'T KNOW what to make of this strange scene. Gamayun sat like a statue, her gaze peering into some unknown distance, away from Antomír and Parfyon. The field stretching before them was riddled with rocks, but it was also covered in bones. Antomír didn't understand that. How could there be bones in the Realm of the Dead? Was it not the land of spirits with no bodies?

For the first time since he had awoken in the Realm of the Dead, Antomír looked at his hands. They were familiar enough, he thought, though he noticed the conspicuous lack of a scar on his left thumb that he had received when he had tried to chop a branch for the first time in his life. He was lucky he hadn't lost his finger completely.

There was no fondness in that remembrance, though. Something about being in Gamayun's presence poisoned all memories associated with Ghavan Isle. She had stolen everything that was joyful in his life and had replaced it with this darkness, this nothingness.

He wished he could muster the strength to be angry. But nothing came, only the pull—nagging sometimes, fading at others—into the comforting oblivion of formlessness.

Parfyon hadn't spoken much to him since they met. He seemed preoccupied with what Gamayun was doing. Some sort of seer-vision, he had explained.

"Parfyon, does it bother you that there are bones there?" he asked, because he felt he should say something.

"Why should it?" He seemed to be thinking of other things, not really listening to Antomír.

"Well, this is a spirit Realm, is it not? How can bodies be present here?"

"They are not really bones, Antomír."

He said it as though Antomír was the stupidest creature in the world.

"Is it an illusion, then?"

"Most things here are an illusion. Your body, my body, the way we look. It is the way of things here. A land of shifting shades and illusions."

"So the bones?" He had an idea. "Are they a kind of symbol for those souls who have faded to oblivion?"

"Symbol, hmm . . ." Parfyon chewed on that idea. "I like it. It seems to fit. If the world of the living is a world of objects and forms with underlying symbols, then . . ."

"Of course!" interrupted Antomír, excited. "Then this world is a world of symbols, with underlying objects and forms. That means . . ."

"Yes," said Parfyon, interrupting him. "In theory, if you retain the knowledge of the symbol, the form and the object remain whole, even in the Realm of the Dead."

Antomír understood. If he held onto his self and didn't fade, it meant that his body wouldn't dissipate and corrupt into earth. Gamayun and Parfyon were hoping to return to the Realm of the Living in their bodies.

"But if you do find the way out," said Antomír. "Won't you simply return your spirit into your broken body? Won't my wound still be there? Won't I just die again?"

"Why do you think she's been sitting here for so long?" asked Parfyon, bemused. "She's trying to find her prophetic voice again. Maybe it will tell her something useful."

"How long has she been here?"

"You're still asking questions about time," said Parfyon with a sigh. "You've a long way to go, little boy."

GAMAYUN REMAINED in her trance state for what seemed an eternity. Her return, sudden and shocking, was announced by a sharp intake of breath and a scream, as though she were being cut open while still alive.

It shocked Antomír back into awareness of himself. He looked down at his hands again. They were different now, thinner somehow. With a sinking feeling, he realized that he was fading into nothingness faster than he thought.

"Parfyon?" said Gamayun, looking around wildly. She had a filmy white covering on her eyes. She didn't see them. "Are you there?"

"I am. And so's your pet."

Antomír seethed, but said nothing.

"Antomír, you are here? Good."

She turned back to staring into the endless fields of stones and bones.

"She does that sometimes," said Parfyon, shaking his head. "It doesn't mean anything. She's just lonely, I guess."

"Does she do that sometimes too?" asked Antomír, pointing.

The bones were scuttling across the sandy, rocky ground like rodents coming out of their holes. Slowly at first, then faster and faster, the yellow shards shook into feverish action.

"What in the name of all that is . . ."

Antomír understood what she was doing. He didn't know whether to be thrilled or terrified.

"She's summoning her own army. An army of forgotten ones."

"What?" Parfyon turned on him. "What do you mean?"

Gamayun's eyes snapped open. They were bright now,

deeply seeing. She smiled at Antomír, and there was even something warm there. Something of shared remembrance. At that moment, he found it hard to be angry with her.

"You were right, Antomír. No symbol is ever fully forgotten, even by those who willingly obliterate them. So many of the dead simply forgot. They needed to be reminded."

"What did you do, you crazy monster?" asked Parfyon, now genuinely afraid.

"I remembered. All the visions of all the lives I have ever seen. And I reminded them all of what they had. What they lost. The symbols of their existence. Their inner, true selves. They remembered, and look, their bodies follow suit."

The bones knit together in front of Antomír, forming skeletal bodies on tottering, unstable legs. Then muscles coalesced from the air, thickening the limbs. Last of all came skin—black, brown, and white, a host of people from countless places and ages past.

Their eyes came alight with surprise and shock. They all turned to Gamayun, their expressions pleading, their hands reaching out, pawing like dogs begging for a scrap of food.

"I am Gamayun. Your mother. And these are my lords. They will lead you back to your homes and your families. To the lands of sunlight and water and dancing."

Comprehension and memory began to dawn on the forgotten ones. Antomír couldn't help it. He laughed with the joy of it. He had never seen anything like it before.

"What an army," said Parfyon. "I think we might actually win this thing."

✻ 15 ✻

The tree swallowed them, the world turned upside down, then it flipped inside out again. Khaidu's spinning head couldn't distinguish between up and down for several minutes. During that time, dark-barked trees with trailing lianas and drooping, waterlogged leaves danced and did pirouettes with a sky that was grey-brown, with neither stars nor sun visible. When everything righted itself, Khaidu saw that she and Aglaia lay on a sward of prickly grass that was closer to yellow than green (if anything that drab could actually be called yellow). Those dark, thick trees were all around them, and next to them ran a brook with water so brown and still and fetid that it might as well have been mud. It was a depressing place. Khaidu sniffed her disapproval, completely sure there would be an accompanying smell of deadness and decay. There was nothing at all. A curious absence of smell. Had something happened to her nose?

She smelled her armpit and was immediately assured that her nose worked fine. But there was something very wrong with Aglaia, she now saw. She was dragging her haunches next to Khaidu, trying pitifully to get up on all fours, and failing. She whined, even barked like a dog half her size.

Khaidu, who had hoped that the transition from one Realm to another might jog Aglaia's human side free, dragged herself nearer Aglaia and caressed her between the eyes in the place that she loved so much. It felt like a foolish gesture, but it was the only thing she could think of doing.

Aglaia shuddered at her touch so sharply that Khaidu recoiled—and then was distracted by another strange sight.

Though Khaidu was still dressed in the clothing that the Hag had given her, several other things were very different. For one, she was wearing her brother Etchigu's best boots—the ones with a thick, solid heel and a touch of silver thread on the toe. She loved those boots. But she hadn't seen Etchigu in what seemed like years. The thought came unbidden—perhaps Etchigu was dead, and her wearing his boots was a witness to that fact?

The second thing was that she had two long, sheathed knives on each hip. And she realized that she knew very well how to use them. That was very strange.

But it was nothing compared to the sight of the wide pantaloons the Hag had given her, lying flat against her legs. Something was very odd about the shape of her legs. They looked rounded with muscle. They looked . . .

"It's just like when Sabíana used to take me to that dream place!" she exclaimed aloud.

There had only been one time and place in her life—outside her childhood—when she had actually walked around on her own two feet. When she had captured her very own Steppe eagle—who had ended up being an enchanted Sabíana, the Darina of Vasyllia—she would appear to Khaidu in human form in her dreams. But they were dreams that were more real than many of Khaidu's waking days. In that dream place, Khaidu had been able to walk and talk freely, as she had not been able to since her childhood.

Since then, the Hag had returned her gift of speech. Had the Hag also given her the gift of her two legs as well?

Or was this part of the Realm of the Dead like Sabíana's dream weaving? Was it just another illusion?

Behind her, Aglaia's yelp had turned into a gurgle and a wheeze. Khaidu pushed up with her arms, ready to propel herself in that half-dragging movement she had long mastered, except her feet caught the ground and her legs pushed her up as though they knew what they were doing. She was standing. The frantic beat of her heart and the tingling all down her shoulders and arms were almost enough to distract her from the horror that lay at her feet.

Aglaia was lying on her side. Her black fur had turned patchy grey, and some of it had been shed onto the grass where she lay. She was fading away right before Khaidu's eyes. And Khaidu, though she was suddenly capable in knife fighting and could run and leap with the best of them, could do nothing but stare at the wolf-woman who had been her salvation many times over.

It happened so fast that Khaidu couldn't quite believe it. One moment, there was an emaciated form of a too-large wolf lying on its side, its breath coming in ragged bursts. The next moment, there was an old wolf skeleton lying under a tree.

"No," Khaidu said aloud. "No, it's a dream. It's an illusion. It's not true. You can't . . . you can't leave me."

She crouched over the bones. Something dripped on them. They were tears. They fell from her eyes.

"Aglaia," she whispered, not trusting to speak aloud without sobbing. "Don't go. I haven't saved you yet."

She sat down on the grass. All the strength that she had reveled in a moment ago faded into numbness. She sat there, her tears dripping onto the grass. She closed her eyes, wrapped her face in her arms, and hid behind her knees. She cut the cord of tightly bound control in her heart, and out came a howl that any wolf would have been proud of.

SHE SAT THERE for a long time. She may have even slept a bit, if sleep were possible in the Realm of the Dead. Finally, an ache in her shoulders and hips became a jab, then a cramp, and she unfurled herself, creaking like an old woman.

She froze in place.

There were little bluebells growing all around her, each tiny flower growing in the exact place where she had dropped a tear for Aglaia.

She sighed, and felt strength flow back into her. The flowers were a sign, she realized. She should have known. This was the Realm of the Dead. It had its own rules. Aglaia might be dead, but she might not. Khaidu had no way of knowing. But whether she were truly dead or not, Khaidu would not rest until she paid Aglaia her final service. She would find her grandson Antomír, and she would return him to the Realm of the Living, even if she had to give her own life to do it. It was the least she could do. Aglaia had already done the same for her.

She felt the fresher for her cry. As she got up, the three bones the Hag gave her jingled in her pocket. She pulled them out. They seemed somehow more substantial here, almost as though they were eggs about to burst, straining to let out the overgrown hatchling come out. She liked that thought—it was right and it calmed her. The egg was a symbol of life and death, after all. She understood symbols. They were way-markers in a dark land.

She put the bones back into her pocket and realized that her left hand was grasping a firm walking stick. Had she just conjured it from thin air? Or were her thoughts and desires transparent in this place? She would need to be more careful.

Turning around in all directions—they all looked equally, hopelessly alike—she closed her eyes and let her heart dictate the right direction. She took three steps, stopped, breathed, and opened her eyes. She didn't know what to expect, but something told her that it would not be what she expected.

She was right.

There was a towering oak growing on both sides of the narrow river, which flowed beneath it. Its trunk was wrapped in a massive black chain. Along that chain, a smiling cat the size of a pony walked back and forth, apparently able to balance on that precarious and ridiculous bridge of chain links. It purred and stared at Khaidu with massive yellow eyes. Just above the cat, a naked woman with long green hair that covered most of her body straddled a branch and brushed her hair with a toothed comb that looked like the jaw of a carnivorous animal. In the shadow of the oak, something moved. It looked like a man might look if he had decided to dress like a tree. And if he had bark instead of skin. And a chestnut instead of a nose. No, Khaidu decided, there was nothing manlike about him except that he walked on two legs. Which were actually tree trunks.

Well, there was no going back now. Khaidu was officially out of the Realm of the real.

She giggled from excitement at the thought.

The cat stopped, hearing that giggle.

It looked up at the naked woman and started to talk.

"Rusalka, is she one of yours? I mean, who else would giggle at the first sight of the Oak of Gates?"

So *that* was a mermaid, a Rusalka—Khaidu recognized the old Vasylli name from stories Aglaia had told the Gumiren children during their long trek to the monastery of Raven's Bane.

Then that tree-man must be . . .

He walked out into the clearing and immediately shrank to the size of a tree stump. The cat laughed so hard it started to cry tears that were comically large.

"You'll never learn, Lesnik, will you?"

"Nope." Squeaked the suddenly tiny tree-man.

Rusalka was pouting on her branch, apparently because the

cat had associated Khaidu with her. But everyone had forgotten about the mermaid, so she harrumphed loudly.

"She has nothing to do with me," said Rusalka. "Can't you smell Hag all over her?"

"You're right," squeaked Lesnik, who was slightly larger than a bear cub now. "Girl, are you with the Hag or against her?"

"How dramatic," drawled the cat. "With her or against her? Might as well ask her if she's related to her."

"I'm just doing my job," said Lesnik.

"You're not thinking it through," said the cat. "The Hag knows we're here. She knows we're keeping close watch on her after that business with the human warrior. What was his name?"

"Voran . . ." sighed the Rusalka, making doll eyes at no one in particular.

Khaidu thought that she glimpsed a bit of fang under her smiling lip. She shivered.

"That's right, Voran," said the cat, then yawned. "Poor idiot. I've heard that he's been up to all sorts of mischief. Have you heard anything of a warrior named Voran, girl?"

"My name is Khaidu of the horse clan of Mamai jani-Beg. Not 'girl.' And I have heard of him, yes. I have even seen him."

"Oh really?" Lesnik was now half as tall as the oak, leaning on the trunk and causing the whole tree to groan under the strain. The cat looked at him with growling alarm and shook its head. "And where would that be, little girl who must not be called girl?"

"In the Heart of the World."

Rusalka yelped and dropped the bone-comb. She looked down, very annoyed, then she stared at Khaidu with an increasingly ravenous expression. Khaidu tapped the handle of her knife to the rhythm of a nursery rhyme. Rusalka subsided.

"So it's true, the rumors," said the cat. "The Raven was foiled?"

"For now," Khaidu confirmed. "But the trees no longer bear fruit."

"That would explain the strain in the walls of the worlds," said Lesnik, as casually as someone discussing the best way to peel a potato.

"And then the Hag sends us some troublesome Gumira from a horse clan I can't pronounce?" said the cat. "The world must really be in dire straits."

"She didn't just send me. I asked to come."

All three of the creatures froze in place, their eyes wide with astonishment.

"Why?" asked Rusalka, her bafflement the first genuine emotion Khaidu had seen on her face.

"I'm going to save Antomír, king of Vasyllia, from the Realm of the Dead."

They all broke into laughter at the same time.

"I haven't heard that one since the Children of the Priest-King!" guffawed Lesnik.

Rusalka laughed so hard that she fell off her branch and splashed into the river. Her hair caught fire as soon as she hit the water. She ran out screaming into the forest. Lesnik rolled his eyes and groaned.

"It's your turn—don't complain," said the cat.

"Fine!" moaned Lesnik and walked back into the forest.

Khaidu didn't know whether to laugh or to cry, it was all so absurd.

"Will you help me?" Khaidu asked the cat, the only one of the strange trio still there.

"Don't ask a cat for anything, unless you're ready to feed it first," said a husky voice coming from the river to Khaidu's right.

"Oh, this is almost too much," chuckled the cat. "If I didn't know we lived in the world of symbols and stories, I would complain about cliché."

Khaidu had no idea what the cat meant. But she had no

time to puzzle it out, because there was crazy-looking old man rowing a boat toward them. He wore dark, flowing robes, a knit cap, a massive sword strapped to his back—how could he keep his back straight with such a burden?—and a kestrel sitting on his right shoulder. She had never seen anything so odd. But the light in his eyes reminded her of someone. The serious, but kind light was something that she had glimpsed in Voran's eyes.

"Yes," said the old man. "I trained Voran."

Khaidu's eyes shot open. Had she spoken her thought aloud?

"No, I can't read your thoughts, little Khaidu. The Hag and I are old friends. She sent me a little message. How's the poor old lady doing? Still running into mischief?"

"Always," Khaidu said, chuckling. She liked the old man's manner.

"Oh, I like the fire in your eyes, little one. No wonder you're a favorite. My name's Tarin."

"Khaidu," she said, pointing at herself.

"Of the horse clan of Mamlai jabini-Belibeg," finished the cat. "Or something like that. Silly unpronounceable Gumiren names. Ugh."

"Now, now, cat. Don't be cross. Just because you won't have your fun with the little Gumira."

"Tarin, you have no idea how boring it is walking back and forth on this chain. I don't care how many poets have written about it. I hate it."

"Well, you might grow to miss it, the way things are going now," he warned darkly. He had made it to a beachhead near Khaidu. "Come on it, Khaidu. I'm to take you the first part of the way."

"Where are we going?" she asked, then felt foolish for saying it.

"Are you one of those silly children who actually want to end up in a fairy tale?" asked the cat.

Khaidu, annoyed at constantly being called a child, shook her head once.

"Well, smarter than most, it turns out. Unfortunately, that's exactly where you are going. Right into the middle of a fairy tale. One of the nastiest, thorniest ones too. Have fun!"

❧ 16 ❧

The journey to Karila was largely uneventful. Still, it was not pleasant for Voran. Though his captors stopped short of full-on beatings, they let him know exactly what they thought of him. A push here, a jab there, once even a short stab of a bread knife into his arm, drawing blood—it was enough to keep Voran constantly off-balance. His sleep was compromised because of the subconscious expectation of pain, and by the fifth day of travel, he was nodding off on his horse. With his hands tied to the saddle horn in front of him, that was a dangerous proposition. Once he almost fell off, which might have resulted at least in dislocated shoulders, if not worse. But he snapped awake just in time, to the general snickering of the company.

Sagynduk avoided his presence entirely. He rode in front with the young messenger from Karila, whose name Voran learned was Arystan, and let it be known that Voran should be as close to the back with the pack animals and the food carts as possible. At first, Voran told himself he didn't mind. But the prolonged lack of any conversation at all, except for the occasional insult hurled at him with a piece of moldy meat, started to wear on him.

Doubt crept into him about his decision to cast his lot with the Raven, manifesting as a peculiar kind of emptiness, an apathy that sapped his joy at people and objects he used to recall with love. With it came a heaviness in the chest that was almost a physical pain, and occasional flashes of something he couldn't quite explain even to himself: a kind of brightness in the mind that made everything seem too vivid for a moment. But that brightness brought no clarity; instead, it was always followed with a pervasive sense of terror and a thumping of his heart that left his chest aching and his breath short.

It worried him. There was something about it that made him think of debilitating diseases and madmen that died with their hands tied to their sides, for fear that they would gouge their own eyes out.

The only thing that helped calm him during those moment was the beauty of the countryside. He was a Vasylli through and through, yes, but he had a special love for the grassy hills and the birch groves of Karila. They were traveling south, so the tundra line quickly gave way to rare groves that eventually became forests further south. The trees were just coming alive —the new leaves were still limp, shivering in the icy wind blowing south from Vasyllia. Every morning, they unfurled a little more. Every morning, the prevailing browns and reds of the landscape retreated a little more before the rising tide of bright green.

Voran remembered how bleak and dead was the landscape in Nebesta. He also seemed to remember that much of Karila had, in the last few years, also been falling prey to the pervasive rot that killed trees and grass alike. But none of that was present here. In fact, there was a newness about the growth, a freshness in the colors and green scents that intensified with each passing day, that suggested to Voran that perhaps something not quite natural was happening in Karila.

He wondered if that were the Raven's doing. But no, the Raven couldn't create. He could only destroy, mimic, and delude. Not for the first time, Voran's heart plucked with the question: Then why are you following him? But he shut down the question before it even finished in his thoughts. He had already answered it. Enough.

The evenings and nights were freezing, the mornings cool and pleasant, especially since there were only ragged clouds that painted the sky orange in the morning and bright red at night. It was beautiful and peaceful, though Voran could rarely force himself out of his own head to gaze at the land and allow his mind to be still long enough to appreciate it the way he always used to in Vasyllia in his younger days.

The sixth day after leaving camp, the towers of Karila came into view—their tips peeked over a hill that gently rose until it seemed to melt into the horizon. It was an odd visual effect, as though the towers were the pointy ears of a monster that waited at the edge of the world, to catch those who dropped off into the abyss surrounding it. The thought was morbid, and it left Voran with a bitter taste in his mouth. Was there something monstrous in old Karila as well as all the other cities?

Then the landscape opened up beyond the rise, and the closer they rose, the better Voran saw the wide, bowl-like plain that stretched in a semicircle for many miles until it ran into the far wilds of the Steppe. In the middle of that plain was a flattened hill that could have been built by men, its shape was so regular for a natural formation.

Voran knew from his childhood studies that it was actually a natural mesa with an unusually wide and long top shelf. Seeing it from this vantage point, slightly above the city itself, looking down on it from the top of the last hill, Voran realized how unlikely it was that such a mesa could ever become the foundation for a city. The walls of the mesa were very steep, so steep that no mounted man could hope to scale it. On foot, it was possible, but dangerous. To imagine hundreds of men actually carrying wood and stones up those slopes to build buildings and roads and walls—it strained credulity.

And yet, there it was, a fortress of pitched wood, roughly pentagonal in shape, with a pointed turret at each angle of the pentagon. Banners flapped on the tips of the turrets. Each of them was a different color, all bright—purple, blue, red, yellow, and green. He couldn't see the sigils on each of them, but he remembered them well enough from previous visits. They were simple designs, embroidered in silver and gold thread—horses in various beautiful poses meant to illustrate the supremacy of Karilan steeds over all others in the Three Lands.

The company of mounted warriors stopped on the lip of the final rise before the dip into the valley where the city stood. Their faces could hardly contain their joy at seeing Karila. Even the Nebesti among them seemed genuinely pleased. As Voran watched, the sun came out from behind a cloud, and the houses behind the walls sparkled. Voran squinted; he couldn't quite understand what would produce such an effect in the sunlight.

"We've warned them of your coming," said Arystan, the messenger from Karila. "They have decorated the entire city for joy at the return of the great traitor."

"You flatter me. I am honored," Voran said, not even trying to hide his contempt for the man.

Voran had noticed on their first day out that Arystan did not wear a sword. A courtier, a professional boot-licker. With disgust, Voran remembered Yadovír. This one was cut from the same cloth—he was sure of it.

"Those sparkling, trailing things, what are they?" asked Voran.

"Lanterns," said the young man. "You should see the city at night. It is a glorious sight."

Voran could imagine. He had always had a soft spot in his heart for Karila, even if he had only visited a few times. Unlike most Vasylli, he never thought badly of the native culture of the Karila, which preserved some vestiges of an ancient history when they were a Steppe-traveling group of nomads. He never felt it was primitive or inferior to Vasyllia. Their culture, their self-worth, always seemed to come from a deep place of heart-love for the past. Something the Vasylli had abandoned, to their own peril.

A clattering noise distracted Voran. He turned his horse around with his knees—he was pleased to see how he seemed to have an understanding with his mount that the humans refused to share—and saw three of the youngest outlaws pull cages out from the carts. Voran hadn't noticed them before. They were filled with brilliant red-throated songbirds with a greenish tinge to their wings. They chittered excitedly, flying from perch to perch inside their cages. The young men opened the cages and lifted them high above their heads. The birds all poured out, like ale from a bottle. Their songs turned into an exuberant chorus as they passed over the heads of the warriors and flew in a sparkling cloud of feathers toward the city.

"They're homing?" asked Voran, intrigued.

"Yes," said Sagynduk, turning to Voran for the first time during that entire journey. "It's an old tradition that had been abandoned in the years of oppression." Voran knew he meant the years of Vasylli ascendancy over the monarchia of the Three Lands. He tried to keep his face calm at the insult. "One of many things we are bringing back, to the joy of our people."

Voran wanted to say how much he loved old Karilan traditions, but he stopped himself. He needed to maintain his distance from Sagynduk. It was part of the way that his plan was going to unfold. If nothing went horribly wrong, of course.

Instead, he stared at Sagynduk and found a different subject to talk about. "Traditions, yes. Is one of the ones you're bringing back the Five Punishments?"

It was a calculated risk, Voran knew. The Five Punishments were the ancient Karilan method of execution, reserved for the most vile criminals. It involved tattooing the prisoner's face with sharp sticks and poisoned ink, cutting off his nose, amputating one hand and one foot, castration, then death. It took five days, with each of the punishments taking place in the morning of each day. All five days, the prisoner remained in the city square on a public stage of execution.

The risk of mentioning the old execution was worth it, though. The Five Punishments were extremely regimented and ritualistic. To prepare the execution stage and the instruments of torture—which had to be newly forged and blessed by the ruler himself—was a process that could take days. And the execution always had to begin on one of the holy days of the old calendar, and there were not many of them in the year. It might be just enough time to bring his plan into fruition.

Sagynduk's face darkened. He was angry. "The Five Punishments? Who knows? I have heard that the Shuudan likes public displays of violence. But these days to believe any rumors is no better than madness."

Shuudan. Voran knew that there had been instability in Karila lately, but he hadn't realized that a woman ruler had taken power. That, more than anything, was telling. The old traditions of Karila always gave preferences to Shuudanai, women khans, as rulers. The Ruling Council of the Seven, who had governed Karila throughout its history as the Third City of the Three, was an innovation. A Vasylli adulteration.

But that was not as interesting as what seemed to be Sagynduk's guarded suspicion of the Shuudan. Voran thought that information could become useful. He knew that Sagynduk, for all his patriotism, was a man of the old order. He had to be— he had given more than two normal lifespans to the service of envoy, a position only possible within the monarchia. And he was a religious man, Voran knew. A true follower of Adonais. Voran had heard that many Karilans had returned to old tribal gods for worship. Sagynduk could not possibly endorse that. He wondered if the Shuudan did.

"The Shuudan," said Voran. "Is she young?"

Sagynduk didn't answer. Arystan was looking at him with a

half-smile, as if waiting for the old man to say something compromising. He didn't.

"The glorious Shuudan," said Arystan, "is ageless, a mother and a wife and a sister to all her people."

Voran snickered. One of the warriors behind him cuffed him with a mailed fist. Voran's head spun. He tasted blood. But he drew himself up and smiled again. Judging by the disgusted expression on the young courtier's face, there was blood on his teeth.

"I look forward to meeting her," he said.

The young courtier guffawed. "Then you are an even greater fool than I thought."

He turned his horse and rode down the hill, as though following the birds. The rest of the horses sprang into action behind him.

VORAN HAD NEVER BEFORE RIDDEN into Karila. He had only walked there, leaving his horse tied in a special stable for travelers near a gatehouse at the foot of the mesa. And so he had never seen, or even known about, the ancient riding path that circled the mesa three times, ascending gradually. There was something about the slow rise that allowed the senses to focus on the subtle changes from below Karila to Karila itself. Voran felt that it was almost like a passage from one Realm to another.

Below the mesa, as the company approached the riding path, Voran craned his neck to try to see the towering walls of the mesa. They loomed over him, nearly as impressive as some of Vasyllia's mountains. Unlike Vasyllia, however, there was a nearly complete absence of wind in this part of the dale. For Voran, it was disorienting. His body and mind associated mountain slopes with driving winds and extreme weather. Here, the air was warm, and the wind didn't even caress his hair—it simply wasn't there. And so, the distant sound of celebration coming from Karila itself was faintly audible, like the memory of a dream.

Voran had had many experiences of higher Powers in his life. The experience was often accompanied by a kind of dissociation between his body and mind, as though he were simultaneously inside and outside of himself. Now, for the first time in his life, he felt the same sensation, but it came from a phenomenon that was clearly not supernatural. The thrill he felt was like a young man's first kiss. His whole person—body and soul—stood in awe and yet rejoiced. That was the closest he could come to explaining it to himself.

Perhaps something unusual was going on in Karila. Something not quite expected.

For the first time since the Raven had left him at the Fang, Voran thought that another force, not the Raven, was guiding both him and the Raven to some unknown purpose. He rebelled against that thought. No more hidden deities acting through him without his knowledge. He would do what he should have done a long time ago. He would seize the rusted blade and wield events himself.

As they ascended, birdsong rose in waves, growing louder the closer they came to the city. At regular intervals, the road was bordered by ancient apple trees. They were just coming into their flower, but that didn't stop the hundreds of songbirds from covering what seemed to Voran every inch of every free branch of every tree. He had never seen so many birds—ruby-throated grosbeaks and indigo buntings and even orange finches the size of large bumblebees. Each had its own songs, but together they sounded more like a symphony than a cacophony.

Voran couldn't understand it. There was something of old Vasyllia here—the same kind of organic harmony between animal and human, between plant and beast, that should no longer exist, not in a world that was coming apart at the seams.

Once again, that ineffable feeling of distant guidance floated over him, gently. It was not of the Raven. There was none of that proud demon's brazenness to it. It was like a lilac-scented breeze compared to the putrid smell of soured ale. Though Voran was clearly outside that reality, he felt that it regarded him with curiosity and openness.

Then he had a terrifying thought. What if what he felt was the presence of the Palymi that protected Rogned, or that seemed to protect him until it abandoned him to the treachery of Yarpolk Dolgoruk? What would that Palymi think of Voran, now that he had abandoned his calling to heal and to serve? Would the Palymi sense that Voran had made a pact with the great enemy himself?

So it was a confused and disoriented Voran that saw the hundreds of Karilans waiting at the gates, holding aloft those lanterns that the courtier had mentioned before. They were all unlit, and the people were standing still, waiting for something. The sense of urgent expectation was heavy on the air. Voran noticed that he was sweating profusely, his breath coming shallow, as though it had been he who had climbed the slope of the mesa, not his horse.

He had assumed that as soon as he came to Karila, he would know what to do. That he would have a clear idea of how to take control of the situation to wield it in his favor. But nothing here was familiar. There was nothing of the old Karila here. This was a new place, a vibrant place that had somehow avoided the ravages both of the internecine war and the inner corruption that came with it. How had he missed this?

Something slithered in his mind. The Raven's presence. It seemed as disturbed as he was. He had not expected Karila to be like this either.

"What have I gotten myself into?" Voran whispered aloud.

The Raven didn't answer. Sagynduk, however, turned his face back to Voran suddenly, as though he had felt or heard something. His eyes, boring into Voran's face with his usual ferocity, lingered there. Voran held his gaze, and something in Sagynduk's face changed. His eyes softened, becoming sad and confused. For a moment, Voran was sure he would ride back to speak to him. But Sagynduk seemed to think better of it and turned back toward the waiting crowd.

Arystan and Sagynduk stopped. The rest of the company stopped with them. All of the Karilans at the gates raised their lanterns, nearly at the same moment. A sense of intense presence overwhelmed Voran. All the lanterns lit up at the same moment, the fires flaring brightly. Voran closed his eyes, and the imprint of hundreds of pinpricks of red remained on his inner eyelids. He was shaking with fear now.

Who is the Power ruling here?

All the people, as soon as the lanterns were lit, started to cheer. Arystan turned around to face the returned outlaws. He had tears in his eyes. For the first time since he met him, Voran thought he might have completely misjudged the young man. There was not a trace of that cruelty that he imagined he saw before. There was something deep and moving in his face. Something like compunction.

Voran looked around him. All the former outlaws, the returned army of Rogned, were weeping, sobbing aloud. The cheering of the Karilans rose even louder. Now Sagynduk turned his horse to face the men he had ruled out in the wilds. His smile was like a sunrise; Voran hardly recognized him. All around, outpouring joy was circulating among all the people, and it seemed only to multiply. Everyone was moved; everyone was in ecstasy.

Everyone but Voran.

"My friends!" called Sagynduk. "Welcome home!"

Voran felt himself being borne on the wave of joy into Karila. He covered his head in his hood and retreated into it. No joy came. No tears came. Nothing but bitterness ached in his chest.

The Raven was nowhere to be seen. Voran was alone.

As they rode into the city, a flash of gold light caught Voran's eye. It was a stela, directly ahead in a small square surrounded by squat buildings of clay with red tile roofs. On top of the stela was a dummy wearing a suit of armor that shone as though it were the source of its own light. Leaning on the golden breastplate, a thin, long sword in the Vasylli style shone even more brightly than the armor.

Voran's heart stopped for a moment, plunged, then raced back furiously into the center of his chest. That was the Blade of Covenant. It was whole again, not a spot of rust on it.

Everything that he had planned had hinged on his ability to restore the Blade of Covenant, with the Raven's help. But by some miracle or magic, it was no longer rusted.

Voran despaired.

End of Part II

PART III

Ordeal

INTERLUDE

Behold, in the days of blood, kings of this earth will fall like wheat at the hand of the thresher. The healer has lost his healing touch. The swan has lost her flight wings. The bear has fallen asleep for all days.

What wonder, then, that one of the sheaves of wheat will come to rule again, in the last of the days of blood!

A Prophecy of Llun

The Sayings, Book XXIII 3:4-5

~

Fifteen years ago . . .

Rogned dreamed often about his ordeal with the serpent of the waters. He ached to speak of it to someone . . . anyone . . . to make some sense of what he thought must have been a kind of prescient vision or prophecy. More than anything, he wanted to ask Voran's opinion of it. Voran had always been like an older brother to him, especially after Karakul's death. But he couldn't bring himself to speak with Voran.

With every passing day, Voran's manner became more and more distant. Rogned sometimes caught Voran staring at him with wide eyes filled with either fear or veneration—or both.

All were distasteful to Rogned. Yet, it was his fault that all this was happening—his own silly vanity to think that the talent of an artisan could summon a Power from the Heights.

Nevertheless, it had worked. And the consequences were not at all what he had expected. Loneliness he could deal with —he was an artisan, after all, and preferred the company of his own thoughts. But the vision of the armor and the sword— that was something that ached inside him. He couldn't help thinking he was failing at some vital task. Worse still was the nagging dread that if he failed at that task—whatever it was— it would be more than just himself who would pay the price. Finally, his latest brush with suicide had done something to him. He could no longer contemplate the possibility of trying it again, even if the Palymi himself appeared to him and told him to do it.

It was all too painful, and at times too wonderful. The vision of the Garden of the Palymi still came to him at odd moments, inundating him with smells of tuberose and soft caresses of otherworldly winds, almost like waves of scented water.

Soon after his ordeal with the serpent of the waters, Rogned led his ragtag host into their first battle.

They faced a militia of former officers of Vasyllia and Nebesta who had gathered some of the most desperate and violent men from both lands to pillage and loot. These were the most dangerous kinds of brigands. They no longer cared what sort of death awaited them, or what sort of hell after death. All they wanted was to enjoy as much as they could from these fading days, no matter who suffered for their pleasure.

In spite of being informally gathered into more of a band than an army, this militia was ferocious and fairly well organized.

Before the battle, Voran privately said, "Rogned, you need to be ready. Our losses, even in victory, may be colossal."

The opposite ended up being true. Rogned's followers—no matter what city their first allegiance was to—pounded the militia like a proverbial hammer of the gods. Rogned couldn't believe the ferocity of his warriors, their almost manic drive to annihilate the enemy. It terrified him. But the adoration in their eyes when they saw him pass by—that was far worse. Such adoration he had seen rarely in other men's faces. When he had, it was on days of worship, directed at an actual deity. Now *he* was the object of adoration.

It made Rogned feel heavy, useless, like a statue of a man instead of the flesh and blood original.

With that heaviness still weighing on him, he joined Voran and Yarpolk—the two had grudgingly agreed to work together for now—at the truce table with what was left of the militia's leadership. The only living warrior of any rank was a Nebesti named Slabomír. He was a giant of a man, almost seven feet tall, with rope-cord muscles that seemed impossibly large, even on his massive frame. He was like a caricature of a demigod in a children's storybook from Vasyllia.

The militia had been occupying the border town of Bskavi in the highlands between Nebesta and Karila. They had come out into the field in front of the town to battle, instead of entrenching in Bskavi as Voran had expected them to do. Rogned had not understood why they came out to fight him, when they had such a clear advantage behind walls.

"Do you expect any reason from brigands?" suggested Voran. "They were probably just itching for a fight."

Yarpolk disagreed. He often disagreed with Voran, Rogned had noticed, and not always for good reasons.

"Your reputation precedes you, Rogned," Yarpolk said. "They were afraid you'd sculpt the stones of the town into monsters and giants that would attack them in their beds."

Voran scoffed, but Rogned thought that Yarpolk might be right.

The expression on Slabomír's face seemed to confirm

Yarpolk's hypothesis. He bowed low before Rogned, then even tried to fall on his knees, before realizing that if he were to do that, the inordinate size of his upper body might simply tip him over into the mud.

Yarpolk's rough laugh seemed to disabuse Slabomír of any further notions of respect. He squared his shoulders and looked ready to deal.

"My men's lives," he said simply, his voice like a bellows, "and you can have the city."

"I believe we already have the city," said Yarpolk. Voran looked like he wanted to slap him for speaking first.

"You have what's left of it, sure."

"What about the people of Bskavi?" asked Voran. "Have you left any alive?"

The giant man shrugged. "Some runts left over, sure. All the pretty ones used up, not worth much, even to you lot."

Rogned's heart dropped at that. He felt sick to his stomach. Was this the substance of ruling over others? Dealing in souls like cattle?

"Food stores? Gold?" pursued Yarpolk. It was a commonly spread rumor that the former regents of Nebesta kept a secret stash of gold somewhere in Bskavi. That was most likely the reason the militia had chosen to take the town in the first place.

Slabomír scoffed. "That's an old story. No truth to the rumors. Not that we could find."

"Well then," Yarpolk turned a little, tugging at his curly chin-beard. It was a flaming red color that still fascinated the artisan in Rogned. Such coloring was very rare in the Three Lands.

Then Rogned realized Yarpolk and Voran were waiting for *him* to make a decision.

Oh, by the Heights . . .

"You may keep your men and only such small weapons as are needed for hunting," he said, trying to sound sufficiently authoritative. He had no idea if he did or not. "Knives and a few bows. And go."

He felt silly speaking these words, even though no one else seemed to think them anything less than an official proclamation. They all jumped to do his bidding without so much as taking another breath.

That evening, the militia filed out of the city in ordered ranks. Rogned, Voran, and Yarpolk were wearing their finest and cleanest kaftans on top of their best mail. Both Voran and Yarpolk had stitched a new coat of arms onto their right shoulders—a rendering of a castle growing out of clouds. Rogned couldn't help smiling. It seemed that everyone had finally agreed on a symbol for their little army. He was a little surprised that Voran's castle had won out over Yarpolk's sun with two crossed spears.

Their horses had been freshly shod, and all three were dancing in place, as though trying out the comfortable feel of the new shoes. As each company of the militia passed Rogned, the militiamen piled their swords into a mound that grew wider and taller as the evening went on.

It was full night by the time the last of the archers had bowed, received leave to keep one bow out of every three, and moved on toward the wilds between Bskavi and the final ridge of mountains between the Three Lands and the Great Wild.

It had gone very smoothly. *Too smoothly*, thought Rogned.

He was soon proved right.

As the drumbeats of Rogned's army sounded the victorious advance into the town, the screaming of women drowned them out. Then came the smoke, edged with orange.

"What's going on?" asked Rogned, knowing and yet fearing the answer.

"Saboteurs," growled Yarpolk. "I *thought* they had given up too easily."

Scouts ran up to Rogned, some of them singed, some simply terrified of the fire.

They confirmed Yarpolk's guess. As the last of the militiamen were leaving, they had tied all the remaining people of Bskavi in the central temple of the town and lit the building on fire.

"Well come on, let's go!" said Voran. "We have to stop the fire."

"Are you mad?" Yarpolk almost laughed. "Look! It's already out of control. You'll just lose men for no good reason. Be practical, Voran!"

"Be human, Yarpolk!" Voran demanded, his eyes round and half-mad with terror and frustrated fury.

Voran looked at Rogned with a frantic expression of pain. Rogned nodded, and Voran rode into the city, calling the men to his aid as he went. Reluctantly, Yarpolk followed, shaking his head and mumbling into his chin-beard.

But the screams were already fading in Rogned's mind. He knew what he wanted. For a brief flash of a moment that left him gasping, Rogned saw the flurry of the Palymi's wings in the clouds. He and the Palymi were united once again in purpose and in craft.

In his mind's eye, Rogned focused on Slabomír, the giant leader of the militia. With his thoughts, he begged the Palymi, whose presence was an invisible wall of tension at his back, propping him up: "Please. For justice." In his mind's ear, he heard assent. Then, as though he stood directly in front of them, Rogned saw the retreating militiamen, led by the giant Slabomír. He was smiling as they rode away. A bag of gold lay half-concealed in a pouch at his side. The fury boiled inside Rogned—or was it inside the Palymi? He hurled his fury at the militia.

The earth at the feet of the entire retreating militia began to writhe. In places, it cracked open like a monster's mouth, ringed with teeth of boulders and tree roots. From the opening abysses, churning forms of dirt and stone and sand grew and morphed into indeterminate shapes on four stubby legs. The legs firmed into black hardness; curved talons grew at the tips of the coalescing toes. The heads lengthened and sprouted scales. Crests of hardened loam rose on the backs of the creatures Rogned formed from the earth itself. Hundreds of giant reptilian monsters now surrounded the militia.

The militiamen all stopped, bristling with weapons, but unsure what to do. Slabomír, mounted on his war-charger, turned back to look at Rogned.

Rogned saw the shapes of each creature he had conjured down to the finest detail of ridged scale and forked tongue. He smelled the freshness of upturned earth in spring—a healthy, invigorating smell. It filled his nostrils like the smell of turpentine and egg tempera on days that he painted. His fingers tingled with warmth; the creatures were soft, like molding clay in his hands. He closed his eyes. Yes—this was right. His skin tingling with ecstasy, he raised his hands over his head.

The monsters, each the length of two men together, fell upon the militiamen.

Now it was Slabomír's men who screamed, not the women and children of Bskavi.

Rogned threw his hands down, and all the monsters and militiamen were crushed as though a mountain had fallen on them. He folded his hands together, interlacing the fingers. His heart was thumping against his chest, and his arms were shaking from the strain. He pressed his palms together as tightly as he could. His jaw ached from the teeth grinding against each other, simulating the grinding jaws of the monsters as they chomped down on the militiamen.

The writhing forms of monsters and men sank into the earth as though it were a bog.

Silence fell.

Rogned breathed deeply and nodded. That would send a message. He turned to see Voran coming back from the city, staring at him with mixed admiration and fear. Rogned smiled at him. Voran smiled weakly, but his eyes didn't respond to the quirk of his mouth.

~

Miraculously, only a few of the people of Bskavi were harmed by the fire. Most were only frightened. When they learned who their savior was, they flocked to Rogned with adoration. The women clutched at him as he rode; the children threw leaves and coins at him; the men stood in rows as he passed, raising their swords and their spears in salute.

For the first time, Rogned understood the lure of power.

He couldn't sleep that night. He kept seeing the brigands writhing in the jaws of the earth monsters. He studied their surprised faces and their final curses. But he found that he didn't regret his decision.

Finally, when the sun began to hint at rising, he fell asleep.

His Palymi stood at the gate of another, even higher terrace. The wall and the gate were entirely of lapis lazuli, which seemed half-liquid, shimmering in the soft light of the red-orange sun of that place. Beyond the gate was a grove of birch trees with bluebells at their feet. Firebirds sang in the branches of the trees. But most beautiful of all were the Sirin. There were at least twenty of them, some perched on the trees with the firebirds, some soaring above the towers in the distance—the towers of the last garden, still four terraces and gates away.

Does that mean that four deaths still remain?

The birds and the Sirin sang, each in their own language and manner. The song was like honey and daggers in his heart—both at the same time.

Rogned looked at the face of the Palymi, who still had not

removed his flaming sword from across the entrance, though the doors were thrown open.

"I'm not yet worthy—is that it?" asked Rogned. It sounded more pompous than he meant it to. It embarrassed him.

The Palymi smiled, evidently more at the embarrassment than the words.

"No human is worthy. But you are certainly doing everything you can to be the first. Tell me: Do you regret taking those lives?"

Rogned realized he was weeping. His heart felt torn in a thousand pieces.

"Yes," he said, sobbing loudly. "I regret it. I am sorry for it. But I am more sorry that I could not live in a different time, when such decisions need not be made. I wish I did not live in a time when justice for the innocent demanded the death of the perpetrators, lest they murder and pillage again."

"Who made you their jury and executioner?" pursued the Palymi, his voice thundering and pressing him down physically into the mossy ground. Rogned held firm.

"They did, when they broke their bond. As the Heights are my witness, I acted in justice."

The Palymi seemed satisfied by that. He moved the sword.

"You cannot enter this garden unscathed, young Rogned. You are still tied to the Realm of Earth. If you pass, your body on earth will die. Only your spirit can go on."

"But I must face the Heights whole, body and spirit! How else will I represent this Realm, if not in my whole self?"

"Then you must wait. Be patient. Your time is near."

He woke up.

The sun shone directly on his face through his tent flap, which quivered with a soft breeze.

Rogned thought he understood. There was one more thing he had to do.

~

"What do you mean, you're sending me away?" Voran complained, his face white with shock.

Rogned sat outside his tent on a soldier's rough stool. Voran stood in front of him, still dressed in yesterday's finest. He had not slept either, it seemed.

"Not away, Voran. I expect you back soon."

"But we are only just beginning. Where could I possibly be of more use to you than here? This is the moment to strike, when the iron is hot!"

"I need you to go to Ghavan Isle."

Voran's face fell. "But I was hoping you'd go there yourself. I wanted to present you to Dar Mirnían, so that we could offer him our swords together."

"I know, Voran."

Rogned was no longer sure that submission to the monarchia of Vasyllia was the correct choice. He tried to tell himself it was not the pleasure he felt, growing with every moment, at being adored by others. No, it was the persistent problem of Mirnían, the Dar of Vasyllia. Was it a good idea to court the favor of a king who hid from the internecine war on an island?

"You haven't changed your mind, have you?" asked Voran.

Rogned sensed that Voran asked the question vaguely on purpose. He was testing him, seeing how he would react. Voran had always been a good judge of people's hearts.

So Rogned breathed deeply and told the truth. Some of it, anyway.

"Voran, how do you think these warriors would react if the first thing we do after such a victory is go north to submit our arms at the feet of a man they don't even know? How many of these people are Vasylli? Hardly any."

"You *will* not abandon the vision, Rogned. You *must not*."

Voran put too much stock in the monarchia. But Rogned understood. It was the lifeline he needed to survive the rigors of war and the constant atrocities going on around them. Rogned was sure Voran would not have understood him, if

Rogned had chosen that moment to explain what his own endgame was.

"I do not abandon the ideal we share, Voran. But would it not be a far better thing if Dar Mirnían came out here to meet us, with his boats and his army? What hope that would give these ravaged lands! You must go to Ghavan Isle and speak of our victory."

He hoped his tone was not too saccharine. You never knew with Voran.

It seemed to work. Voran bowed. Rogned got up and stretched out his arms. Voran fell into his embrace. He was weeping.

Rogned's heart was like a stone in his chest. He knew he was embracing his friend for the last time.

❧ 17 ❧

Voran sat in a garden whose very existence was ridiculous. It seemed to be hanging from the clouds instead of being perched on the top of a walled turret in Kari-la's highest tower. Flowers of every conceivable shape and size —bluebells, lilies of the valley, irises, roses, black-eyed Susans, forget-me-nots—filled every nook and cranny between shrubs of hawthorn and chokecherry, small apple and pear trees, and larger maples with dark purple leaves and trailing yellow flowers like Vasyllian temple rings.

In the middle of this gorgeous absurdity was a one-room hut made of large grey stones. The roof was nothing more than thatch, but it was evidently well maintained. Inside was a straw pallet on the floor—nothing else. There was no door. It was a prison that no prisoner would ever want to leave.

Voran certainly did not. Here, he tried to convince himself, he could simply ignore the despair that kept rising inside him every time he thought about his predicament. So he sought out memories instead, the more painful, the better. Anything was preferable to the present.

He remembered Rogned's final goodbye, and for the first time, he thought he understood why Rogned had sent him away to Mirnían. He had phrased it so well, but it had all been a ruse. Voran now thought that Rogned had expected Yarpolk to take advantage of Voran's absence. Rogned probably knew that as far as Yarpolk was concerned, Rogned was a dangerous free agent, someone that Yarpolk could never control. That suggested to Voran that Rogned may have given himself up to be the sacrificial lamb. He had allowed his execution at the hands of Yarpolk to happen willingly.

The more Voran considered it, the more he thought it was a distinct possibility. He recognized behind it the perplexing and unbreakable law of sacrifice. He himself had seen it in action more than once, beginning the moment he had healed Mirnían near the tree that wept tears of Living Water. Mirnían had wanted to kill him, and Voran had submitted to the sacrifice. That submission, as the Harbinger later explained, was what gave Voran the power to heal Mirnían. And Voran became the only one in the Three Lands with the hands of a healer.

That memory made Voran wonder: Was Karila's apparent state of prosperity, at least in some small part, due to the sacrifice of Karila's son, Rogned? If so, then it might be that Rogned's tragic death had been worth it. Karila was an unexplainable paradise in the midst of war and pestilence. There had to be divine protection here. Was it that Palymi that Rogned had talked about once?

And if so, where did that leave Voran? He had willingly allied with the Raven, the king of illusions and traps. He had bonded himself with that demon willingly. And the creature had great hopes for him, he knew. The Raven wouldn't let Voran go without a fight.

Nor would he let him remain here too much longer, Voran suspected. He needed to do something. But all the certainty he had felt when he first found Sagynduk's band was gone.

And seeing the Shuudan, in all her glory, did little to calm him. In any other circumstance, Voran would have been astounded at her, at the vivid contradictions in her, which seemed to be an image of the contradictions in Karila itself. She was probably not much older than eighteen or twenty, but her bright green eyes were those of a much older woman. Still, they danced with sincere joy at the sight of Sagynduk's return, almost as though she had wished it for a long time.

Those eyes. Set in a soft, round face of dark brown complexion, they shone even more brightly than they would have in a Vasylli face. And they had looked at Voran for a long time. There had been no joy there. Quick, fiery anger—of that there was plenty. But curiosity, too.

Or so he had thought. Still, a week had passed, and no one had visited him, least of all the Shuudan.

This morning, as he sat on one of the many benches shaded by the fragrant purple leaves of the maple-like trees, was the eighth of his imprisonment.

He was just beginning to think about the symbolic significance of eights. All Three-Landers, no matter what their city, understood the number eight to be symbolic of the idyllic age to come after the final death of all creation, what used to be called the final coming of Adonais to earth. Well, he had come. And no blissful eternity had followed. Quite the opposite.

It was at that moment that Voran heard the gate to the walled garden creak open. There had been no sound of a lock. He realized with some amusement that he could have left at any point. The thought made him laugh bitterly. He had never before been more of a prisoner than now.

The Shuudan, her hair bound in a headscarf of pink silk that made both her skin and her eyes shine as though with their own light, came into the garden alone. Her long, trailing dress was also of pink silk, with embroidery of gold seeming to dance up and down her skirts as she walked through the sunlight toward his hut. It was only when she was in front of him that he recognized that the gold thread had been embroidered in the shapes of Sirin flying.

Voran sighed. He had always been so sure of Vasyllia's standing as Mother of Cities. The Sirin's presence, to him, had always suggested it. The words of the Palymi he knew as the Pilgrim-Harbinger seemed to confirm it. Karila had never been anything but the last sister, the runt of the litter. And yet, a Vasylli was the prisoner. A Karilan was the queen. Everything was wrong. But perhaps, for the first time, everything was right.

"You are comfortable?" she asked in slightly accented Vasylli. Her accent was even less than Karakul and Rogned's, and they had both known the Vasylli tongue since childhood.

Voran looked her in the eyes. She didn't look away, though her eyebrows gathered slightly in evident disapproval of his rudeness. He looked away. Nodded.

"That's too bad," she said, her fingers starting to play with the yellow blossoms. Was it Voran's imagination, or did the blossoms actually lean in toward her fingers?

"Why?" he asked. "Isn't that the point of this prison?"

"Quite the opposite," she said, chuckling. Her eyes lit up when she laughed, even more than when she scowled. It was mesmerizing.

But again, he looked away. It was like trying to hold fire. It burned very quickly.

"What will you do with me?" asked Voran.

She laughed again, a soft laugh at a comical memory. "You're really something, you know?" she said. Her manner was comfortable, informal—dangerous. "The Five Punishments? Really? When Sagynduk told me, I didn't know whether to laugh or cry. So I did both. One right after the other."

Voran wondered if the tears were for him or not. He immediately blushed, feeling embarrassed at the thought. Her presence threw his self-assurance off in ways he could hardly remember feeling. She was very young, and yet . . . not at all.

"Yes, the tears were for you, Voran. For what you've become."

There truly were tears on her eyelashes. The speed with which her moods changed was dizzying, and yet each of them was entirely right. Entirely sincere.

"I hardly know what to say."

"Good. Baby steps," she said. She sat on the bench next to him. "Sagynduk would not come with me, by the way. He really is very mad at you."

Voran felt even more ashamed. All of it—his bluster, his rudeness, his show of bravura—it was all intended to take control of a situation he was sure he could grab like the reins of an unruly horse. He had fully intended to make it up to Sagynduk later. Instead, he may have alienated his only friend in Karila.

"You let Sagynduk back," said Voran, carefully. "That means that I am a kind of payment, yes? So execution or at least some form of public punishment would only seem logical."

"Sagynduk is an old man, bowed low by grief. He only needed to come back. I would have taken them all in with open arms. I had even sent him envoys, telling him that. He, like you, refused to believe that I could be anything but a conniving witch, thirsting for his blood."

She said it with such evident relish at the absurdity of the thought that she got up and almost started dancing. She was in nearly constant movement around him, going from shrub to tree to flower, touching, smelling, whispering, enjoying.

Voran was utterly bewitched and lost. He had no idea how to relate to this woman. All his long-built skills at speaking to men in all walks of life were useless. He had never met anyone like her.

"That's not to say that you *won't* be executed, Voran." She said this with perfect calmness. "But you have not been tried. Yet."

Voran breathed deeply. They had come to the crux of the matter.

"What sort of court do you have in Karila? Is it anything like the Vasylli Council of the Reaches? I don't suppose you still have the Seven in situ?"

"In situ . . . what an interesting phrase."

"Old Vasylli, I think."

She sat down again and smirked at him. Leaning on her arms, she raised her eyebrows. It was clear what she was saying: *Stop trying to impress me as a man impresses a woman. You're out of your depth.*

He certainly was.

"No, the Seven set down their burdens when the blade rusted. When it was restored to us, they were the first to beg for the reinstatement of the Shuudanate."

Voran hoped she would go on, tell him about the restoration of the Blade of Covenant. She looked at him with a half-smile, chuckling softly, daring him to ask, playing with him like a cat with a captive mouse.

He didn't want to capitulate. Not yet. "So . . . who sits in judgment in the Shuudanate? Do you? Queen, mother, sister, daughter . . . judge? Executioner?"

A shadow flitted across her face as her smile was wiped away. He found himself wishing it would come back.

"No. It would have been better for you if I *was* your judge."

She got up again and stretched, almost like a cat, though she also seemed to grow in importance and dignity.

"I have heard rumors that you are no stranger to the Powers. Perhaps that will help you. But I do not know. Rathúdiel is not like the others."

Even the name pressed on him. He had never heard it, but he was sure it belonged to a Palymi, the highest of the Powers serving the Unknown Father in the Heights. Voran had had encounters with two Palymi. One—the Pilgrim, sometimes the Harbinger—was more or less pleasant. The second, a warrior of the Heights named Athíel, was more painful than anything he had experienced before or since. And he was an intimate of pain.

Athíel had purged Voran of the consequences of the first breaking of his Sirin's soul bond. But that silence between hearts had only lasted weeks. This time it was worse. He had not seen or heard from Lyna, his soul-bonded Sirin, in many years. Voran's whole body ached in the expectation of the pain that was sure to come if there was to be some sort of purification from the Palymi.

He was so consumed by memories of his past that it took him a moment to realize that the Shuudan had stopped moving or speaking. She had also taken off her head-covering, revealing waves of curly black hair. Voran felt vaguely indecent at seeing her uncovered like that. But that feeling passed. As with so much of what she did, there was a rightness to that action in that moment, as she looked away from Voran into some distant point.

Voran turned to see what she was looking at. The sun, which had been shining unimpeded up to that moment, hid behind a cloud. Or that was what Voran's mind registered the form to be at first. But it moved fast, spinning in on itself like a top or a wheel within wheels, while also seeming to remain immovable at the same time. What his mind perceived as a disconnect registered in his heart with warm familiarity, followed by fear. He knew what such contradictions to the senses always meant. Powers from the Heights.

The spinning form was no longer cloudlike. It was like a mountain with wings—six wings in constant motion. In the whorl of wings, Voran saw what looked like a brand of fire. His stomach dropped. More pain, he knew. He looked at the Shuudan for a moment, and he saw her assessing him. He couldn't give a name to her expression. There were too many different emotions there, though all of them were contained, not excessive, like the distillation of pure emotion. Like a statue, but a living and breathing one.

He couldn't look at her anymore. She was shining, though whether it was from her own inner light or because she reflected the Palymi, he didn't know. He didn't dare guess. He had always prided himself at being comfortable with the presence of the divine. He had been a fool. The Powers, he now knew, had merely tolerated him all his life. Here he was in the presence of a woman who had been transformed by contact with the Powers into something . . . he struggled to find the right words in his mind . . . It wasn't that she was no longer human. No, she was truly human, in a way that very few ever achieved. Perhaps she was the first and only one, at least in this blighted time.

Rathúdiel stood towering over them, his feet on opposite sides of the wall, straddling the garden. He was also like a living statue, his skin marble-like in color, though obviously not cold or solid in the way of stone. Voran didn't doubt that if he touched the skin, his hand would burn to ashes.

"This is the Healer?" he asked, his disdain pushing Voran physically down on his knees.

The Shuudan didn't answer. She merely adored, with eyes, with body, with upraised hands, with joy pouring out of her eyes.

"I am no longer the Healer," said Voran, barely able to get the words out through the sense of presence that made even the air feel solid, difficult to breathe into his puny lungs.

"We begin with truth," said Rathúdiel. Was that approval in that terrifying voice? "To begin otherwise would be . . . unwise."

The Shuudan smiled. Had Rathúdiel made a joke? Did the gods make jokes?

In a blast of clarity, Voran realized that he knew nothing about anything. How would he ever find his way again?

"And it seems we also begin with humility," said Rathúdiel,

his voice impossibly resonant and deep. "Not quite what my brothers suggested."

He wanted to protest, to say that he was known by the Palymi, that he was friend to the Harbinger himself. But all that was a lie. His entire life was a lie.

"In the spirit of good beginnings, Voran, son of Otchigen, I offer you first word," said Rathúdiel.

Voran understood and was even more pushed down by the presence. The Palymi was offering him the mercy of unburdening his heart. So this was to be the judgment. Voran had to condemn himself.

It was the hardest thing he had ever done in his life.

"I will speak," said Voran, though it came out like a croak. "It will take time."

"In some sense, we are outside time, Voran," said the Shuudan. "While the Palymi is with us, it is as though we are between time and eternity."

He nodded. He didn't understand with his mind, but her words had the intended effect—he felt lighter, able to speak more than two or three words at a breath.

"I have willingly allied with the Raven. At first, we were companions of chance. I tripped into one of his many snares. I was sure he was destroyed by the Harbinger in the Heart of the World. But some part of him persisted, continued to live. Perhaps inside me, I don't know. He offered me something no other Power has ever offered. He offered me a chance to face the Unknown Father as I believe Rogned did. I had to take that chance. I had nothing left. Everything I had ever believed, my entire life, everything that I fought for—it had all crumbled to dust in the Heart of the World.

"Not the Harbinger, not Athíel, none of the Powers we revered as good ever offered me an answer. I had been given a gift. A healing hand to do my part in restoring the order destroyed by the fall of Vasyllia. But how could I do that if I did not know why I should?

"And now I see that Karila seems to have achieved what Vasyllia lost—some measure of that beauty and order and harmony that we Vasylli always believed was our own calling. Were we not intended to be the hammer, the axe, the sustainers of the Covenant between mankind and the gods?

"But now it seems I have labored an entire life in vain. Must I simply be content with the death of Vasyllia? Did the Harbinger not tell me that Vasyllia is *everything?*"

He realized he was beginning to feel that old sense of betrayal that had started him on the path with the Raven, that had gotten him into this mess. He breathed deeply, tried again.

"I have failed—I know that. But I think I know now that the reason for my failure is not fate."

The Shuudan put a hand on his shoulder. It seemed to pulse warmth and comfort into his body. He felt tears rise.

"I allied with the destroyer of my city . . . thinking to save my city. I was wrong. I renounce him. I deny him. I cast him out."

Voran's heart twisted in itself with pain that was like being ripped apart by fire-edged thorns of steel. He opened his mouth to scream, but held it in. The Shuudan's hand was still on his shoulder, and though now her comfort was a trickle, it was still there. And so was his mind, whole, his own, distinct from the poison of the Raven.

"You won't get rid of me so easily," wheezed a pitiful voice next to Voran. A shriveled old man in dirty robes lay in fetal position on the ground. All the greenery, even the grass, shrank from touching him. He stank.

Rathúdiel did nothing. Voran expected him to strike the Raven down with that firebrand in his right hand. But he stood, impassive, waiting.

"You lied to me," Voran said to the Raven, lamely. The creature cackled.

"I lie by nature. But I told you nothing of untruth. Ask the Palymi. They cannot lie."

Voran's heart was still racked by ripping pain, but he looked up at the face of the Palymi. He thought he might die if he asked. But he could not continue to live like this. He asked.

"Is the Throne of the Gods real? If I sit in it, will I hold the power to summon the creator himself?"

Rathúdiel didn't answer. He looked at Voran with eyes like sapphires, if those stones could burn with living fire. Then he nodded.

Voran's despair hurt even more than the physical pain in his heart.

"See?" wheezed the Raven. "For once in my existence, I told you the truth. And you still won't believe me."

Rathúdiel continued to be silent and do nothing. Voran couldn't understand it. The Raven was a sniveling rat at his feet. Why did he not kill him? Why did he not rid the Realms of this creature?

He stood and he waited. Voran's pain was now like fire boiling all the blood in his body. He hugged himself and groaned into his own arm, biting it until it bled.

"We can still go, Voran," said the Raven. "Look. They don't dare do anything to me. They know they can't kill me. Come with me. I will take you away. We don't need them."

"But what about the way of Rogned?" Voran could barely get it out through clenched teeth. His jaw seemed permanently shut.

"I will find another way. I am a king of the ways—you know that." The Raven chuckled, making his writhing, stinking form all the more horrible.

Voran focused all his attention on the feel of the Shuudan's hand on his shoulders. It held him harder now. He thought he felt the sharpness of her nails through his shirt. It was all he could hold on to. He held on like a drowning man holding a tearing wheat stalk.

"No," he finally said. "I will not. Go back to the hell you came from."

The Raven screeched, then dissipated into a foul, brownish mist. It surrounded Voran like a cloud of biting flies. He felt his entire body go rigid, then his mouth opened of its own accord. The screeching mist flew inside his mouth and into his body.

The Raven was inside him.

At that moment, Voran knew that the Raven had always been inside him. Ever since he had allowed him in, thinking to destroy him in the Heart of the World. He had failed.

Rathúdiel still stood in place, his eyes still boring into Voran.

Now Voran understood why he had been seeing strange dreams and why the Raven had been invading his own dreams. They were bonded, like Sirin and human. He had not yet possessed him. But if they ever came to the Throne of the Gods, the Raven would certainly possess him. Then the world itself would fall under his slavery. And Vasyllia's plight would be the plight of the whole world for all times.

Voran looked at the Shuudan. Her face was splotchy and red. She was weeping, trying to keep it in, but failing. It gave him a small comfort, and he took a free breath. Enough to face Rathúdiel one more time.

"Rathúdiel. Tell me. Did Rogned find his way?"

Rathúdiel's eyes softened. He nodded. Voran sighed.

"Then I wish to take his path. Will you lead me?"

"I cannot. You have bound yourself to the Raven willingly. If I take you to Rogned, then you will lead the Raven to the gates of the Heights themselves. That is what he wishes."

"Is there nothing I can do?"

Rathúdiel looked away at the Shuudan. For a moment, doubt crossed those immovable features. "There is only one possible way to break the bond."

The Shuudan's hand shuddered on Voran's shoulder. She removed it. Voran thought he knew why.

"Execution?" asked Voran. "What use am I to the world dead? Or has all this been a farce? A torture preceding an eternity of darkness?"

"You have to understand, Voran," said the Shuudan, urgent. "The Raven's connection to you is tenuous. He can only hold onto the bond through your body. Your spirit is untouchable."

"Thanks to the Sirin," guessed Voran.

"The soul bond, yes. It is never truly broken, once established."

Voran looked at her, trying to understand what it was she was not telling him. He looked back at the Palymi, but he was looking at the Shuudan, inscrutable.

It was almost as though they were expecting him to *do* something.

Then it dawned on him.

"You need me to submit to the execution. To ask for it, even."

"Even that is not enough," said the Palymi. "You need to desire it."

To desire his own execution. How was that even possible?

"I need time," Voran said.

Rathúdiel nodded. "I will return in a week. I place no compulsion on you, Voran of Vasyllia. If you choose to remain here, to rest your wounds of body and mind, you may."

Voran's laugh was bitter. "It will be a torture. He will never leave me alone, will he?"

Rathúdiel shook his head.

"One week," said Voran. "Very well."

He crawled into his hut and barely made it to the pallet through the shocks of after-pain. He lay in a stupor there until sleep took him.

❧ 18 ☙

If Sabíana had thought that lying half-dead in a filthy turret room in the third reach was the low point in her life, she did so no longer. Once again she was lying half-dead in a filthy room. But it was not in a turret of a palace. It was in a whorehouse.

These past few weeks had been the worst of her life by any measure. As the dog-men had carried her through the double wall separating the first reach from the rest of Vasyllia, they had called out to the denizens of that shut-in place: "Vasyllia, receive your Darina. She has risen from the dead! Behold the miracle."

Or some such nonsense.

Sabíana didn't know what the dog-men expected would come of it; what did happen would have been unpleasant whether or not she had been announced as Darina. The people waiting at the double door tried to claw past her to reach into the passageway between the two walls. Some managed to get through as the door closed on them. Sabíana didn't see what happened to them, but their screaming was indication enough that it was nothing good.

The stinking, threadbare, and angry men and women who had not made it through decided they needed a scapegoat.

"Look at her finery," one of them had said. "Darina or not, she's a lady all right."

Sabíana, remembering it now, was still astounded that she had not been raped, only beaten and robbed and left to bleed on the dirty cobbles of the first reach. She didn't know how long she had lain there. Her head had struck the cobbled streets during her first fall, and she'd lost track of her body, time, everything.

She had awakened to the rough handling of a man who was tattooed obscenely all over his body and who had only one eye, as well as two slit nostrils. She had tried to escape him, but her body hardly responded. And any effort had been stopped by a rough woman's voice, directed at her: "Take it easy. He's harmless. Unless I tell him not to be. Up to you."

At that point, the man had opened his mouth to show the stump of his tongue. She had heard of the punishments that Aspidían had doled out over the years, and she knew that if those punished remained in Vasyllia, the only place of employment they could usually find was in the pleasure quarter, among the newly established brothels. Local muscle for the suddenly thriving whore markets of Vasyllia the great.

Then came the days of darkness, pain, and humiliation. She had been left in a bed of convalescence for only a single night before the woman, the madam of the establishment, had forced her to do grunt work—cleaning and washing and other tasks for which she'd never been properly trained. The threat of beatings by the mute giants with slit nostrils—there were at least five of them—was not merely theoretical. The first evening of her new work, Sabíana had been beaten, in spite of the fact that she had worked conscientiously the whole day.

"That's so you know what to expect in case you don't do your work," the madam had said. It was an effective, if cruel way of doing business.

Sabíana's head injury was worse than she had initially suspected. She found that entire sections of the day would disappear from her memory—something that led to more than one beating. But worse was the persistent sense that she was slipping back into a kind of acceptance of horror that had been her refuge during the many years of her sickness in the palace. She had to force herself to care, to go through the motions, even when blank despair seemed a far more logical, more human response.

One time, she had seen a knife lying around in one of the rooms where the young, pretty things plied their trade. It was a piece of solid workmanship, probably belonging to a carver or a butcher, though in this Vasyllia such a knife could belong to anyone. The denizens of the first reach had no illusions about their chances at surviving the coming invasion. So even the poorest tradesmen came to squeeze the last bits of enjoyment from their empty lives.

She had lingered too long, thinking about the owner of the knife and what his tragedy might have been. Before she could have hidden the knife on her person, one of the mutes found her. The beating that night was short, but severe. She had remained in bed the next day.

That night, she took stock of her situation. She thought it must have been two weeks or so since she had come to the first reach. Though her head still throbbed constantly, she was pleased to notice that her body had grown harder and more resistant to exhaustion. The blanks in her day were still distressing, but they seemed to have been getting shorter, at least before the last beating.

She knew, at that moment, that she needed to get out. It didn't matter where. Just not in the center of the misery of the first reach.

Sabíana had no intention of waiting for a good moment. She would try to escape that night. She hoped and assumed that the madam was more interested in guarding against men coming in during the night hours than in preventing anyone from leaving. Sabíana had noticed that none of the girls had ever tried to run away. Neither did any of the hired help. And truly, where would they go? Madam provided everyone with food and shelter, when there were plenty of homeless and shelterless and hungry people prowling the dark corners of the pleasure quarter, and indeed all of the first reach.

So Sabíana slipped out of her window. The landing was painful, and she almost yelped from the jabbing suddenness of something that felt like a knife-thrust in her leg. But there was no time to see what it was.

The moon was full and the night was unseasonably warm for late spring. She crept across the back part of the grubby courtyard and over the short wall separating the whorehouse from the high street. No one grabbed for her or raised any alarm. Everyone seemed to be asleep, even the guards she had assumed would be there.

As soon as she was in the street, she realized why the guards weren't at their posts. They were lying on the ground, tied up. And there were warriors prowling the streets in groups of three and four, fully armed. Had the walls been breached already? Was this the invading army?

But no, they were Vasylli, clearly. Before Sabíana could make sense of the strange contradiction of Vasylli warriors attacking Vasylli citizens in the middle of the night, someone noticed her. Without a sound, she was seized, her mouth was covered, and she was carried—gently, but firmly—to a back alley and into a warehouse. She tried to bite the hand that held her mouth closed, but the soldier obviously had experience with this sort of thing. She managed little more than a frustrated wheeze.

As soon as they entered the warehouse, a staircase yawned before them. It led down, underground.

They rushed through passageways barely lit with dying torches, going against the flow of warriors rushing up toward the city streets. There were more warriors than Sabíana thought possible. Now she was completely confused. None of this made any sense.

A few dizzying turns, and her guards deposited her in a room full of women and children. That was strange enough, but when Sabíana stopped to actually look, she realized that many of the women were sick or maimed in some way. Even some of the children showed signs of abuse. Immediately she flared in anger. She was just about to storm out of the room to demand a reckoning when she realized that there were white-hooded women and men walking among the sick and wounded. She hadn't seen any of those white hoods since before the fall of Vasyllia.

They were brothers and sisters of the Temple complex that used to be—the Order of Healers.

She felt a sudden compulsion to know what was happening. Something vital, something urgent was going on.

"What's this?" she demanded of her escorts before they left the room.

The guards turned back to her, surprised. She couldn't understand why, at first, then realized that her tone of voice didn't match what she looked like—a dirty, probably smelly charwoman in black rags that were closer to faded brownish-green from being washed so many times.

She took advantage of their momentary confusion. "Why do Vasylli fight Vasylli? Have we stooped so low?"

One of the guards, a boy probably no older than eighteen or nineteen, had turned bright red from anger and embarrassment. "We do nothing but free our city from the filth."

"So say all self-righteous butchers of men," said Sabíana.

It was a quote from the Sayings. The boy recognized it, and it confused him even more. That suggested something to her. It wasn't normal for warriors to know the Sayings by heart. She pounced again. "I think I know who you are," she said. "You're the Sons of the Swan, aren't you?"

The older guard, though taken aback, seemed to have had enough of the conversation. "Come on, we're going to miss it!"

"Miss all the fun, you mean? The fun of killing your bothers in cold blood?" she said, in the haughtiest voice she could muster. "What would your leaders say if they knew that you had the Swan herself in your hands, and you treated her like a common wench?"

The younger one's eyes were nearly all whites now. But the older one pointed at her clothing. He laughed derisively.

She pointed at him instead. He wasn't even wearing armor, only what looked like a retooled kettle on his head and a butcher's leather apron on his chest. She laughed at him, mocking his manner. "And should I judge you by that armor, soldier?"

She said it with such command that he straightened without thinking.

"Who are you?" said the younger man.

"I am Sabíana, daughter of Dar Antomír, sister of Dar Mirnían, and Darina of this city in his absence. I have been healed by the Powers, and I have come to help my sons."

The entire room was quiet. Everyone was looking at her now—the children, the women, the old men and their wives, the white-hooded Healers. Sabíana knew this was the knife-edge moment. Either everyone would laugh, or—

"What was the name of our lady Sabíana's childhood nanny?"

This came from the older guard. It seemed at least he had decided to give her a chance.

She looked at him more intently. Yes. There was a clear resemblance—he had Nanny's eyes. She imagined that he probably "tut tutted" exactly like she had, in his unguarded moments. Son? No. Too young.

"You're Nanny's grandson, aren't you? We called her Nanny, Mirnían and I. But I prayed for her in the Temple by her godsname. She was Predislava."

His expression changed. Remembrance struck it like a mailed fist across the face. It was clear—he recognized Sabíana.

"Highness," he said, then fell on his knees. "What is this miracle? How can you walk? We had heard that you were dead . . ."

"You will hear much more than you thought possible, young man, by the time all this is done. Now quickly, tell me. Why are my Sons out in force tonight?"

His gaze flitted over the women and children. Quite right. Who knew what sort of people were left in the first reach these days? Even the wounded could harbor a traitor or two, or simply someone who would sell information for a loaf of bread. She walked out of the room back into the torchlit hallway. The steady stream of warriors had lessened somewhat, and now there was a pervasive sense of expectation and waiting in the air, thick as musk.

The guards followed her.

She faced them, just out of earshot of the women and children.

"Tell me, quickly."

"My lady," said Predislava's grandson. She now saw that he was not that much older than the other one. He just had a fuller beard. But his eyes danced and his entire manner was that of a young boy on his first hunt. "How much of the city's present situation are you aware of?"

"Speak plainly, young man. I'm not your military commander. Just tell me in your own words. All I know is that the first reach is quarantined. Evidently not for disease, but to be a buffer against invasion. But who is invading and why? Remember: I have been gone for a long time."

"Yes, lady. We've had some of Vasyllia's best scouts—you remember Tolnían, surely, he's still at his work—monitoring the lands of Vasyllia for weeks. It is an exceedingly confusing picture. Aspidían had sent out a strong force of the army loyal to him—this is weeks ago now—into the mountains. At that point, the information we had was that they had been sent to stop an invading force of Nebesti, led by a man named Parfyon Kryvoshey. He had styled himself knyaz of Nebesta."

"Knyaz?" She thought hard and fast. "That would mean that Nebesta has finally decided to cut even any symbolic connections to the Three Lands. But I've never heard of Parfyon. Some minor noble?"

"From what we can tell, not even that. A commoner raised by the Veche of Choosing."

Sabíana laughed. "Well, we do live in interesting times, it seems. So he was intent on conquering Vasyllia for the Nebesti? That sound more like Yarpolk Dolgoruk's style."

"There are rumors that Parfyon killed Yarpolk, or had him killed, in any case. But the information flow is very spotty, you understand. And that's not even the strangest of it."

The younger guard, excited by the conversation, butted in: "The Nebesti were turned back by another army that had come up *behind* them. An army of strange, dark-skinned warriors riding bears. Or perhaps they are bear changers. They dealt the Nebesti a decisive blow, routing their army entirely. Parfyon was, by all accounts, killed in action. After the Nebesti remnant retreated with their tails between their legs, the bear riders pushed further into Vasyllia."

The other guard, not to be outdone, pushed back into the conversation.

"Only to be faced with—and I still don't believe this—an army of giant serpents. Or giants with serpents. Or both. The serpents initially looked like they would fight the bear riders. But then they joined them to attack Aspidían's Vasylli. And the bear riders and serpents routed the Vasylli! That's why we're out tonight. Aspidían's remnants are not far from the city."

"So many different armies?" Sabíana thought that perhaps

rumors were painting the real situation with shades of implausibility. "Sounds unlikely."

"That's not even all of it," said the younger one, excited again. "You won't believe this one, my lady. Your brother. He's back. And he's brought an army of *both* Vasylli and Gumiren. Fighting together. They've joined the bear riders and the giants."

Sabíana was so shocked by this that she skipped a breath, then her breath caught as she overcompensated. She fell into a coughing fit.

It gave her just enough time to try to process all the strange information. Sabíana had long assumed Mirnían, who had disappeared twenty years ago, to be dead or hiding out somewhere, waiting for someone to hand his crown back to him. But no, he was alive, and evidently he came with an army.

She was surprised to find out that her first thought was not relief or joy. It was resentment.

He will pry the crown of Vasyllia from my dead fingers.

The thought came even before she had a chance to analyze it. Her blood chilled as she realized where her thoughts had naturally tended. Perhaps her illness had left her worse off than she thought.

"Who leads the Sons now, my warriors? Take me to him. I have much to think of."

THE CORRIDORS, like rabbit warrens, seemed never-ending. Everywhere they were feebly lit by torches, but nothing adorned the earthen walls other than the occasional brace of wood and stone. It was exactly what Sabíana needed for her mind to wander, making connections.

She let the warriors lead her, and she abandoned herself to her racing thoughts. The situation as described by the warriors was absurdly complicated. Three armies allied together against

Vasyllia. At least one of the leaders of that army, if not the one spearheading everything, was Mirnían himself. Mirnían, her idiot brother who had insisted on leaving Vasyllia during a time of war, in search of Living Water, and who had never come back to the people who expected him to be a worthy heir to the greatest Dar in living memory, her father Antomír.

Mirnían. He had never been good at his war studies. He had never been particularly quick on the uptake at all. Sabíana knew that their father's greatest wish had been that Mirnían would make an excellent public figure, with Sabíana behind him, telling him how to rule well. Mirnían did have an intangible talent—a magnetism that attracted people of all classes to him, neither making them feel subservient to him nor allowing them to be too familiar with him. She had nothing of the sort. She remembered how badly she had offended Yadovír after a riot in the Temple, twenty years ago. It had been a misstep that may have helped push Yadovír to embrace a path of treachery, a path that had led to his own brutal assassination.

No, she had never been a charmer. But she knew how to rule. Without her, Mirnían was nothing. And she had been here, with the people, when the siege of the Gumiren began. She had bled with her people. And when she was struck down with her strange illness, she had continued to bear the sufferings of her people in her own body and mind. With the power of Feína, the Sirin of fire, she had appeared to many of her people in dreams and premonitions, helping them, giving them strength, reminding them of the ultimate importance of Vasyllia as a symbol of good in the world.

Yes, she had finally chosen to die and clothe her spirit in the form of an eagle. But she had come back, hadn't she? She had faced even the Raven himself in the Heart of the World, standing side by side with her beloved Voran as he had tried to do the impossible—to stand between a demon and immortality.

Where had Mirnían been all this time? What had he been doing with himself? And why was he coming to Vasyllia with an army of Gumiren?

There was too much to process. Too much to consider. Little of it made sense. What sort of giants were these? Giants, particularly giant serpents, had only evil roles in the *Old Tales*. But if they were truly evil, why did Mirnían ally himself with them? And where did dark-skinned bear riders fit in all this? Nebesti invading Vasyllia—that made sense to her. But all these other armies? Why?

She was frustrated by lack of information. Add to that the uncertainty she was rushing toward. What if the current leader of the Sons of the Swan didn't accept her claim? What if he didn't believe she *was* Sabían? Would the word of a common soldier be enough? Even if he did remember her?

She hated being in such situations. Information was every-thing to her. With information as a tool, she could inspire men to do the right thing, either for her or for Vasyllia. But without information, she was no better than a supplicant. And a desperate one at that.

For the first time, she wished that she had taken the Harbinger's advice and gone to Raven's Bane. She would have been in a position of power then. But would she have reached Vasyllia in time?

They had arrived. The elder guard ran inside, while the younger kept a soft hand on the crook of her elbow. They waited.

It took her a moment to come out of her thoughts and see where they were. They stood in front of a wooded archway leading into a cavern whose width and breadth she couldn't even begin to guess. Stalactites dripped everywhere, audible even over the whisper of men and the constant rustle of leather and feet and weapons. Wrought-iron lamps seemed to float in the darkness above. They were exquisitely made, almost as though they had been grown, not crafted—organic shapes of leaves and small animals and clouds and stars.

She knew, then, who led the Sons of the Swan. She didn't know whether to rejoice or not.

"Welcome, Sabíana, the Swan of her people. We have been waiting a long time."

Yes. She had been right. The voice was that of Llun the smith.

SABÍANA DIDN'T KNOW Llun personally, but she nevertheless felt she knew him like a brother. They had encountered each other once, about fifteen years ago. It was during the early days of the Gumiren ascendancy, just as Aspidían and the Consistory were coming into their power. Llun had been the last of a uniquely Vasyllian phenomenon—the first-reacher, low-caste artisan who followed an ancient discipline of mind and body to create objects of intense, unrepeatable beauty.

The Raven had singled him out to create an object of power, a container for Living Water that would never go dry. At that moment in time, no one understood the Raven's endgame, and it seemed simply like a power move by an already ascendant Raven to ensure his continued dominance over Vasyllia, and eventually the rest of the Three Lands. Now, in retrospect, it was clear that it must have been intended to serve a different purpose, something to do with the Heart of the World.

In any case, Sabíana, with her rare power to create dream-scapes and include people inside them, was able to warn Llun and to prepare him for the torture of the Consistory. He had remained firm long enough not only to create the flask to contain the Living Water, but also to have it smuggled outside the city, with the eventual purpose of finding Voran. She had no idea if he had succeeded in that last part; what she did know was that he was taken by the Consistory and became one of the dog-men.

She had tried to reach out to him in dreams again—around five years ago—but he had rebuffed her with a hatred that had surprised her. He was not taking well to the conditioning of the dog-men. That was the last she had seen of him, but she had always hoped he would break the conditioning and join the resistance in Vasyllia—the so-called Sons of the Swan, named in her honor—which had persisted over all these years, in spite of the fact that they kept getting rooted out by Aspidían's men.

The idea they stood for was immortal. They wanted not simply a return to old Vasyllia, but a return to a life in concert with the Powers of the Heights. They wanted to embody the ideal of Lassar and Cassían for a new age. And so, they continued to survive.

But how Llun had come to rule them—that must be quite a story, she thought.

Unfortunately, now was hardly the time to ask about it. Now, as her warrior guards led her toward a slightly raised area in the middle of the cavern, she felt the eyes of hundreds on her. To either side of this rise lay two cave pools that had been illumined from within by some kind of cunning lamp that shone even underwater. Knowing Llun's talents, she recognized that this was probably child's play to him, even if it seemed impossible to her. On top of the raised stone floor was a metal chair with a high back.

It seemed to be some kind of torture device, she thought, judging by the metal restraints that she saw attached to the legs, arms, and neck area of the chair. But the restraints lay limp and unused. Perhaps they were a reminder of something in Llun's past.

As he sat in that chair, Llun himself looked hardly at all the young, bearlike man she had known fifteen years ago. He was white-haired, now more portly than muscular, and with a face so scarred that it was unclear where the scars ended and the lines of age began. He couldn't be much older than Sabíana herself, but he looked not a day younger than sixty.

Still, his eyes had the same direct, unflinching blue intensity, and his beard was still mostly black, though not as well kept as it had been when he was a working artisan in occupied Vasyllia. What astounded her most, perhaps, was the emotion behind the eyes. She hadn't expected it. She didn't quite have a name for it. The closest she could come up with was calm dispassion.

It was not the traditional, expected face of a war leader. She didn't know what to do with that realization yet. She set it aside, and instead focused all her attention on the room.

It was utterly silent, even of the usual rustlings of casual movement. All eyes were on her. There was even a kind of smell in the room—sharp like new cheese. It was fear.

"Should I ascribe some special grace to your appearing in Vasyllia at this time, Highness?"

Llun remained seated in his chair as he addressed her formally. Clearly, he was testing her.

"If you wish, Llun. Personally, I consider every event in my life to be accompanied by some special grace. Life itself, is it not a grace?"

"Philosophy. Not my cup of tea." He got up, and she saw that he only had one leg. Only one arm, too, it seemed. *The tender mercies of the Consistory*, she thought. No, such a man would not be won with clever words. She rethought her approach.

"Llun, you, more than anyone, must know that all the wars of men, all these battles, the vying for power—it is all only the surface. You know that even if the Sons are victorious in every field of every battle from today to the day of reclamation, it will be in vain, unless . . ."

She let the pause hold for a long minute. The silence lengthened. The drops of water shattered it, again and again.

She felt the fear rising around her. She leaned into it with her words and her emotions.

"In vain . . . unless the Heart of Vasyllia is secure. And I do not speak in metaphors."

Llun frowned in puzzlement, but he nodded. "Explain, Highness. What do we fight for, if not the heart of our city?"

"Not the symbolic heart, my warriors. The literal heart. There is a place, deep inside Vasyllia Mountain, where a source of Living Water flows out to all the Realms that make up the known and unknown world."

She waited. Some started whispering to each other, but she sensed little resistance to her words. She had been right—these men had been fighting for a generation, and they were ready to hear about the deep truth for which they had fought. It was in their bones.

"The Heart had been the Raven's goal all along. He didn't care about the city, about the monarchia. I would even guess that a few months ago, the Consistory itself stopped performing any of its dark rites to appease him and to maintain their power over the populace. Is that right, Llun?"

He nodded curtly, once. "Go on."

"He sought the lifeblood of all the Realms. For immortality. For permanent form. But he failed."

She waited again. Confusion reigned in their eyes.

"Why has nothing changed then?" It was one of the warriors in the crowd. A man without an eye. "We've been fighting the same fight since the day the Raven stole Vasyllia."

"It is worse than you think, my warrior," she said. "The Living Water is losing its power. Life itself is running out. We may be at the end of our world."

"Then what is the point?" asked Llun, quietly. "Why not simply give up? Live a life of pleasure. Or simply commit mass suicide?"

"Help is on its way," she said. "The Living Water only assumes its life-giving properties after it is sowed with seeds from the fruit of a sacred tree. There were three such trees in the Heart of the World. They have all died. But there is a final fruit, still living, as far as I know, in a hidden place. The Sirin have gone there, to bring the fruit back and to plant it in Vasyllia's soil once more."

The whispers grew louder now. This was what they wanted to hear.

"But if the city is unprepared," she said, after the necessary pause, "how long will the fruit survive? I do not know."

"We must free the city," said someone, as grunts of assent rose all around.

"As I said, Highness," growled Llun. "Should I not ascribe some special grace to your coming now, of all times?"

"Why now, Llun?" she asked carefully. "Is it because today is the day you planned to take over Vasyllia from the Consistory?" Her thoughts were a blur. What day was it? There was something significant about today, and not only because of the invading armies approaching Vasyllia. It was a special day.

Then she knew. Or hoped she did. Llun waited for her to answer her own question. He was tense. They all were. Her answer would determine a great many things.

"Today is the day of your namesake, Llun the prophet. In the words of Llun, I declare that today is the day of blood, the day of carnage, when the stars themselves shall weep red. Today is the day when the true Dar of Vasyllia comes into his ascendance."

Llun's eyes were wide, and she saw that his breathing had gotten ragged. Still, he waited.

"The only thing Llun the prophet got wrong was this. Today is the day when the true *Darina* of Vasyllia comes into *her* ascendance."

She smiled. Llun smiled back, sincerely and warmly. It had worked.

"Men!" he bellowed. "Welcome your Darina Sabíana back properly."

He fell on his knees before her and extended a hand. She took it, and he pulled her toward the chair. Before she sat down, he took the restraints on the arms and the back of the chair and tore them off with his own hands. They clattered on the stone floor.

She sat down. Before her, in the dancing yellow light of the lamps, hundreds of armed warriors stood on their knees, their heads bowed before her in silent expectation.

"Rise, my Sons!" she exclaimed, raising her right hand.

The thunder of her army rising was deafening. Their faces shone; their eyes sparkled with unshed tears. They exclaimed, as though with a single voice: "Long live Sabíana, true Darina of Vasyllia!"

She breathed deeply. Once, long ago, such a spectacle had caused goose flesh to rise on her skin. She had thought herself blessed and specially chosen by the Heights then. Now, she only felt the compulsion, like an ache in her bones. She wanted the blood of the traitors. She wanted it now.

"Go, my Sons," she said, standing up. "Win me back my city!"

❧ 19 ☙

Over the course of the next two days, the Artisan killed two more warriors, both Vasylli. Adelaida's connection to his presence had grown stronger, and so both times she had managed to come before they died. The terror of the first was so pervasive that she could do little but hold him down physically, trying to will some measure of calm, which she didn't feel, into his body. It was all in vain. He died in agony, his mouth frozen in mid-scream. She closed his mouth, but his teeth remained protruding and horrible.

The Artisan hadn't come out to gloat the first time.

He did the second time. His second quarry was hardly out of his childhood, probably no older than seventeen. Adelaida had been tending the wounded after a long day of marching, and so she was close when she felt something like a tearing in the air around her. A gurgling scream followed soon after. She found the young man with the Artisan on top of him, doing something horrible she couldn't quite make out. She pushed him aside, and to her surprise, he gave way.

But as she prepared lavender water and cooled the young man's brow, the Artisan giggled obscenely behind her. She refused to look, even though her skin crawled at every one of those sounds. She focused on the face of the young warrior. He was in terrible pain, but there seemed to be less terror in his eyes than in the previous victim's. She sang to him—an old song she used to hear the fisherwomen sing on Ghavan's shores as they mended nets—and his eyes fluttered closed, even as he still spasmed with pain.

O you bright sun,
Come, peek out
From behind the hills!
Look out, my sun,
Until the time of spring!
Have you seen, my sun
The beautiful spring?
Have you met, my sun,
Your sister-true?
Have you seen, my sun,
Old Woman-Winter?
Have you seen how she
Ran away from spring
From the Beautiful One?
Has she carried the frost away in a bag?
Did she shake the cold over the land?
Did she run away,
Hiding under the mountain?
Did she meet the spring,
The beautiful sister of the sun?

The sensory details that came with the song threatened to overwhelm her—the salt on the warm breeze of late summer, the shuffling of whitecapped waves on pebbles, the light in the eyes of the fisherwomen's children as they ran up to the retreating waves, only to run away, screaming joyfully, as soon as the waves advanced. She closed her eyes. The tears were gathering, but she willed them to remain unshed. It hurt to do so. But it was necessary.

The young man was slowly fading away. Truly, there

was not much she could do for him. But she was over-flowing with shared pain, with a need to transmute that pain into relief that she could see. Because only when he was visibly relieved, only then could she also relax some of her internal strain, which had been steadily growing into agony. So she continued to sing, to wipe his face with the cool, fragrant rag, to lean with her upper body against his, so he could feel the warmth of human contact as he died.

She had become so absorbed in her task that hadn't realized, until he spoke to her, that the Artisan had stopped cackling.

"There were some beautiful moments on Ghavan Isle over the years, were there not?"

She turned to look at him, baffled by his question.

He had a strange look in his eyes, almost a softness, as though he needed something from her.

"It was my entire life, Artisan. You know that it was beautiful."

"I gave that to you, didn't I?"

"Did you?" She wondered. Was he capable of giving good? "It was mother and father who made our world for us, not you."

He didn't answer, his eyes retreating into a dark place of recollection. She steeled herself against him, because he looked so pitiful that she knew she was about to feel sorry for him. But that was what he wanted. She wouldn't do it.

"Why are you here, Artisan?" she asked. "Why won't you leave these people alone?"

His face twisted into a monkey-like grimace. "Do I begrudge you the dead cows that *you* eat?"

She shook her head. Of course he would say something idiotic like that. She had been wrong to expect him to speak truth to her.

She redoubled her efforts at focusing on the young warrior.

He was looking at her now with eyes lacking any coherent thought behind them.

The Artisan remained silent behind her.

The young man, after a spasm of pain that seemed to rack his entire body in a single convulsion, breathed raggedly out. A long, pained breath. Then, his breathing stopped.

He was dead.

The Artisan sighed with what sounded like contentment.

"Is there no other way you can feed?" she asked, turning on him. She felt the jagged emotion of her question, as though she were cutting both him and herself at the same time. "And why must it be my people?"

"You wouldn't understand." He still grimaced at her, but she sensed a shadow of doubt creep into his voice. She pushed into that place, probing.

"Help me understand."

He sighed, no longer content with whatever sustenance he had received from the young man's death.

"I must enter Vasyllia, Adelaida. It is . . . the heart of the matter."

"So the giants seem to think as well."

"The *giants*," he scoffed. "They are pitiful, lesser creatures. A deformed fetus of a first attempt at creation."

She felt sick at his words, but forced herself to be still. He was skittish like a scared deer, and she needed him to speak. She needed to understand.

"Adelaida, you humans are so small, so . . . so childlike. You simply don't know about the vastness of life. Of what it truly means to experience the fullness of existence. I . . . *we* had that once. And it was torn from us. Can you imagine?"

No, she could not. But she nodded, encouraging him to continue. He was growing more aroused, more agitated as he spoke.

"Have you ever felt closeness to another of your kind, closeness so intense that you can finish their sentences? The kind of thing when you look at them and know . . . not suspect, but *know*, exactly what emotion fills them? Is that not a wonderful, powerful intimacy?"

She nodded again. She only guessed at what he meant, but as soon as he said it, she thought of Batuk, and it made her heart warm.

"Can you imagine how much more thrilling and intense it is to be completely united to another being of your kind? So much so that there is an intermixing of your essences, but without you losing a single atom of your own self? Twice the joy, twice the pleasure. It is . . . I think you humans would call it intoxicating."

"Is that what you had? With others of your kind?"

He nodded. "It is not usually given to our kind, this sort of gift. Only after much, much labor. But some of us found a way to quicken the experience. Adelaida, you cannot imagine what that feels like."

"No, I don't suppose I can."

"But try to imagine what sort of pain there is when that union, that intimacy, is ripped away by someone else. Someone . . . jealous of your pleasure."

His gaze shifted away from her at that moment. He wasn't telling the whole truth. But she didn't react in any way, even trying not to breathe. She needed him to finish his thought.

"Then, not content with breaking that union, imagine if that *someone* had the power to then strip you of your body. Leaving you with nothing but a formless spirit, wandering around all the places you once loved, seeing all the people you once loved, without being seen, not being able to feel the same intensity of joy or pain or fear or anything . . ."

He stopped. His breathing was labored. Her own breathing had gotten shallow. She felt his distress like a nagging ache in her chest, growing in intensity with every second. It was becoming excruciating.

"Would you not do everything in your power to restore that union?"

He stared at her, his eyes boring into hers, waiting for her reply. For the only possible reply. She nodded. He sighed with evident relief.

"And so I do. Vasyllia is the key to it."

"But to do so, must people die? Innocent souls? Aren't you just doing the same thing that was done to you? Ripping out souls from bodies, leaving them to the Realm of the Dead?"

"It is *worth* it!" He growled. "I must remain alive! Without food, I will perish."

So he was not immortal. Now she knew. It was valuable knowledge. She must find a way to use it to her advantage.

"Adelaida."

He had made some decision, she suspected. His manner had changed, his body tense, but now with expectation of pleasant reward.

"Adelaida, I want to give you a taste of it. Will you let me?"

Before she could say anything, he had reached into her thoughts and grabbed her. It felt as though a cold fist held her heart and the inside of her head with a metallic grip. Then, she was drowning.

Not in water. In emotions too powerful for words. The joy she felt wasn't joy, so much as the apotheosis of joy. If every wedding night, every first birth, every childhood present, every moment of love awakening, every song sung at firesides with friends were distilled into a single cup of dark, velvety wine—it would only have been a taste of what coursed through Adelaida like a waterfall.

"This is what I offer you," his voice, deeper and kinder than before, resonated inside her. "I want you to share this with me. With us. You will be blessed among all women. And you can give it to others too. It will be yours to give to all you choose, and its source is endless."

But it was all wrong. There were faces behind that coursing

joy, that rich intimacy. Faces of dead men and women and children. Distinct among them was Derzhava, her body whole, standing on two firm, strong legs. Tears coursed down her face. She pointed at her feet, as though reminding Adelaida of what had been taken away from her, even before she had been born.

Adelaida screamed, but no sound came out. The Artisan fell back. There was a sound like a huge soap bubble popping. A smell of rotten meat followed it.

Adelaida put both her fists into her mouth and bit hard. The pain was sharp. But it was hers. Not the world's. Her own pain—*that* she could manage. She focused on it, on the metallic tang of blood on her tongue. She was Adelaida. And she would never, never follow the Artisan's way.

"How can you ever be joyful," she said, wheezing from the effort of simply breathing, "or happy? How can you feel any pleasure in that union, if you know that it was achieved through the suffering, the death, the agony of others?"

His eyes shot open in surprise. "Don't you realize anything, Adelaida? They would have died anyway. But I have made their deaths a sacrifice for future blessedness."

"Whose blessedness?" she almost shrieked. "Yours? Your kind's? What sort of pathetic creature are you?"

His face darkened. "I will give you this chance once. And since you have partaken already, you are beholden to me."

She struck him across the face. The face recoiled, just like a human face. And there was a palm print on it, as though he were truly human. How deep did his illusions go?

"My life is not mine anymore, Artisan, if it ever was. But neither will it be yours. Not ever."

He grew still. But it was the stillness of a predator before the lunge. She braced herself, not knowing what would come. Would he kill her? Did he consider it his right to snuff out the life he himself had created?

But no. She realized something then. He might have created her. But she lived, her brother and sisters lived, not because of him. His domain was the egg-reality in Ghavan. It had been destroyed, and yet they remained. That was not him. Someone else gave them this new life.

A *someone* who was good, she was sure of it. A someone whom she wanted to know. A someone to whom she wanted to give her life. All of it.

Was that the Unknown Father?

No answer came, but there was something like the after-echo of a love song in Adelaida's mind. A soft caress without hands. A cooling relief.

She was no longer carrying everyone's pain. It had been washed away.

The Artisan was shaking with impotent fury. His hands, clenched like talons, reached for her face, but he couldn't seem to bring himself to attack her. And it made him even more angry.

"You will regret this. I will make you hurt. Like I hurt. Worse."

He disappeared. Adelaida, completely exhausted, fell back on the hard ground. Her hands were shaking. She closed her eyes and lost consciousness.

ADELAIDA DIDN'T REMEMBER WAKING up the next morning. Something like a fog inside her head obscured everything. The first thing her conscious mind recognized was the smell of burning wood, then the warmth of wool wrapped around her, then a regular breeze on her cheek.

She saw that her head was cradled in Lebía's lap. Her mother looked away absently, her eyes inscrutable, her eyebrows drawn together in concentration. She was breathing through her nose, which was the source of the intermittent breeze on Adelaida's face.

"Mama?" Adelaida said, her voice groggy. "What

happened?"

"You had passed out, my dear," said Lebía, still looking away. "You're taking too little care of yourself. Too much care of the men. There are other nurses here, you know. You don't have to do everything."

There was something she was keeping back. Something horrible.

"What is it? Tell me."

Lebía looked down at Adelaida. Her eyes were hard like flint. "I think you should stay out of sight of the Ghavanites for a day or two. Batuk will take you with his brothers."

"What are they saying about me?" she asked, though she was sure she knew the answer already.

Lebía sighed in exasperation. "War addles people's minds, my dear. Pay it no mind."

"Tell me!" Adelaida snapped.

Lebía's eyebrows jumped up in surprise. Adelaida wanted to apologize, but she forced herself not to.

"There's some sort of sickness passing through camp. It's acting very strangely. It burns through the men over hours, not days. As though something is eating them from inside. Some of the more superstitious think that . . . Adelaida, I can't."

There were tears in her eyes.

"I have to hear you say it," whispered Adelaida, her heart like a stone in her chest.

"They think you are killing them. They think you are a witch that is feeding on their life force."

Lebía's face turned slightly green as she looked away from Adelaida again.

"Mother, do you believe them?"

Lebía's head snapped back toward Adelaida. The old fire was back. It washed over Adelaida like a cooling spray of water. She hadn't lost her mother yet, at least.

"If you ever say anything so stupid to me again, I will spank you like the child you are," Lebía said, her tears falling on Adelaida's forehead.

Adelaida smiled, but the smile felt insincere.

"And Father?"

Lebía sighed and looked toward the tent entrance. "He doesn't know what to think."

Adelaida found that she didn't blame him. It hurt, but she understood him.

"It isn't me," she said. "I can't tell you what's actually going on, Mama. It's for your own safety. But I'm trying to stop it."

Lebía caressed Adelaida's head. She seemed to be searching for the right words.

Another whiff of burning wood reached Adelaida's nostrils.

"What is that smell?" she asked, trying to get up.

Lebía kept a firm arm over her shoulders, pushing her back gently.

"They're burning Derzhava's body."

"Without me?" She pushed against her mother, but Lebía kept the pressure firm.

"It would . . . not be a good idea for you to be seen right now."

Adelaida's heart twisted, like someone had gouged out a piece of it with a blunt knife.

"Please," she whispered.

Lebía looked at her intently, breathing all the while through her nose. Finally, she nodded.

THEY STOPPED at the tent opening. As before, Mirnían had had his roomy war tent pitched on an escarpment. The tent, on the outside, was a deep blue with golden stars. Two posts rose from it, pointing to heaven, each holding a banner of Vasyllia and Ghavan. The inside of the tent reminded Adelaida more of a room filled with velvet tapestries hung for effect than a spartan war tent. It was one of the few things that Adelaida knew helped Zabían and her sisters retain some semblance of calm amid the storm of war preparation.

Adelaida was grateful that the children were still sleeping on their pallets on the hard ground. It astounded her how quickly children became accustomed to the physical rigors of living on the march. Even children who had been sheltered their entire lives on an island with no way off.

From the slight rise where the tent stood, the flat lands of the Vasyllia River Valley stretched out before Adelaida for miles. On either side of the river, war pavilions and yurts stood like a plantation of hastily grown trees, shuddering in the constant mountain winds. It was early morning with a bright sun, so the predominant colors Adelaida saw were golds and silvers—fringes of tents, heraldic devices on banners and on warriors' chests, helms with peaks as sharp as Vasyllia Mountain herself.

"Look, Adelaida," said Lebía.

As the wind blew her hair across her face, bringing with it hints of cherrywood on fire, Adelaida saw a distant cloud part, as though on cue. The sun, also as though directed by an invisible hand, shone brightly onto the thing that revealed itself behind the unrolling clouds. It was so perfectly timed that Adelaida felt like she was watching one of the Ghavan village doll shows, with their elaborate scene settings painted in bright reds and oranges and purples.

She didn't understand what she looked at, at first. She had no frame of reference for it. It was massive, even from this distance, and it glittered like a collection of gems set in different kinds of stone settings, each of which was carved elaborately, down to the minutest detail. She couldn't shake the sense that she was looking at something artificial, some illusion or play of the light that would wink out as soon as her mind made sense of it.

"What . . . is it?"

Lebía laughed a little. "Of course. You've never seen a city. Not a proper one."

"That's . . . Vasyllia?"

Then it started to make sense. But rather than diminishing in her estimation, it grew. Things she couldn't make out at first now fit together into a harmony of shapes and colors and suggestions—no, not a harmony, a symphony—that came together to form a single work of art. It staggered her in its scale, its beauty, its sheer audacity. This could not be the creation of man alone. This had to be a divine city, a city where gods dwelt together with men.

Then, she understood, as though another cloud had lifted, this one in her mind.

"Mama, did Father wait to have Derzhava's funeral until we could see the city?"

Lebía's eyes were brimming with tears, even as she still smiled at Adelaida, and nodded. She closed her eyes, sobbed softly, dropping a few tears. One of them stubbornly hung to the tip of her slightly curved nose. Adelaida gently picked it up with a tip of her finger, strangely fascinated by this expression of Lebía's grief. It had been days since Adelaida herself had cried, even though she felt the need to release her pent-up emotion almost on an hourly basis.

She saw the sun contained in its fullness inside the drop—a sphere of incredible brightness and beauty, visible in its wholeness to her eyes.

Something moved in her heart at that moment. Small, delicate things could contain the full image of overwhelming beauty, and that beauty wouldn't diminish because of the size. The sun itself, still the sun, was visible in a drop of water. Both were true. Both existed. Maybe that's what happened to her. While she lived on Ghavan, she was like the sun in the droplet—tiny, not giving any warmth, insignificant to the wider world, an expression of the Artisan's guile. But she was outside in the world now, fully alive, like the sun in its sky. She was no more dependent on the Artisan than the sun was dependent on the size of the droplet of water.

He could threaten her all he liked. He could even harm her, probably. But he would not change her. He could not. She was Adelaida, daughter of Mirnían, the Dar of Vasyllia. She was herself, and her self was expressed through her actions. And if those actions were good, then was that not a testament to her self being good as well?

She believed it to be so. Derzhava did as well—Adelaida was sure of it.

And so, as Mirnían himself applied the final torch to the bier of Derzhava the Seer, Adelaida thanked her friend silently.

"I promise, Derzhava," she said, "that the Artisan's poison will not touch my people. I will stand between him and them. Even if it means . . ."

But to finish that thought was dangerous. As though in confirmation, something slithered in her mind—a presence.

I am here, the Artisan was saying. *And I will not let you stand in my way.*

$$\text{❧}\quad 20\quad \text{❧}$$

"The Hag had said that you wouldn't be alone," said Tarin the old warrior, behind Khaidu, as he gently rowed in the stern of his skin-covered boat.

"Aglaia," confirmed Khaidu, not looking back at him, but instead at the never-ending forest of old willows trailing both edges of the never-ending river. "She . . . she's dead."

"Dead? What do you mean?"

With a sigh, Khaidu explained what had happened as soon as they had landed in the Realm of the Dead.

Tarin remained silent for a long time, deep in thought. Finally Khaidu looked back. It still felt strange to perform such formerly impossible motions with her body.

His eyebrows were scrunched over his lumpy nose. He scratched his black woven skullcap, then turned to the kestrel still sitting on his shoulder and started to twitter at it. The kestrel keened back at him, as though they were conversing.

That's exactly what they were doing, Khaidu realized. *What a remarkable old man*, she thought.

"Khaidu, you've noticed the strangeness of this place, yes? As soon as you arrived?"

"Well, I can walk, for one. And apparently I'm a master at the art of knife fighting."

Tarin chuckled. "Well. Lucky you."

"It's some sort of illusion, I think. Sabíana—you know her?—used to weave half-substantial dreamscapes and take me inside them. I imagine the Realm of the Dead is something like that?"

"That's an interesting comparison, yes. But not all that useful. Because you'll be second-guessing yourself at every turn. Is this real, is this not? Am I right, am I wrong?"

Khaidu nodded. He had hit the problem squarely on its head.

"No," he continued. "This isn't a land of illusions. It's a land of symbols."

That gratified her immensely. She pulled out the three bones that the Hag had given her, remembering how she had imagined them to be more like eggs in this Realm. And she had been right. They weren't bones anymore. They *were* eggs.

"So the symbolic overlays the real in this world, is that it?" she asked. "But how can you know what's real, then? How do you navigate this place?"

"It's not as difficult as it might seem," he said, in a singsong voice. This was clearly a favorite topic with him. "The world above—it's literally above, by the way, in case you didn't notice—the world above is a world of objects with underlying symbolic meaning. We wouldn't know what to do with an egg, unless we understood its symbol—that it holds the power of life in it. So we eat it. Not because it tastes good—it does that, I'll grant you—but because by eating it, we partake of the life inside it. No one would ever have thought of eating an egg until he had understood that underlying symbol."

Khaidu liked this very much. It fit closely with the way the Gumiren used to live. Every thing had its purpose in their daily life. But that purpose, though utilitarian to some degree, was always given deep meaning by the symbol behind it. If given a choice between a fork with two prongs or a fork with three, the Gumir would always use the three-pronged one. Not because it secured food better, but because three is a number with greater symbolic significance than two. Three are the divine attributes of Sky, Earth, and Fire. Three are the parts of every human being—soul, body, and spirit.

"So in the Realm of the Dead," Tarin continued. "The opposite is true. What you see is not the object. The object is dead, or faded, or passed into oblivion. It's not even the memory of the object or the person, because memories can fade as well. What lives here is the symbolic meaning of the object or the person. That is what you see."

"So," Khaidu raised the three eggs in her palm for him to see, "in the world above, the Hag gave me three bones, magical artifacts, she said. But here, they are eggs."

"Ah! Power in potential. Very smart. I've always liked that Hag, even if she can be perfectly dreadful some centuries. The way she hounds the poor Ivans . . ."

Then it hit Khaidu.

"Tarin, are you saying that Aglaia's disappearance is not physical death?"

He clicked his tongue and whistled. The kestrel chittered in answer.

"I suspect that's exactly it."

"But . . . how can someone with as rich a sense of self as Aglaia fade away in a Realm of symbols?"

"What was she like before you came here? Was she her usual self? I've never met her, but I've heard much about her. Quite the character. As you said, a very rich sense of self."

"The giant Buyan had deprived her of her human speech. A parting gift, he said. And, I think, he had suppressed her human self deep within the wolf."

"He can do that?" He whistled his astonishment on a low, protracted note. The kestrel beat her wings in disgust. "I didn't know the giants had restored so much of the old magic."

"I'm not sure they have," said Khaidu. "She had been under the their power before, so perhaps . . . perhaps she was more suggestible than most? I don't know."

"But that does explain how she could die here. What was her death like, if I may ask?"

It was a brazen question, Khaidu thought. She didn't answer, trying to unclench the sudden tenseness in her shoulders—the old, familiar strain of her earthly, crippled self. But the moss trailing from the gently swaying osiers on the river-banks, the bright silver of their under-leaves that in the absence of sunlight seemed to shine with their own light, the rich earthy smell of soil that pervaded all other senses like a persistent hum—all this calmed her. She felt her body, though it was a symbolic body, as solidly as she had ever felt anything. And so she could look back at the memory of Aglaia suddenly dying, and her heart did not break.

"She faded, as you said. Into an old skeleton of a wolf."

Tarin was silent a long time. Every once in a while, he hummed into his nose, then blew out of it sharply. Other odd sounds included a flick of his fingers against his teeth and an occasional slap of his palm across his thigh. He was a very loud thinker, evidently. The kestrel seemed to be as fascinated by his loud silence as Khaidu was, staring intently at him the whole time with cocked head, occasionally rousing, seemingly just for the purpose of doing something while the crazy old man made up his mind.

"I'm not sure what it means," he said finally. "But it very well may be that you will find her somewhere here. In a place where her self is most . . . most meaningful."

"She'll be with Antomír, then."

"Very possible, very possible," he said, musing still.

"Which only begs the question, old man," she said, a little annoyed. "How are we going to find him?"

"Oh, didn't I say? Silly me. This landscape is very soothing to me. I grew up in mountains mountains mountains, but my heart lies in lowland river-valley forests. Not enough of those in dear old Vasyllia. Ah, Vasyllia, Vasyllia . . ."

Khaidu harrumphed loudly, and was gratified to hear him jump in his seat.

"The Hag *did* warn me you're an ornery creature sometimes," he said, but there was laughter in his voice. Khaidu wasn't sure he was capable of being insulted at all. No wonder he was such a solid presence in the land of shadows and symbols.

"Yes, the journey. Right. I don't know much about Gumiren culture, little one, so you'll have to forgive the stupid question. How is your cultural memory passed on through the generations?"

Khaidu smiled. It *was* a stupid question.

"Songs and stories, of course. Isn't that how it's done in your land too?"

"Well, yes. I suppose it might be true of all peoples, but I had to make sure."

He hummed a ditty to himself in a raspy tenor that was surprisingly pleasant. She even forgot to be annoyed with him for getting distracted again.

"Stories, yes." He cleared his throat loudly. "Well, maybe you can work it out. To get to your goal, what do you need to do?"

Oh dear. She knew what was coming now.

"You have to journey to it. But all symbolic journeys are . . ."

"Yes, they're ordeals. Quests, if you like."

"So we're going on a quest to kill some monsters, is that it?"

"Oh, I have no idea which story we'll end up in, but I'm sure it'll be properly dangerous. And don't think you can't die in the land of symbols, little wolf. You can."

Lovely, she thought, with an internal grumble.

~

NOW THE SKY seemed to grow darker, from a pale brownish color to a dark of moonless night. They could only see by the sickly glare of floating globes of light that looked like too-large fireflies. They cast jagged shadows, making the formerly pleasant osiers loom over them like old men with knives in place of fingers. Silence fell, punctuated by hissing noises like hundreds of snakes that moved around too fast for snakes. Sometimes the hissing was right behind Khaidu's ear, making her jump. The change into a land of nightmare was so quick that Khaidu had hardly noticed the transition.

No wonder she needed that skill with knives, she realized.

Tarin seemed to have a completely opposite reaction to the fall of nightmare. If before he had hummed to himself, singing occasional snatches in between conversations, now he broke into full-throated song. He had an old man's voice, but it was still resonant, thick with exactly the right combination of longing and excitement. She began to lose herself in the rhythm of that song as it rose and fell like the boat on the rapids.

With a lurch, she realized that's exactly where they were—rapids. Stones jutted out everywhere. And she could see them more clearly than before. She looked up to where the sky should be. Instead of a star-speckled expanse, she saw something like a ghost of a river, glimpsed from underneath. It flowed like water, diffusing soft white light all over the landscape, silvering it. The intensity of magical presence filled Khaidu. Her muscles tensed, especially in her hips, as she anticipated jumping out with knives bared at some monster that lived in the waters.

She wasn't disappointed.

Two translucent creatures covered in silver scales jumped out of the water on either side of the boat, their women's heads and torsos glowing in the darkness, their teeth sharp and jutting over their thin lips. If they had eyes, Khaidu didn't see them. They were more like pits of emptiness.

With the quickness of a cat, Khaidu was up on her legs—she had a split second to rejoice at that gorgeous feeling of strength in her thighs—her hands doing bizarre twisting motions with the knives, arms flailing around almost without her controlling them. Before she could say "Dear me, there are vila in this boat," one was back underwater, the other lay bleeding on the bottom of the boat. Khaidu's knives were hilt-deep in black blood.

She reached down to throw the vila back overboard, but she froze in place instead.

The vila had Sabíana's face. Khaidu felt the blood draining from her face, leaving it cold. Her hands shuddered. The vila with Sabíana's face opened her eyes and looked at Khaidu with recognition. She started to speak, but only gurgling came out.

It was loathsome. Khaidu, her whole body shaking with disgust, grabbed the vila by her legs and pitched her overboard. As the vila fell, it cried out in Sabíana's voice.

"What on earth?" Khaidu exclaimed, her breathing unsteady.

"Not earth, dear one," said Tarin, chuckling. He hadn't even made an attempt to get up from his perch. The kestrel was standing on one foot, both eyes closed, as though it was mildly annoyed by the presence of the vila and was hoping they would just go away.

"So that's how it's going to be?" she asked, furious. "I'm going to fight, and you're going to sit there?"

"That depends on the story we're about to enter."

She groaned. She was trying to keep Sabíana's face out of her mind, but was failing miserably. Worse was the thought—why Sabíana? Why had the vila chosen that aspect? What did that mean in the land of meaningful symbols?

Tarin swerved the boat toward a landing space of what looked like white sand. Beyond it was a plain of short, yellow grass leading on for miles. There was a massive stone in the distance. And yes, even at this distance, Khaidu saw that it had writing on it.

"Good grief. Not a waystone? Here too?"

Tarin laughed.

~

THE WAYSTONE WAS unlike the ones in the real world. It was more a stela than a stone—sharp-edged, made of something like obsidian, shiny and imposing. The letters on it shone in gold, as though they were growing on it like luminescent moss, not engraved into the surface of the rock. The writing was pretty much what she expected.

~

IF STRAIGHT YOU GO, cold and hunger await
If left you go, you will die, but your horse will live
If right you go, your horse will die, but you will live

~

"I DON'T HAVE A HORSE," she said, "So I suppose the only one left to try is the straight path."

Turning to Tarin, she jumped. Tarin wasn't there. Instead of him, a white horse with a mane of gold—not simply gold color, but actual spun gold—stamped in place with hooves that sparked silver. Everywhere the sparks fell on the ground, snow-drops grew.

Flowers again, Khaidu complained internally.

"So not the straight road, eh, horse-man?"

The horse tossed its head and spoke in Tarin's voice. "Think sideways, Khaidu. Remember, consider the symbols."

She looked at the waystone again and tried to remember

the stories. There were different ones, of course. It wasn't a waystone in the Gumiren stories, it was always an old, gnarled man sitting on a stump at a crossroads. But the idea was the same. Usually the hero took all three roads, but there was only ever one road that really mattered.

"Well," she said, smiling slyly at the horse-Tarin, "I liked you from the first. So we're not going to seek your symbolic death. Let's go left. If there's nothing left of me, it's up to you to finish the quest—you do know that, right?"

The horse snorted. There was more than a little of Tarin's laugh in that snort.

"Get on my back, wolfling," he said.

She was unexpectedly comforted by his use of Aglaia's diminutive for her. She got on the horse's back, and it flew over the waystone in single leap, bearing leftward.

But as soon as it landed, a mountain sprouted in front of them. Khaidu kicked the horse to the right of the mountain, but the mountain moved with them. She rode left, and the mountain moved with them again. It was a mountain you couldn't ride around. She remembered that there was something like this mountain in more than one Gumir storybook. She looked closer at the mountain and saw that the surface was crawling with predatory animals—lions and tigers and chimeras she had no name for.

Now what?

She remembered the Hag's gift. Reaching into her pocket, she looked at the three eggs. But which of them was which? She knew eagles hatched from eggs, but wolves and bears didn't.

Think sideways.

One of the eggs was speckled, dotted with brown and black spots. One was an almost furry dark-grey. The last was furry and brown. She took the first of them and popped it into her mouth. The shell melted. So did Khaidu.

She fell off the horse and flipped inside herself, then

popped back out as feathers appeared on her arms and her nose became bone-hard. She reached for it with her fingers, but it was long flight-feathers that came in front of her eyes. She was an eagle.

Flapping her wings, she lifted up into the air. The mountain grew with her. She flapped harder. The mountain grew a little less insistently. She flapped until her entire body felt like it would burst into a thousand shards of glass. At the top of the mountain was a jagged peak, bathed in swirling colors of a purple so bright and vivid that it no longer had a human name. Khaidu realized she was looking at warm air, swirling over the top of the mountain. She could *see* wind and air currents.

But she was quickly distracted. Her brother Batuk stood on top of the mountain, straddling the sharp point of the summit. He was holding a Gumir longbow. Even from here, Khaidu saw that it was a well-crafted bow. In the hands of someone as good as Batuk, the arrow wouldn't miss.

"I killed your eagle once, little wolf, and now I'll kill you," he said.

She saw his face again, the dark, twisted way it looked on the day when he had almost killed her in the Steppe. It had been the last day she had seen any of her family.

Panic overwhelmed Khaidu as Batuk stretched the bow. She hung in the air, slapping wildly, like a swimmer treading water. Swirls of teal and orange-colored currents ran around her, spinning in wild curlicues. She closed her eyes, ready for the killing stroke.

But she was an *eagle!* She didn't need to float in the air, waiting for death. She would deliver it herself!

The arrow came, but her eagle eye saw it flying in slow motion. She spun in midair, letting the arrow graze her tail feathers ever so slightly. As she spun back, she fell down, wings bent, directly at Batuk's face. It had gone white in abject terror.

Something was wrong. He had both his eyes open. There was no scar.

Khaidu pulled back at the last moment.

It wasn't really Batuk, she realized. This was a test.

She flew around Batuk and plunged down the other side of the mountain, headfirst. The mountain tried to shuffle backward to block her way, but she was too fast. At first as small as a pebble, then growing larger and more golden as she dove, the Tarin-horse reared and stamped and kicked out his back legs, enjoying himself far too much.

As she spread her wings for the landing, flapping them gently, she molted out of her feather skin and grew back into her Gumira skin. Her legs felt even stronger than before, and her heart beat triumphantly, pulsing pure energy through her body. She hopped onto Tarin's back and they were off along the brownish grass.

"Do you understand now, little wolf?" asked the horse-Tarin.

"Yes. The ordeal is mine. I have to face my own fears, my own vices, my own failings. Only then can I find Antomír."

"And, maybe, a way out of this place."

She was glad he had said it. Until that moment, the thought of the *afterward* had only lurked, while she consciously pushed it out. Perhaps there was hope for them all. More than that, perhaps they could come through this ordeal stronger, more fully themselves.

Or perhaps they were all imprisoned here for eternity. In a land of shades and nightmares.

THERE WERE TWO MORE ORDEALS. The first was a stampede of frightened deer running roughshod through an open plain, directly at the horse-Tarin and Khaidu. She ate the wolf egg and transformed into a monstrous wolf, larger even than

Aglaia. Just the sight of her caused some of the deer to run the other way, but she was forced to attack a few bucks who had decided she was the source of all their woes.

The temptation at that moment, she was surprised to realize afterward, was an intense desire to eat to satiety. She had always lived in relative abundance, but the life of the Steppe was harsh, and Mamai never allowed anyone to eat their fill. The Gumiren way was the way of self-discipline in matters of food. As the wolf, Khaidu felt an intense desire to eat for the future, as though overfilling herself would somehow protect her from future deprivation. As she started to feed, she realized this gluttony was her own, not the wolf's. She recoiled and embraced Mamai's rebuke, which rang in her head from childhood.

"Always be a little hungry when you finish," she had said. "It will make you strong. Stronger than the so-called warriors in the Western lands."

And she felt the better for it once she was in her own body again.

The third ordeal was the strangest of them all.

The Tarin-horse had been strangely quiet for a long time, as though he knew that what faced them would be especially difficult.

They rode up to a wall of white stone. There was one gate only. It was open, and beyond Khaidu saw a garden of flowers that could not possibly have existed in the Realm above. Everything was larger, more fragrant, much more bright, and much more varied than in the world of the real. Over it all towered an oak tree with leaves of gold. It was three times taller than the largest oak tree Khaidu had ever seen. The effect of the whole garden was dizzying. It was as though the essence of flowers had taken idealized form. Or it was something like a poet's vision of a garden of paradise made flesh.

Khaidu dismounted carefully. She expected something horrible to jump out of the flowers. But there was no one there, not at first. Then she saw that two people stood facing each other in the shadows of the oak. One of them was a woman of unparalleled beauty. She had curling, bright red hair and milk-white skin. Her features were perfectly symmetrical, in a way that almost made her look like a statue. But her eyes were almost too alive. They were a peculiar shade of green-blue that danced with an inner circle of yellow near the pupil. Khaidu could have stared at those eyes for hours, mesmerized.

Khaidu took one look at her and thought, *I will never be that beautiful.*

The man standing facing the young woman was Antomír. His side still bled, but his face had regained its living color. He smiled wanly at the beautiful woman, reaching for her with tentative hands. She smiled and blushed, just enough to keep Antomír from stopping his advances. He took her hand and raised it to his lips. He looked so happy.

Khaidu wanted to scream. She had not known until that moment how much she wanted Antomír. She had suspected something of that sort, of course, from the moment in Raven's Bane when he spoke to her not as a crippled sub-human, but a person. But now, she knew it for a fact. And now, it seems she was supposed to . . . what? Let him go?

Never!

Khaidu looked at her last egg. The bear egg. What would a bear do here? What was the symbol she was missing? What was the fairy tale?

Something growled in the trees. Khaidu looked up and felt the blood drain from her face. A seven-headed red-scaled dragon had been sleeping in the crown of the tree, and now it woke up.

Khaidu didn't even think. She popped the bear egg into her mouth. This time, the transformation was unpleasant. She tasted blood, lots of it, and the stiffening of her muscles was like she was being stretched to a ripping point. It made her angry, and she roared.

Antomír stood under the tree, brandishing a sword, one hand reaching back toward the woman in a gesture of protectiveness. The seven-headed serpent raised wings that looked like fire incarnate and flew up into the sky, until it seemed to fill all of it with its bulk. Antomír's face drained of color, but he only gripped his sword the harder.

This was ridiculous. What could he do against a dragon like that?

But what could she do? She was only a bear, after all.

Wait . . .

She looked down at her paws. They were not bear paws. She roared again, and it was not a bear roar. She flapped her . . . she had wings! She shook her . . . she had a mane!

She seemed to be a flying lion.

Gently nudging Antomír away, she flew up toward the writhing mass of toothy, red-scaled heads. She wouldn't have much time or chance, but she knew her stories. Dragon heads grew back. Dragon hearts, once wounded, quickly bled out.

She flew straight at the monster. One of its heads lashed out at her, grabbing a chunk of her left forepaw. It hurt. There was nothing symbolic about it. It was real, pulsating pain. Gritting her teeth, she flew around the bulk of the dragon, looking for some sign of where the heart might be. She had read stories where the dragon heart is conveniently marked by some differently colored scale pattern. There seemed to be nothing like that here.

The dragon struck her again. And again. One wing was now broken, and she teetered in midair, only able to stay in flight through sheer force of will. It was over—she knew it.

Then she saw it. Nothing unusual, nothing special. She just saw that the dragon was a lizard. A very large, revolting, many-headed lizard. But a lizard nonetheless. All lizards, like all other creatures, hid their hearts in their chests. She plunged straight at the mass of the dragon body.

It was suicide. But it was also what the dragon least expected. So even as both wings were ripped from her lion body, Khaidu launched herself, teeth-first, at the chest of the beast. The force of her landing was so fierce that she felt the breastbone shatter under her paws. She sank her fangs into the creature and held on for dear life. The flowing of blood over her muzzle was warm and pleasant to the taste. It reminded her of buttery, salty Gumir tea.

She was growing delirious. But her jaws stayed firmly on the creature. Her vision dimmed. She could no longer move anything, and a brief glance showed that her lion body was mostly a ragged carcass of red. She closed her eyes and held on with her teeth. Slowly, slowly, the pulsing of the dragon's blood lessened.

Khaidu . . .

She held on, ignoring everything but the feel of her jaws clamped on the heaving monster.

Khaidu . . . is that you?

She opened her eyes, but only one worked. Everything was blurry and red, but it seemed she was no longer flying. Had she brought down the serpent?

"You stubborn wolf-child! Wake up!"

Khaidu woke up. Aglaia loomed over her, her face concerned.

Wait . . . Aglaia?

Khaidu shot up, almost smacking Aglaia with her forehead. Khaidu was lying on a green sward. Another mountain loomed to their right. Thunder sounded in the distance. There was a sharp, acrid smell on the air. She couldn't quite place it. Something like spoiled milk.

Khaidu pushed herself up. Tarin was nowhere to be seen. Instead, Aglaia stood in her human form, dressed like an ancient queen of Vasyllia—in layer upon layer of heavy gold fabric, her curling, grey hair elaborately intertwining with a circlet of gold, from which temple rings of swans in flight drooped and tinkled. She had found her human form again, it seemed.

"Took you long enough!" complained Aglaia.

"What?" Khaidu said, bewildered. "Where are we?"

"At the battlefield, can't you see?"

Then Khaidu did. As far as the eye could see, the green field was covered in dead bodies of warriors in armor. She recognized none of them, except one.

At Aglaia's feet, propped against a boulder, lay the grey-faced, wounded form of Antomír.

🕊 21 🕊

For the last two days, Adelaida had done as Lebía asked. She had traveled with Batuk and his brothers, in the middle of the host of Gumiren. The ten brothers had even surrounded her with their bodies, for good measure. But it was not as gloomy as it could have been. Etchigu and some of the younger brothers—Adelaida had long despaired of learning any of their strange, guttural names—constantly made a joke of it. Most of the time, they called her by a strange name: "the queen who walks the skies." They thought it was a wonderful joke, but whenever they brought her up, Batuk would stop smiling and his face would turn dark.

Adelaida suspected he was thinking of Khaidu, the sister whom they all lost in the wilds. He seemed to be the only one to remember her. Adelaida added that thought to the store of things about Batuk that she had begun, almost unconsciously, to shut in a special chamber of her thoughts, to be returned to in calm moments of pleasant introspection.

Those times, however, were precious few.

Every hour of their marching seemed to bring new revelations, each more shocking than the last.

The first was the return of the rot. Vasyllia, when they

entered it, had been unnaturally green and verdant, filled with all manner of life. Whether it was the destruction wreaked on nature by the vicious battles, or whether there had been a sudden change in weather, or whether it was something darker —it hadn't been obvious at first.

But soon it became clear that the trees were less and less green, the closer they came to Vasyllia. Then they saw that some of the smaller growth—shrubs and berry bushes and scrub pines—was sickly, covered in black slime-mold and infested with rot. Everywhere, the browns of mushrooms and other fungi started to predominate. The late spring flowers had all turned brown as well, and the smell of sickly sweetness predominated where lilac and lily of the valley had been before.

Soon after that change occurred in the landscape, the first bodies appeared. They were Vasylli, probably soldiers of the army that had blockaded the advance of the allied forces of bear riders, serpent-giants, and Ghavanites. But their deaths initially seemed not to be from battle. Many of them were already half-skeletons in appearance, and some were covered in creeping mold of a greenish-brown color that slithered away at the slightest movement of air around it. Adelaida felt there must be a malevolent force at work, even if Batuk and the others thought the idea unlikely.

Then it became clear, as Vasyllia loomed larger and larger ahead of them, that there had been a battle. There were new bodies, not touched, yet, by the rot. Their blood was still fresh, their eyes still clear, not filmed over in death.

"Perhaps they turned on each other in panic?" Etchigu mused aloud, making sure to include Adelaida in the conversation by looking at her.

Batuk shook his head and pointed at the bodies.

"Look at the direction," he said. "The corpses."

Adelaida saw it then. "Most of them seem to be running *away* from the city—is that it?"

Batuk smiled, looked at her with something like pride, and nodded. "It's the regularity of the pattern, see? They must have been attacked by a force coming—"

"From Vasyllia itself?" Adelaida interrupted him. "How likely is that?"

Batuk shook his head, but with an expression that seemed to say, "With you Vasylli, anything's possible."

The possibility seemed real enough to Mirnían, because the entire army was ordered to halt, not even half a day's march from Vasyllia's gates. Batuk and Etchigu were summoned to Mirnían's tent.

"I'm coming with you," Adelaida told Batuk.

"I don't think that's a good idea," he answered, and Etchigu's shoulder shrug seemed to confirm his agreement with Batuk.

"Batuk, do you think I'm some kind of vampiric harpy?"

Batuk's eyes widened in confusion. He didn't understand those words in Vasylli, evidently. But then it seemed he decided that it didn't matter whether he understood what they were exactly or not.

"I think you are wonderful," he said. Her heart skipped a beat at that. "But your white-skinned idiot people are more superstitious even than us Gumiren. They seem to think you are . . . vampiric, you said? What a word!"

"Batuk, you understand that the fate of entire nations is being decided here, yes? I want to see it. I've never seen anything but a single village on a tiny island. And now my parents are deciding things that will determine history. I *need* to be there."

Etchigu laughed his short laugh and looked at Batuk with a glance that said, *Will you ever understand these women?* Batuk smiled back. In his ugly, flat face, it was like the sun rising.

So she came with all ten brothers to Mirnían's tent. There was such a commotion of raising tents and pounding pegs into the ground and digging latrine ditches and setting up campfire pits that hardly anyone noticed Adelaida in the midst of the knot of young Gumiren nomads.

As they approached Mirnían's tent, Adelaida saw that Zmei and Veles were already there, and that they were doing everything to keep as far away from each other as possible. Mirnían was sitting on a sawed-off log between them, his chin in his hands, poring over a map that looked like it had just been drawn that morning. Lebía stood slightly behind him, her hand on his shoulder, her fingers absently playing with the ends of his curly hair as she also examined the map.

It looked like the kind of scene that would later be painted by iconographers to memorialize the return of the exiled Dar Mirnían to his city. Adelaida even felt the tears begin to gather, before she pushed back the sudden emotion.

As she did, Mirnían looked up and his eyes locked with hers. They were tired, and Adelaida noticed lines on his forehead and down the sides of his mouth that hadn't been there before. At first, as his gaze focused on her, he didn't seem to recognize her, but then his eyes softened. He smiled. It was a smile of deep remembrance and gratitude. She felt her heart turning into a puddle of molten gold at that look from him.

It disappeared as someone said something in his ear. Immediately, it was as though someone had clapped their hands sharply, breaking a moment of transcendence. Mirnían conferred with those around him, not looking back at her anymore.

Adelaida felt like something precious had been broken in the world, never to return.

Why the dour thoughts? She chided herself. Now was no time to be mawkish.

As Adelaida and the Gumiren approached, all eyes turned to them. For some reason, the conversations among the adjutants and minor nobles surrounding Mirnían fell silent. Zmei stared at her with eyes that didn't blink. Veles's eyes were blinking back tears at an alarming rate. It was uncomfortable and strange to be the center of attention. She began to regret demanding to come.

But as soon as Batuk and Etchigu took their places in what was supposed to be an informal circle of allies, Mirnían began to speak, and all attention shifted back to him. Adelaida could breathe again.

"Batuk, Etchigu, have your scouts come back yet?" asked Mirnían, without preamble.

Etchigu nodded, but Batuk answered.

"The gates of Vasyllia are shut. There are clear signs that the first reach is armed. At this moment, it seems they arm against you, Dar of Vasyllia."

"Then why did they kill their own?" asked Lebía.

"Another faction has taken power in the city?" suggested Veles.

No one had any better suggestion, even though Adelaida thought that there was probably a better reason, one that no one was considering. Something obvious, something true. But what it was kept evading her, like a word that sits on the tip of the tongue but refuses to be spoken.

Silence descended on the group. Zmei, who had been growing more and more restless as the silence stretched, finally stomped on the ground. His foot stuck calf-deep in the earth. He swore.

"Why are we waiting?" he boomed. "What difference does it make to us if another faction has taken over in the city? No faction can stand in our way. My serpents will have that wall down in minutes. We can have the entire city burning in half an hour."

"And you ask why I wait?" Mirnían scoffed. "That is why, Zmei. We are nearing our objective. But I still do not know what yours is. Not really. Are we even allies?"

Zmei stewed in his own silence.

"There's another thing," said Veles. "The rot in the trees,

and the suddenness of its appearance. I don't like what it suggests."

"What would *you* know?" Zmei boomed, then subsided back into stewing in his own thoughts.

"I would know more than you think," said Veles, smiling bitterly. He turned to Adelaida. "Child, have you heard of my brothers' and sister's journey through the Realm of the Dead?"

Adelaida, holding firm against the natural retraction of her inner self at all the eyes turned on her, nodded. It was an effort simply to make her head move.

"Yes. Derzhava spoke of it to me."

"So do you believe me if I tell you that this creeping death stinks of the lands of the dead?"

The Artisan's voice growled nearby. That convinced Adelaida. She nodded, her eyes wide in fear that the Artisan would choose Veles for his next victim.

"What are you suggesting?" asked Mirnían.

"I don't quite know," said Veles, after a pause. "But if the Realms truly are collapsing in on each other, and I don't think anyone can possibly deny that, then perhaps the lands of the dead are bleeding into the lands of the living?"

"On purpose?" asked Lebía, as Adelaida's heart skipped a beat. They were getting too close to guessing the Artisan's endgame. "Tell me truly, Veles. You have more experience of that strange place than anyone else. Is this the work of the Queen of the dead?"

"I fear that it could be," said Veles.

"That's all very interesting," grumbled Zmei, "but how does it help us with our current problem? And do remind us, what is our current problem again, oh Dar?"

"I don't like not knowing what I'm getting myself into before I attack," Mirnían said.

"Is that why you remained on your little island for all those many years of the internecine war?" Zmei challenged.

The air turned frosty as Mirnían stood up to face Zmei.

Batuk and Etchigu moved to either side of Mirnían and crossed their arms as they stared at the imposing figure of the giant warrior. And yet again, to Adelaida's shock, Zmei seemed to grow a little smaller before the bravery of the Gumiren. She wondered what sort of power the brothers had over the serpent-giants.

"I propose that we send a delegation to the gates under a flag of truce," said Lebía, clearly trying to diffuse the tension.

Mirnían smiled and turned back to her. "Yes. I will lead it."

Veles immediately began to protest. "Highness, we've already lost one Dar. I won't let it happen again."

"Then you will come with me and protect my life with yours," said Mirnían.

"I will come as well," said Zmei.

"No," said Mirnían. "This is a truce parley. Not a show of force. Better to keep our best weapon hidden, don't you think?"

Grudgingly, Zmei conceded the point. But he looked about ready to burst into flame on the spot.

"Father, may I go?" Adelaida said, her voice tremulous. "As representative of Ghavan Isle? As a natural-born Ghavanite?"

Lebía's face had gone white, and she had gone completely still. The Ghavanites around Mirnían had grown tense, as though ready to pounce. But Mirnían smiled.

"It is fitting," he said. "You will come, my dear."

Good, growled the Artisan somewhere nearby. *Almost there.*

As quickly as the camp had been pitched, it was broken twice as fast. Adelaida marveled at the speed with which the men worked. But their objective was in sight, she understood. Soon the issue would be resolved, either by battle or by truce. She sensed that the men hoped for a battle, having been largely denied one in the first encounter, being more a rear-guard than a frontal assault.

Even before the breaking of the camp had concluded, Mirnían, Veles, Etchigu and Batuk, Adelaida, and an honor guard of twenty warriors picked from all three armies, rode along the now visible highway leading through the last, straight part of the valley directly toward Vasyllia Mountain and the gates of the city. It was early morning still as they embarked, and the cold of a nearly freezing night clung to the tips of Adelaida's fingers and nose as she tried to keep pace with the rest of the entourage. She had been given a stout Gumiren pony to ride. It had a chestnut hide with a bright blond mane that kept falling in front of the poor pony's eyes, and it seemed too small at first to keep up with the war-chargers that Mirnían and the warriors rode. The chargers had not been ridden in weeks, and the first glance at a straight, unimpeded road seemed to drive them mad. They rode like the wind incarnate.

But her pony kept up better than she expected. She preferred to ride with Etchigu and Batuk in any case, and their own ponies were not as eager to ride like the wind as the Vasylli horses. The first hour of riding, Mirnían and the Vasylli gained a sizable lead on the Gumiren and Adelaida, but the ponies were hardy beasts. After the war-chargers spent their initial rush of speed, they slowed down considerably. By the time the gates were visible as a thing distinct from the rest of the wall of Vasyllia, all the riders were together as a group. The Gumir ponies seemed ready to ride another few hours, while the war-chargers' flanks were foaming, their eyes almost all whites.

Adelaida found that she had to constantly remind herself to breathe. The sight of Vasyllia growing by the minute before her shocked her. She had no words to express the sheer scale of what she looked at. But that was only part of it. The city had clearly been built to be a symphony for all the senses.

Trees were as numerous as houses, and many of them were flower- and fruit-bearing. Cobbled streets were lined with chokecherries and frothing hawthorns, and their sweet smell interwove with the ubiquitous, resinous tang of fir and spruce. Even as they rode up, clouds of birds with red breasts and yellow wings and blue heads and aquamarine beaks sang and cavorted and made impossibly complicated designs in the sky with their murmurations. She even thought she could hear singing, like an afterglow of the sun as it sets below the horizon.

But all that was corrupted by the sight of dead bodies, by the insistent smell of slime-mold, by a palpable sense of wrongness that was like a low droning in the air, just beyond hearing.

Adelaida felt like she was being cloven in two by the idea of what Vasyllia must have been and by the encroaching deadness all around them. It was almost like she was in two places at the same time. Or in two times at the same place. It was profoundly disturbing.

Finally, they approached near enough to see the two stone-carved trees on either side of the massive gates of Vasyllia. There were half-hidden turrets in the crowns of those trees, and even at a distance, tree and turret both bristled with what looked like porcupine quills.

"Spears," confirmed Batuk to her questioning glance.

"Arrows too," said Etchigu, pointing at the walls. The porcupine quills pointed out of narrow slits in the wall proper as well.

What were they getting themselves into?

"Raise banners," said Mirnían softly. Ten spears rose around them, all of them bearing the ancient banner of the Dars of Vasyllia.

"Now we see if the gambit pays off," said Batuk.

Adelaida understood. It was a calculated risk, but if the new faction in Vasyllia was even slightly disposed to the monarchia, this banner would speak more eloquently more than any master negotiator.

As soon as the banners came up, something seemed to have happened behind the walls. The quills seemed to shudder, some of them moving back and forth. It was almost a comical sight.

The gates opened. Adelaida gasped aloud. She had not expected that to happen. Nor had anyone else, evidently. A ripple of excited anticipation passed through the entourage.

"Look!" said one of the warriors in shock.

A white horse led a delegation of five warriors and two white-robed clerics out of the city at a swift canter. The rider of the white horse shone like burnished gold. Adelaida's eyes were fixed on the rider, who looked like something out of a legend come alive in all the glory of the Old Tales. It took her a long time to realize that the rider was a woman, dressed in chain mail from head to foot, with a massive wolf fur thrown over her shoulders, secured in place by brooches in the shape of swans in flight. She wore a crown of gold with red gemstones that seemed to shine with their own light.

"By all that is holy . . ." said one of the warriors.

"It can't be . . ." said another.

Mirnían's face was inscrutable to Adelaida. There were many warring emotions there, clearly, but she couldn't decide which was winning. There was a good deal of fear there, but the joy was almost as vibrant, especially in his eyes.

"Sabíana," he said, quietly, as if to himself.

Adelaida's jaw dropped at hearing that. That was impossible. Sabíana was dead.

But whatever joy Mirnían might have felt at seeing her, Sabíana seemed to share none of it. She rode up to within easy speaking distance, but showed no inclination to dismount.

"Come back to your throne, have you, Dar of Vasyllia?" Sabíana challenged with a rich, alto voice that carried years of suffering in its tone. Adelaida could almost feel that suffering as she listened. She found herself mesmerized by her aunt, whom she had never met. She was strikingly beautiful, but that beauty was more in how she held herself, not in any unusual harmony of features.

"Sabíana?" Mirnían said, quietly. He seemed no older than a young boy before Sabíana's steely presence. "Why do you greet me so, after so many years? Why do you not come and embrace me, as befits a sister?"

Her face flushed, but she made no move to either dismount or ride away.

"Sister. Yes. I had almost forgotten. I was sure that you had long forgotten."

Mirnían sighed, then dismounted. He handed his reins to the nearest warrior, then did something that Adelaida had never seen him do in his life.

He fell on his knees and bowed his head.

"Your anger is justified, sister. Forgive me. I have many sins to atone for."

Sabíana, if it were possible, got even more angry.

"What use have I for your atonement? What need have I for your groveling?"

It sounded almost too formal, like an incantation. Not a conversation between equals. Certainly not a conversation between brother and sister who had not seen each other in twenty years.

"You selfish bastard," Sabíana said, quietly, though her fury made her tremble visibly. "Not only do you expect to be the savior of the fallen city. But you even dare to bring this city's enemies—no, mankind's enemies!—within sight of this hallowed ground?"

Mirnían stood up. His shoulders straightened a little more, and his voice was no longer plangent.

"This is war, Sabíana. Are you trying to tell me that you've kept your hands clean all these years? Compromises are necessary."

"Don't lecture me. You have no conception, not the faintest idea, of what I did for *your* people. Well, they are your people no more. I have never been deposed as Darina of this city. And you have never been crowned Dar. So we have nothing to say to each other until you surrender your forces to Vasyllia."

Veles, who looked like he was in intense physical pain, moved his horse forward.

"Lady Darina, may I speak?" he said.

Her face lost none of its fury, but she nodded. "Name and rank, soldier. Then speak."

"Veles, of the Children of the Priest-King, my lady."

Her severe expression lessened. "I have heard of you. Feína spoke of your feats many times in the unbearable evenings. Your courage gave me courage."

Veles lowered his head slowly, then continued. "The creeping death, my lady. You have seen it, yes?"

She nodded once, making no other move, as though she were a barely animate statue.

"It is a sign, my lady, that time is running out. The line of succession . . . does it matter, when the land itself may die unless we do something to stop it?"

It was only a slight change in her tanned complexion and the furiously brown eyes, but it was enough. Adelaida felt that the severe queen was ashamed.

"It matters less."

A silence fell, tense, interrupted only by the whickering of the horses and the jingling of harnesses.

Adelaida looked at all the faces, especially those surrounding the brother and sister of the Dar's family. All of them were set, hard, ready to do whatever their masters demanded. So much dedication here. So much strength. Could it be that all these people, who should be working together against the darkness, would allow it all to shatter—over who would sit in what chair in a dusty old hall somewhere in old Vasyllia?

No. She could not let it happen.

Her hands shook, and her stomach was trying to eat itself, but still, Adelaida spoke,

"Aunt Sabíana, my queen. My name is Adelaida. I am the daughter of Mirnían and Lebía."

Sabíana's eyes went wide at this, and she looked at Mirnían in confusion. "I didn't . . . I never heard . . ." Then she looked back at Adelaida, and there was something broken in her eyes.

Before Mirnían could answer, Adelaida forced herself to continue: "My lady, Veles here speaks more truth than even he knows. It is far worse, and far later than you know."

The Artisan's presence loomed behind her like a suddenly grown mountain. Her fear nearly made her choke on her words.

"We have very little time indeed. If we do not come together now, then there will be no one to stand before the great enemy of our time."

Sabíana frowned. "The Raven is gone. He abandoned—"

"A ruse," Adelaida interrupted, stuttering. "And he is not the only danger."

If you do this, you will regret it for every moment of your short, remaining life.

The voice was inside her head. She gritted her teeth.

"There are three great formless ones who seek union, who seek permanent form. And they are near. Very near. What they seek is close. Possibly in Vasyllia or near it. Unless we all come together . . ." Her head spun as the Artisan screamed inside it. She couldn't go on.

"We have little time to explain now, my lady," said Veles. "But there can be no doubt of it. The Raven is only one of three. All three, if joined together, may be unstoppable."

"But who are the other two?" Sabíana asked, perplexed.

"One of them is the Queen of the dead lands."

Sabíana blanched . . . "So the creeping death . . . it is . . ."

"Yes, we think she is close."

Adelaida felt like the inside of her temples were crumpled metal foil being squeezed by a fist.

Don't do it. The Artisan growled.

I must. She breathed deeply. *I do it for my family. And I do it for you.*

"The third, my lady," said Adelaida, her heart threatening to burst from the speed of its beating, "is a demon called the—"

She didn't have time to finish before her own voice gave out. She couldn't breathe. She couldn't speak. She couldn't scream, even though she wanted it more than anything else.

Mirnían stared at her, but it was not him. The Artisan's eyes stared back at her.

"Ah yes," said Mirnían in a voice hardly his at all. "We come to it at last. My so-called daughter. The source of all the discord. The secret traitor in our midst."

Everyone stared at her with horror.

"Sabíana," he began, "we must—"

Mirnían's face twisted in pain, and he turned white. His hair began to fall out in chunks, and his skin clung to his skull as though someone were sucking the life out of him.

"Stop her!" he wheezed, pointing at Adelaida.

All the warriors of Ghavan rushed to grab Adelaida. Batuk and Etchigu were pushed aside and kept away at sword-point.

Mirnían gasped for air that wouldn't enter into his lungs. "Kill her. Before it's too late."

He fell to the ground, writhing in pain.

Then, the writhing stopped. Everything stopped. Mirnían was dead.

❧ 2 2 ❧

Antomír savored the pain, the blood flowing out of him from countless wounds. He no longer worried about the nature of those wounds. He had, for a fateful moment, when he was pierced through the first time—a moment of shocked indecision had cost him his life. Again.

But the intensity of this sensation was worth it. Before, blankness had lain behind all of his half-felt perceptions in the Realm of the Dead. Every time he had thought he remembered a taste of fresh venison falling off the bone or thought he heard a woodpecker torturing an oak tree, the memories were like mist burned away by the sun. Now, as he lay propped against a boulder, he reveled in the flow of blood, the fiery agony of every moment of his spirit-body's final fading away. Every moment, as he bled out, was a glory.

But the blood flow stopped. The agony faded. Perhaps he should have expected that the second death of all those who had fallen in battle with the Queen of the dead would be more final. There would be no coming out of this formlessness.

Still, he was at peace. He had accomplished what he had set out to do. He would never become a mindless, formless pawn of the dread Queen. He would simply fade out of existence. That was not the ideal way to finish his journey, but it was enough.

"You know," said a chiding voice that he found vaguely familiar. "I would have thought that a grandson of mine would have a little more fight in him than this. Mirnían's son, indeed."

Antomír's eyes shot open, and the profusion of color dancing before them boggled his mind for a moment. Two figures stood before him, both bedecked in florid, ancient clothing that would have been well suited to an illustrated book of the Old Tales. He felt that he should know both of the faces looking down at him, one with an expression of tense concern, the other with open annoyance.

The annoyance was what snapped him back to full awareness.

"Gr . . . grandmother? Khaidu? I . . . don't understand."

It looked like Grandmother Aglaia, for sure. But what was she doing here? Was she dead as well?

"It's complicated," she said, and had the grace to look abashed at her lack of an answer. "And . . . No, no. I won't explain. Won't even try. It's not for us to do it, anyway. I've had enough of explanations to last me at least . . ."

She huffed, evidently at a loss for the word to make her point sufficiently clear to the dimwit at her feet. He smiled. This grandmother of his would probably have been the life of the feast in calmer times. Khaidu smiled with him. She still had that crooked grin that he had loved so much in the monastery of Raven's Bane.

He looked around. He was still on the battlefield, and the battle had been very much lost, judging by the field of sowed dead. Already, many of the bodies of the slain had begun to fade back to the bones from which Gamayun had summoned them.

He shook his head. It was throbbing with pain, and he was surprised to find that he wasn't being sucked back into the deadness that had characterized his existence in this Realm.

He looked back at the women, who were still waiting for him to say something. Now even Khaidu looked like she was about to get annoyed. *How much they suited each other*, he thought. The wolfling and the old wolf-woman.

"Oh, very well." Aglaia subsided and seemed to float down to a seated position. It looked vaguely like the petals of a flower closing in on themselves for the night. "Shall I frame the narrative?"

Khaidu chuckled. "Aglaia, be nice. You've only died once. Antomír was on the verge of dying a second time. It's bound to be a little . . . disconcerting."

"How would you know?" said Aglaia, still annoyed. "You haven't died yet at all!"

Aglaia put on a very innocent expression that seemed far too guileless for her years, and sighed as though she were the most put-upon person in all the Realms combined.

"She's not saying anything," Khaidu said to Antomír in a conspiratorial tone, "because she has no idea what's going on."

Antomír, only at that moment, realized that Khaidu was *standing*. On her own two feet.

Aglaia guffawed, then crossed her arms and turned slightly away from Khaidu.

Khaidu chuckled and winked at Antomír. This was getting stranger and stranger.

"Would you please put us all out of our misery, Antomír?" said Khaidu. "What happened here? This battle?"

He sighed and began his tale.

~

Antomír's Tale

My dears.

I'm not afraid of calling you both that. You are both dear

to me, and my best memories of this past, horrible year are of moments with you. Raven's Bane. The quiet before the storm.

What both of you do not know is my dark secret. I have been soul-bonded to Gamayun, the Day-Seer, for a long time. No, it isn't like the Sirin bond at all. That is love. This is more like rape.

The Raven's plan, eons in the making, was many-sided and very subtle. One part of it involved the subversion of Gamayun. He is, as you know, a trickster. But to weave an illusion that would trick the one who sings all times into being? That was something masterful—I admit it freely. He trapped Gamayun, leaving her only one way out of a future so terrible, she nearly went mad as it began to weave itself into existence. He gave her a way out: my body for her freedom.

He wanted to possess me. You see the delicious irony in it, don't you? From his point of view. To finally possess the heir of Cassían, then to eat the fruit of the trees of life. To become the Deathless, and to rule over a kingdom of death, the Realms transformed in his image, in the undying body of Antomír of Vasyllia, animated by the soul of evil incarnate.

Except he overplayed his hand. He acted too quickly, or was forced to by Voran's coming—I don't know. He wanted my body for his eternal form, but he also needed the other two parts of his wholeness—the Artisan and the Queen of the dead. The Great Changer. Together, bonded into a single being of power inside my body, and given eternal life by the lifeblood of the worlds, they would be able to topple the foundations of the Heights.

Gamayun played her part. She brought me, trussed up like a festal chicken for the table, to the Heart of the World. But I would not do her bidding. I took the only way out. I took my own life.

Don't cry, Grandmother. It was necessary.

Gamayun died as well. But the Raven should have known that he wouldn't be able to dispose of her so easily. Gamayun continued to plot, even after her death. I found her, here in this Realm. She had allied herself with a singularly ambitious man named Parfyon of Nebesta.

Ah, you know of him. Good.

Then Gamayun did a remarkable thing. She raised an army for herself out of the denizens of the dead. She invited me to join her and Parfyon. They were going to defeat the Queen of the dead and take over this Realm for themselves. Then they planned on invading the Realm of the Living. How, I don't know. We never got that far.

The Queen knew of our plans. She seems to know everything that happens in her Realm. And she may have even allowed Gamayun to form the army for her own purposes. I don't know. All I know is that we met them here on this field. It was not a battle at all. It was a slaughter.

The formless spirits that serve the Queen can take any form and can change that form as they wish. They have no minds of their own, but are guided by her intelligence. She sees through each of their eyes, feels with each of their hands. It's like she's a single monstrous creature made of many different bodies, all of which do her bidding without question.

There was, of course, no hope of victory.

But I embraced the battle. I had no intention of ever becoming one of her formless ones. I preferred to die the second death—the death of utter oblivion and forgetfulness. Yes, like these poor souls here. See how they're nothing but bones again? Horrible.

And I thought I had died. I felt the bite of the death steel. I felt the pain of life ebbing from me again. This time, I thought, for all eternity.

Apparently not.

Oh, Gamayun? I fear that something far worse has happened to her. And to Parfyon. The Queen took them. I fear that she has added their essences to herself. Added the prophetic vision of Gamayun to the ambition of the Formless One.

Yes, it is terrible. Perhaps this truly is the end of all things.

KHAIDU LOOKED over at Aglaia and shook her head while rolling her eyes. Antomír couldn't help finding the gesture endearing, even as he felt a little stung at its being directed at him.

"Are all you Vasylli so dramatic?"

Aglaia chuckled dourly. "Some more than others," she answered. "I blame his father's side of the family."

Antomír couldn't believe how calm they seemed.

"Didn't I make it clear?" he said, a little louder this time. "The Queen not only hasn't been stopped, she's gotten much stronger. The tenacity of Parfyon of Nebesta and the vision of Gamayun? This is catastrophic!"

"Oh, we know that," said Aglaia.

"So what do we do?" Antomír almost screamed.

"Well, it looks like that's about to be determined for us," said Khaidu, looking over the field of slaughter.

Antomír turned to look.

A mountain stood in the middle of the battlefield, where the bones of the dead had been. Instead of lying in heaps on the plain, the bones had been assumed by the mountain, and now they formed a kind of macabre design on the slopes, interspersed with stone and greenery and what looked like . . . fabric.

Oh no . . .

He looked up to the summit of the mountain and saw a face, crowned with a boulder-strewn peak. Beneath the crown, two eyes like pits of fire burned above the features of the face, which before had been little more than a suggestion etched in the natural shapes of rock and trees. But now, that face had become more familiar, more human. Its eyebrows were dark and too thick for beauty. Its mouth was slightly open, in a mocking expression that Antomír knew all too well. And then he realized that the crown had two vulture wings rising from each side.

All hope fled. The Queen of the dead had subsumed Gamayun, the Day-Seer. He shuddered to think what that meant. That she could see the future, or at least some possibility of it, seemed inevitable. But would this abomination of amalgamation be able to sing the futures into being as Gamayun had?

"Well, that feels . . . wonderful," said the Queen of the dead.

"She can speak," said Antomír, in the dour half-humor of those convicted to death.

"I have not spoken in . . . well, I've lost count. All thanks to you, little princeling. Take them."

Shadowy figures bristling with sharp limbs like knife-edges appeared out of the corner of his vision. With icy gauntlets, the dead warriors herded Antomír, Aglaia, and Khaidu closer to the Queen of the dead. As they walked toward her, the landscape seemed to blur past them, as though it were not they who moved through it, but the landscape that moved past them.

Finally, they stood in the place where Antomír had first seen the final sparks of the fruits of life and the pouring down of the lifeblood of the worlds into the Realm of the Dead. He looked up. The roots of the trees in the Heart of the World above them were insubstantial, like nightmare shapes made of fog. There was no light, except for the dark red glow of the eyes of the Queen. In that lurid light, the moor-like landscape looked like a huge bowl of blood surrounded by a rim of stones, like the lip of a monstrous goblet. Antomír, Aglaia, and Khaidu stood in the exact middle of it.

All around them, rising from the ground, looking like

something foul being birthed in the red-flecked mud, the shapes of the dead rose to take their place of worship before their queen. Antomír tried to see if any of them looked like Parfyon, but they all seemed to lack distinct features. He had last seen Parfyon felling the dead warriors like trees, but no one could have stood up to their onslaught for long. He saw no sign of Parfyon.

For some strange reason, that gave him hope.

"It is time!"

This time, the Queen of the dead spoke both with her lips and with that inner voice that pierced all the way into the depths of his being.

As she spoke, she raised her hands and began to grow. She grew and grew, until the tips of her fingers touched the roots of the trees of life, far above. At her icy touch, the roots shriveled, turned black, and writhed into slimy shapes that looked like mirror images of the twisting forms of the dead in the mud around Antomír.

The Queen grew even more.

Her hands tore at the firmament separating the Realm of the Dead from the Heart of the World. It shattered like ice. The waters of the lifeblood of the worlds poured over her head. She screamed in elation. Colors flared in her face. It became flesh-colored, human, except for its monstrous size. The waters continued to pour over her body and her rocky skirts, transforming them into a gigantic facsimile of an ancient dress of gold-embroidered cambric in deep red and purple tones. Her crown was dark gold, and Gamayun's wings were encrusted with blue and green gems.

The waters continued to pour down, filling the bowl that they all stood in. All the Queen's faceless and indistinct followers firmed up into individual faces and bodies of all different shapes and sizes. They all shared one thing in common: expressions of fierce loathing, their eyes directed at the world above as though they could immolate it with the power of their hatred.

The lifeblood of the worlds lapped at Antomír's feet, and he felt a jolt of electricity. Pain, joy, anger, the smells of salt sea and cinnamon tea, the taste of roasted boar with currant sauce, the sparkle of early sun on the waters around Ghavan Isle—they returned to him. He was whole. He was alive.

The waters passed through them and into the ground. The ground flowered, the grass transformed from grey to green, the trees reveled in mottled bark. Even the turbid waters of the dark land turned bright blue.

But it didn't last.

There was not much water left in the Heart of the World. And now it ran out.

The Queen, as she turned back into stone and wood, screamed again. Her followers looked like barely animated statues frozen in poses of terrible longing. And the deadness pulled at Antomír again, dulling his sensations, confusing his mind, lulling him to sleep.

"You see what they have taken from us?" exclaimed the Queen. "Well, no more. Now is our time to take."

She grew even more. The rest of the separation between the Heart and the Realm of the Dead shattered. The earth bubbled at Antomír's feet. All around him, the forms of the dead scrabbled to climb up the skirts of their queen.

"Come on!" whispered Khaidu. Then suddenly she had two knives in her hands and had felled two of the dead guards still holding them. She moved faster than a deer running away from a wolf. All five of the guards lay in an indistinct heap at her feet. How had she done that?

Then it came to him: she must still be alive, truly alive. An anomaly in the Realm of the Dead. Perhaps they might escape from this disaster yet.

Khaidu ran up the stone skirts of the Queen. Aglaia immediately began running after her. None of the Queen's servants so much as budged. Their attention was wholly focused on their queen. Antomír tried to follow Khaidu, but his feet were like cotton wool. They would not move. Aglaia returned to him.

"One last fight, my boy. I know you have it in you," she said. Her eyes were soft, gentle. They reminded him, dimly, of what it meant to be alive.

He found his feet and lumbered behind Aglaia until he reached the growing mountain. As soon as all three had set foot on it, they were launched upward with the rest of the still-growing peak. They passed the groves of the Heart, the once luminous trees now shriveled and black. They rose toward the far sky of the Heart, which Antomír now saw was also of light-colored stone. They were about to crash into Vasyllia Mountain itself. But the rock-sky shattered at the touch of the Queen's black-gauntleted hand. A black, star-flecked sky beckoned to them as to a long-lost sister. Finally, the mountain stopped growing.

Antomír, Khaidu, and Aglaia were still too low on the mountain to see where the Queen had stopped.

"Hurry," said Khaidu, even as she continued to run up. Antomír wanted with all the power of his will to sit still, to become one with the mountain, to melt his self into the singular will and intention that was the Queen of the dead. But he followed Khaidu.

They climbed for what felt like hours. The ever-present forms of the dead, who paid them no attention, littered their path like jagged boulders on a mountain pass. But the three of them steadily made headway, coming closer and closer to the shoulders and head of the monstrous Queen.

Before they reached her, Khaidu stopped. Antomír reached her level and gasped at the sight.

"Is that . . . Is that a throne?"

23

The eight days passed like a single afternoon. They were pleasant days, all in all, filled with the kind of quiet introspection that Voran had had no time for during the last twenty years. In his youth, he had always been the kind of man to disappear for days in the wilderness, ostensibly for the hunt, but actually to breathe in the resinous air of a pine grove and to lie on a tree branch staring for hours at the slowly moving stars. But that sort of indulgence had not been his since the Vasyllian days.

So he tried to enjoy the hours now, even as they sped by him. But the spectre of death, and worse still, the need to accept it with joy, haunted him, even during sleep. He had dreams that began as ambles through fields of gold and ended with decapitation. By the third or fourth day, even the mixed fragrance of lily of the valley and chokecherry that greeted him every time he woke up could no longer give him joy.

The Shuudan didn't return. He was left entirely alone. He didn't even see any servants, though food was left for him every day. No matter how early he woke up, it was always already there—a platter of fruit, bread, nuts, and a bit of dried meat—delicious and filling, if simple fare. He hardly finished half of it—not that he wasn't hungry. As death faced him, he was finding a renewed appetite for everything that reminded him of the fullness of life—memories of joys and failures both, the pleasure of food and drink, the touch of chokecherry flower filaments between his fingers.

How was he supposed to give it all up? Especially now that he had, for the first time in so many years, been able to enjoy life, if only in solitude, if only for a short time.

But such thoughts never lasted very long. He knew, with the clarity of rational thought, that he must do this. He must be the Healer to the end, especially if that end were to be life-giving.

After all, if Rogned's willing self-sacrifice caused the prosperity of Karila, could not the self-sacrifice of Voran cause the prosperity of all Three Lands?

That thought kept coming, no matter how many times he felt guilty for it. He couldn't help it—he had been forced, he felt, into the role of a chosen savior of the world. Except now, when his moment was at hand, he wanted nothing more than to lie on soft grass and dream about the past.

So it was with relief, mixed with fear, that he heard the door open on the eighth day to admit the Shuudan. This time, Sagynduk had come with her. Voran got up from the bench where he had been sitting the whole morning, and almost ran to Sagynduk.

The white-haired old man had no expression on his face at all, or at least none that Voran could distinguish. But Voran no longer looked for signs in others' faces to determine his best course of action. He was done playing the role of Voran the Healer. He would simply be himself. And so, he almost fell on the poor old Karilan in his haste to embrace him, but also to fall at his feet.

"Sagynduk, I'm so sorry," he kept trying to get out, in between sobs and laughs. "I never . . . you have to understand . . ."

"Oh, the Vasylli," said Sagynduk, not smiling, though there was a chuckle lurking in the corners of his eyes. "So emotional."

Voran laughed, embraced the old man's knees, and abandoned himself to weeping.

It felt like being reborn.

"Voran," said Sagynduk finally. "I forgive you. We all do. Come. I wish to be with you at your test."

"Test?" asked Voran, not quite comprehending.

"It may not work, after all," said the Shuudan. "Without your fervent desire, without your willingness, this sacrifice will be empty."

She had not meant it to make him feel guilty, he knew that. But the weight of the world was once again on his shoulders. It had once been a comforting burden, reminding him of his calling. But he was heartily sick of it.

"Let's go," he said, hearing the heaviness in his own voice.

He caught the Shuudan's glance as he passed her. She looked frightened. That only made him feel more guilty.

A CROWD of people met Voran at the base of the tower. They were hushed, nearly silent except for an unusual amount of whispering and rustling of fabric and shuffling of sandaled feet on the dusty paving stones of Karila City. Expectation hung on the sunny air like a fog you couldn't quite see. Voran stopped, struck dumb by the looks on their faces. None of them were at all negatively disposed toward him. No one seemed to want him to come to harm. But why? He had been the reason for Rogned's death! They would still have their favorite son, if not for him.

What a pair those two would have made, thought Voran. Rogned and the Shuudan. Truly, a Karila ruled by them would be like a renewed Vasyllia of the elder days.

Without any visible sign, the crowd parted in front of Voran and the Shuudan. They left him a straight path through the center of the city directly to the stela at the gates.

"Go, Voran. You must prepare yourself," said Sagynduk behind them.

He meant the suit of armor and the sword—Voran knew it instinctively. He began to walk toward it, the Shuudan by his side, never lagging though she was much shorter than he. She seemed to be floating over the surface of the paving stones while he lumbered like an animate lump of rocks. He felt coarse next to her.

That feeling receded, and behind it came a dread he felt like a sucking in the pit of his stomach, spreading out to his chest, then to his head. He thought he might faint. He had nearly given his own soul to the Raven for a chance at the Blade of Covenant. And now, he was to receive it freely? Was this irony, or simply how things must be?

He saw, as he approached, that the stela had a narrow set of stairs carved into it, curving upward. Too narrow for two people side by side.

"You must go alone," the Shuudan said. "And be careful."

She still looked frightened, and Voran wondered what sort of test there might be at the top of that stela. He nodded once, feeling like he should smile for her, but then sensing that he was now beyond any need to conform his emotions to the needs of others. There was nothing between him and his death, save his own will. He needed to focus on that.

He climbed up. The stairs were narrow, even for him, and a few times the same dread he had felt moments before flared inside him, and he tottered in place, nearly falling backward to his death on the pink paving stones. He imagined the sight of his own body splayed in a pool of widening red amid the dusty pink. But he climbed on. It took longer than he thought it would, as though there were some illusion at work making the column seem shorter to the eye, an illusion unable to fool the tired legs that kept churning upward and upward. Finally, he stood before the dummy that wore the armor. The sunlight gleamed off the helmet—peaked in the Vasylli style, but with no hair plume.

He realized with a stab of shock that the golden breastplate had the engraving of a white moon, a sister in style to the sun that adorned the chest of Adonais in the Heart of the World. The terror flared inside him.

Was he being set up? Was this another ruse of the Raven? Had the entire encounter, the confession before Rathúdiel and the Shuudan, been another sham spectacle of the trickster? He must not put that mail on. He must not take hold of that sword. It would mean the Raven's final victory—he was sure of it!

But the Shuudan's eyes flashed on his memory. Her fluid grace, the way she seemed to dance through life—that was no illusion. There was nothing of the Hag's seductive vileness as he had experienced in the Lows of Aer, so many years before. No. As soon as he breathed deeply and descended into his deep heart with his mind, he found that place he had lost so long ago.

For the first time in months, he remembered the word.

Saddaí . . . Saddaí.

And he realized what it was. It was an invocation. More than that. It was a naming. And with the naming came knowledge, or the beginnings of it. Knowledge of the Unknown. The Unknown . . . Father?

Is that his name? Voran wondered.

"It is one of my names," said the voice in his deep heart.

Silence and peace flowed out of his chest. He tarried no longer, putting on the mail with the practiced hand of an old warrior. He left the sword for last. He gripped it, raised it, and its weight and balance were perfect for him, as though the original blade had been made with Voran exactly in mind. He laughed from the perfect absurdity of the thought.

Fire leaped down from the clear blue sky: flames of white gold. They danced and spun and alighted above the heads of each person assembled in the crowd below him.

Voran suddenly knew that time was short, that Rathúdiel was coming down from the Heights of Aer to this place. He rushed down the stela, almost flying in his joy.

THEY WALKED to the other end of Karila almost in a straight line. There, in a quiet square behind the Shuudan's palace, a place overgrown with moss and ivy and trailing flowers of gold and pale blue, stood an old hawthorn tree bursting with white blossoms. Just at the point where the trunk of the tree met the branches, it looked like someone had grown the hawthorn into the shape of a high-backed chair. The shape hadn't been carved out of the tree—that much was clear. It looked like a natural part of it, even down to the footrests and handrests.

In that chair sat Mirodara, the dendrite, niece of Llun the smith. Her eyes were closed, her head lolling in sleep that could have easily been mistaken for death. Voran hardly recognized her. She was thinned out, almost to her skeleton. Her hair was white and brittle, and the nails on her hands and feet had begun to curl in on themselves. She was a horrifying sight, especially as Voran remembered the astonishing vision of a pink-cheeked thirteen-year-old girl sleeping under an arbor of sweet-smelling vines, grasping the vial of Living Water.

How could this be the same person?

Then she opened her eyes. They were filmed with white like a blind person's, but with a ring of intense blue shining through the opal translucence. She looked directly at Voran, and he shivered in spite of the sun bearing down on his already warming mail.

"You don't have to do this, Voran," she said, in a voice more like a ninety-year-old woman's.

"Of course I do," he said, and at that moment, all doubts, all fears dissipated. He realized he wouldn't have to force himself to give his life for Mirodara. He would do it with pleasure.

Rathúdiel materialized out of nowhere, like a mist softly rising at morning. His presence was no longer like a hammer pushing Voran down. He was hardly even there: an echo of a hymn sung by a priest during midnight vigil.

"Will she finally find her peace?" asked Voran.

Rathúdiel smiled. It was confirmation enough.

"I know you have never felt true peace, Mirodara," said Voran. "You deserve it more than any of us, I think."

"Voran, I have peace to give you first," she said, her eyes now distant, pensive. "A vision, a final gift to you. Llun lives. And he is with Sabíana. They are both alive."

It was enough. He remembered the calm moment he had shared with Sabíana inside Vasyllia Mountain, only days before they had learned the true nature of Adonais in the Heart of the World. He remembered the intimacy of their simple conversation, the softness of her paralyzed body as it melted into his embrace. That moment held everything in it; he had suspected it then in his inner heart. Now he knew it for truth.

He would never see her again.

Llun would take care of her, he knew.

"Thank you, Mirodara," he said. "I am ready."

He gave the sheathed Blade of Covenant to Sagynduk and approached the hawthorn tree. Carefully, as though she were a newborn baby, he lifted her from her throne. She weighed hardly anything, but even the slight movement made her wince and cry out in pain.

"At the roots," said Rathúdiel to Voran's unasked question.

Voran laid her at the foot of the tree, just where the roots began to dig into the earth. Stepping over her carefully, he reached for the lowest branches and pulled himself up to the chair. It had fit her body perfectly, so he assumed it would be small for him. But he fit it just as well as she had. Somehow, that didn't surprise him all that much.

Rathúdiel now stood before Voran. He was smaller than he had been, though he still shone with power and presence. Now he was no taller than the hawthorn. Reaching his living-marble hand toward Sagynduk, he pulled out the formerly rusted blade. As he grabbed it, Voran saw that it had a familiar mark just under the handguard. It was a feather, all aflame. The sign of the Warriors of the Word, the same sign that Tarin's sword had had.

It was fitting.

From that brand, fire leaped forth and covered the entire length of the blade, though it remained sharp and shining in spite of the flames.

"Are you ready, Voran of the Vasylli?" asked Rathúdiel, solemnly.

Voran nodded. He kept his eyes open.

Rathúdiel stabbed him in the heart.

Several things happened at once. The blood spurted out of him like a river, falling directly on Mirodara's emaciated body. A foul brown mist seeped out at the same time and seethed like a cloud of hornets, circling over Mirodara's body. Voran felt his own body go rigid. He knew the Raven was preparing to possess Mirodara. And he knew there was nothing he could do about it.

At that moment, he caught the gaze of the Shuudan. She was weeping. But she wasn't looking at Voran. She was looking at Rathúdiel.

"Forgive us," she mouthed.

Rathúdiel blossomed outward. It was like the unfurling of a banner, or the sudden flowering of a thousand roses. He was a column of white fire and wings, spinning in every direction. There were eyes—thousands of eyes—all over the column. And there was a thunderous song in the air, like a choir of a thousand Sirin.

"For the Realms," he thundered. "For these little ones."

Then the wings enveloped the mass of the Raven's brown, seething mist. The hornet-like writhing of that mist attacked Rathúdiel, and the majestic wings of white and gold shriveled. Some of them flared into lurid flame, then winked out.

In a blast of bluish flame, Rathúdiel vanished. So did the remnant of the Raven. The Shuudan fell on her knees, weeping.

Rathúdiel was dead—Voran knew it. But was the Raven? Somehow, he doubted it.

Voran felt his life bleeding out of him. He looked down at Mirodara. She was young again, asleep with exactly the same expression of half-smiling mischief he had seen at the wall of Vasyllia. She opened her eyes and smiled at him.

It is fitting.

He closed his eyes and felt his spirit leave his body behind.

It was a whirling sensation of being sucked inside out, then outside in again. With a shock, he realized he had eyes to open. He opened them.

End of Part III

PART IV

Eucatastrophe

INTERLUDE

If man is to sit in the Throne of the Gods, he must endure the seven baptisms of fire. The first is the soul bond with Sirin. The second is the passage from the Realm of Earth to the Lows of Aer. The third is the shedding of the skin of the old man. The fourth is the purification. The fifth is the first death. The sixth is the second death. The seventh is . . . (illegible)

An apocryphal and incomplete variant of "The Emulation of the Powers"

The Sayings, Appendix 10D

~

The assassins came for Rogned on a night of the full moon. That was Yarpolk's one mistake.

Rogned had always had a special love for the moon, and not only because the Karila of old had seen her as a queen of the night, a demigoddess of purity and virtue. She was also a being of white fire. And it was that fire that saved him.

The moon's light silvered the entirety of the moor where Rogned's army encamped. It was a high moor between ragged bits of mountain, but the place he chose for their rest had no sight of mountains in any direction, just uninterrupted sky. His Karilan side, the one that probably had some kinship with the Steppe people like the Gumiren, found peace in the gentle roll of the hills and dales, especially at night.

His army had spent a week resting between fierce battles—both victories—on their steady march closer and closer to the city of Nebesta. Voran had been gone for three weeks, and Rogned expected him back any day. The closer Voran's anticipated arrival, the more obviously anxious Yarpolk became.

Rogned had never been very good at reading people, but Yarpolk's state was unmistakable. He was afraid of Rogned, afraid of what he would do to Nebesta, his birth city, if there were even nominal resistance to the army's coming. The fervency of Rogned's followers' killings probably didn't help allay Yarpolk's fears. Even Rogned wondered at how his followers were capable of superhuman feats of valor, but equally inhuman acts of cruelty. So far, he consoled himself, they had not hurt women and children. It was no small comfort to him.

He had never sought out this kind of power, and it was grating on him almost constantly, like a shirt that persistently rubs at the same place on the neck, no matter how many times you wear it. The adoration in the faces of his people only got more pronounced. He knew his history; he knew where such adoration of human leaders always led: to holy war. And that was the one thing that the Three Lands could not survive—not now, not after so many years of internecine bloodshed.

Such thoughts, and others more gloomy, tortured him that night under the full moon. But because of them, he saw the assassins.

At first they were furtive shapes trying to move from shadow to shadow behind the tents. Then, they became bolder, coming out and hoping speed and surprise would be their ally. They shouldn't have tried. They should have known that such treachery could in no way touch Rogned. Not now that his connection with the Palymi named Rathúdiel was so intimate. He felt the god's presence, even in the middle of the day, when there was no sign of him anywhere. And at this moment, he felt Rathúdiel's gentle prod, like an iron brand between the shoulder blades, pointing him in the direction of Yarpolk's killers.

They had to be Yarpolk's men. There was no other explanation. Who else would have dared to try to kill him? Who else had so much to lose when Nebesta would fall, inevitably, to the unstoppable army of fanatics?

Rathúdiel spoke to him: "You cannot defeat them alone. There are too many."

Something stirred in Rogned's mind. The moon called to him with a woman's voice.

"The moon," said Rogned. "Her fire will make a fitting weapon. She has always been a beacon of virtue and goodness."

"Is it fitting to use such a beacon to kill?" asked Rathúdiel.

"Is there any other more fitting?"

Rathúdiel exuded doubt and confusion. It was profoundly disturbing to sense such things coming from one of his kind. They were always so sure of the how things must be.

"Have you considered that this may be a setup?" asked Rathúdiel.

"Something like, 'Rogned has gone mad and begun to kill his own'?"

"Moon-sickness," confirmed Rathúdiel.

Rogned chuckled. Perhaps he was right. But what could he do? He could only travel the road before him, turn along the paths presented to him. And there seemed only one now. He knew where it would lead, eventually. And he welcomed it.

Closing his eyes, he reached out with his hands toward the moon. Her fire was warm, supple, like fresh clay in his hands. He abandoned himself to his fury, and fire rained like arrows from the heavens down on the assassins of Yarpolk.

The assembled armies looked at Rogned with hatred.

What a change. And how quickly it occurred. Only now did Rogned appreciate the subtlety of Yarpolk's plan. Now, as he stood on a quickly built platform, his neck already in the noose.

"Look at him, all of you who come from all Three Lands!" boomed Yarpolk, in complete control of the situation, striding back and forth in front of Rogned like a predatory cat sizing up its prey. "This is what happens when you follow a madman."

It had all been quite brilliant. Yarpolk had apparently started to spread rumors of Rogned's moon-sickness on the night that Voran had left. It was a cunning move; after all, Rogned rarely slept now, and never when the moon was visible.

"He claimed to have been guided by a Palymi," continued Yarpolk, playing on the crowd like lutist on a twelve-string. "The wonders he accomplished—he said they were of the Heights. And perhaps they were. But he is only a man, as we all are. And no man can expect to walk with the gods and remain himself. Remain sane."

Rogned had assumed that Yarpolk miscalculated by sending the assassins during the night of the full moon. That had been a fatal mistake. Yarpolk knew that there was no possibility he could assassinate Rogned, not while Rogned enjoyed the protection of the Palymi. So Yarpolk had counted on Rogned protecting himself, and he had hoped it would be in spectacularly glorious fashion. Rogned's burning of the assassins with arrows from the moon had been a work of art perfect for Yarpolk's designs.

"But no more," Yarpolk said, his voice softer now, edged with sorrow. Truly, he was a brilliant orator. "No more shall we follow this poor man. No more can we be subject to the whims of a moonstruck mad creature. I pity him, as I'm sure you all do."

He paused, gloriously, for effect. No one even breathed.

"But no one is above the law. And murder must be recompensed with equal blood."

When Rogned's followers had found the corpses, Yarpolk had put on a show worthy of song. Shock, surprise, horror—he had clearly prepared for this moment, but no one saw it other than Rogned. Yarpolk had always been an effective leader of men. Now was his moment.

Rathúdiel, invisible to anyone save Rogned, spoke quietly as Rogned stood, the noose around his neck, awaiting the final horn call signaling his execution.

"The law of sacrifice. Had you been planning on it all along?"

Rogned thought about it. He had twice before tried to rush the encounter with the Heights through a hastening of his own death. But that had been inspired by arrogance and self-indulgence. He was grateful now that Voran had saved him. But this was different. All unjust deaths, he knew, were rewarded by outpourings of unmerited and unexpected grace from the Heights. That was as true as the fact that the moon came up at night. He hoped his death would be found worthy.

"No, I had not planned it. Not really. But it is the only way."

"There is always a multiplicity of ways. But you do have a flair for the dramatic."

"Always," agreed Rogned.

The horn call sounded. The platform fell away. Rogned dropped.

❧ 24 ❧

Voran's eyes took several minutes to make sense of the bizarre surroundings. The first thing he saw was a hearth, but it wasn't in the middle of the room. It was in an indentation in the wall, surrounded by a brick-layered pipe that led up to the paneled ceiling, and apparently allowed the smoke to leave the room by expelling it through the roof. He had never seen anything like it. Then he noticed that the darkness of the room was at least partly due to dark wood paneling that covered all the walls. The panels were intricately carved, down to the smallest detail, depicting moments in history.

He saw battles, victory feasts, many scenes of kings on thrones, a few encounters of High Beings with kings and commoners alike. It was like a history lesson of the Three Lands from the moment of the Covenant to the reign of Cassían and his capture of the Raven.

Nothing more recent than that. Voran found that very interesting.

It almost distracted him from the fact that he was dead. Or was he?

Then he realized that he sat in a tall chair with ridiculously comfortable velvet cushions. There were two other chairs, both facing the same wall hearth. A young woman with dark eyes and dark hair pulled back into a severe arrangement of layered plaits sat in one. She seemed incapable of smiling, but she exuded goodness in the way that some people do, even when physically repulsive. Not that she was repulsive at all. She was a classic Nebesti beauty, complete with dark eyebrows on pale skin and sharp features that complemented each other perfectly.

He inclined his head toward her. She returned the gesture, but did not smile.

The other chair also had a figure sitting in it. It was . . .

It was Rogned.

Voran flew up, then realized he had hands and feet and could feel them. This was not what he had expected of being dead. Rogned, seeing his confusion, laughed heartily, his mouth open and his entire body shaking with contagious mirth. The woman smiled, and her eyes danced.

"Rogned . . . are you . . . good Heights . . . what is . . . I don't . . ."

Rogned got up and embraced Voran. He felt warm. He felt solid. He felt alive.

What was going on?

The woman cleared her throat, as though slightly embarrassed. Rogned disentangled himself from Voran and looked at her with a flush on his young face.

"Yes, of course, Alienne. We don't have much time, I know."

"Please, I don't begrudge you your joy," she said in voice like low wind chimes. "But time waits for no man, as they say."

Voran sighed with intense contentment. But still, something remained. Something more wonderful was coming. Rogned spoke.

"Voran, you must be very . . ."

"Confused, yes," Voran answered. "But I think I can guess. All three of us accepted a death of sacrifice willingly."

"Even joyfully," said Alienne. Voran wondered about her story, but it was not the time to ask.

"Surely there have been more than we three?" asked Voran, but chided himself immediately. The answer was obvious.

"We represent our cities and our people. Vasyllia, Nebesta, and Karila are all present."

"And this place?" Voran pointed at the panels. The figures seemed to dance in the low firelight.

"A threshold, of sorts," said Alienne.

Of course. A threshold to the encounter. The reckoning that all of them had wanted. The answer to all their questions. He looked around again. It was a strange, surprising place. He had expected something more imposing. A mountain peak, perhaps. Something like the place where the tree had wept tears of Living Water. Nothing quite so domestic.

He turned around. There was a door behind them. It was shut, leaving the entire room in shadows and firelight.

Then, the door burst open. Hail and sleet and wind rushed into the room. They three were drenched to the bone, but the fire continued to burn. The weather faded. Then came lighting and a burst of sunlight so hot, the panels began to glow. Voran was dried in an instant and began to grow unbearably hot. Then, the door slammed shut. Silence fell. Voran looked at the fire in the hearth, and realized he had missed something.

There was a sapling in that fire—a tiny aspen with shivering orange leaves. The fire danced on the branches, through the translucence of the leaves, but the tree was not consumed.

He was in the presence of the Heights. Perhaps this was the Heights of Aer, or some form of it that he could understand with his human mind.

As Voran stared silently at the sapling, he heard the voice. It was the same voice that had spoken to him on the top of the column in Karila. It seemed to be inside him. He turned around, but saw no one. The room was totally dark now, save for the sapling and the fire. The panels seemed to have melted into darkness. The chairs were no longer there. Voran saw that all three of them were on their knees, their entire selves intent on the sapling and the fire.

"Welcome, my children," said the voice. "Do you come to seek your rest?"

None of them dared answer. Both Rogned and Alienne seemed to be waiting for Voran to speak first. Perhaps because Vasyllia, for all its fallenness, was still Mother of Cities.

"No, Father," he said. "We seek justice for our innocent dead."

"Ah . . ." The voice sounded infinitely sad. "You do well to seek this. The laments of countless sufferers have come to my ears, and now I hear all of them, even those yet to come, in your voice, Voran of Vasyllia."

He said no more. Voran did not feel anything but warmth from that presence, nothing but encouragement. So he spoke.

"Father, can justice be found in the Realm of the Living?"

"Oh my Voran," said the voice. "I could enforce justice in a split second of your time. But there is justice, and there is freedom. Yet even with both of these, there is still a lack."

"Mercy," said Alienne in a half-whisper.

"Mercy must season justice, yes," said Rogned. "But freedom dictates that there may always be someone to choose neither one."

"Why must it be so, Father? Why did you not create us to desire nothing but mercy and justice?"

"Because of love."

Voran didn't know who said it.

"Love is impossible without the freedom to reject it," said Alienne. "To reject mercy and justice too."

"Has there ever been a place or a time when people have always chosen love freely?" asked Voran.

"No," said the Father, and the sorrow in his voice was mountainous.

"I don't understand, Father," said Voran. "Would it not be

better to create all of us with no capacity for anything other than love?"

"A world of automatons," said the Father, using a word Voran didn't understand.

"There is another fate awaiting us, isn't there?" asked Rogned, his face shining.

"Union," said the Father. "Oneness in multiplicity. Endlessly growing love."

The onion that, once peeled, grows ever larger with each successive layer—Tarin's model of the Realms—that was what the Father was talking about.

"You are always calling us, and not only us," said Voran. "All created things. Onward and upward, for all times. A helix always moving toward you, but never arriving."

"Can we see you?" asked Alienne.

"Not in this age," said the Father. "There will come a time . . ."

But he didn't finish his thought. He changed the subject.

"My children. The Realms balance on the tip of the knife. I have never destroyed my creation for the sake of its rebirth. But if I must, I shall. You can prevent it. If you do not . . ." He let the rest trail off.

"What must we do?"

"You must sit in judgment."

Voran gasped. The Raven had lied. Or he had not known. The Throne of the Gods was not a tool to force the hand of the Heights. It was a judgment seat.

Oh, Gods, no. Voran thought. How could he ever do such a thing?

He looked at Alienne and Rogned. They waited for him. So, apparently, did the Father. Why him?

But there could be no answer to that. It simply was.

"Father, we will sit in judgment."

Relief welled up inside Voran, and he saw it reflected in Alienne and Rogned's eyes.

"I will be your mouth, my children. Do not worry about what to say. You will know."

The fire flared brighter than their eyes could endure. The sapling grew, and they seemed to be drawn into it. Into the fire. Voran relaxed his muscles and closed his eyes. In his deep heart, he felt an overflowing of water. Living Water. And he knew what they must do.

He opened his eyes. He stood on a high spur of rock, under a sky of intense cerulean with not a shred of cloud anywhere to be seen. Before him was an ocean, rimmed like a half-moon on his side by ragged rocks, the tips of a high mountain range. He turned around. He stood in front of a stone throne with no back to it, the seat large for any human being. Behind the throne rose an oak tree so immense that its top was invisible to the eye. Alienne was at his right, Rogned at his left. Voran walked to the other side of the throne, and almost lost his breath.

Below the roots of the oak tree, which seemed to be hanging on nothing but air, Voran saw Vasyllia, far below him. It flickered with red, amid a torrent of grey-white steam. To either side of him, the twin falls of Vasyllia poured down into what looked like a cauldron. Vasyllia was on fire.

He turned to Rogned. "The Throne of the Gods is on the tip of Vasyllia Mountain," he said.

Rogned shrugged his shoulders. "I suppose you've always been right about Vasyllia." There was no rancor in his voice.

"And that, my brothers," said Alienne, pointing across the ocean, "is the tower of Gamayun. This is the Sea of Time."

"The crown of the Realms," said Voran, not quite knowing how he knew what to say.

An opalescent tower did stand in the midst of that ocean, its top intertwined with the branches of the world-oak. As the sun played on the waves lapping the shores of the tower's distant island, Voran saw that the current had different colors and shapes, though mostly the sea was a churning dark grey, close to black.

"But what is that?" said Rogned, pointing to their right.

Voran turned to see a large cone of rock, higher than the rest of the peaks ringing the Sea of Time. There was something vaguely human-shaped about it, as though it were a colossal monument to some ancient queen.

Then, it moved. Arms rose above what Voran now saw was a head, crowned in stone, with black wings extending up and out like horns. A horrible stench rose from that creature, inundating Voran.

"I am the Queen of the dead," said the abomination. "I come to sit on the throne. Get out of my way. Or be annihilated."

$ 25 $

A delaida stood alone in a circle of brandished spears. Just outside her peripheral vision, she felt, more than saw, Batuk try to break through the circle to reach her. He didn't, whether kept behind by the Vasylli or Etchigu or both, she couldn't tell. She had no time to guess. Any minute now, some frightened warrior of her father's would simply run her through. Then there would be no one to stop the Artisan's designs.

She was so intent on surviving that she had no time to think of what had just happened. Her father had just died.

"Don't move!" someone yelled at her, though she hadn't so much as twitched.

Afraid to look at anyone, lest they think she were trying to bewitch them, she looked down. She immediately wished she hadn't. Mirnían was hardly recognizable as human—more a jumble of bones with skin sticking to them. A few tufts of white hair jutted at odd angles from unexpected places. The opulence of his clothing, the shine of his royal mail and helmet —it was like a mockery of kingship.

She heard Sabíana shout something, but she couldn't make it out. Instead, she dismounted, slowly, her hands extended palms-out in surrender. Whether it was her movement or Sabíana's command, her father's men looked shaken. She could easily see this, even with quick, furtive glances. She chanced a longer look. They were mostly not staring at her anymore at all, but at a circle of Vasylli warriors that seemed to have appeared out of nowhere, who were encircling *them*. Two concentric circles now, with her at the center. Amid the shouting of all the men, chaotic and more akin to the braying of hounds than rational speech, Adelaida locked eyes with Sabíana.

Sabíana's eyes were overflowing with shared pain, so much that Adelaida almost lost what remained of her self-control. Could it be that Sabíana believed her innocent?

"Don't move!" commanded Sabíana, her words directed at Mirnían's men. "If you do, you will be cut down."

Mirnían's men were outnumbered three to one, and now Adelaida saw more warriors hurrying out from the gates of Vasyllia toward the confused scrum near their Darina. Even with her limited experience, Adelaida knew this could turn catastrophic very quickly for all concerned.

Batuk and Etchigu retreated, raising their weapons and indicating their readiness to move back, away from Vasyllia. Their fellow Gumiren joined them. At a gesture from Sabíana, they were allowed through. Batuk looked at Adelaida with wide eyes, but his expression remained contained. She knew how hard it was for him to contain himself, and she looked away, for his sake. The bear riders—five of them—were next to leave the field. That left ten of Mirnían's Ghavanites, men Adelaida had known since childhood. All of them looked ready to skewer her like a boar.

"Disarm!" commanded Sabíana. "This child is under my protection. She is guilty of no crime. This is Raven's devilry—can't you see?"

A few of the men wavered, and their spears tottered. But a few others looked like one wrong move from Adelaida, and they would kill her in a second, with no thought for their own lives. Such was the loyalty Mirnían had earned from his men.

Adelaida lowered her hands and breathed out. Her head spun, and she knew that soon, no matter what, she would simply collapse. But events were outside her influence, finally. The Artisan had played his last card. Whether he won or not did not depend on Adelaida. She almost smiled at the rush of relief she felt, even as she stared at bared steel.

"Retreat!" Sabíana raised her hand, and her face was dire. "Or I give the final word. I do not want to spill Vasylli blood, but by the Heights, I will!"

They retreated. The spears clattered to the ground, dropped by all of Mirnían's men nearly at the same moment. Their faces had turned grey, and they seemed unable to tear their eyes away from the corpse of Mirnían at their feet.

Sabíana dropped her hand, and four mounted warriors surrounded Adelaida and led her away from her father's body.

Something tore inside Adelaida. And it was as though all that had kept her together disappeared in a single moment. She heard herself, almost outside of her own body, screaming something about her dead father. The warriors forcefully took her toward Sabíana, who had dismounted. She took Adelaida in her arms and embraced her, hard. She was weeping too.

Adelaida grabbed Sabíana's shoulders and shook her violently. She screamed and screamed. Sabíana's red-rimmed eyes were bursting with tears, but she said nothing. She only looked at Adelaida with large brown eyes that tried to absorb Adelaida's pain, siphoning it off her.

Adelaida stopped shaking her and dissolved, nearly insensate, into the arms of her aunt. She remembered nothing else for a long time.

~

IT WAS with a mind incapable of making connections between things that Adelaida saw that she was being taken under honor guard into Vasyllia. The scale of the city no longer moved her. The sparkling of the waters coming from the chalices that caught the falls no longer inspired her. The ever-present color of growing things, though even here the fading was taking hold, ceased to make an impression on her heart. She saw. She did not understand.

A palace with seven broken towers, a courtyard with cracks in the paving stones, a series of staircases in hallways hung with tapestries over the cold stone—all of this her mind registered, but her heart did not make sense of. Only when her body hit the softness of a down mattress—then, for a brilliant second, she felt physical relief that burst like a sunrise into relief of her heart's pain. But then, she fell asleep—which felt like complete oblivion.

COMING OUT OF IT, Adelaida had the sinking sensation that she had no body, that her spirit was floating around in unfamiliar places. Then, pinpricks in her hands pulled her attention downward, and she saw two long-fingered hands, unexpectedly clean and wearing an unfamiliar silver ring, resting on a coverlet of the whitest white she had seen since Ghavan.

Ghavan. Her home. She was Adelaida. And she would never again see her home.

The room came into focus. Next to her bed stood a solid wooden table with a high-backed chair that had a red velvet cushion on it and a muslin throw draped over the back. A simple clay jug of something that smelled sweet and sour at the same time stood on the table, next to a plate of the same kind of solid, unadorned clay that was covered in cheese and grapes. She hadn't had grapes in what seemed like years.

Suddenly, she realized she was famished and thirsty. She almost fell out of bed in her haste to get to the table, for a moment disoriented by the unfamiliar feel and look of the pale linen underdress that she was wearing. It was softer than anything she owned, and very pleasant on her body.

With a lunge of terror, she had a thought: *Have I died?*

But that was absurd. Everything here was the height of the sensual, not the spiritual. She sat down and wrapped herself in the muslin throw. She ate, and she drank, and she almost paid no attention to the tears that dripped into her drink, and the sobs that racked her body at uncomfortable moments, causing her to choke on her grapes.

"I didn't mean to kill him," said the one voice she wanted to hear least in all the world. It sounded like the Artisan stood behind her, around the area where the door was still shut. Adelaida suddenly felt that this place was a prison, not a paradise for the senses.

She didn't answer him. But now the food was ashes in her mouth, and the mead was too sour to drink.

"I'm worse off than I thought," he continued in a voice that mimicked sincere regret. He did that so well. "I should have known. Every new body I took—it fed me less and less. I burned through each one more and more quickly. Now, it seems I can no longer hold a body at all."

She wanted to throw the clay jug at him, just to see something physical strike him. To hurt him in some way. But he had no body.

"I only meant to . . . to scare you. I wasn't planning on possessing . . . your father . . . for any longer than a few moments."

"It was . . . it was enough." She croaked out, barely recognizing her own voice.

Silence filled the room. She felt his discomfort with it, his desire for resolution, but she refused to indulge him. She held onto the silence like a drowning woman holding onto a piece of driftwood.

"Well, I suppose you'll be happy now. There is no possible way for me to join with my brother and sister, the Raven and the Queen. I am dying. My spirit is in tatters now. Can't grab onto anything anymore."

She persisted in staring at the stone floor. She noticed that the corners were covered in piles of dust and woodshavings.

"And at the last possible moment, too," he said, persisting. "I don't suppose I need to keep silent now. The Raven and the Queen are here. In Vasyllia. Or rather, on the summit of Vasyllia Mountain. At the Throne of the Gods."

Slowly, dimly, Adelaida felt the old stirring of life back in her chest. She looked at him. He was an old, withered man with a matted beard of yellowish white and black hands with too-long fingernails. This is what he would have looked like on Ghavan if he had been abandoned there for thirty years alone, living off scraps like a scavenging beast.

She couldn't help it. As much as it made her physically ill— she was sure she would hurl right onto the floor—she pitied the Artisan.

With that pity came something strange inside her. A light, warm and satisfying, inside her chest. With it came insight. She knew. How? It didn't matter. Then she saw, in her mind's eye, the face of Derzhava, and she smiled knowingly at her. Seer to fellow seer.

"It is too late for them," she said. "They have found no bodies either. Voran, Mirnían, and Antomír are all dead. The only heir of Cassían left is Sabíana. And you know that the Sirin of fire protects her from you."

He had been standing. Now he crumpled onto the floor like an exhausted child, all arms and legs akimbo. He was pitiful.

"But it is not too late for you," she said. She knew what she had to say now. Her heart threatened to fail her before she did it, but it was too late to care about pain. There was not much time left—she knew it.

"Father," she said. The Artisan didn't look at first, then something in his expression changed. It focused, and his eyes shot up at her in shock. "Yes. I accept you. You created me. You are my father."

She needed to cry again, needed it like air to breathe. But the tears wouldn't come. The tearing inside her was unbearable.

"And I want you to know this, Father. You have nearly killed me by killing Mirnían. But you can give me, and the world, life again. By sacrifice."

His eyes grew into nearly all whites. He shook his head frantically, almost like a small child faced with some imagined terror of the night rising from the shadows painted by the moon.

"You are dying," Adelaida said in a whisper. "You know this. Everything you touch will die with you. That gives you a great gift. You can save me."

There were tears in his eyes. They fell on the stone floor, and actually left wet impressions, almost like real tears. That gave her the needed strength to continue.

"You made me," she said in a whisper that barely came out. "You know what that means, don't you?"

He shook his head, once, though his eyes couldn't leave hers.

"That there is some good left in you."

She could speak no more. Her head spun, and the world did a strange somersault around her. There was a dull thud, a flash of pain in her head, then . . .

❧ 26 ☙

S abíana rushed to Adelaida's room. The servants had been incoherent with worry. One had said she was dead. The other said she had fainted. The third had fainted herself.

It was Sabíana's eternal curse to be surrounded by incompetent fools.

But she found that her heart was doing frantic things in her chest as she started running down the hallways, incapable of maintaining the dignity demanded of a Darina. What did any of that matter? The world was turning itself inside out, miracle piled on top of catastrophe, and she was supposed to somehow maintain control of everyone else, not to mention herself.

The revelation that Mirnían had other children had shaken her. She had been sure that Antomír was the only child. His death was catastrophic, therefore, for the line and for Vasyllia. But this other child. Where had she come from? When had Mirnían managed to have a child who looked not a day younger than Antomír himself? Were they twins? But that was not possible, no.

Something about Adelaida made Sabíana feel intensely sad. That feeling only increased a motherly instinct she hadn't known she possessed. When all the men turned on her as though she were the cause of Mirnían's sudden—and clearly demonic—death, Sabíana had never felt surer of anything. She needed to give haven to this wonderful girl. She would have done it even if she had been a complete stranger. But Adelaida was dear to her. How? Sabíana could hardly understand.

She stopped at Adelaida's door, suddenly shaking all over. She looked at her hands like they were snakes slithering away.

Grab hold of yourself!

It was almost impossible. She needed to face the possibility that one of the servants had been right—that Adelaida was hurt, or worse, dead. Nothing was impossible.

She pushed the door with her whole self, not just her hand. Adelaida lay in a heap on the floor, her eyes half-open. A small stream of blood trickled down her cheek. Sabíana took a deep breath and plunged into the room. Gently, but firmly, she cradled Adelaida's head in her lap and felt her forehead. It was warm.

Adelaida twitched and moaned.

Thank the Heights.

The relief nearly made Sabíana faint. She closed her eyes while the room danced around her, then called loudly for the servants.

As they bustled around Adelaida's bed, Sabíana remembered an eerily similar scene, twenty years ago, when she had also encountered an impossible person—Otchigen, Voran's father, who had disappeared in the wilds years before. She had taken care of him personally in a room similar to this one. Like Adelaida, his appearance was unexpected. But he had turned out to be essentially a corpse animated by the Raven. Adelaida was not that. Surely not that.

The color had returned to Adelaida's cheeks by the time the servants had brewed, and brought, some mulled wine for her. She had drunk it with such evident surprise at its taste, just like a small child eating a sweet for the first time, that

Sabíana couldn't help but laugh aloud. Adelaida responded in kind, smiling for the first time since she had met her. It made an already beautiful face turn luminous.

"My father," Adelaida said, then turned greenish for a moment, before stilling herself and taking a long breath. Her self-control was almost preternatural, Sabíana thought. "Mirnían was sure that Vasyllia was in the grip of enemies. What happened? How did you become Darina again?"

"It's a long story," said Sabíana as she leaned back in her chair.

"I would welcome a long story," she said. What she left unsaid, but what Sabíana guessed, was that she needed a long distraction.

So Sabíana offered it. She told her of the nearly miraculous victories that the Sons of the Swan had over the Consistory's dog-men. How Aspidían's plan to control the population of the second and third reaches by spreading rumors of a false epidemic had made all the Vasylli so frightened that most of them didn't even leave their houses as battle raged in the streets of the city outside their very windows. How the first reach, through the long work of the Sons to serve and minister, as well as to fight, had won the commons back to the ideal of the monarchia. How Sabíana herself had been hailed as a savior returned.

It had been easier than she could have hoped.

Of course, that worried her more than anything else. There was likely another disaster just around the corner.

"What have you done with the Consistory men?" asked Adelaida, with an expression that made it seem that she felt sorry for them, too. Was there no end to this child's compassion?

"They're in the prisons they built themselves. A fitting punishment, don't you think?"

She smiled wanly and shook her head softly, more at her own thoughts than at anything Sabíana had said.

"Adelaida, I will soon go and parley with Mirnían's army. Anything you can tell me about them, about who will likely take power, anything at all . . . it will help us make a lasting peace. I do not want there to be any more bands of dispossessed warriors roaming the Three Lands, harassing peaceful people."

Adelaida nodded, all business now. She was about to speak, when she was distracted by something in the window.

"Is that?" she began . . . then her face turned ashen. "Oh no . . ." she breathed.

Sabíana was already at the window, her body braced for anything. She saw . . . she didn't understand what she was looking at. It looked like ten . . . no, fifteen suns were floating in the air above Vasyllia, growing larger and larger. Then, they unfurled, like a massive parody of chicks pecking their way out of shells and stretching themselves out into full length.

Except they weren't chicks. They were serpents with wings and jaws ringed with swordlike teeth. And they breathed fire.

Vasyllia was already burning before her eyes.

❈ 27 ❈

"I am the Queen of the dead," said the abomination with the voice of Gamayun. "I come to sit on the throne. Get out of my way. Or be annihilated."

Khaidu felt the thrum of the mountain beneath her, as though it were not a mountain, but a living body. This was a bit too dangerous, even for her tastes. Together with everyone on the mountain, she was intent on the massive throne on the upthrust of rock to their left, both sides of which were shrouded in mist as the Sea of Time fell in prismatic waterfalls behind it. Truly, it could be called a Throne of the Gods—it could easily seat three people of uncommon height, not just one. Still, she didn't quite see it as a throne—it looked like an organic thing, more a part of the mountain than something carved or created.

The tower over the Sea of Time was to their right. It was a conical, thin spire of white rock that reached into the world-oak, to disappear in its heights. Scalelike, iridescent designs played up and down the nearly sheer walls every time the sun shone from behind a cloud. There were no windows or doors or openings of any kind. Just a spire of rock, leading into the clouds.

The scale of everything was almost overwhelming. The Throne of the Gods to their left, mountains everywhere, and the Queen herself growing to a gargantuan size—what could Khaidu, or any human, hope to do?

And yet, everyone saw that three human-sized shapes stood on the throne, and haloes of color and power pulsed around them. She tried with all her strength to make out their faces, but they were too far away. All she saw was what looked like two men and a woman.

"Let's go see who they are," she said to Antomír and Aglaia.

Aglaia looked ready enough, but Antomír seemed to turn to stone at the suggestion. Why were Vasylli men all so sensitive? She scoffed quietly, trying to not show it openly.

But it wasn't some sort of masculine weakness. There was something wrong with him. He did seem actually rooted in place.

"I can't," he said, finally. "It seems . . . well, the dead cannot travel outside the Realm of the Dead. And the Realm of the Dead is . . . limited . . . to where the Queen is . . . it seems."

Well, that's annoying, thought Khaidu. If only he were to push a little harder, to desire it a little more intensely. She was sure he would be able to make it.

"Worship me!" screamed the Queen.

One of the three figures on the throne, a man, stepped forward. When he spoke, his voice thundered as though he were not a man at all.

"Worship is fitting only for the Most High," he said. "Abominations like you deserve only pity."

"That's . . ." Aglaia had turned pale, even though she smiled. "He made it."

Khaidu had recognized his voice too. Voran, Aglaia's son.

Something—a kind of foul-smelling brown mist—swirled around the face of the Queen with Gamayun's wings.

"Well, you're very late," said the Queen and opened her mouth wide. It grew and grew until the jaw looked unhinged, like a snake's mouth opening before sinking its fangs into its prey. Khaidu was disgusted, but fascinated at the same time, as the brown mist, which was now more like a cloud of shrieking bats, flew into the Queen's mouth. She closed her mouth, and her face . . . shifted. A beak grew in the middle of the Queen's face—a raven's beak—and the voice that now spoke to Voran was not one voice, but many.

"Well, my rat," the monstrosity said, looking at Voran and the other two, whom Khaidu still did not recognize. "It didn't happen quite the way I wanted it to. But we have done what we planned all those ages ago. We have united again. True, we have no body. But that doesn't matter as much as we thought it did."

Voran stood straight as a brandished blade, but he said nothing. Khaidu wished she could see his expression. She felt entirely useless.

"Are you so faithless that you would not wait for me, Raven?"

This was a new voice, one Khaidu did not know. An old man stood below them, on the rocky shore of the Sea of Time. He was almost bent over in half, utterly withered and wretched.

"Artisan? You're still alive?" boomed the Raven-Queen-Gamayun.

"Barely," said the pathetic figure. "But I made it. I am ready."

He closed his eyes and extended his arms out toward the abomination. He seemed to dissipate into fine, crystal-like sand that flew upward in swirling eddies and currents in fantastic shapes that reminded Khaidu of birds and flowers and trailing vines. Upward and upward the sand flew, toward the open beak of the monster. Finally, he was also consumed.

Khaidu wanted to get off the mountain more than she had ever wanted anything. This was the absolute worst place to be —she knew it. But Antomír's pale, miserable face—it decided her. She wouldn't abandon him. Not now, at the end of all things.

She took his hand in hers and faced him, ignoring all the madness around them.

"I'm sorry, Antomír," she said, looking him in the eyes, not looking away. "I wanted to take you out of the Realm of the Dead. I failed."

He smiled wanly. Truly, he looked more exhausted than she had ever seen him.

"Go, little wolf," he said with gentle affection. "I do not begrudge you your life."

"You stupid Vasylli," she said. "I'm staying with you."

Awkwardly, quickly, before her good sense could stop her, she kissed him on the lips. Antomír looked shocked for a moment, then he smiled, and for the first time since she encountered him in the dead lands, there was pink in his cheeks.

He cupped her face in his hands and stared at her for a long time. She thought she would explode from the insistence of that stare. Then he leaned in and kissed her. His lips were slightly salty. She closed her eyes and leaned in.

The mountain quaked. Khaidu found herself in Antomír's firm embrace. She chuckled to herself. If he thought he needed to protect her, he was a greater fool than she'd first thought. But there was something pleasant about letting him think that he should protect her. The mountain quaked again, and now, chunks of it fell off and over the heads of Khaidu and Antomír.

"Look!" Aglaia said, pointing up at the abomination.

The creature was smaller, definitely, and there were cracks in the skirts of the Queen. They widened, and the earth under their feet quaked again.

"What's happening?" exclaimed Antomír.

It didn't matter what was happening. Khaidu had changed her mind. She was going to pull Antomír and Aglaia out of the grasp of Queen of the dead, if it was the last thing she did.

She grabbed Antomír's hand and yanked, as she jumped down and away from the mountain. The shapes of the dead around them were transfixed, staring at their queen in utter terror. None of the dead tried to stop Khaidu.

The earth quaked again, and now, it wasn't chunks, but boulders that broke off the Queen's body. As they ran, Khaidu chanced a backward glance at the Queen's face. The Raven's beak had cracked, and only shards of it remained. The Queen's face had lines in it, as though she were a hundred-year-old woman on her deathbed. Gamayun's wings were shedding stone feathers at an alarming rate.

"Wolfling!" cried Aglaia as they stumbled over protruding rocks, closer and closer to the edge of Queen's skirts, where good, hard, beautiful mountain stone of a dark purple and grey color beckoned to them. "Did you do something?"

Khaidu laughed as she ran. "Thank you for the compliment, old lady," she taunted. "But even I can't do *that*."

They were no more than twenty feet away from the edge.

Then, the mountain collapsed in on itself. There was a horrifying screech of many hundreds of voices as the entire massive body of the Queen broke and fell in, back into the Realm of the Dead under the earth.

Khaidu and Aglaia were on good, hard, Vasylli ground. Antomír wasn't. He was on the last remaining ledge of the Queen's skirts, which held on stubbornly to Vasyllia Mountain. It teetered dangerously. But he couldn't get off it. A man stood between him and the Realm of the Living. A man holding a bared sword, pointed at Antomír's heart.

"Parfyon," said Antomír to the man. "Hurry! Come with us. There is our escape."

But the man didn't answer. He had no expression on his face. If he ever had a personality, it seemed to have been erased with the fall of the Queen.

"Please, Parfyon. We can have life!" Antomír looked at Khaidu in desperation, but she felt her entire body go rigid. No, this was his ordeal alone.

"Parfyon!" A voice thundered from the throne. A woman's voice that echoed with power, but also with regret and pain.

The man turned around to look, even as cracks appeared between his feet. Any minute now, the ledge would collapse to fall back into the Realm of the Dead.

"Parfyon!" the woman called again, in a voice full of unshed tears. "Be the man you could not be before."

Parfyon's eyes seemed to take an eternity to focus, but then some cold, dreadful certainty covered his face. He dropped his sword. Antomír ran past him and jumped. Aglaia and Khaidu both steadied him, as his knees seemed barely able to bear his weight. He grimaced, and his face was stretched in pain. He looked down to his side. Blood seeped through his clothing.

"Damn," he said. "I knew it was too good to be true."

With a final crash, the last ledge collapsed. Parfyon was nowhere to be seen.

❦ 28 ❧

Voran watched the abomination of the Great Changer fall apart and collapse back into the abyss. The knowledge came over him with the stamp of certainty, as the Father had said it would. He turned to Rogned and Alienne.

"The third of the three changers, the one called the Artisan. It seems he had a change of heart."

"He sabotaged his own plan?" asked Alienne, uncomprehending.

"Yes!" said Rogned, understanding lighting up his features. "The evil ones never do account for the miraculous power of love."

"The Artisan was always a crafter, a creator," Voran told Alienne. "It seems that he created a simulacrum of life on Ghavan Isle. But the Father gave that simulacrum true life. She is named Adelaida, daughter of Mirnían and Lebía. And she loved her creator, though he was a creature of evil. It broke his heart, it seems."

"So is the Great Changer dead?" Alienne asked, her eyes filled with tears. Voran knew that the second loss of Parfyon would be more difficult than the first.

"No," said Voran. "He cannot die. But his judgment is coming swiftly."

"But first," said Rogned. "Vasyllia."

"Yes," they all three spoke at once and turned away from the Sea of Time. Below them, Vasyllia still burned. Below them, the serpents still spewed fire on everything that lived in the fallen city.

"And so they come at last," said Rogned, his gaze intent on a dark smudge in the distant sky.

"The Sirin have returned," said Alienne.

"And with them come the monks of Raven's Bane, bearing the final fruit of the trees of life."

Like the first drops of a spring rain after weeks of drought, the Sirin's song appeared with the whistle of wind rushing through reeds.

The serpents all stopped spewing fire from their mouths. Cries of frustration and agony erupted from them as they flew up, higher even than the peak of Vasyllia Mountain. They spun in on themselves and became fifteen suns of whirling fire. All save for one, who saw the three human beings standing on the Throne of the Gods. With a baleful eye, he snorted and joined the rest of his brothers.

"We will meet again, Zmei," said Voran, with the certitude of prophecy.

The waves of the Sea of Time rose on either side of the throne, reaching almost to the seat where the three stood. Voran turned back.

"The tower . . ." said Alienne.

"It's gone," said Rogned.

The crash of the broken stones had caused the water to rise. Voran turned back to watch it fall on Vasyllia. The chalices, tiny in his vision far below them, couldn't contain the rush of the waterfalls anymore. They cracked and broke under the strain. Wave after wave fell on a burning Vasyllia. Steam mixed with cloud until Voran saw the city no more.

He turned around, back to face the Sea of Time. He felt Rogned and Alienne behind him like a comforting hand on the shoulder.

"Come!" he commanded. "We call all the Powers, High and Low. It is the time of judgment."

They came. Palymi, Alkonist of all sizes and shapes, Majestva with wings like vast sails, living vessels bearing all the human beings who were called to the judgment. Last of all came the Sirin, with Lyna at their head. To his left, Voran saw Sabíana, Lebía, Adelaida, Batuk, Veles, and the other Children of the Priest-King. To his right, he saw Khaidu, Antomír, Aglaia, and the monks of Raven's Bane. Antomír bled from his side and leaned heavily on Khaidu. He looked like he had only moments of life left.

They were all here. It was time.

"Children of the Father Most High," Voran said, and his voice echoed. "Hear his judgement. Palymi, bind the abyss with chains unbreakable. Majestva, weave cords of fire around the chains. Alkonist, stand guard before the chains of fire. The Raven and his changers are forever banished to the abyss at the pit of the Realm of the Dead, there to await the final judgment of the Father at the end of all time."

A few of the Palymi, Majestva, and Alkonist bowed before Voran, then exploded into the unfurled movement of thousands of wings flying at once. He felt his eyes grow wide at the sight, but the torrent of prophecy did not let him wonder at it. He continued to speak.

"All those who seek to emulate the Darkness in life will join it in the abyss after life ends. There to await the final release, or the final punishment. The Realm of the Dead will once again be sealed from the Realm of Earth, and a guardian shall be placed there."

Veles, Almira, her husband, and Severuk, their golden wings burning like fire, walked forward.

"We shall go, with our people, who have lived lives too long extended by the Fountain of Youth," said Veles. "We shall shepherd the dead until the final days."

"I go as well," said Alienne, and now she had wings like the four guardians did. Voran felt a surge of sadness and affection for her. "I will try to find what is left of Parfyon. I must. I still love him."

In a moment as quick as thought, she stood with the winged guardians of the Realm of the Dead. They bowed to Voran. A Majestva of fire and wings enveloped them and disappeared in a flash of wings and eyes. After them, the Children of the Priest-King all bowed to Voran and disappeared as well. The torrent inside Voran was even stronger now, a waterfall that would burst out of his chest if he tarried.

"Vasyllia was once the seat of Covenant. But Vasyllia fell, and no longer can such a Covenant stand. And neither can Vasyllia stand. Vasyllia must rise. And you all, children of the Father Most High, will rise with Vasyllia. You are worthy. You have fought and come through the endless war. With Vasyllia you will rise. But not yet."

All the people who remained stared at Voran in expectation. He hardly felt himself anymore. Just the words spilling out of his lips. His heart hammered the steady rhythm: *Saddaí, Saddaí.*

"For Vasyllia will be set apart from the world. It will be a city on a hill above the clouds, a place no human being can reach by his own will. It will be a haven, a garden of anticipation for the coming of the One, the Mediator, who will unite not only the Three Lands, but the Three Realms of Death, Earth, and Aer."

Voran no longer felt his body. There was a glow about him, like white fire. He caught Sabíana's eyes, and they were filled with tears. Lebía was on her knees, her face in her hands.

"Until the One comes, Vasyllia will stand as a reminder to all who live in the Lowlands. A reminder that virtue is rewarded, and vice is given to the abyss. A reminder that though human life may be filled with bitterness and loss, there is a place where rest shall be given. A place where all who are worthy may await the coming of the Mediator and his final judgment."

"But who is worthy?" asked Antomír, and there was a challenge in his voice.

The answer was obvious, and Voran knew it himself—as Voran, even though the torrent of prophecy continued to impel him.

"All those who have a soul bond with the Sirin may find rest in Vasyllia the New, to await the coming of the One."

Antomír, with a groan, fell on his knees.

"Dar Antomír of the Vasylli," said Voran. "Your time is not yet come. The Father gives you second life. You must lead the exiles, the people who have not yet heard the Song of the Sirin, into the Lowlands. There, you must kindle the fire of Vasyllia the New in the hearts of all who will hear you. There, you must establish a new kingdom. There, all Three Lands will unite under your banner."

Antomír stood up, and there was color in his face again. He bowed before Voran.

"The monks of Raven's Bane go with the Dar of the Vasylli," said one of the monks.

Antomír, Khaidu, Aglaia, Adelaida, and Batuk were taken by another Majestva. The monks bowed, and disappeared in a blaze of white fire. No one was left at the foot of the Throne of the Gods, except for Sabíana and Lebía.

Lebía stared at Voran, and her eyes were red with pain and weeping.

"Voran," she said. "They killed my Mirnían."

The torrent of prophecy left Voran, and he was himself again. He came down to Lebía and Sabíana, and he enfolded them in his embrace.

Then the sky filled with Sirin, and they burst into song.

Feína flew down from the choir of her sisters and hovered

over Sabíana's head. Sabíana smiled for the first time. Aína flew down from the choir of her sisters, and she wept golden tears. The tears fell on Lebía's head, and she sighed. Lyna, last of all, flew down from the choir of her sisters, and she laughed for the first time in a millennium.

Voran felt tears falling down his face—hot, sweet tears that washed out the last vestiges of pain in his chest. He was himself again. And he was with his beloved.

Sabíana, her face assuming that soft rebuke that he had loved so much in his youth, inclined her head toward the throne. The unspoken words were clear: Have you forgotten Rogned?

No, he hadn't. He turned to him, arms around the waists of his beloved and his sister.

"Rogned, will you stay in Vasyllia?"

Rogned smiled his mischievous smile. "No, my friend. I have not yet stormed the Heights of Aer. How can I stop now?"

He laughed as fire enveloped him, filling him, until he was consumed in a blazing glory.

Antomír awoke extremely disoriented. He was lying in a field of new grass so bright green that it was nearly translucent. Khaidu lay near him. One of her eyes was open, but she seemed to have no interest in opening the other one. Antomír turned around and saw . . .

Well, *everyone.*

He stood up.

Behind him was a field of bodies. For a moment, he thought he had returned to the land of the dead. But that couldn't be. They were not bodies. They were sleeping forms, coming awake. He recognized hardly anyone at all, except for Aglaia. They all looked as confused and groggy as he felt.

The field sowed with awakening sleepers reached for at least a mile all the way to a wall of rock that was far higher than any mountain Antomír had ever seen. It was as though all the mountains of Vasyllia had been combined into a single peak so high that even the distant, wispy clouds of summer barely reached its ankles, so to speak.

"Is that what Voran meant?" asked Khaidu, still on the ground, though both eyes were now open.

"That Vasyllia the New is a place no one can reach by his own will?" Antomír asked with a rueful smile. "I imagine so, my love."

She blushed at that declaration of his. They had kissed, but it was in the Realm of the Dead, technically. They had only just awoken to the living world. And they had not spoken the words to each other yet.

He touched his side, where the killing wound had been. There was nothing there but unbroken, healthy skin.

"I love you too, you silly, pathetic excuse for a Dar," Khaidu said, the roses in her cheeks and the fire in her eyes suggesting she hardly thought him pathetic at all.

He didn't care that all of the surviving Vasylli were behind him. He lay down next to Khaidu and kissed her. She embraced him, smiling widely. He had never seen her smile like that. It changed her face, making it soft and beautiful. Then, it struck him.

"Khaidu?"

She understood. With a sigh, she rolled over and tried to stand up. She did. She stood on her own two legs.

Then, Khaidu bawled like a baby. He hid her face in his chest. It made him feel inexpressibly safe and warm.

Aglaia had come up by that point. She looked younger by at least twenty years, full of vigor in spite of her grey hair.

"Grandson, while you're busy with very important affairs, perhaps you can spare a glance over that way." She indicated with her chin.

Antomír and Khaidu turned around, away from the imposing sight of the new Vasyllia Mountain.

The landscape was somewhat familiar, though the absence of the rest of the mountains made the now gentle, rolling nature of the grass-clad hills seem strange, almost sea-like. Just down the slope of one of those wave-hills stood a towering mesa with a walled city fortress on top of it. It was built of dark wood, in the shape of a five-pointed star. A pointed turret shone with gilding at each angle of the pentagon. Banners of spectacular colors flapped on the tips of the gilded towers. The entire space of the mesa outside the city was filled with people. From this distance, they looked like ants, but they glittered like fireflies at night.

Lanterns, thought Antomír. *They're all holding lit lanterns.*

"It seems all Karila has come out to greet us," said Aglaia.

ADELAIDA FELT no pain in her chest. All she felt was an intense relaxation flowing out from her chest to the tips of her fingers and toes. She opened her eyes. There were clouds like banners stretched across an azure sky of early morning. She even noticed one or two stars persisting in the blue.

She felt his presence before she saw him. Batuk sat on the ground, facing away from her, among the many other sleeping forms surrounding them. He didn't sleep, but made no move to turn to her.

She reached out and touched his shoulder. Then she noticed the quiver. His entire body was shaking softly.

"Batuk, what is it?" she asked, getting up to sit cross-legged behind him, her hand still on his shoulder.

He sniffed loudly, then turned around. It was much like a boulder trying to move, she noticed with a smile.

Then she felt her eyes grow large in surprise.

"Your eye!"

Both eyes were whole again, and he had no scar left on his face. He smiled for the first time since she met him. Although he was not a handsome man, that smile illumined something she had always suspected that he had inside him.

"Thank you, Adelaida."

"For what?" she asked, her eyes dropping down automatically, before she got annoyed with herself and looked back into his face.

"For showing me that there is life after death."

He looked away from her pointedly at that moment, toward a young man and woman standing apart from the rest. There was a stately old woman with them, dressed like a Vasylli princess. Batuk stared at them with fiery intensity, tears gathering in his eyes. The young woman was a Gumira, Adelaida saw. She would have to ask Batuk about that later.

But now, she leaned into his chest. She had to. Her own tears were coming again, and she was heartily sick of everyone seeing them.

After a moment, Batuk's rough, iron-like arms encircled her like she was a precious artifact made of glass. In spite of her tears, she smiled.

"Can you hear it?" he asked.

She listened. Birdsong. Distant, but growing closer.

They stood up. Adelaida felt her mouth drop at the sight of a city on a hill, directly ahead of them. From that city, a multi-colored cloud of birds was rising and flying directly toward them.

Adelaida had never seen anything so heartbreakingly beautiful.

She and Batuk approached the young man, just in time to hear him speak. She recognized him. Voran the Bright had called him Dar, but she would have recognized him anyway, for he looked like a young Mirnían. This was her brother, Antomír.

"Well, shall we?" he said, smiling to his Gumira bride. "Our new home beckons."

~

VORAN AND SABÍANA walked in the fields of tall grass outside the walls of Vasyllia the New. The landscape had changed completely after Vasyllia had separated from the rest of the world. Now, Vasyllia Mountain was a lone peak in a high plateau that extended into a forest of dark firs. That forest went on for miles, until it ended, suddenly, at what Sabíana had begun to jokingly call the end of the world. It was a sheer fall, thousands of feet deep, into a distant landscape below the clouds. Down there was the rest of the world, so far away as to almost be a dream.

Voran always felt a little wistful when he thought of those who were not yet ready to come to Vasyllia the New, especially Adelaida, whom he had wanted to come to know. Sabíana had nothing but praise for the girl, and Sabíana had never been one to praise lightly.

They had found many people in the streets of the new city, some they had never expected. Siloan the potter was there. Otar Gleb was there. Derzhava the Seer, walking on two firm, strong legs, was there. Marinka, Kachinka, and Zabían were all there with their new soul-bonded Sirin. They were an endless comfort to Lebía, who still mourned Mirnían bitterly. Tarin and his kestrel appeared at odd moments, when least expected, always with some mischief in mind. Even Dar Cassían himself was there, larger than life, as Voran had expected him to be. Life in the new city was indescribably peaceful and beautiful. It was the fulfillment of the longing that had awoken inside him so many years ago when he first heard Lyna's song.

But none of that compared to simply being with Sabíana. She was young again, as was he. But it was a youth different from how they were twenty years ago. They lost nothing of their years of experience, but the aches disappeared, the tiredness was swept away, the wounds were healed, the lines of worry and care faded completely. They were ageless.

He found himself staring at her again as she walked through the waving grasses. She turned back to look at him, her head cocked to one side quizzically, as though she didn't understand why he was staring at her.

Then she looked up at Vasyllia, and her face changed. Wonder grew in her eyes, so unexpected that Voran turned around himself. The fires of the giants had scoured the surface of the city, burning away all the trees and the wooden houses and gardens. But the stone bones of the city, the buildings, palaces, archways, and bridges carved out of the mountain itself—they had been untouched. The true Vasyllia had been revealed, without the defilement of the centuries of the false covenant.

"Can you see it?" she asked, her voice hushed with awe.

He did. From this vantage point, in the middle of a grassy field, the stone city looked like a bearded and crowned face. A kingly face. In the middle of the crown rose the fiery aspen that had grown already to incredible heights, even though the Sirin had only planted the fruit from the last tree of life a week ago. The old king of stone had a crown with a fiery jewel in its center.

Then Voran remembered that Vasyllia the Old had been there even before the Vasylli had come with Lassar from the Lowlands. It had been called the City of the Gods, once. It seemed the Powers had actually carved this city, all its buildings and arches and bridges, as an image. An image of a great king.

"Who do you think it is?" asked Voran.

Sabíana didn't answer. They stood there, hand in hand, drinking in the wonder until the sun began to set behind them, and the image of the king faded in the gloaming.

"Let's go home," said Sabíana.

Voran embraced her and they went.

ACKNOWLEDGMENTS

Thank you to Nicholas Bergin for his wonderful editing work, to Maria Kotar for her invaluable proofreading and advice, to Stuart Bache of Books Covered Ltd. for his amazing cover design work.

Thank you to Coco Wiel for her long-standing support and financial help, and to her father Calvin (Nicholas), who continues his support even from beyond the grave.

And a special thank you to all my patrons over at patreon. com/nicholaskotar. I couldn't do what I do without you!

Here are all my wonderful patrons, so you may know them:

Harlan Kellem

Jack Keoseyan

Eleni Tsagaris

Jeff Muter

Nina A McDonald

Brittany A Sprunger

Jacob Russell

Remington Sloan

Trever Arnold

Theodore Cooke

Faeli Kathryn Heise

Konstantin Graf
Алексей Ковинский
Anastasia Brodeur
Brianna Henderson
Lisa Parrott
Jesse Rimshas
Fr. Matthew Smith
Gabriel Wilson
Aham Svarupa
Nina McDonald
Patrick Wilcox
Robin Morris
Randall Born
Julie Gould
Bob Pfeiffer
Steve Litteral
Jamie Patrick
Mary Feldman
John Parker
David Moser
Mary Maceluch
ChristianRPG
Zoe Turton
Daniel Austin Burnett
Joachim Wyslutsky
Svetlana Birthisel
George Luimes
Kevin Zalac
Anna Lytle
Stephen Jones
Angel
Tim M Dwyer
Dn. Andrew Wilson
Ben Andrus
Michael Cook

Jason Aumen
Ralph Sidway
Kimberly Hancock
jane g meyer
culianu
Caitlin
John Hyde
Fr. Anthony Perkins
Maria Kotar
John Considine
Nicholas Medich
Robert Hegwood
Blake Paine
Dianne Hatfield Combs
Jo Navarre
Anthony James
John Simmons
Elise Roberts
Zoe Kaylor

ABOUT THE AUTHOR

Nicholas Kotar is a writer of epic fantasy inspired by Russian fairy tales, a freelance translator from Russian to English, the resident conductor of the men's choir at a Russian monastery in the middle of nowhere, and a semi-professional vocalist. His one great regret in life is that he was not born in the nineteenth century in St. Petersburg, but he is doing everything he can to remedy that error.

www.ingramcontent.com/pod-product-compliance
Lightning Source LLC
Chambersburg PA
CBHW051629180726
48284CB00006B/1661